To Jeanett[illegible]
So glad [illegible]
this!! Love, Dar

The Amazing Graces

A Novel by
Darlene Shorey-Ensor

Silverlining Press
Talent, Oregon

The Amazing Graces

darleneshorey-ensor.com

ISBN-13: 978-0615763460
ISBN-10: 0615763464

Library of Congress Control Number: 2013932300

Cover Art & Book Design: Silverlining Designs

Silverlining Press
Talent, Oregon

Acknowledgments

To the Haywire writing group of Ashland, Oregon, with special thanks to Leanne Zinkand and Cynthia Rogan, without whom this book would not have been possible (or is it "who?").

And thanks to my parents, Bette and Wes Shorey, younger sister Deborah Roach and especially to my older sister, the poet and song-writer Deena Shorey, who wrote the wedding poem. Love you all.

To Rick,
who knew I could write
long before I did.

1

Jennifer

On October 1, 1965, my mother plowed her brand new Cadillac into my father and his fiancée as they crossed the street in front of his office. Daddy died instantly. Leslie flew through the air, landed on her head, and passed away two days later.

My parents had split up a couple of years earlier, when I was 11. Dad found an apartment in town, near his law office. At first Mom said he just needed to be closer to work. But as the weeks passed, and she got more and more mad at Daddy, calling him a "bastard" all the time, my three sisters and I gradually figured out what was happening. A year later, he started dating a younger woman.

Leslie Tilson, who my mom called "that skinny slut," was a paralegal in Dad's office. In her late twenties, she was single but had a three-year-old son, Ben. When we first met her, the four of us vowed to rally against her and we snubbed her whenever we could. But the more we got to know Leslie, the more we began to like her, and we eventually came to adore her.

Mom had grown fat over the years. She always complained that she gained twenty pounds with each kid. But Les, who was slender, pretty and drove a little green MG seemed very chic to us. She and my dad were always fun to be around because they laughed a lot and never yelled at each other. We were much happier and had a lot more fun with them than at home with Mom. And Ben was the little brother we'd always wished for but never had. As his real dad was no longer in his life, we encouraged him to call our dad "Pops" which we found hilarious.

On the day my father died, they arrested Mom and charged her with murder. Dad and Leslie were well liked in the legal community, and people said they "threw the book" at Mom. Sentenced to twenty years in prison, she'd probably get out in ten, with good behavior.

So, there we were. Within a few short weeks, we lost our father, our mother was in prison, and we were four little girls, adrift.

* * *

When my father, Jeffrey Grace, married my mother, Janet, in 1948, they began popping out baby girls at the rate of one every three years. My older sister was named Jacqueline, which she was very proud of, because she thought it sounded sophisticated, like Jackie Kennedy. She looked nothing like the former First Lady, a fact I reminded her of repeatedly, just to make her mad. Usually, I called her Jacki, unless I was in the mood to bug her. Then I'd call her "jack-off," an expression I heard from a kid at school. Of course that drove my parents up the wall, though I had no idea what it meant.

I showed up in 1952, three years after Jacki, and was named Jennifer, usually shortened to Jenny, or Jen. After three more years, Julie came along. Most of the time we called her Jules, or Ju, which sounded like "Jew" so, of course, we'd get yelled at if we called her that in public. Jules became the very bane of my existence, and after I heard that expression, whenever she provoked me, I called her "Bane," which always made Daddy smile. The youngest of my sisters, Johanna, arrived three years after Julie. Johanna was a long name for a baby, so we just called her Joey, which irritated my mother to no end. The folks around our neighborhood referred to us as Jacki, Jen, Jules and Joey, or the Grace girls. We liked to call ourselves "The Amazing Graces."

My dad, a successful tax attorney, worked in a law office in San Jose, California. We lived in a large, rambling house out in the country, in an area south of San Jose called New Almaden. My mom's younger brother, Joe, and his wife, Sally—both school teachers—and their three sons lived twenty miles south of us, in Morgan Hill. Kevin was my age, and the twins, Michael and Matthew, were the same age as Joey. Our only cousins, we spent most holidays, vacations and weekends together, the seven of us splashing around in the pool in our backyard, laughing, yelling, fighting, singing and generally being silly.

The only problem I remember back then was the fighting between Mom and Dad, usually over money. My mom loved shopping. Like her younger brother, she'd been a schoolteacher before she started making babies, but quit her job to raise us kids. My father earned a good income, but complained a lot that he couldn't keep up with Mom's spending. We shopped for school clothes in the most expensive stores. Mom took us to Hawaii on vacation a couple of times, even though my dad had to work and couldn't join us. And she went all-out on our birthdays and Christmas. We took tap and ballet classes, swimming and piano lessons, and got to go to a horseback riding camp over the summer. My girlfriends complained that my sisters and I were spoiled rotten.

* * *

The day of the accident, a Friday, I sat in my eighth grade English class, looking forward to the weekend because my best friend Sharon and I planned to go horseback riding at the local stable. As I focused on writing a book report, my teacher approached my desk, leaned down and whispered to me that I needed to report to the principal's office, where my Uncle Joe was waiting. A short, bald man with broad shoulders, we used to tease him that he looked like the guy from the Mr. Clean commercials. He always wore a white T-shirt and white pants. That day, he didn't seem too happy. In fact, my uncle wouldn't even look at me.

"I need to talk to you, Jennifer," he said softly. "Let's go sit in my car."

We walked out to his old, yellow Studebaker. On the way, I frantically tried to recall what I'd done that was so awful Uncle Joe would come to my school. *Why not Mom or Dad?*

We climbed into his car and sat in silence for a few minutes. I looked out the window and watched as gold and orange leaves swirled down from the trees, blown about by the wind. I started biting my fingernails which I did a lot back then. When he finally spoke, my uncle's voice was crackly.

"There's been an accident," he said. I thought maybe Joey had fallen off the monkey bars again. She'd broken her arm the year before.

"Your dad. He and Leslie were hit by a car earlier today. He didn't make it…I'm sorry, honey, to have to tell you this. Your dad died this morning."

Daddy died? Those two words don't even go together! Daddies don't die. Your cats die. They get run over in the driveway all the time. You come out in the morning and find your pet lying stiff as a board on the cold ground. But your *dad* doesn't get run over.

"You're joking, right?" I asked.

"No, I wish I were, Jen. And there's one more thing. I don't know any other way to say this. But... it was your mom. She hit them with her car..." His voice trailed off into a sob. I'd never seen my uncle cry before. We sat there for a while, neither of us saying anything. Then he started the engine and we drove away slowly.

My mom hit my dad with the car? This can't be real!

He continued: "I didn't want you to hear about it at school. Or on the radio. I'm taking you to our house. Jacki's already there. Sal's picking up the little ones. You'll be staying with us for now."

"There's no room at your house," was all I could think to say. Uncle Joe and Aunt Sally lived in a small, three-bedroom house, barely big enough for the five of them. Where would we sleep?

We drove the twenty miles to Morgan Hill without speaking. I kept thinking any minute he was going to say "April Fool!" even though it was October. At thirteen, I knew he wouldn't come to school to play a joke on me, but I kept hoping he was kidding.

When we got to the house, I walked through the front door and into the kitchen. Aunt Sally was making something on the stove. I smelled the rich scent of garlic bread in the oven. To this day, that smell still makes me sick. Julie, Joey and the twins all sat around the table, eating spaghetti. Everyone was quiet, watching me.

"Where's Jacki?" I asked.

"In Kevin's room," Aunt Sally answered, her eyes red and swollen.

I walked down the hallway and opened the door. Jacki, lying face down on Kevin's twin bed, turned over and sat up, wiping her eyes. Used Kleenex lay scattered all over the bed.

"That bitch!" she said.

"Who?" I asked, momentarily confused. Jacki almost never swore.

"Mom, of course, you ninny!" she said, blowing her nose into a tissue. "She ran Daddy over with her car!"

"Well, it must have been *on accident*," I protested. "Maybe her foot slipped off the brake. She wouldn't do it on purpose!"

"Don't be a spaz, Jen. Of course she did it on purpose. She's already in jail!"

Whenever Jacki was upset, she had a tendency to take it out on me. But seeing her in tears set me off. I started wailing. I don't think I even understood the enormity of the situation, but seeing my older sister cry was too much. We held each other close and wept.

We cried a lot over the next couple of days, and even more when the news came that Leslie had died. Jules, always hysterical about everything, would sometimes be laughing and then burst into tears. She kept saying, "We're almost orphans now!" Joey cried when she saw us crying, but at seven, she was just happy with all of us being together. She kept asking when Mom was coming home from jail, until Jules socked her hard on the arm and she stopped. I thought constantly about little Ben. Would he even remember his mother?

For the first few days, we stayed home from school. It was kind of an adventure, sleeping on mattresses shoved together in the family room. I wanted to tell my friends everything that was going on, but Aunt Sally made me stay off the phone because a lot of people were calling the house. I worried about our cat, Pookey, who was still at home, alone. They said our neighbors were feeding her.

One afternoon, while sitting alone in the living room, desperately wishing I had my cat there to comfort me, I started weeping. Aunt Sally saw me and asked, "What's wrong, honey?"

"I miss Pookey," I sobbed.

"Oh, for crying out loud!" she said. "He's just a damn cat!"

I know now that my normally sweet aunt must have been

feeling overwhelmed at that time to say such a mean thing to me, but I resented that remark for years.

At night, after everyone was asleep, I lay on my mattress, thinking about Mom being in jail. I really missed her a lot. I tried to imagine what it was like in jail. I wondered if she was missing us. I tried not to think about Daddy, but images of him lying in the road kept creeping into my mind. *What's it feel like, to get run over by a car? Did he know it was Mom who hit him?* I thought a lot about Leslie, too. And sobbed myself to sleep.

It was hard with all of us living in my uncle's house. My Aunt Sally, a short, chubby woman with prematurely graying hair, was usually pretty cheerful and used to make us laugh a lot. And she'd do this thing where, when she laughed, she inhaled through her nose, causing her to snort like a pig. Every time she'd do it, we'd all start laughing and imitating her. That would embarrass her and make her snort even more. One time, she actually laughed so hard she peed, right there on the kitchen floor.

But during the weeks after my father's death, she wasn't in a very good mood. One afternoon, Matt was fighting with Joey over a yo-yo when Jacki snatched it out of his hand and gave it to Joey. He stormed off, mad, and called back to us, "So what? Your dad's dead and your mom's in jail!"

As he walked by, I shoved him hard, knocking him into the wall. He ran crying to his mother, his little face distorted with rage. She came out of the kitchen, yelling at me.

"I pushed him because he was talking bad about my mom!" I defended myself.

"I don't want you pushing him!" Aunt Sally yelled at me.

"I didn't!" I shot back.

She stormed into the kitchen and was angry all night, not speaking to anyone.

"You're such a little ratfink!' Jacki said to Matt.

The memorial service for my father was held four days later. My aunt and uncle decided against an open casket because it would be too hard on us kids. Uncle Joe suggested we pick out a song to sing during the service, because Daddy loved it when the four of us sang together. Jacki had started playing the guitar a few years earlier, and she strummed along as we sang. Sometimes, the four of us stood in front of the big mirror in my parents' bedroom, singing folk songs. We liked to pretend we were on the Ed Sullivan show.

Jules thought about it for a while and then offered up, "What about 'Hang Down Your Head, Tom Dooley'?"

"You moron!" I yelled. "That's about a guy getting hanged for killing someone. How could you even suggest it? Everyone will think we're singing about Mom!"

"Oh," she said.

"I know! I know!" Joey broke in. "Can we sing the song from the Beverly Hillbillies?" It was her favorite song. She started singing, "Come and listen to the story 'bout a man named Jed..."

"You're a bunch of retards!" Jacki yelled. We eventually decided to sing 'Kumbaya,' except Jules kept singing it her way: "Someone's farting, Lord, kumbaya," and we decided to drop the whole idea.

I don't remember much about the funeral except riding in the limo, which was fun. Lots of people I didn't know came up to talk to us about what a fine man Daddy was. Afterward, his law partner, Norman Green, and wife Deena invited everyone to a gathering at their home, where a huge buffet of food sat waiting for us. It seemed silly to me.

"Isn't it ironical?" I whispered to Jacki. "Everyone brings food at a time when you're not hungry at all. 'Uncle Pete died? Okay, have a tamale!'"

That night, after everyone was asleep, Jacki and I laid on our mattresses, talking about the funeral. She suddenly said,

"I wonder if we should have sung the Beverly Hillbillies song." Somehow it struck both of us as funny and we started giggling, and then laughing, louder and louder. Finally, Uncle Joe had to get up and tell us to quiet down. I'm still amazed that sometimes, in the midst of overwhelming grief, we could find something to laugh about.

The days following the service were hectic, with Uncle Joe making arrangements for Mom's legal defense and Aunt Sally trying to manage us kids. They both took a short leave of absence from work. Jacki, angry and in tears a lot, upset the younger kids and got them crying, so she went to stay with our Aunt Mimi, a friend of Mom's from college. I think she spent a couple of weeks there. I overheard my aunt and uncle talking in low tones about having her seeing some kind of doctor, a psychiatrist, I guess, but eventually she came back and seemed better, although quiet and sad most of the time. And absolutely determined she'd have nothing to do with my mother.

"You go see her if you want to," she said to me one day. "I don't care what you do. But I'm never going to talk to her again. She can rot in hell, for all I care!"

My feelings were mixed. I sometimes raged at Mom and hated her for what she did. But I also wanted her home, taking care of us. I wanted us all back together again. She ruined everything with her lousy temper. But even surrounded by all my siblings and cousins, something big was missing. It was my mom, and I needed her.

2

My parents met in college at San Jose State. They say opposites attract, which was definitely true for them. My dad was tall, slender, and handsome, but a little on the serious side. His own father died when Dad was four and his younger brother, Kenny, was still an infant. When Dad was ten, his mother married an alcoholic, and soon she started drinking, too. Their stormy marriage lasted only a couple of years before his stepfather died of a heart attack. Daddy graduated from high school and attended San Jose State, majoring in law. His mother still drank a lot and developed diabetes. She died while he was in college. Kenny moved up to San Francisco and he started drinking heavily and we never heard from him much.

Daddy met Mom at a party one night. He told me once, "She absolutely knocked my socks off!"

Janet Sutherlin was a beautiful blonde bombshell, Dad said. "Highly energetic," "outgoing" and "vivacious" are words people used to describe my mother. She and Uncle Joe came from a wealthy family and wanted for nothing, my grandparents having made money from real estate. Headstrong and determined, when she met my dad, she decided right away that she would marry him. They dated off and on during college and broke up several times because he was too serious for her. Mom wanted to party and have fun and wasn't interested in studying. She planned to marry a rich guy and didn't see that she'd be using her college degree in the future.

Daddy must have had some reservations about marrying her, because they obviously had nothing common. But she was beautiful and sexy, even if she was "quite a handful," as he described her later. They got married after he graduated from law school and, a year later, Jacki was born.

My oldest sister takes after my mother physically, more than the rest of us. She inherited Mom's thick blonde hair, big blue eyes and curvy body. People used to say my sister looked like the actress Tuesday Weld. Even as young girl, I noticed that everywhere we went, guys looked at Jacki and commented on how pretty she was. She always turned a lot of heads. But she had Daddy's personality—quiet, introspective, and serious.

I used to complain that I got the "leftovers." Skinny like Daddy was when he was young, I also ended up with his, thin, mousy brown hair. I did inherit his green eyes and his intelligence, but the boys didn't care about that. As the only sister who wore glasses, and the only one with braces on my teeth, I often felt that life wasn't fair.

My sister Jules was the exotic-looking one. With her light brown, curly hair and sharp features, I would often hear her described as "alluring." I asked Mom one day, "So who's Julie's father, anyway?" and she just laughed. Jules is the one who ended up with my mother's personality. Short-tempered, always flying off the handle, and a total pain in the butt. It seems like I spent my entire childhood either trying to irritate her or trying to get away from her.

And Johanna, the baby, was the only one who seemed to inherit parts of both my parents. Pretty, like Mom, her soft features, fair skin and golden blond hair always made her look younger than she was. Unlike the rest of us, she had a tendency toward plumpness. But her gentleness and good-nature came directly from Dad. I was six when she was born, and even though I was bitterly disappointed she was a girl when I desperately wanted a baby brother, I loved her instantly and tried to mother her. It was me who started calling her Joey, against my mother's wishes, but everyone liked it, and the name stuck. I fiercely protected her, and when I thought Jules was picking on her in any way, I jumped in and pounded her into the ground. Then one of my parents or Jacki would have to pull me off, and we'd both get grounded.

Never one to be intentionally cruel, my dad, as a young parent, didn't realize how sticking labels on his kids could hurt. He referred to Jacki as "The Pretty One," he called me his "Smart Girl," Jules was the "Rebel," and Joey was "The Sweet One," or his "Sunshine Girl." I hated those references. I never told him, but I always wished I could be the "Pretty One," or the "Sunshine Girl."

In spite of the labels, I knew both my parents loved me, but I always had a special relationship with my dad. He introduced me to reading, and gave me my favorite book, *To Kill a Mockingbird*. After I read it, I decided I'd name my first child Scout, after the main character.

When I was only ten, I read *Lord of the Flies* and was deeply disturbed by it. I remember sitting in the den with Daddy, talking to him about the book.

"I don't understand the part where the pig's head is talking," I complained. "Pigs don't talk. Especially if their head is stuck on top of a stick."

"Well," Daddy said, "I think he was talking symbolically."

I thought for a moment. "Then I still don't get it. I think I'll write to the author and ask him about it. Do you know where I could get his address?"

My father smiled and said he'd help me find it. He always encouraged me to write and said I could be a famous writer when I grew up if I wanted. I said I hoped to be a lawyer because I thought he'd like to hear that. But it was a lie. I really wanted to be a jockey or a cowboy.

Daddy also taught me to play chess, although I didn't really enjoy it that much. I preferred checkers or Candyland, but I loved spending time alone with him when we played. He was a busy man, with a thriving law practice, a demanding wife, even more demanding daughters and an occasional round of golf—so any time I got alone with him was special. I was good in school, mainly because I knew it pleased him. Being with him meant a lot to me, and I loved the times when I could make him laugh.

My mom was unpredictable. At times, my girlfriends thought she was the perfect mother. Generous and fun-loving, she'd pick us up after school, take us clothes shopping, and buy us candy and records. Every year, on our birthdays, she'd allow my sisters and I to completely redecorate our bedrooms. One year, I did my room in a cowboy theme, with pictures of horses on the wall. Jules picked poodles, Joey's room had ballerinas, and Jacki chose butterflies.

As we got older, our parents fought more and more over money. One day Jacki pulled me aside just before my eleventh birthday.

"We should tell Mom we don't want to change our rooms this year," she said.

"But why?" I argued. "I'm tired of my room, I want unicorns next."

"Because we can't afford it. I heard Daddy say we're up to our eyeballs in debt. Mom spends too much money."

Well this was news to me. I didn't know anything about being in debt. But I grudgingly agreed to her plan. Later that year, when Jules changed her room to bunny rabbits, and Joey got bumblebees, I seethed with jealousy.

As I look back on it now, my mother was starting to have some pretty serious mood swings back then. One minute, she'd be laughing and planning a party or a vacation; the next, she'd be yelling and swearing. One time she went into Jacki's room and broke all of her Beatles albums in half, not an easy thing to do. Another time, when she was mad at my dad, she picked up his suits from the cleaners and threw them in the pool. This only happened maybe once a month, although Jacki would tell you it was more often. You never knew when Mom was going to go off, but I think, as kids, we were relieved that most of her anger was focused on Daddy.

Growing up with parents who were constantly fighting didn't seem unusual to us. I just assumed that was how families were. We were focused on so many other things; none of us spent much time dwelling on the constant bickering. We simply never realized the depth of Mom's anger, especially after Daddy left and took up with Leslie.

But Jacki, the eldest, knew there was something wrong with Mom, and often called her crazy or "psycho." One time Mom overheard Jacki call her that, and she stopped cooking for us for a week. The tension grew worse between Mom and Jacki after that, but it might have been because Jacki, being a teenager, was into dating boys, driving around with friends and wanting more freedom. She'd always been closer to Daddy anyway, which I think made Mom jealous. And Mom's jealousy was a thing to be reckoned with.

* * *

After the tragic event, we stayed out of school for two weeks. My sisters and I constantly pestered Uncle Joe with questions. Where were we going to live until Mom came home? When were we going back to school? Who was feeding Pookey? When could we visit Mom? Finally he'd had enough and said he'd give all the information to Jacki, and she would share it with us. It was obvious we couldn't stay out of school any longer.

Uncle Joe decided to move us back to our house in Almaden until after the trial. He and Aunt Mimi would take turns staying with us. Aunt Sal would be at her place with the boys. We couldn't wait to go back home, not really thinking about whether it was a good plan or not. We just wanted to get back to our own house, sleep in our own rooms, and, hopefully, get back to normal.

But walking into the house for the first time since the "accident" felt funny. It was like everything had changed, and yet it looked exactly the same. Pookey was skinnier but he was happy to see us.

That night, Jacki and I stayed up late. I washed my hair and she set it in rollers for me so that it would look nice on my first day back at school.

"Jacki, can I ask you something?"

"Sure."

"Do you miss Mom?"

She ignored the question for a while. Then she said, "Well, of course I do. But I'm never going to forgive her. She ruined our lives, as far as I'm concerned. Just because she was jealous..."

Jacki's voice started to crack, so I let it drop for a moment. She continued to divide my wet hair with a comb, wrap up a section in the curler and hold it in place with a bobby pin.

"Do you think they'll really send her to prison?" I asked.

"Well, she did kill two people, dope. What do you think?" she answered.

"So we'll end up living at Uncle Joe's? Will we have to change schools?"

"I don't think they want us there. There's no room. Besides, they already have a family."

"But where else would we go?" I persisted.

"Jeez, I don't know. They called Uncle Kenny. He lives New York now, and it sounds like he can't take us. Nana and

Papa are in a nursing home. They're both going senile and all their money's gone, anyway. I don't know..."

"I wonder what happened to Leslie's car," I mused.

"Yeah, that's something we need to think about," she responded sarcastically. "I really worry about little Ben. I wonder who's taking care of him now."

"You know what scares me the most?"

"What?"

"How this is going to affect Joey. If she'll grow up insane or something."

"Joey's too young. She'll do okay. You don't have to worry about her."

"Jacki? I still think Mom did it by accident," I said.

"I know you do, Scout," she said softly. Sometimes she called me that, when I was hurt or sad.

I was actually excited about going back to school the next day. I'd really missed my pals, especially my best friend, Sharon. I'd only been able to talk to her a couple of times, briefly, on the phone. But I was a little nervous, wondering if the kids would ask me a lot of questions, or if they would look at me or talk about me behind my back. Aunt Mimi drove me to Sharon's that first morning and we both squealed and hugged each other when she opened the front door. Then we walked to school together and Sharon filled me in on all the gossip.

"Everyone's been asking about you, Jen," she said. "We all feel bad about what happened. I really wanted to come see you."

"I really don't want to talk about it, okay? 'Cause I don't want to start crying again. That'd be so embarrassing, to cry at school."

"I know what you mean," she sympathized. "By the way, your hair looks really cute."

I enjoyed my newfound popularity for almost two days. My teachers were all sweet to me, and the kids were especially nice. On the third day, things settled down to normal, with one exception. There was a girl in my class named Maria whom I'd always ignored because she dressed kind of shabbily. She was short and thin, with long, black hair and big, dark eyes. Someone told me her dad was Puerto Rican. She seemed really shy and didn't have many friends. One day she came up to me while I was sitting in the cafeteria having lunch, and said, "You know, my mom's in prison."

"Really? What'd she do?"

"Drugs."

"Oh." I didn't know what she was talking about. In 1965 I thought drugs just meant medicine.

"I live with my grandma now—just until Mama gets out of jail."

"So where's your dad?" I asked.

"We don't know where he is. He took off before I was born. He might even be dead!"

This was all shocking to me. I'd never heard of a father just taking off. But I liked Maria and would frequently sit and talk to her when my other friends weren't around.

I'd been back at school for almost two weeks when I came home one day and Aunt Mimi announced that Jules, Joey and I would be going to visit my mom on Saturday. I was so happy I jumped up and down. We were all excited, but when Jacki came home, I pretended I didn't care that much. I tried to talk her into it, but that Jacki had a stubborn streak a mile long, as Daddy used to say, and she wouldn't budge.

"She'll be upset if you don't come!" I said.

"*She'll* be upset? *She'll* be upset?" she shrieked. "She. Ran. Daddy. Over. With. Her. Car. Do you understand that? How stupid are you?" She was really hollering.

"Okay. Okay," I muttered defensively. "I get it! Don't blow a head gasket!"

Jacki stormed up to her room and refused to come down

for dinner. I felt guilty and tried to make up with her. She told me to just leave her alone. Finally, she let me into her room and allowed me to brush her hair, the signal that she'd forgiven me.

I hardly slept at all that night, and was up early to get ready for the visit. I brushed Joey's hair and picked out an outfit for Jules to wear. We wanted to look our best for Mom.

Finally, it was time to go, and Uncle Joe loaded us into the station wagon. It took half an hour to reach the county jail in downtown San Jose. It wasn't at all what I had expected. I thought Mom would be behind bars, and we'd be sitting in chairs next to her cell, life out of a scene from "The Rifleman." Instead, a policeman led us down a long hallway and into a room where we had to wait while Uncle Joe signed some paperwork. I sat there, biting my fingernails. After what seemed like forever, the door opened and Mom came into the room, accompanied by a lady in a police uniform. Jules and Joey both screamed and ran to hug her while I hung back, feeling shy with the officer in the room.

Mom looked a little tired to me. She wore blue slacks and a blue shirt and no makeup but her hair looked nice and shiny.

I finally gave her a hug. She cried as she clung to the three of us.

"So Jacqueline decided not to come after all?" she asked Uncle Joe, wiping her eyes.

"She was really busy, Mom," I said. "She had a lot of homework this weekend." By the look on my mother's face I knew she didn't believe me. I wished I hadn't said anything.

We all sat down at a long, wooden table. I looked around the room. The floor was covered in grime, and the pale green paint was chipping off the walls. I shuddered.

"So tell me what you girls have been up to," Mom said.

Jules and Joey were both talking at once, telling her about our experience being at Uncle Joe's and missing school. Joey asked her when she was coming home.

"Soon," she answered. I wondered how she knew that.

"Mommy, where's your stripes?" Jules asked.

"What stripes, honey?"

"You know, the stripes you have to wear..."

"Jules, shhhh." I knew she was referring to something she'd seen on TV.

"Mommy, you're lucky, you got new clothes," Joey said brightly. "But why is that lady watching us? Did she run over somebody, too?"

The girls kept pestering her with questions until Uncle Joe took them down the hall to buy some RC colas.

When they were out of the room, Mom asked, "So how are you really, Jennifer?"

"I miss you. I miss Daddy. I want you to come home!" I was in tears and very embarrassed. "It's been awful." I sobbed.

"Honey, I will come home as soon as they let me. But please don't be angry with me. You know this is all your father's fault. He's the reason I'm in here. None of this would have happened if it weren't for him and that slut. I'm sorry it turned out this way. But I don't know what else I could have done."

At the time, she seemed so sad I didn't even question her words. I just hugged and held onto her. I never wanted to let go. I wanted her to tell me everything was going to be all right. But Uncle Joe came back and soon we had to leave. Jules started crying then, so of course Joey did, too. Mom was sobbing and said her life had gone to hell in a handbasket. The officer took her out of the room and we were led back down the hall and out into the parking lot.

As we walked out to the car, Joey asked, "Where's Helena Handbasket?"

After we got home, the girls told Jacki about our visit, but I didn't say anything. It took a while, but after a few days, she finally came around and asked me how the visit had gone. I'd been sadder than usual after the visit, but I didn't know why. I wasn't hungry at all. I felt like sleeping all the time, except at night, when I finally went to bed, and I couldn't sleep at all. My friends at school helped cheer me up. The song "Nowhere Man" by the Beatles was really popular then and Sharon bought me the 45 record, which I played over and over again.

When Jacki asked me about the visit, I said, "She blamed it all on Daddy." I couldn't understand why Mom wasn't sorry. Jacki just shook her head. And as sad as I was, I had no idea of the coming changes that would turn my world even further upside down.

3

One evening Uncle Joe announced that Jacki and I had an appointment to meet our social worker after school the next day.

"I didn't even know we *had* a social worker," I said to Jacki.

"We were assigned one right after Mom got arrested," she explained. "She was the one who gave the okay for us to stay at Uncle Joe's. But it's stupid! We don't need a social worker! It's not like we're criminals or anything." For some reason, the idea really bugged her.

The next afternoon, Uncle Joe drove us over to the Department of Social Services, where we were introduced to Miss Simmons. In her late twenties, she was tall, with long, blonde braids and big, green eyes. She told us to call her Beth. I liked her right away.

We sat in Beth's office and talked about how things were going. Jacki was unusually subdued, and Uncle Joe kept wiping his eyes while I chatted about school and needing some new clothes.

Finally Beth said, "I know you girls have been through a lot in the last few weeks. This has been a terrible experience for you. Your aunt and uncle have been wonderful, but they can only do so much." She paused, and I wondered what was coming.

"Unfortunately, your uncle's going to have to move back home soon. And as much as they'd like to, they simply can't continue to care for all four of you." My heart stopped. She continued, "It's been decided that, because Julie and Johanna are the youngest, they'll go back to live with your aunt and uncle. And until this situation with your mother is resolved, you two will go the children's shelter for now, and probably on to a foster home at some point."

"What's the children's shelter?" I asked.

"An orphanage," Jacki said, through gritted teeth.

"This is just a temporary solution for now, girls," Beth continued. "A lot depends on what happens with your mom."

"Jacki," Uncle Joe said, "you know it's just too crowded at our house."

"Why can't we all just go live at our place?" I asked. "Jacki and I could share a room, Jules and Jo could be together. We'd all fit."

"Honey," Uncle Joe answered. His voice suddenly went soft. "The big house has to be sold. Your mom needs the money for her legal defense."

I sat back, speechless. The idea we'd all be separated had never entered my mind. And we were going to lose our house? Where would we keep our stuff? Where would we live when Mom came home?

"But why can't Jules go to the orphanage? She's the bratty one!" I argued.

Beth addressed me. "Jenny, no one is being sent away because they're bratty. But you and Jacqueline are older, more mature, and more capable of dealing with this situation. Julie is only ten; do you really think she could handle this better than you?"

I sat with tears rolling down my face.

Uncle Joe said, "I'll bring you girls back to the house every weekend. I promise. We'll be together on holidays. I'm so sorry, kids. But this is the best we can do for now." He looked so sad right then. I wanted to hug him, but I was too mad.

"I know this is really hard," Beth said, "but your aunt and uncle will keep in touch, and so will I. I will need you girls to pack up a couple of bags of clothing tonight and I'll pick you up tomorrow."

Uncle Joe then tried to lighten the situation by telling us we'd be getting new clothes for the trial, but that really didn't help at all.

On the way home, neither Jacki nor I spoke. It was all too new, too sudden, and too overwhelming. Uncle Joe gave us some large suitcases for our stuff. I realized, as I was packing, that I might not ever see this house again. With tears stinging my eyes, I emptied out my drawers and closets. Anything that didn't fit into the suitcases, I crammed into pillowcases—all my stuffed animals, books and albums. Even my old tap shoes. I gently removed the Beatles posters from the walls and rolled them into tubes. Aunt Mimi was home by then and came into my room to help. But I was too upset to accept any comfort from her. She pointed out I shouldn't take my bathing suits right now, as it was early fall, but I would need my pajamas, robe and slippers. Finally, she left to go help Jacki, and I closed the door and locked it. Then I lay on my bed and cried.

In the morning, I felt a little better. Even though I was upset about leaving home, I was also curious about the children's shelter, and as long as Jacki was with me, I felt like we were going on an adventure together. I convinced myself this was a temporary situation, and when Mom got out of jail, we'd move to a new house together. I'd always written short stories about interesting things that happened in our lives, and I thought this might end up as part of a really great story.

The next day, Beth picked us up after Jules and Joey left for school. Uncle Joe said he'd explain the situation to them later that evening. As we drove in her car, Beth told us about her life. She'd gone to the same college as my parents, and always wanted to be a social worker. Her boyfriend, Ken, was a therapist. She was open, friendly and funny. I asked her a lot of questions, but Jacki stayed quiet.

The first thing we saw at the children's shelter was the locked gate in the front.

"Why is there a gate?" Jacki demanded.

"Because some children need to be protected from their parents," Beth explained.

"It feels like we're being penned in," Jacki complained, as Beth rolled down her window and pressed a button on the intercom. The gate slowly swung open. I'd never heard of kids needing to be protected from their own parents.

We entered an office, where we met with a woman who introduced herself as Ann. Beth stayed with us while Ann "processed" our paperwork. I learned the shelter was divided into separate dormitories for boys and girls, but they did share a common living area, dining room and patio. The "residents," as we were called, were also divided into age groups. Jacki would be housed with girls aged fifteen to eighteen, while I would be in the eleven to fourteen section, which I immediately protested. I'd thought for sure I'd be in a room with Jacki. As it turned out, I was just down the hall from her, so I felt better. We learned that we'd take a bus to a new school that was closer to the shelter. Ann went through our belongings, telling us what we could keep and what things we'd have to send home. Jacki was upset that she couldn't keep her guitar. Ann gave us a printed copy of the rules of the house and took us on a tour. I wondered if they thought it would make us feel better by calling this place a "house" instead of a "shelter." It didn't.

Afterward, she took us to our rooms. In each one there were four twin beds, four small dressers and four very small closets. You could draw a curtain around your bed for privacy. Down the hall was a large bathroom, with several toilets and showers. It reminded me of the hospital room Joey was in when she broke her arm, except here there were posters on the walls above the beds. Everywhere you looked, you could see the smiling faces of the Beatles, the Dave Clark 5, and Paul Revere and the Raiders.

Jacki sat on her bed sobbing. "This is so humiliating," she said. She slowly began to unpack and put her belongings in the tiny closet. Then we went to my room and did the same. After that we were free to watch TV in the "rec" room, or play ping-pong on the patio. Jacki didn't want to do either. She asked Ann if she could call one of her girlfriends, but found out she was allowed only two phone calls per week! I thought she was going to have a spaz attack, but she just went back to her room and lay on her bed.

"This kind of reminds me of the year we went to summer camp, remember?" I said. "I was all excited to meet new kids, but you were really crabby at first because you didn't want to leave your friends. You thought summer camp was stupid. But then we got to ride horses and go swimming and you met that really cute guy. Remember? Badger?"

"Beaver. His name was Beaver. Just like the kid in that dumb TV show. He gave me my first kiss," she answered, staring off into space.

"Really? On the mouth?"

"Yes, on the mouth."

"Did you like it?" I asked eagerly. She had never shared this with me before.

"Not really. He tasted like tobacco. And he tried to put his tongue in my mouth. It was yucky."

"Why'd he do that?" I asked, horrified.

"I don't know. It's just what boys do. It's called French kissing."

"Do all French people kiss that way?"

"I guess so. I don't know. Stop asking me questions. You're

giving me a headache."

Jacki frequently ended our conversations by saying I was giving her a headache. She had more headaches than anyone I knew.

I wandered out of her room and down the hall to the rec room, looking forward to seeing the other kids when they got back from school. That afternoon, I was totally floored when the school bus arrived and I saw Maria get off. She gave a yell when she saw me and we threw our arms around each other.

"What are you doing here?" I asked.

"My grandma's in the hospital. She has sugar diabetes. So I had to come here. I been here a few times before. It's no big deal. The staff's really nice. Except you can't stay up late. When I'm at home, Grandma lets me stay up as late as I want. But the food's pretty good. We get pizza on Friday night. And sometimes they take us to the movies."

"So how long have you been here?"

"About three weeks."

I felt guilty that I hadn't even noticed she wasn't at school all that time. But then, I hadn't been there recently either.

"They say I might go to a foster home," I said.

"Yeah, that's too bad. I wish you could just stay here with me. They won't put me in a foster home because I'm going back to Grandma's soon. But I been to a few foster homes. I can tell you all about it. Some are okay, but some are real nasty. I bet you're in my room. We're the only girls in junior high here. Did you bring any posters? I just got a new Herman's Hermits poster. I just love Herman. He's so cute! My grandma says I talk a hundred miles an hour," she added, as if I hadn't figured that out.

And she was right: we were in the same room. We sat on our beds, talking, until a bell chimed and we went to the dining room for dinner. Jacki was sitting at a table with a couple of older kids, and I introduced to her to Maria. Even though my sister looked kind of sad, she did say, "I'm happy you have a friend here."

As we sat down for dinner, I realized Maria had lied about the food. We always had good food at home. Even with my mom's craziness, she was a great cook, and liked to use lots of fresh fruit and vegetables and whole grains. It wasn't uncommon at our house to have Lobster Thermidor with a warm spinach salad for dinner, followed by Baked Alaska for dessert. That night, they served a bland beef stew with a slice of white bread, and fruit cocktail for dessert. I hardly touched my plate, but Maria scarfed hers down, went back for seconds, and then finished off my plate. I sat and watched in disbelief. She said she always gained weight whenever she was at the shelter. "At home, we usually have fried potatoes and wienies," she explained.

That evening, after dinner, was game night in the rec room. They had all kinds of games set up, like Monopoly and Life, and served root beer and pretzels, but Maria and I went back to our room and went through our clothes. By the end of the evening, I had given her several of my blouses and T-shirts, since I knew Uncle Joe could always bring me more. She thought they were wonderful and kept asking me which one she should wear the next day. In exchange for the clothes, she gave me a necklace that she said was real silver. I knew it wasn't, but it was pretty and had a little heart on it, so I put it around my neck. I wore it all the time until it gave me a rash and I put it away.

For the rest of the week, I was busy adjusting to my new school, making friends, writing stories about my adventures, and hanging out with Maria. I missed my sisters and Sharon, but being at the shelter was like having a sleepover every night. After lights out, Maria and I would talk. She liked to imagine what she would be when she grew up. First she wanted to be a dentist, but the next day, she wanted to be a dog trainer. Then a bartender. Every day, it was something new.

She asked a lot of questions about my family and was envious that I had three sisters. She was really impressed when I mentioned our swimming pool. "Guy, you're so lucky!" she said many times.

One day she let it slip that her mother had been in jail once before, when Maria was about three years old. Her mother had slapped her so hard she knocked her off the bed and broke her collarbone.

"My mama's not really bad," she explained. "She just got in with the wrong crowd. Grandma says it's the drugs that make her do things. It's not her fault. When she gets out of jail, she's gonna be a model and make lots of money. She told me so! We're gonna move to Beverly Hills and live in a big house!"

It felt weird hearing Maria talk that way. She was a year older than me, already fourteen, and I didn't get how she could believe all that baloney.

"Hey, Jen," she whispered one night, right as I was falling to sleep.

"What?"

"Do you know much about sex?"

"You mean how babies are made?" I asked.

"Yeah."

"Jeez, of course. I'm not an infant, you know," I answered, irritated.

"Well, there's one thing I don't get." When I didn't respond, she continued, "How do the sperm thingies know when to pop out of the man?"

I rolled over. "What do you mean?"

"I mean, you know, when the man *goes* into the lady, how do the sperms know when to come out?"

I thought for a moment. "Man, I'm stumped. I'll have to ask Jacki."

"Go ask her now. I bet she's still awake."

"No, it's after 'lights-out'!"

"Go ahead, chicken," she urged.

"If you want to know so bad, you go ask her!"

"Dare ya," she said.

"Double dare ya," I answered.

"Triple dare ya."

"Okay," I said. "I dare you to infinity!"

"Dare ya to infinity and back!" she challenged.

"There is no infinity and back. You can't go further than infinity!'

"You wanna know what I heard? Boys always do it with animals, like with a dog or a goat, before they have sex with a girl. For practice."

"You lie!"

"No! For reals! My uncle even told me!"

"Go to sleep, you perv." I rolled over and closed my eyes, wondering what boys who didn't grow up on farms would use for practice.

Uncle Joe collected us on the weekend and took us back to Morgan Hill as promised, but it was an odd two days. The house was overcrowded as usual, and Jules kept whining and having temper tantrums because she wanted to go back to the shelter with us on Sunday. Jules hated being left out of anything Jacki and I did. She always had to tag along. And Joey kept clinging to me, which was sweet in the morning, but by afternoon was really bugging me. Jacki was grouchier than usual. There was talk of the upcoming trial, which she did *not* want to attend, but Mom's lawyer was telling Uncle Joe to make sure we were there.

Somehow it seemed like we didn't fit in there anymore. They'd moved the twins into Kevin's room and put my sisters into the twins' room, so the house seemed less crowded, but more than ever it felt like there was no room for us.

On Sunday afternoon, I sat on the patio, talking to Kevin.

My cousin had always been fat, irritating and immature. At a time when most boys were starting to grow their hair long, in typical "Beatle" fashion, Kevin kept his cut short, and he always dressed like a square. We called him "The Boy Scout" behind his back. Instead of being interested in music, he preferred to sit on the back fence and shoot at birds with his BB gun. Jacki always said he was "a total waste of human protoplasm."

"So what's it like at the *orphanage*?" he said, just to rile me.

"Oh, it's not too bad. The food's really good," I lied. "We get ice cream every night."

"For real? What kind?" he asked, his eyes wide.

"Any kind you want. Sometimes they take us to '21 Flavors' and we can each bring a whole gallon home! And we get pizza, sometimes three or four times a week."

"You lie!"

"Ask Jacki." I knew she'd back me up. "We have pizza so often I'm getting a little tired of it, actually. And we get to stay up and watch *The Man From U.N.C.L.E.*" That was Kevin's favorite show, but he rarely got to watch it, since it came on after his bedtime. "In fact, the guys who play Napoleon Solo and Ilya Kuryakin might come to the shelter to visit the orphans!" I knew I was laying it on thick, but it was so much fun I couldn't stop. When it came time for Uncle Joe to take us home, the jealous look on Kevin's face made me grin from ear to ear.

On the way home in the back seat, Jacki whispered, "I heard what you said to Kevin. You can be a real wisenheimer, you know that?" We both grinned.

4

THE NEXT WEEK passed uneventfully. Jacki was on the phone a lot, hoping one of her friends would take her in. Somehow she got around the rule about two phone calls a week. She hated being at the shelter, saying it made her feel degraded. And that it was all Moms' fault her friends turned her down.

"No one wants anything to do with us," she grumbled. "They're all afraid Mom's going to run them over." I knew she was exaggerating, but it was true. After my parents separated, and my mother went off the deep end, a lot of our family friends stopped coming around.

On Friday evening, my sister seemed more anxious than usual, and right after dinner, she pulled me aside.

"There's a possibility I might be able to go live with Aunt Mimi," she said quietly.

"Why just you? Why can't we both go?"

"She can only take one of us because she just has a studio apartment. You know she sleeps on a fold-out couch so I'll have to sleep on a cot. She asked me because I can drive now and she wants to get an old car so I can get myself around. That way, I'll be able to go back to my old school. But is it okay with you? I hate leaving you here..."

"Well, I guess so. And if you have a car, maybe you can come get me and I can stay with you on the weekends?" I asked hopefully.

"That'd be boss!" she said, throwing her arms around me. She smiled for the first time in weeks. I wasn't sure how I felt at that moment, but I knew Jacki was desperate to get out of the shelter, and she really missed her friends. She was just starting her junior year when all this happened, and it meant a lot to her to stay with her class. I guess I felt happy for her. I still had Maria to hang out with.

But that weekend, back at Uncle Joe and Aunt Sally's, I felt even more out of place, like my whole family was falling apart. I tried not to look miserable, but I was in tears a lot more than usual. I spent my time avoiding Jacki and the adults, mostly playing with the twins.

Unlike their older brother, Mike and Matt were small for their age with cute little pixie faces. Being identical twins and hard to tell apart, they were frequently addressed by members of the family simply as "Twin." Someone might say, "Twin, pass the ketchup." Or, "Twin, stop looking at me or I'm going to slap you into next week!" I played Cowboys and Indians with them a lot that weekend.

After they went to sleep on Saturday night, I spent time going through the bags of clothes Uncle Joe had stored in the basement. I pulled out several blouses I thought Maria would like, and some small stuffed animals. She was a sucker for little things like that. Any small item could keep her happy for days. Jules wandered down the basement steps and sat watching me for a while. In a rare act of kindness, I passed a few of my things on to her. There was no room for my stuff at the shelter, and Jules now had her own dresser and closet. For some reason she wanted my albums, but I wasn't ready to part with them yet. At ten, she wasn't that interested in music anyway. I gave her my Mickey Mouse ears and she was happy. She'd destroyed her own set a long time ago. Then she started picking her nose and I sent her back upstairs.

Uncle Joe took us kids to The International House of Pancakes for breakfast on Sunday morning. While we were gone, Aunt Mimi came over and picked up Jacki. They thought it would be better if we weren't around when she left. I was moody and depressed afterwards, and asked Uncle Joe to take me back to the shelter.

On the ride there, he tried to cheer me up by promising that on the next weekend he'd take me horseback riding at the local stable. I hadn't been on a horse in a long time and I missed it a lot. That cheered me up a little. Then I asked him if I could get some new, white go-go boots, since mine were getting worn out. Go-go boots had become all the rage ever since the TV show *Hullabaloo*. He said to put them on my Christmas list.

Uncle Joe dropped me off at the shelter, but when I walked through the front door, Ann greeted me with terrible news.

'Honey," she said, "I'm afraid Maria's gone home. Her grandma got out of the hospital. She picked her up this morning. I'm so sorry!"

I was crushed. Sitting on the bed, I stared at the wall. Why did all these bad things happen to me? What had I done to deserve this? I got up and dumped the bag of clothes I'd brought for Maria into the trashcan in my room. Then I crawled back into bed and pulled the covers over my head.

Carmen, one the housekeepers, sat on the bed next to me and patted my back. She didn't speak much English, but she tried her best to comfort me. I refused dinner. Carmen had to go back to work, so I closed my door and wept. For my Dad. For my Mom. For Jacki. For Maria. For Pookey. But mainly I wept for me.

The next morning, I found some little cards and gifts the other kids had made for me and left outside my door. It was sweet, but I was too miserable to appreciate it. I still wasn't hungry and didn't go to breakfast. Back in bed, hidden under the covers, I just wanted to sleep forever. Ann came in to talk to me but I ignored her.

Right before lunchtime, Beth came into my room. I guess the staff was worried about me and had called her. As soon as she sat down on my bed, I started blubbering like a baby. She held me for a long time.

"You need to cry, Jenny," she said. "It's okay, just let it out. Anyone in your shoes would feel the same way."

I cried even louder. I was mortified to be seen carrying on like that, but couldn't help it. Finally the tears dried up and Beth put a cold washcloth on my face, which made me feel better.

"Why don't you go take a shower, get yourself ready, and we'll go out to lunch." I gave her a big hug before I headed for the bathroom.

We went to one of those drive-in restaurants where the waitresses were on roller skates. They brought your food on a tray and hooked it over the driver-side window. My sisters and I never went to that type of restaurant, since my parents thought it was low-class. We ordered hamburgers and French fries that came in red, plastic baskets, and root beers served in large, frosty mugs. I was starving and wolfed down my French fries, which were my all-time favorite food, after Butterfingers.

"You look thin, honey," Beth said. "Have you been eating?"

"No, I'm just not hungry. But, yeah, my pants are getting baggy."

"Well, I have some interesting news. I think I've found a foster home for you."

I stopped eating, but said nothing.

She continued. "Their names are Shelly and Bob Wright. Bob's a mechanic. They're fairly young, late twenties, I'd guess. They have two little kids, and foster daughter who's about your age. They don't live in the best neighborhood in town, but the good news is you'll get to go back to your old school. And next year, you'll start high school with Jacki!"

I grinned. It was the best news I'd heard in a long time.

Then the realization came. "So you think I'll still be in foster care next year? You don't think my mom will be getting out, do you?"

She looked stricken. "Jenny, I just don't know, I guess it could go either way, but we have to be prepared. I hope, for your sake, she does come home, but in all honesty, there's a real possibility she could spend a few years in jail."

That wasn't at all what I wanted to hear, but I'd suspected for a long time Mom wasn't coming home. Especially when they refused to let her out on bail. I had hoped for a miracle, that she would get out somehow. That they would realize she didn't mean it. That her kids needed her. But that obviously wasn't going to happen.

"So you think I might be able to get some new go-go boots?"

She smiled. "We'll see."

Beth picked me up the next morning from the shelter and drove me to my new home. She was very chatty on the way over, but I stayed quiet, feeling all shaky inside.

When we pulled into the neighborhood, my heart sank. Cars were parked on the front lawns, if there were any lawns at all. The driveways were covered with oil stains. Bicycles, old toys and junk were strewn about. Mom would have called these people "white trash."

We pulled up to the curb in front of a plain yellow house. Beth was still being very chipper, but she kept looking at me nervously. We carried my two large suitcases to the front door and knocked. A short, fat lady opened the door and introduced herself as Shelly.

"Not Shelly like the poet, Shelly like the actress. Shelly Temple! Get it?" She had long, stringy, blonde hair, with dark roots, blue eyes, and bright pink cheeks from too much rouge. She was wearing a baggy T-shirt and pedal pushers.

"Hi, honey, come on in," she said, ushering us inside.

I quickly looked around the house. The floors were bare linoleum, with a few threadbare bathroom rugs scattered here and there. The walls hadn't been painted in years. The furniture was shabby. In the corner of the room sat an old TV that was turned on to *Queen For A Day* in black and white. The house was messy and the floors needed to be swept and mopped.

"My, but you are a skinny one! We're gonna have to fatten you up! Well, take a look around. It ain't much, but it's home. I'm bakin' a cake. You like lemon cake? I ain't much of a cook, but I love to bake!"

I looked through the small living room into the kitchen and noted the box of Betty Crocker cake mix on the kitchen counter. I could hear my mother snorting from fifty miles away. You'd never find a cake mix in her kitchen.

"You all go on and have a look around while I pop this in the oven," Shelly said.

Beth and I walked down a hallway and looked inside the first room. A little girl, the very image of her mother, sat on the floor playing with paper dolls. Her hair was messy and she was barefoot, but she was actually quite pretty. A little boy with a blond crew cut sat on the bed, coloring in a coloring book.

The little boy said, "Hi, I'm Bobby Junior. This is my sister Punkin. Her real name's Paulette, but we just call her Punkin. She's four and I'm almost six." We said hello and moved on.

We opened the door to the next room and I was in for a shock. The floor was yellow-checked linoleum and the walls were also painted yellow. The twin beds were covered by a red and yellow plaid bedspread, with curtains on the windows to match. It was the ugliest room I'd ever seen. Dozens of pictures of horses, obviously ripped from magazines, were taped to the walls with Scotch tape. I was horrified. Beth quickly shut the door, muttering something about the brightness of the room.

The last room was the master bedroom, which we didn't go into, but I could see the bed was unmade and there were clothes all over the floor. Beth took a quick peek into the bathroom but I decided against it. I'd seen enough.

Shelly came out of the kitchen, wiping her hands on a dirty dishtowel.

"You folks want some iced tea?" she asked. "Go ahead and have a seat."

Beth and I sat on the sofa and I stared at the TV screen, chewing my fingernails. A woman being interviewed was telling a sad story about her house burning down. She was competing with several other women over who had the saddest story. Then the audience would applaud for the woman they felt the sorriest for and the response was recorded on a meter on the TV screen. Whoever got the most applause would be crowned *Queen For A Day*. My mom always laughed at these women. *"They're all pathetical,"* I thought.

Shelly returned to the living room with two plastic glasses filled with ice tea. "Want some cookies?" she asked. We both declined. Shelly and Beth chatted for a few minutes while I watched TV. I hadn't seen a black and white TV since I was little.

Then Beth had to go, and I felt abandoned all over again. As I walked her out the door, she leaned over and whispered to me: "Just remember, you'll be back at school with your friends on Monday."

I sure won't be bringing any of my friends over to this dump.

"And you can call me any time. Remember that, okay?" I nodded and gave her a hug. Then Shelly and I watched her drive away. I desperately wanted her to come back and get me.

"Well, Becky'll be home pretty soon. She's your roommate. She's kinda cranky, but she's okay. She's a colored girl. I hope you don't mind."

"You mean she's a Negro?" I asked. We'd been taught not to use the expression "colored."

"Yeah."

In the neighborhood I had been brought up in and the schools I had attended, there'd only been white kids. The only Negro I had ever talked to was our family physician, Dr. Alexander, a man Daddy had gone to college with.

"Well, why don't you go unpack, honey? Get yourself organized. I got to hang the wash on the line and get supper goin' pretty soon. Bobby'll be here shortly, and he likes to eat as soon as he gets home."

I went back to the god-awful bedroom and began to shove my things into any dresser drawers that were empty. Then Bobby Junior, or BJ, as he liked to be called, and Punkin came into the room and showed me which bed was mine, and where to hang my clothes in the closet. They both liked to talk at once. Then I heard the front door slam, and footsteps coming down the hallway.

A tall, dark-skinned girl came into the bedroom, threw her books onto the bed and said, "Just what we need: another damn cracker in this house!" Then she stomped out.

"What's a cracker?" I asked the kids. They just shrugged.

I finished unpacking and went into the living room. Becky was sitting with her chair pulled up close to the TV, her legs thrown over the arm.

"You like *Dark Shadows*?" she asked, staring at the TV.

"I never watched it," I answered. We didn't get to watch a whole lot of TV at our house. Daddy said we were better off reading.

"It's really cool. It's about a vampire. Shelly likes to watch *The Edge of Night*, which is stupid. This show's better."

I sat down on the couch, not knowing what else to do. I could hear Shelly in the kitchen, making dinner. That's when I noticed a basset hound lying next to the couch.

"Who's this?" I asked, leaning over to pet him. He lifted his head and licked my hand.

"That's Elvis. He's a pain in the butt. I never liked dogs," Becky answered.

"You must like horses, though," I commented.

"Yeah, when I get big, I'm gonna get me twelve palominos. All of 'em just like Trigger," she said.

I was so pleased they had a dog. Mom had never allowed us to have one. Pookey was the only pet we'd ever had. It turned out that Elvis was pretty old and never did much except eat and lie on the floor.

I heard a car drive up. Becky rolled her eyes and said, "That'll be the master of the house."

The screen door swung open and a short, heavy-set man entered the living room. He had a crew cut and he was wearing greasy overalls.

"Hi, I'm Bob. I guess you must have met the Princess here," he said grinning. "How're you doing? I'd shake your hand but I'm covered with grease. Where's my bride? In the kitchen? Hi, baby. I'm home!" he yelled, and then said, "Got to go wash up. Becky, you help Shelly set the table." Reluctantly, she got up and sauntered into the kitchen. I went in to help.

Bob came out of the bathroom with the kids following him. We all sat around the Formica table and Bob said grace. We never said grace at our house, but I had friends who did. Dinner was Chef Boyardee ravioli, canned string beans and mashed potatoes. Shelly filled our glasses with cherry Kool-Aid as we loaded our plates. Bob asked the kids about their day and they both answered at the same time. Shelly asked Becky if she had fed the dog. She said no. Shelly told her to get up and feed him before eating her own dinner. Becky got up and started slamming cupboard doors.

"Don't mind her," Shelly said. "She fell out of the wrong side of the bed this morning." I was to learn that Shelly had a curious way of saying things. Everyone ignored Becky and continued to eat.

"I baked a lemon cake today," Shelly announced proudly.

"I bet you did, sugar-britches," Bob answered. "She bakes a cake nearly every damn day! My woman knows how to keep her man happy. In more ways than one." He winked at me. I looked away, unsure if I was supposed to be offended or not.

After dinner, Bob told me to go sit in the living room while the girls did the dishes. He came in and sat down in the easy chair with a beer in his hand.

"So I hear you do real good in school," he said.

"Yeah, I get good grades," I answered.

"Well, it'll be good to have someone with some brains around here! Now, my wife, and don't get me wrong, she's as sweet as pie and I love that woman to death, but she's about as sharp as a bowlin' ball, bless her heart. And I wouldn't trade her for nothin'. No sireee, bob. I was a foster kid, too, ya know?"

"No, I didn't know."

"Yep. From the time I was about eight. I was in about ten different homes. Ran around a lot. Got into a little trouble. Stole a car. Nothing serious, mind you. The judge said I could go to jail or join the Navy, so I enlisted right then and there. Did my four years. Got out. Met Shelly and married her as fast as I could. Didn't want her gettin' away from me. Got me two beautiful kids. Yep, I'm a happy man. Don't make no money, but I'm a happy man. You'll end up okay. I can tell."

I smiled. For some reason, I liked this guy.

We all sat around the living room watching TV that night until the kids fell asleep and Bob put them to bed. Then he and Shelly said goodnight and disappeared down the hallway.

I was surprised she didn't tell us when to go to bed.

Becky and I stayed up late and then she fell asleep on the couch. I went into the bathroom to wash my face, but couldn't find a washcloth. So I brushed my teeth and put on my pretty lavender nightgown with the matching robe and slippers I had gotten on my last birthday. They looked out of place in the red and yellow bedroom. I just shook my head as I pulled back the covers. I wondered if there were cooties in the bed. I didn't really know what cooties were, but I'd heard about them.

The bed was lumpy and uncomfortable. The springs creaked every time I moved. I could hear a dog barking in the neighborhood. I imagined Jules and Joey asleep in their room in Morgan Hill, and Jacki in her bed at Aunt Mimi's. It was the longest, loneliest night of my life.

5

THE NEXT MORNING AT BREAKFAST Bob brought out cereal bowls for everyone, a box of frosted corn flakes and a container of Tang. When I poured the milk over my cereal, it came out lumpy. I mentioned this to Becky, who said, "Yeah, powdered milk does that sometimes. You have to stir it up real good." I'd never heard of powdered milk, and when I tasted it, I gagged. So I ate my cereal with nothing on it, and it wasn't bad.

I learned that Saturday was "chores" day in the Wright household. I imagined that meant working all day long. But Shelly only cleaned her house once a week, and for no more than a couple of hours. One time I heard her say, "Housework is dumb. You work from sun-up to sundown, clean everything in sight. But six months later, you just have to do it all over again!"

She put a Smokey Robinson album on the stereo, and cranked it up real loud. I'd never listened to Motown before, but I loved it! We quickly swept the floors, did a minimum of dusting and mopping, rinsed off the draining boards and bathroom counters, and in no time at all, Shelly declared we were finished. She asked if I would mind going grocery shopping with her. When I agreed to go, Becky jumped in and said she wanted to go, too.

As we were driving to the store, Shelly said, "I meant to mention it last night, but my kid brother Tony's gonna be moving in with us for awhile. He just lost his job at the fillin' station. They said he kept comin' up short. But really, they just wanna cheat him out of his pay, the thievin' bastards. Forgive me, Lord." She made the sign of the cross over her heart. Whenever Shelly said anything bad about anyone or used foul language, she always said, "Forgive me, Lord" and crossed herself. I looked at Becky, who rolled her eyes.

"Anyway, Tone is one handsome devil. You girls are gonna love him. Of course, he's a little old for you. He's almost twenty-two. But still, he's real cute. Anyways, he was living with his girlfriend—her name is Lolita, if you can believe that, just like the movie. But she's a *Mexican*!" When she said the word "Mexican," she lowered her voice. "I couldn't believe it when he started up with a Mexican gal. You coulda knocked me over with a fender! But she's real nice. Anyway, they couldn't afford the rent so she had to move back in with her folks, and Tony's gonna stay with us for awhile."

"Where will he sleep?" I asked.

"Oh, we got a little room down in the basement where the washing machine is. There's a bathroom down there, too. He lived there for a while after he dropped outta school. Our place is like home to him."

As we shopped, Shelly filled up the cart with stuff we rarely had in our home. Packages of cookies, hot dogs, potato chips, Jell-O, bologna, and TV dinners. Cans of spaghetti and chili and vegetables. Nothing fresh. No fruit, except bananas. And lots of cake mixes.

That afternoon, several of the neighbors came over and Bob barbequed hamburgers. They brought cases of beer with them and as the evening wore on, the backyard filled up with the sounds of men laughing and arguing. Bob fell asleep on the grass with Elvis snuggled up against him. Shelly said she'd had too much to drink, crossed herself, and headed off to her room.

I put the kids to bed and Becky and I stayed up, talking. She told me she was one of thirteen kids, and that her mother had been married four times, but had had several kids in between husbands.

"Where's your dad?" I asked.

She shrugged. "I don't have a dad" was all she said. She'd been in a couple of foster homes before she came to the Wrights and this was the best one so far.

"They're not bad, for white folks," she said. "They don't care what time you go to bed. Or if you do your homework. And they don't make you do a lot of work around the house, neither. Shelly will ask you to baby-sit them kids sometimes, when she wants to go out with her girlfriends, but I don't mind. My brother, Carlton, when he gets out of the army, is gonna come get me. Unless my mama dries out before then."

I didn't know what she meant, but felt too shy to ask. So I told her about my Mom being in jail. Becky said, "I didn't know you white folks ever did stuff like that. My mom hit my stepdad in the nose with a beer bottle once and then had to drive him to the emergency room 'cause he was bleeding all over. We still laugh about that."

"Did she ever go to jail?" I asked.

Becky started laughing. "Oh, you bet! Everyone in my family's been in jail at least a couple of times. The cops pick on us all the time. It's how we live. But you wouldn't know that, now would you?"

"Well, my mom didn't mean to do it. It was an accident. She was just upset," I said.

"Yeah, I heard that before!" Becky muttered.

Eager to change the subject, I asked, "I don't get it. With thirteen kids in the house, how do you all fit around the dining room table?"

She looked at me like I had rocks in my head. "We don't got no damn dining room table. Everyone just grabs a plate and sits anywhere. But not all my brothers and sisters are at home anyway. Two of my brothers live with their dad. My sister Lorraine, she's seventeen, she lives with her boyfriend. They have a baby. And an other one comin'. We're sorta scattered all over."

We sat in silence for a few minutes.

Then, for some dumb reason, I said, "Our family doctor is Negro."

Becky gave me a hard look. "That's very helpful," she said.

I glanced away, embarrassed.

The next morning, the Wrights were up early, slightly hung over. But they showered, got dressed and cleaned up the kids. Then they headed off to church. They asked me to join them, but I politely declined. We hadn't been raised to go to church, both of my parents being agnostic. And besides, if there was a God, right now I'd be plenty mad at him.

I hoped Uncle Joe was going to take me horseback riding, but when he didn't show up, I called him. The Wrights had just one telephone-- a big, black thing that sat on the end table by the couch. The first time I picked it up, I heard people talking. Shocked, I hung up and told Shelly about it.

She said, "It's a party line, honey. On this side of town, we share the line with three other families. You have to wait till they're done talking. And you only answer the phone if it's for us, which is three short rings. Didn't you guys have a phone at your house?" she asked, sympathetically.

I turned away from her. *Yes, we had a couple of phones. Pretty white Princess phones that hung on the wall. We also had a color TV and a dishwasher*. But I didn't say anything. Why make her feel bad?

When I got through to the house, Aunt Sally answered. She sounded in a hurry and said that Uncle Joe was too busy and couldn't come today. I asked to speak to Jules, but as soon as she came on the line, she started whining and carrying on, so I said I had to go. I called Aunt Mimi's number, but got a busy signal. Bored, I sat down and turned on the TV.

I fell asleep and woke up with a start to the sound of the screen door opening. A tall, handsome young man walked through the front door, carrying a cardboard box. His hair was blond and curly. With big, brown eyes, and a smile on his face that showed beautiful white teeth. I stared at him.

"You must be the new kid," he said, putting the box down on the coffee table. "Looks like they got a cute one this time."

I think I must have turned bright red. It was the first time a guy ever called me cute. People always said Jacki was cute, not me.

"Hi, I'm Jenny," I said.

"Hi, yourself. I'm Tony. Shelly's brother. Half-brother, really. We have the same mom but different dads. So how do ya like it here?"

I was taken off-guard by the question. "Well, it's different," was all I could think to say.

He laughed and said, "They're good folks, Shelly and Bob. Took me in when my old man threw me out. They'd do anything for you. I think you'll like it here. It's real mellow. You got a smoke?"

"No, I don't smoke, sorry."

"I was just joshin' ya. Don't even think of takin' up smoking. It's real bad for ya. They must have a pack around here somewhere. Well, I got to unload the truck. Ya wanna give me a hand?"

As we walked out to the truck, he said, "What are you, about fifteen?"

"I'll be fourteen in a couple of months."

"Damn, baby, you look good. You're gonna be a knockout!"

He called me baby! I fell totally, one hundred percent head over heels in love at that very moment. I couldn't think of a single thing to say. We unloaded a few boxes from the back of his truck, then he said a quick goodbye and took off. I walked back into the house, totally stunned, but with a big grin on my face. Maybe being here wouldn't be so bad after all.

That night, I washed my hair, and Shelly set it for me. She sat on the couch and I sat on the floor in front of her. One of my favorite TV shows, *Bonanza,* was on. It made me think of home. My sisters and I all had a crush on Little Joe, so every Sunday evening we sat, glued to the TV. But I found that watching in black and white was kind of boring.

Shelly told me she had almost completely finished beauty school before she got pregnant and had to drop out, but she hoped to go back when the kids were bigger.

"You should think about goin' to beauty school, too. I'd bet you'd be real good at it!" she said.

"Well, I'm actually thinking along the line of going to college and becoming a reporter," I answered. "And maybe raise horses in my spare time."

She went on to tell me how she had come from a broken home, and how her step-dad used to abuse her and Tony. It sounded like she'd had a pretty hard life.

"But then I met Bobby and everything changed. We started going to church and believing in the Lord. Now we're Christians, and we're on the right path. I think the same could happen for you. You just have to accept Jesus Christ as your Lord and savior. It's as easy as falling off a bicycle."

I made a mental note that I needed to start writing down some of the things that came out of Shelly's mouth. But not the religious stuff.

The phone rang a little while later, and it was Jacki. Since the phone was right in the middle of the living room, I didn't have a lot of privacy.

"How're things going there?" she asked.

"Ummm, okay I guess. I'm really looking forward to going

back to school tomorrow."

"Yeah, me too!" she answered. "I'm thinking that next weekend maybe we can come pick you up and you can stay here for the weekend." Then she told me she loved me, which she had never done before. I was embarrassed to say it back, so I just said, "Me, too." And hung up.

The next morning I was up early, picking out my best outfit. Shelly helped me with my hair. I hadn't told Sharon that I was coming back to school. I wanted to surprise her. Shelly even put a little bit of mascara on my lashes and let me wear a dab of lipstick.

Being back at my old school was great. I had a lot of homework to make up since I'd already missed so much. But being able to hang out with all of my old friends really helped.

Shelly let me have a sleepover one night at Sharon's and I told her everything that had happened. She said, "I can't believe what you've been through," and we both started crying. Sharon had the most normal family of anyone I knew. Her dad was a plumber, her mom a nurse, and she had two older brothers. They lived in a pretty house in the suburbs. I never saw her parents fight.

It was hard for me to get back into the swing of things at school. It was like everything in my life had changed, and yet for everyone else, life was just the same. My friends would be chatting about what boys they had crushes on, and who was wearing a padded bra, and which one of the Beach Boys was the cutest, and I was thinking about my dad, or missing my sisters, or worrying about my mom. I was too embarrassed to tell them anything about living in a foster home. When Sharon asked if she could come spend the night at my house, I just told her that Shelly didn't allow sleepovers.

* * *

I gradually got used to living with the Wrights, and settled into a pattern: school during the day, followed by homework, supper, clean-up, playing with Elvis and the kids in the backyard, and talking on the phone with Beth, who called a couple of times a week to check on me. I could stay up and watch TV however late I wanted.

There were almost no rules. BJ and Punkin frequently fell asleep in their clothes and were put to bed that way. You ate when you felt like it, whatever was in the cupboards. The first week I was there, I went on a cleaning frenzy. I scrubbed the bathroom, the kitchen, and did a thorough job of mopping the floors, but soon the house was a mess again, so I gave up. No one else cared, so I tried not to let it bother me either. And, after a while, it didn't.

One thing I noticed about the Wrights was that, in spite of being poor and unsophisticated, they really loved each other and loved their kids. They were a happy family. Bob would come through the door after work and holler: "Where's my woman?" and Shelly would come out and give him a big hug and kiss and he would pat her on the rump.

And they played a lot with their kids. I frequently walked in on Bob sitting on the floor, playing paper dolls with Punkin. One night she begged to paint his fingernails with bright red polish, and he finally relented. Later that night, he went looking for some nail polish remover to take it off but couldn't find any, so he had to go to work the next day with bright red fingernails. He was that kind of dad.

One afternoon, while wrestling with the kids in the living room, Shelly joined in and all four of them were rolling around the floor, trying to hold Bob down to tickle him. I was envious of them. My family was never physical like that. We went to plays, to the symphony, and once Mom and Dad took just Jacki and me to an opera, but we never got down on the ground and played together. I wanted to join in, but didn't know how, so I just watched. Then Bob stood up with a smile on his face and said to Shelly, "Honey, let's go change the sheets." He asked if I'd mind watching the kids for a while and winked at me. He and Shelly went into the bedroom and closed the door.

For a moment I was taken aback. I knew they were probably doing it. But I always thought sex was something you did at night, in the dark. It never occurred to me it might happen during the day.

Neither Bob nor Shelly were shy about sex. Shelly frequently made comments about Bob's "package." One day she said to me, "He's hung like a rhino," but I thought she said "albino" so it took me a while to get what she meant. Another time she told me she had "become a woman in the backseat of a '57 Plymouth." I was still embarrassed when it came to sex, since we never talked about it much at home, but I enjoyed listening to their banter. It made me feel more like a grown-up when they talked about things like that in front of me.

Of course, they did have squabbles every now and then, particularly over money, but once the tiff was over, they were back to being lovey-dovey again. Bob would yell, "Scooter-Pie, I need some lovin'," and she'd yell back, "OK, go ahead and get started, Stud-Muffin. I'll be there in a minute!" It always made me giggle. They never seemed to hold onto their anger, like Mom did.

The only person in the household who bothered me was Becky. Sometimes she'd follow me and want to hang out, but other times, she was mean and rude. She frequently got into my stuff and wore my clothes without asking. I complained to Shelly about it several times, but nothing changed. Becky was only twelve years old but already a couple of inches taller than me. One day I got so mad I punched her in the back with my fist. Shocked, she burst into tears and sat there, bawling her eyes out. I thought for sure I'd be in big trouble, but all Shelly said was, "Good. Maybe she'll learn something. Sometimes ya just got to nip these things in the butt."

The next weekend, Uncle Joe came and picked me up, and then we drove over and picked up Jacki. I hadn't seen my sisters in a couple of weeks and we spent a pleasant weekend together. But I knew Tony was going to be moving in, so I was in a hurry to get back to the house. I told Jacki about him and she only said, "He's way too old for you. He sounds like trouble. You better keep your distance."

Jacki then told me she'd met a boy at school that she really liked, Doug Palmer. Tall and skinny, but real cute and smart. He also had his own car.

"And guess what? He loves poetry! I actually played the guitar for him one day—he really wanted to hear me play. So I just did some Peter, Paul and Mary songs and he thought I was great. He said we could write songs together!"

"That's far-out," I said. "When do I get to meet him?"

She said one day they might be able to drive over to see me. Maybe even take me to the drive-in movie with them!

That afternoon, Jacki and I watched Joey playing in the backyard with our cousins. Earlier that week, Jules had taken a pair of scissors and cut Joey's hair all crooked. Aunt Sally took her to a beauty parlor to get it fixed, and they had to cut it shorter to make it even. Now her long, beautiful blonde hair was gone and she looked like a little boy. But I noticed she seemed really happy, and it bugged me. I wondered if she'd forgotten our parents. She ran around the yard, laughing and yelling, and then came over and climbed onto my lap.

"So, how are you are doing, squirt?" I asked her.

"Good," she answered, playing with my wristwatch. She twisted it and tried to pull it off my hand.

"Are you happy here?"

"Yeah." She tugged the watch off and was trying to pull on

the stem.

"Do you miss Mommy and Daddy?" I asked.

"Jen," Jacki said sharply. "What are you doing? Why are you asking her that?"

I set Joey down. "Because I don't want her to forget them!"

"She won't forget them. But she's happy here, so leave it alone!"

"Doesn't it bother you she's so happy? I mean, I know it sounds silly, but she never seems sad about Daddy."

Jacki thought for a minute and said, "It's because she's so young. Little kids just bounce back better. You should be happy for her. Would you rather that she was behaving like Jules? Driving everyone crazy?"

It was true. Uncle Joe and Aunt Sally were having a lot of trouble with Jules. She was constantly getting grounded.

I guessed Jacki was right, but still, it troubled me. Before I went back to my foster home that day, I asked Aunt Sally for any pictures she might have of my family, particularly Mom and Dad. I planned to put them on Joey's dresser, but I didn't tell my aunt that. She promised she'd look for some.

As Uncle Joe drove me back to the Wrights that evening, he said "All this driving around was getting to be too much. I want to get you girls together as much as possible, honey, but I'm going to have to cut down to every other weekend. It's costing a lot of money for gas, and the station wagon needs a ring job. Do you understand?"

"Sure," I said, although I really didn't.

As we pulled onto our street, I saw Tony's truck parked in the driveway. I was eager to get into the house, but Uncle Joe said, "Wait a minute. I've got something for you." He reached into the back seat, pulled out a box and handed it to me. It was my new, white go-go boots.

"Thank you, Uncle Joe! You're hunky-dorey!" I kissed him on the cheek and hopped out of the car.

"So I've been told," he smiled.

"See you in two weeks!" I yelled as I closed the car door, and walked towards the house.

Tony, Bob and Shelly were sitting in the living room, watching the Ed Sullivan show. Topo Gigio was on. When I walked through the door, Tony looked up and said, "There's my beautiful baby doll!" and my heart soared. I sat down on the couch to watch TV with my new family.

6

Five months after I moved in with the Wrights, my mother went on trial. Thanksgiving had come and gone. So had Christmas and my fourteenth birthday. The holidays were weird, without my parents around. My aunt and uncle tried to make them special for us but it wasn't the same, and we were in tears much of the time.

We visited with Mom a couple more times, but I always came away feeling sad, disappointed and angry that she never took responsibility for causing so much unhappiness. All she did was blame Daddy. More and more, she focused on her own life and didn't seem interested in mine.

Uncle Joe suggested I start writing to her so I could sort out my feelings, and I enjoyed doing that. By talking to her in a letter, I could say what was on my mind without having her interrupt me. I told her all about school and my friends, but I didn't share much about my home life. Occasionally she wrote back, commenting on things I had shared, giving me advice and asking questions about my sisters. The one person I never told her about was Tony.

From the moment he moved in, Tony and I had a special relationship. We talked a lot, and he could always make me laugh, even when I was really down. He flirted with me, called me his baby girl, and teased me about the boys at school. He was also really sweet and generous with BJ and Punkin, and he even spent time helping Becky with her homework.

Unfortunately, he was gone a lot of the time. He finally landed a job in construction, so he was at work all day, and sometimes he delivered pizza on the weekends. His relationship with Lolita, Lola for short, was on and off. He brought her over to the house a couple of times for dinner, but I didn't really like her much. I thought she was kind of snotty. He had several buddies who'd stop by the house sometimes, and it was always fun to have them there, even though they smoked, drank beer and left pizza boxes around the living room. Shelly didn't seem to mind. She really adored her brother, and as long as no one used profanity around her kids, she was pretty easygoing.

Tony was there the day Uncle Joe called to say Mom's trial would begin on the first Monday in May. I knew it was coming, but it still upset me to hear those words. In a way, I wanted it to be over with, but I was also afraid of the outcome. Uncle Joe and Beth tried to prepare me for the worst. And as the weeks went by, I gradually came to accept that, in all likelihood, my mother would be spending the next few years in prison.

That night, after supper, while the kids were in the bath, we all sat around the living room and talked about the upcoming trial. I cried a lot.

"I don't know if Mom did it on purpose. I hope she didn't. But I don't care. I still love her and I want her to come home."

Everyone was sympathetic. Tony even rubbed my back. But there wasn't much anyone could say or do that would make me feel better.

Becky was unusually quiet. I noticed with surprise that her face was wet with tears. She stared at the floor and then whispered, "At least you had a daddy who loved you."

I didn't know how to respond. Bob cleared his throat and said, "Well, maybe one day, Beck, you'll be able to track down your dad. Maybe even spend some time with him..." His voice trailed off.

Silence filled the room. Becky said "I did meet my Daddy once."

That was a surprise. She always said she didn't have a daddy. "It was the summer I turned five. I was staying with my Aunt Gert in a tiny apartment in Oakland. I don't know where Mama was but it was just me and her there that summer. Gert was Daddy's older sister. Somehow she tracked him down and got him to come over for dinner on my birthday. I'll never forget: he gave me a card that had balloons on the front and it said "Happy Birthday, 5 year old!" And inside was a dollar! A dollar! That was a lot of money to me. All I ever got before was a nickel, maybe a quarter, if I was lucky. So Daddy said, 'Now put that dollar on top of the TV set so it don't get lost.' And I did.

"Then we had supper and afterwards, a cake with blue and pink sprinkles all over it. It was so pretty. It was the first cake I ever remember having. Anyway, it was late and he had to go, I guess. So after he left, I went to get my dollar. I just wanted to look at it, you know? And it was gone! I tore the place apart looking for that damn dollar, but I couldn't find it no where. He took it! My daddy took my dollar! I cried and cried. Aunt Gert said never mind, she'd just give me a dollar, that he must've took it on accident, and I guess I might have believed her for a while. But, you know, over the years, I'd think about that day and I knew it wasn't no accident." She was quiet for a moment and then softly said, "Daddy took my dollar."

We sat in silence while Becky cried some more. "I don't know what's going to happen to me," she said between sobs. "I don't think I can ever go home. There's never enough money. Mama can't hold down a job. She spends all her money on booze, like it's more important to have Jack Daniels in the house than feed her kids. I don't want to be in foster care 'til I'm 18!"

I went over to the couch and sat next to her. I tried to put my arm around her but she stiffened up. "I thought Carlton was going to come get you when he gets discharged from the Army?" I offered.

She wiped tears with the back of her hand and then said, "He's not in the army. He's in prison."

We tried to comfort her. Shelly brought in a plate of cookies. Bob told her she could always stay with them, which made her laugh.

That night, when we went to bed, I whispered to Becky, "I really hate your daddy."

"Yeah, me too," she said. I felt closer to her that night than I ever had before.

* * *

Mom's attorney wanted my sisters and I to be at the trial every day, so Aunt Sally took us shopping for some new clothes. Uncle Joe said he thought it would be good if my sisters and I wore matching dresses on the first day of the trial, but Jacki put her foot down and said, "Not a chance!" She didn't want to be at the trial at all, but I guess she got talked into it. She wasn't happy about it, but she would go.

On Monday and Tuesday the jury was selected so Wednesday was the first day we actually saw the inside of the courtroom. Beth brought me to the courthouse early that morning and I waited in the judge's chambers with my sisters and Uncle Joe. Jules and Joey had puzzles and coloring books to play with, and I brought a notebook to occupy myself, plus a new Nancy Drew book.

The first thing I learned about trials was there were a lot of delays, and motions to be made. A great deal of time was wasted, it seemed to me. We were left in a room with tables and chairs and they brought us some snacks. Jules had been bugging Jacki a lot to ask Aunt Mimi if she could go live with them, and Jacki was getting irritated. She'd already told her no many times. Then Jules came and sat with me and I put my arm around her.

Normally, Jules doesn't like to be touched. But she snuggled up against me and then asked if she could come live in the foster home with me.

"Why don't you like living where you are?" I asked her. "You have family all around you. Why would you want to leave Joey?"

"I hate it there," she whined.

"You should be happy you're with family and stop being a brat all the time," I scolded. She moved away and I realized I had hurt her feelings. I apologized and offered to read to her. But she shook her head and went over to stare out the window.

A couple of hours later they finally brought us into court. Mom was sitting at a table with her lawyer, Mr. Morgan. We sat in the first row behind her. She was wearing a pretty green dress I'd never seen before. She turned around and smiled at all of us, acting like nothing was wrong. I smiled at her, and Jules waved. Joey said, "Hi, Mommy!" Jacki just stared straight ahead.

The prosecutor made his opening remarks and said some really nasty things about Mom. It was horrible having to listen to it. He made it sound like she had done it on purpose, and had planned the whole thing. He called it a "cold and calculated crime." I'll never forget those words. I hated him right off the bat.

Then Mr. Morgan got up and spoke, and he made it sound like it was all Daddy's fault. That my dad had abandoned his family to go and be with another woman. A younger, prettier woman. That my mom had been left on her own to raise four rambunctious daughters. I didn't like him either. I was disappointed that neither of them reminded me of Atticus Finch.

When he was done speaking, there was a moment of silence as he sat down. Just then, I got a whiff of an obnoxious odor. And before I could stop her, Joey said, in a voice loud enough for the whole world to hear, "Okay, who cut the cheese?"

I gasped in horror. Mommy turned around and said, "Shhhh." I'm not sure, because the judge had his hand in front of his mouth, but his shoulders were shaking and I think he might have been laughing.

My sisters and I were only in the courtroom for two days. Most of the time, we were bored. Jacki sat there without moving, while I wrote in my notebook. Jules squirmed around, tapping her foot and letting out loud, dramatic sighs. Joey fell asleep with her head in Jacki's lap and slobbered all over her dress.

On Thursday night, just as Shelly was coming in the door with a pizza, the phone rang. Becky reached it first. She'd been in a foul mood for a couple of days. I think she was jealous because I got to miss school. When the caller asked to speak with me, she said, "Whom the fuck is speaking?"

She handed to phone to me and Shelly started yelling at her, telling her, "I ain't gonna tolerate no language like that in this house!"

It was Uncle Joe on the phone, saying I wouldn't be coming to court in the morning, because Mom was making some kind of deal and there wouldn't be a trial. I was a little disappointed. For one, it meant I had to go back to school the next day, and for two, I was interested in watching the court proceedings, even if it was boring a lot of the time. There was always a small group of reporters hanging around the courthouse, trying to get pictures of us, and everyone but Jacki enjoyed the attention. She kept saying she was "mortified," but I think sometimes she just liked using big words.

On Friday morning, my mother went in front of the judge and pleaded guilty to a lesser charge—two counts of first-degree manslaughter, I think it was--and sentencing was set for a later date. After all the weeks of anticipation, I felt a little let down. A month later, my mother was sentenced to twenty years in prison. Mr. Morgan said she'd probably get out in ten.

The day I heard the news was probably the worst day of my life. Even though I had tried to be ready, it was a shock to realize I'd be twenty-four years old the next time my mother was a free woman, if she behaved herself. I cried and cried. Uncle Joe took me home with him for a couple of days. I needed to be with my sisters.

We had one more visit with Mom at the county jail before she was to be transferred to Frontera, the women's prison in Southern California. Mom had requested to see each one of us individually. Again, Jacki refused to go. Mom saw Jules and Joey first. Then it was my turn.

Mom looked pale to me, with more lines in her face. But she didn't seem as high-strung as she usually was. As I look back on it now, I guess the look on her face was of resignation. She tried to act cheerful, but her eyes were bloodshot and her face was swollen, so I knew she'd been crying a lot.

"I'm really sorry for this mess, honey," she said. "I know you all must be really mad at me."

"Well, Jacki is," I said slowly. "But I'm just sad. I don't want you to be here. Did you tell the judge you're sorry? I don't get how he could send you away when you have four kids to take care of."

She just smiled and held my head against her chest. I felt like a baby.

I needed to know something. "So, are you sorry?" I asked.

She held me for a long while before she spoke. "I'm sorry your dad stopped loving me. I'm sorry he fell in love with someone else and abandoned us. I'm sorry for a lot of things. But you have to understand, at that time, I was just so sad.

I didn't know what I was doing. I wish it had never come to that. But I was so confused and so angry, I just couldn't stop myself."

It wasn't what I wanted to hear. I just wanted her to say she was sorry for killing Daddy. But she never did.

When it was time to go, I hugged her and then started to walk away, and then I burst into tears and clung to her. Crying hysterically, I refused to let go. I *couldn't* let go. It took Uncle Joe and two of the police matrons to pry me off of her and lead me away. I was embarrassed and shocked by my behavior. It just wasn't like me. I cried all the way home.

The thing about crying is, after a while, you get bored with it. Little things distract you, and you start crying less. Then you'll think of something, like your mom's cooking, or the fact that your youngest sister would never remember the good times with your mom and you might start crying all over again, but not quite as long this time. There are other things to occupy your mind, like chores and homework and friends and parties. There are horses, new clothes, and boys to fall in love with. Pretty soon, a whole day has gone by, and you realize you didn't cry all day. Not even once.

* * *

Back at the Wrights' I realized school would be out soon and I had the summer to look forward to. Shelly had taken a job three evenings a week as a cook's helper in a nursing home, and she offered to pay me fifty cents an hour to watch the kids during the day until Bob got home. That gave me enough money to buy records when I wanted to, and to go horseback riding occasionally. Uncle Joe also slipped me some money every now and then, and one day he even gave me a twenty-dollar bill.

The day after school let out, I got to go with Sharon's family for two whole weeks on a camping trip to Yosemite. We did a lot of swimming and hiking and I had a fantastic time.

When I got back, Becky was spending a few days with her aunt. I was happy to have her gone at first. It was nice having the bedroom all to myself. But I started to miss her after a while, especially at night, when we usually stayed up talking. On the days Shelly worked, she left the house around two thirty in the afternoon, so I was home alone with the kids until Bob got there, around five.

About a week later, Tony came home from work early one day. He'd been laid off when the construction job was over. He was all covered with dust and dirt, and, as usual, went downstairs to take a shower. The kids were napping and I was watching *Dark Shadows*. I needed to do some laundry, so I carried a load down to the basement. The bathroom door was open, and Tony was standing at the sink, combing his hair in the mirror with a towel wrapped around his waist. He saw me walk by in the mirror and called out, "Hey, baby girl. What'cha doin?" I stood at the entrance of the bathroom and watched him comb his hair. Since he'd been working out in the sun, his back was golden brown, and his long, curly hair was blonder than ever. He turned to face me. His chest and arms were bronze and muscular. He had almost no chest hair.

"So," he said, smiling at me, "you ever seen a man's pecker before?"

"Ahhhh, no," I answered slowly, looking away.

He paused. "Well, do you want to?"

"I guess so." I hadn't really thought about it much. He unwrapped the towel. I had seen my cousin's penises when they were babies, but it never occurred to me that as boys got bigger, so did their penises. His hung long and thick. It reminded me of the horses out at the riding stable. The end of it was cute, like a fat mushroom.

"So, what do y'think?"

I didn't know what to think. "Groovy!"

"Y'wanna touch it?" he asked.

"Okay, sure." I would've never thought to touch it, but since he offered...

I reached out and grasped it in my hand. It jumped a little, and I yanked my hand back.

"It's okay, Jenny, it's not going to bite you."

I took it back in my hand and was amazed at how it responded, growing bigger and harder. Jacki had told me, "When a man gets excited, his thing gets hard." But she didn't mention it also stood up and pointed to the ceiling. I was impressed.

"Where are the kids?" Tony whispered.

"Taking a nap," I said, pulling away from him.

He reached over and lowered the toilet seat lid, and had me sit on it. He took my hand again, put it around his penis with his hand covering mine, and moved it up and down.

"This is how you please a man," he said.

His hand continued to move mine up and down, slowly at first, and then faster. After a minute or so, he groaned, and some white stuff shot out the end of it. His head was back, his eyes closed, and he continued with a couple more short strokes before he released my hand, which was covered with slime.

"Yuck, *what is that*?"

He opened his eyes and looked at me. "What do you think it is? It's called semen. It's the fluid the sperm live in."

I looked closer. "I don't see any seeds in it."

He smiled and shook his head. "They aren't exactly seeds. They're more like little polliwogs. They're too small to see. Now you better wash up."

I scrubbed my hands with soap and water while he went in to dress.

I heard the kids stirring upstairs and went up to check on them. They were watching cartoons. I sat on the sofa and wondered what had just happened. One minute I had been doing laundry, and the next thing I knew, I had Tony's thing in my hand. I didn't know what to make of it.

Tony came upstairs and watched TV with us.

"Are you okay?" he asked.

I just nodded, staring at the TV. I didn't know if I should be mad or happy or what. Somehow I felt I was *supposed* to be ashamed, but I wasn't.

In the distance, I heard the sound of the ice-cream truck. BJ and Punkin jumped up from the floor and begged Tony for a couple of dimes. He dug some change out of his pocket and told them to get four ice creams. They raced out the door.

Tony leaned over and rubbed my cheek with his finger. "Are you sure you're okay, baby girl?" Again, I just nodded. "I really enjoyed your visit. I hope you'll come down and visit me again."

"Okay," I said.

"Now, you won't go tell nobody, right? It's just between you and me, okay?" I nodded. I still felt too embarrassed to look at him.

"You're so beautiful," he said.

He leaned closer and kissed me on the mouth. I was so startled I didn't even respond. I had never been kissed before. But I definitely liked it!

The kids came back into the house. Tony squeezed my thigh with his hand and then moved away. We all sat on the couch, watching Yogi Bear, sucking on root beer Popsicles.

Two days later, Tony was down in his bedroom, so I went down to do another load of laundry. As soon as I loaded the washer, he was behind me. He turned me around and kissed me. On the lips. On my cheek. On my neck. Then he led me to his bedroom.

He was wearing just a pair of cut-off jeans, which he slipped off as he lay down on the bed.

"Touch me," he said, and I reached down and fondled him like before. He arched his head back and closed his eyes. "Oh, God!" he gasped. In just a few minutes, he was done. He had some Kleenex by the bed, which he used to wipe up with.

"Now I want to make you feel good," he said softly.

"Just kiss me," I told him. And he did. He kissed me long and passionately. I loved being in his arms, with my head on his chest. It was the sweetest thing I had ever known.

After a while, he said, "I can't believe this is happening. This is wrong. You know what jailbait is, right?"

"Yes, of course." I was running my fingertips across his chest. His friends often teased me about being jailbait. "I don't care."

"I don't either, truth be told. This just feels so good. I been wanting to lay down with you for such a long time." He paused. "You know I'd never hurt you. You need to trust me, okay?"

I nodded.

"Now, baby, will you take your clothes off for me?"

I thought for a moment. "No, I don't want to."

He laughed and sat up. I watched him as he lit a cigarette and blew the smoke out of his mouth. "That's okay. We'll wait until you're ready."

I didn't want to tell him I wouldn't be ready for a long time. I was only fourteen. And as much as I adored him, there was no way I was ready to go any further. I loved kissing him. I loved being held by him. The other stuff I did because it pleased him. But I was very happy to leave it at that. For several weeks, I made lots of trips down to the basement.

The only part of our "romance" that bothered me was that I couldn't share it with anyone. I was dying to tell Sharon. I remember thinking that half the fun of being kissed by a cute guy was telling your girlfriends about it later. You get to relive the excitement all over again. But I couldn't do that. At school, all of my girlfriends had crushes on certain boys, but I wasn't interested in anyone but Tony.

Then there was the problem of Lola. Tony was still going with her. I was so mad when I first realized he planned to continue seeing her. But he said that since we had to keep our thing a secret, it would look funny if he weren't dating. Plus, there was very little time I could actually be alone with him, especially after Becky came home. She was around every afternoon when Shelly left for work, unless she went over to a girlfriend's house, which wasn't very often. And then Tony got another job in construction and was gone all day. My trips down to the basement to visit with him just about came to a stop.

At night, I tossed and turned, thinking about him. I would hear his truck pull up in the driveway, hear him come into the house and go downstairs. I so wanted to be with him. The nights he didn't come home were the worst. I didn't know where he was or who he was with, but I guessed he was with Lola. It was torture.

Frequently, in the evenings, Jacki would call. She'd tell me all about her adventures, the job she had taken over the summer at the donut shop, and her relationship with Doug. They drove over to visit me one afternoon, and my sister was horrified at the way I was living.

"I cannot *believe* you haven't made Beth move you to a nicer home! This place is a dump! These people are pigs!"

I couldn't bring myself to tell her that I actually liked living there. "It's not that bad," I said. "They're really nice here. Becky says most places are a lot worse."

"Well, I'm going to have a talk with Beth. I am totally appalled!"

"No, it's okay. Really. I've settled in here now, I don't want to get moved again." Of course, I couldn't tell her about Tony.

She promised she'd come get me more often and bring

me over to Aunt Mimi's to spend the night, which she did a couple of times. Aunt Mimi's apartment had a swimming pool. I've always loved lying out by a pool, reading a good book. But with her work schedule, and seeing Doug, and going to the beach with her friends, she didn't spend that much time with me. And I wanted to be home as much as possible, just in case Tony was around.

Then, the weekend before school started, we were having supper one night when Tony said he had a surprise for me. Talking to Bob and Shelly, he said one of his friends from high school, a guy by the name of Buddy, was working on a dairy farm over in Fresno, and they had a couple of horses. He'd invited Tony to come over for a ride and said he could bring me. I was thrilled! I'd get to go horseback riding and spend the whole day with Tony! Becky jumped in and said she wanted to go too, but Tony said they only had two horses. She got real bratty when she heard she couldn't go. Shelly finally sent her away from the table, and while that was going on, I heard Bob say something to Tony, who responded with, "Jesus Christ, Bob, she's just a kid!" I knew they must have been talking about me. Bob relented but added, "You just better take good care of her." I wondered if he was suspicious. But Tony did a real good job of acting innocent.

7

We left early on Saturday morning. It was a two-hour drive to Fresno. I was so excited the night before I barely slept. As soon as we got out to the countryside, Tony said, "Hey, why are you sitting way over there?" and I scooted next to him. He put his arm around me as we drove. I loved being in the truck with him. It felt like I was just driving down the road with a real boyfriend. Sometimes he'd tell me to get a cigarette for him, and I'd put one in my mouth, light it, take a puff and hand it to him. I never inhaled, but I felt like a grown-up. I had deliberately worn my tightest blue jeans and a T-shirt that showed off my bust. Tony had mentioned there was a river ran through the property where we'd be riding, so I'd worn my two-piece bathing suit underneath my clothes.

It was going to be a hot day, and soon we stopped for gas and Cokes. Getting back in the truck, Tony pulled me close and kissed me. Then he groaned. "Jesus, Jenny, you have no idea what you're doing to me."

When we finally found the ranch, it was almost noon. Buddy and his girlfriend were there. They had two large, chestnut horses saddled and ready to go. Buddy was a short, dark-haired guy with a thin, black moustache. I'd met him a couple of times at the house but didn't care for him much. His girlfriend, Tina, was small, with fair skin and dark hair. Buddy called her his "Port-a-gee." She wore tight jeans, cowboy boots and a cowboy hat. I heard Buddy say to Tina, "Tony likes 'em young."

We mounted the horses and rode down a dirt road along the river. I sat in the saddle, while Tony sat behind me. Our horse was a little rambunctious, so Tony took over the reins, which meant his arms were around me. I didn't mind. I was ecstatic, riding in the sunshine with Tony. This was the happiest I had been since before my father died.

We stopped after a while, at a clearing near the river, and tied up the horses. Tina and I stripped down to our bathing suits. The guys stripped off their jeans and jumped in the river, wearing just their underwear. Tina and I tiptoed into the water, getting used to the temperature gradually. Then I dove under. I felt so refreshed after the hot drive in the truck. We swam around and splashed each other, and then Tony carried me around the water on his back. It was the most fun I'd ever had. I wished every day could be like this.

Eventually, we got on the horses and rode back to the barn. The guys unsaddled them while Tina and I fixed our hair and put on a little makeup. She told me that Buddy carried a little tube of Vaseline with him that he'd rub into his hair before he combed it. She said he thought he was Elvis Presley. Then she said to me, "I don't mean to pry or anything, but don't you think Tony's a little old for you?"

"Oh, we're just friends," I said. I could feel myself starting to blush.

She stared at me for a minute. "That's not what I hear," she said.

The guys decided to take us to a little diner close to town. Tony and I hopped into the truck and followed Buddy and Tina to the restaurant. The guys ordered beer, while Tina and I had Cherry Cokes. When the waitress came back with our drinks, we ordered cheeseburgers and French fries.

The guys were talking about things they'd done in high school, and the whole time Buddy kept looking at my chest.

It made me really uncomfortable. I was eager for us to finish up and get out of there so I could be alone with Tony again. Finally we said our goodbyes, and we were on our way. By that time, it was after dark. I was so disappointed for the day to be coming to an end. A little way out of town, Tony pulled off the main road and onto a narrow dirt lane between two fields.

He stopped the truck and turned off the engine. "Oh, baby, I been wanting to kiss you all day." We kissed for a long time. Then he was lying on top, pressing his hardness into me. He shoved my T-shirt up and grabbed my breasts. It felt so good that I let him continue for a few minutes, before I finally said, "Tony, no, stop!" I really did want him to stop. I knew I couldn't let him go any farther, or I'd be in real trouble.

"No, honey, don't make me stop. Please. I love you."

While I was digesting this information, he pulled down my bathing suit top and started kissing my breasts. It felt fantastic, but also a little scary.

"No, Tony, stop! Please!" But he didn't. He kept touching, squeezing and kneading my nipples. It felt so incredible. Okay, I thought, just this. Just above the waist. It'll be okay. So I let him. But Tony took this to mean I was okay with anything. He reached down to undo the zipper on my jeans.

"No, no, no!" I pushed his hands away. "Tony, stop it!"

Finally he sat up. "Baby, I don't understand. Don't you love me?"

"Yes, I love you!" It was the first time I'd ever said it to a boy and it felt funny. But I really did love him.

"Then what's the problem? I promise I won't hurt you. I would never hurt you, I told you that."

"I'm just not ready for this," I answered.

"Look, we love each other. It's the right thing to do. You can't just keep me waiting. I need you so bad."

"Well, let me just touch you..." I reached for his crotch.

"No," he said. "That's not what I want. I want to see you. I want to touch you. Please, baby, I want to look at you. Don't you want to make me happy?"

Well, just looking wouldn't hurt, I thought. Reluctantly, I let him pull my jeans off. He reached for my bathing suit bottoms but I grabbed onto them in one last effort to stop him. But he was stronger than me, and just yanked them down.

"Oh, God, look at you in the moonlight. You're fucking beautiful. I am so lucky to have you. I love you so much, baby."

Just at that moment, I thought about my family. I wondered what Jacki would say if she knew where I was right now. What would my mom think about me if she knew? I felt like crying.

Tony kissed my face, my neck and then put his tongue on my nipple again. With his right hand, he reached down and touched my pubic hair. I tried to squirm away from him.

"Honey, spread your knees for me a little," he whispered.

"No," I protested.

He reached down and separated my legs. And then touched me down there. Where no one had ever touched me before. "There, see? Isn't that nice? Don't it feel good?"

I didn't say anything. He continued to touch me.

"Oh, sweetheart, you feel so nice. I been wanting to touch you there for so long. You make me so happy."

Then he grabbed his pants off the floor and I thought he was going to put them back on. Instead, he pulled something out of the pocket and I heard the sound of paper tearing.

"Tony, what are you doing?" I whispered.

"Shhhh, baby, it's okay." I couldn't exactly see what he was doing in the dark.

Then he shifted himself so that he was on top of me, between my legs, and I could feel him pushing himself inside me. "No, no, stop it!" I yelled.

"It's okay, honey, I won't hurt you." He kissed me hard on

the mouth and I couldn't pull away. He shoved himself in. It was uncomfortable. Not really painful, but unpleasant, like he was too big. He thrust a few times, then cried out "Oh, yes! Oh God," and collapsed on top of me. I lay there quietly. He kissed me again and told me how much he loved me.

Finally he sat up and lit a cigarette.

"Are you okay, baby doll?" he asked, and I burst into tears. "Awww, honey, don't be upset. I'm sorry. I just lost control. I couldn't help myself! It's just that I love you so much. Next time, it'll be better, I promise."

"I wasn't ready," I sobbed.

"I know, but it's always like that the first time, for a girl. Come here, snuggle with me. You just don't know how happy you made me. Now shhhhh. You're okay." I laid my head on his chest and he held me tight. After a while, he said, "I better get you home before old Bob sends out the posse." He started the motor and we drove home. I was quiet the whole way. I was happy that Tony loved me, but I felt so confused about what had happened. I wished he could have waited.

Before we reached our street, he pulled over and kissed me again. He asked if I was feeling better. I said yes, but I wasn't so sure.

That night, as I lay in bed, I missed my mother more than ever. Why couldn't she be here for me?

The next morning, Tony was out of the house when I got up. Jacki and Beth were coming over to take me school clothes shopping, so that helped to distract me from what had happened the day before. Tomorrow was going to be my first day of high school, and I'd be able to see Jacki every day. That should have made me happy. But I was still feeling weird about Tony. I just couldn't get it out of my mind, and didn't understand what I was feeling. Tony had said he loved me over and over, but I still felt sad.

* * *

High school was better than I thought it would be. Jacki had a lot of friends, both male and female, and they gave me a lot of attention. Because I was hanging out with seniors, I earned the admiration of a lot of my own classmates. Frequently, her friends gave me rides home from school so I didn't have to take the bus. I ended up being a lot more popular than I had been in junior high. Sharon and I were having a blast.

At home, things weren't quite as rosy. Becky spent a lot of time with various relatives, and each time she came back from a visit, she'd be angry with her foster family, calling us crackers and honkies. It would take a few days before she would settle down. Shelly and Bob talked about having her moved to a new home, but decided against it. She still got into my stuff a lot, and always tried to listen in on my phone calls. But sometimes we talked about things at night, especially if one of us had just returned from visiting with our mothers. She only had supervised visits with her mother, and her social worker had to be present. Becky didn't get along with her social worker, so frequently she just didn't go.

We went to see Mom about once every six weeks after she went to prison. She seemed more resigned to her situation by then, and had made friends with some of the other inmates. She didn't seem as angry all the time and she asked me more questions about myself. But she really wasn't part of my life anymore. It was hard to talk to her. I couldn't tell her about Tony. She didn't know any of my new friends. I didn't like to talk about the Wrights, because I knew she would just say things to put them down. So mainly I just asked her questions about the other inmates.

After school started, I saw Tony a lot less. I still babysat the kids three days a week, but usually Becky was there.

We had the opportunity to be alone maybe once every two weeks, if that. I'd go downstairs to his bedroom, close the door and strip off our clothes. Since we'd already gone all the way that night in the truck, there didn't seem much point in going backwards, so I continued to let him have sex with me, although I didn't enjoy it very much. It always felt rushed and I worried about getting caught or getting pregnant. I did love cuddling with him afterwards, when he would kiss me and tell me how much he loved me. I lived for those moments.

But sitting in class the next day, I'd look at other girls and wonder if any of them were having sex. And if they enjoyed it, or just felt guilty. I wondered if Jacki had done it with Doug yet. I couldn't help but worry about what she would think of me if she ever found out.

Once again, Halloween and Thanksgiving rolled around. I spent the holidays in Morgan Hill and enjoyed being with my sisters and cousins, but one thing really upset me. Joey had started calling Uncle Joe "Daddy." When I heard it the first time, I yelled at her. When she did it again, I burst into tears. Uncle Joe pulled me aside and we had a long talk. He said he'd wanted to talk to me for a while, because he and Aunt Sally were thinking about asking Mom's permission to adopt Jules and Joey. I was horrified. But he said that Joey missed having a father. She wanted to call him Daddy, just like the boys did. And if they all had the same last name, they would feel like more of a family. And then there was the problem with Jules.

It had been a rough year for my sister. She not only lost Mom and Dad, but Jacki and me as well. She was fighting with kids at school, and seeing a therapist who initially suggested the adoption. It all made sense when he explained it, but it felt like my younger sisters would now be a part of my uncle's family, not mine. I cried and cried, and got a bad headache. And then cried some more. The thought occurred to me that they would become Julie and Johanna Southerlin. We would not be the Amazing Graces anymore.

"You're taking them away from me!" I accused Uncle Joe. But it wasn't true. They were no longer mine, anyway. Jacki came in and sat with me and we both wept. Our sisters were part of a different family now. Nothing was going to change that.

In December, Shelly announced that she and Bob were taking the kids over Christmas vacation to visit with her mother, who lived up in Crescent City. Becky and I were welcome to go with them, but we both declined. I didn't know her family very well. We'd only met them a couple of times, and I didn't want to ride in a cramped car all that way. Besides, I'd be spending a few days in Morgan Hill, I told them. But the real reason was that, if we could get rid of Becky, I'd have the chance to be alone with Tony. And then I got a lucky break. Becky was going to go on a trial visit with an aunt she had in San Francisco, and, if things worked out, she might live there permanently. I asked Shelly, if Becky moved out, would I have the room all to myself, or would she take in another foster kid?

"Don't know," she said. "We'll jump off that bridge when we get there."

I couldn't wait for Christmas break! The first two weeks of December were the longest weeks I'd ever known.

I had to admit, things with Tony had been a little weird lately. He wasn't at home much, so I was always cranky with him when he did come around. I missed him. I hated it when he went out at night or didn't come home after work. I knew he was going out with other girls and it made me miserable. I told him if he loved me, he wouldn't want to be with other girls.

One night he made the comment that he was "tired of changing my diapers." When I demanded to know what he meant by that, he said, "You're just so young. You need to be with boys your own age." I threw my hairbrush at him when he said that. I kept thinking that if we could spend a few days together, I wouldn't be so bitchy. I just wanted to be with him, to curl up with him at night, and wake up next to him in the morning. I liked to imagine us living in a little apartment together. He'd be working during the day, and I'd be at home, cooking for him and ironing his shirts. We'd be so happy!

As it got closer to winter break, Shelly told me I'd have to make arrangements for some place to stay while they were gone, because she knew I wasn't supposed to be left home alone for two weeks. I assured her I would be spending most of my time at Sharon's, and that was good enough for her. Shelly didn't always abide by the rules, anyway, but she said she just wanted to "cover her ass." Then she said, "And don't have no parties while we're gone, neither." I promised her I wouldn't.

Uncle Joe called the morning that Shelly and Bob left because, for some dumb reason, Shelly had told him they were going to be gone, so I also told him that I would be at Sharon's most of the time. He said to be careful and that he'd pick me up later in the week. So the coast was clear.

When Tony came home from work that evening, he got cleaned up and took me out to dinner. We hadn't been out together since our horseback riding date. Once again, I was so happy just to be with him. I wanted him to take me dancing, but there was no place I could get in without an ID card. I wanted to go someplace romantic, but we just headed back home. Once we got to Tony's room, we made love, and it was much better than it had ever been. I was still pretty shy about my body, even though he kept telling me how pretty I was. Finally, he made me stand in front of a mirror and look at my body. I didn't want to, I kept looking away, but he made me look at my full frontal image in the mirror.

"Look at how gorgeous you are!" he said. "I don't know

why you always compare yourself to Jacki. She's cute and all, I won't deny that, but babe, take a good look at yourself. You are really beautiful! A total knock-out!"

I couldn't stop smiling. We took a shower together and then went upstairs in our robes for ice cream.

Later that night, Tony said he wanted to take some pictures of me. He had a new kind of camera that took pictures instantly. No need to take them in to be developed! You just snapped a picture, it slid out of the camera and you could watch it develop right before your eyes. I would have been flattered, except he wanted me naked in the pictures. I put my foot down and said "not on your life." But he persisted. He promised no one would ever see them but him, and said he needed the pictures of me for the times when we couldn't be together. He even said that he wouldn't need to be with other girls if he had these pictures.

He had me pose in several embarrassing positions. I tried to hide my face whenever I could, but he said he wanted to see my beautiful mouth. I was glad when he finally put the camera down and we could go to sleep.

The next day was Saturday and I spent the day helping him move a friend into an apartment. That evening, we had a cookout in the backyard and again I spent the night in his room. On Sunday morning he said "I got some things I got to take care of so I'll be back after awhile."

"Why can't I go with you?" I asked.

"I'd rather just get these things done on my own," he said.

"I don't get why I can't go with you," I argued. "I hardly ever get to see you any more."

"Look, stop smothering me, Jen. I said I'll be back a little later."

That really stung. He took off without me and I stewed about it all afternoon. But when he showed up later with a large bouquet of flowers, I forgave him. We made love for hours and then took a shower together. We were just climbing into bed when we heard a loud pounding on the front door.

"Who in Sam Hill is that?" Tony said, and then we heard Uncle Joe calling my name. I pulled my clothes on and rushed upstairs. I opened the front door, and Uncle Joe pushed past me into the room.

"What are you doing here?" I asked.

"I ran into Sharon's mom this evening at the grocery store. It seems she was visiting some family in Morgan Hill. I thanked her for keeping an eye on you. She said she hadn't seen you in weeks."

"Well, I…had some baby-sitting jobs that came through for me this weekend, so I just stayed here."

I knew it sounded lame, but it was all I could think of.

"Are you here alone?" he demanded.

"No, Shelly's brother is here. He's downstairs."

"Call him up here." Uncle Joe was never upset like this. It scared me.

I called down to Tony and eventually he came up the stairs. He was wearing just his jeans. I wished he had thought to put on a shirt.

"Has my niece been here all weekend?" Uncle Joe must have thought I was out riding around with boys.

"For the most part, yes, Sir, except when she's been baby-sitting." Thank God he'd overheard that.

Uncle Joe looked from Tony to me. I realized then that both of us had wet hair. I hoped he wouldn't notice. He seemed unsure what to do next, and then he said, "Go pack up some clothes. You're coming home with me."

I ran into my room and started shoving clothes into a paper bag. I was so scared about almost being caught that it didn't occur to me, until we were in the car, that my vacation time with Tony was over.

Uncle Joe drove for several minutes in silence and then said, "I need the truth! Did that boy lay a hand on you?"

"No, of course not, Uncle Joe! He's way too old for me. I swear!"

"Are you sure you're being straight with me?"

"Of course! I would never lie to you, Uncle Joe! Honest! In fact, I have a crush on a boy in school named Timmy. He has horses and everything!" The lies were flying out of my mouth. I had no idea where they were coming from.

He was quiet for a few minutes. Then he said, "It's just one damn thing after another with you kids." I had never heard him speak that way. Since the day my dad died, Uncle Joe had been nothing but kind and sweet to us. It would break my heart if he ever found out I was lying.

The rest of Christmas break was spent in Morgan Hill, though I did spend a couple of days at Aunt Mimi's with Jacki. I got to pal around with her and Doug, which was fun. I kept imagining what it would be like if Tony and I could have hung out with them. I would've loved that.

8

Six months later, my relationship with Tony came to an abrupt and disastrous end. In the middle of class one day, I was called into the principal's office once again. I half-expected to see Uncle Joe waiting there with bad news.

But it was Beth. She looked really angry. "Let's go," was all she said. As I got into her car, I could see all my belongings in the back seat.

"What's going on?" I asked her.

She took a long, deep breath. "Shelly found pictures of you and Tony."

Oh, no!

"Apparently your uncle called Bob and Shelly after Christmas. He was worried something was going on between you and that kid. Bob said the thought had crossed his mind as well. Shelly was positive her brother wouldn't get involved with a minor, but recently she decided to do some snooping, and found the pictures. She didn't want to get Tony into trouble, but Bob was livid and insisted they call me. Jennifer, I need to know. How long has this been going on?"

I was completely dumbfounded. I didn't know what to say, so I said nothing.

"You are my responsibility. I put you in that home."

Visions of my uncle finding out the truth spiraled inside my head. And Jacki. I was horrified that anyone had seen those nasty pictures. This was the worst thing that could have happened.

Then I panicked and said the only thing I could think of, the one thing that would get the blame off me. I said, "I didn't want to. He made me." As soon as I said it, I was sorry. It wasn't exactly true. I loved Tony. I didn't want to get him into trouble.

"Oh, Jenny, why didn't you tell someone?" Beth wailed. "I would have taken you out of there. I could have protected you."

Now that Beth was feeling guilty, I wished I could take it back. But then I would have been in big trouble again. I was so confused; I didn't know what to say. "I don't want to talk about it," I said.

"Well, you're going to have to talk to someone about it. We're heading back to the shelter. You can't live at Shelly's anymore. And a police report has to be filed."

"I'm not talking to no police!" I was damn sure of that. There was no way I'd say anything else to get Tony into trouble.

"They have the pictures. That's pretty good evidence you were being abused, honey." Now that she thought it wasn't my fault, she was being kinder to me. I wanted to break down and tell her everything because I had never been able to talk to anyone about my first love affair. But I had also heard Tony and his friends talking about "jailbait" laws, and I knew that, in order to prosecute a guy for statutory rape, they needed the testimony of the victim. I knew I would never, ever testify against him. No matter what.

But other things besides Tony demanded my attention right then. Beth pulled me out of the foster home where I'd lived for the last eighteen months, and where I had grown close to my new family. I thought about Bob and Shelly and felt so incredibly embarrassed. I thought about BJ and Punkin, who I would never get to say goodbye to. And I thought of Becky who, in spite of being a major pain sometimes, had been like a sister to me. Where would I go now? Would my new foster family know what I had done with Tony? Would they trust me? In just a couple of hours, my life had once again been turned entirely upside down. Only this time it was my fault.

I was at the shelter for only two days when my old buddy, Maria, walked through the door, carrying a paper bag with her belongings. We almost didn't recognize each other. I felt a little bit shy connecting with her again. But in no time at all, we were back to being best friends.

Maria had changed a lot over the last year and a half. Almost sixteen now, she was taller and a little heavier, wearing makeup and long, dangling earrings. She had taken up smoking recently, and complained bitterly that she really needed a cigarette. Her grandma had suffered a pretty serious stroke, and it was doubtful that Maria would be able to go back there to live.

"It don't matter," she said. "Me and Eddie are getting married, as soon as he gets a job."

"Maria, no! You're too young!" I argued. It was after lights-out, and she and I were once again talking about our futures.

"I don't care, I love him and we're gonna get married. We can live with his aunt. We'll both get jobs. It'll be fine."

"But I thought you were going to go to college. Be a veterinarian or something."

"I can still do that. Maybe Eddie can support me while I go to school. But right now, I just want to drop out and go to work. I want a big wedding, with lots of bridesmaids."

I figured that she probably loved Eddie as much as I loved Tony, but still it seemed like a stupid plan. However, I didn't want to tell her that. I had enough to worry about.

"Hey, Maria," I said. "Did you ever figure out how the 'sperms know when to pop out of the man'?"

She was quiet for a second, and then she burst out laughing. "I sure did! I got firsthand experience, if you know what I mean!"

"Yeah, me too," I said softly.

Two days later, Beth came to the shelter, accompanied by a young police officer. He wanted a statement about my "physical relationship" with Tony. At first he was really nice to me, being all sweet and sympathetic, but when he realized I wasn't going to say anything, he started getting a little nasty.

"Why would you want to protect someone who's been abusing you?" he demanded.

I refused to say anything.

"You know," he continued, "if he was abusing you, there's a good chance he was doing the same to other kids in the house."

That was so ridiculous I almost laughed. Still, I wouldn't say anything.

Finally, he gave up. As he was preparing to leave, he turned to me and said, " You really need to think about what you're doing. Do you actually want to let him get off scot-free?"

I looked away from him. None of this really bothered me, since no one had a clue as to what had gone on between Tony and me. Beth was disappointed that I wouldn't cooperate with pressing charges, but she said she understood. She assumed I was afraid of Tony and I let her think so. It was just easier that way.

Then I asked if she had told Uncle Joe why I had been moved from the home. She said he knew I'd been moved because something inappropriate had been going on. Now he knew I had lied to him. I was so ashamed. How could I face him? I started crying and told Beth, "Tony made me promise not to tell!"

She hugged me for a long time and said she was sure Uncle Joe would understand.

I stayed at the shelter for another two weeks. I was glad that Maria was there because it made me less lonely. We both missed our boyfriends constantly. One night I told her everything about Tony, from the very beginning. When I told her about the night in the truck, she got really upset.

"Jenny, that's not right, I don't care if you're in love with the guy, he's not supposed to just *do it.* Man, that's really cold. I held Eddie off for almost four months, but when we finally did, it was so sweet and special!"

"That's so romantical," I said slowly. A sense of sadness engulfed me. I wished my first time had been like that.

Two weeks later, Beth surprised me by saying that she'd applied for an emergency foster license so I could live with her and Ken. They had a small house in an area of San Jose called Willow Glen. She wanted to keep me in the same school, so she'd have to drive me there in the mornings before she went to work, and I'd take a couple of city buses home in the evening. I wouldn't get home until after dark, but I didn't mind. As Shelly would have said, "Don't look a gifted horse in the mouth."

9

Jacqueline

When I got the news my younger sister Jennifer had been molested for over a year by the brother of her foster mother, I took a head-dive right over the edge. Back then some people called it a "nervous breakdown." I don't know what they'd call it today.

Actually, my psychiatrist, Dr. Wheeler, said, "There's no such thing as a nervous breakdown. There's no way nerves *can* break down." He paused and then he asked if I knew anything about camels. I answered, "No, not really," wondering where this was going.

He continued, "The camel has the amazing capacity to carry a load that is over twice its own weight. But if you try to make him carry one more stick over that weight, the camel will just sit down, and nothing can entice him to get up. Take away the stick, he'll get right back up."

"So," I concluded, "the straw that broke the camel's back..."

"Exactly," he said, smiling. "Human beings are a lot like camels. We can carry only so much. Once we get overloaded, we just collapse."

I wasn't so sure I cared for being likened to a large, ruminant mammal, but I got the point. The last eighteen months of my life had been one horrific load after the next: my wacko mother murdered my father and was sent to prison, which she justly deserved, and then my sisters and I were separated. Jenny and I had to go to the children's shelter. I was eventually rescued by my Aunt Mimi but, in the process, had to abandon Jenny. She was placed in a foster home where she was living with a bunch of lowlifes. She didn't seem to mind it that much. She'd even started to sound like them. She'd say, "I didn't do no homework last night" and I'd say, "Jeez, Jen, you're talking like a hillbilly."

The thing about Jenny is that she never really shows what she is feeling. She was very shy about crying in front of people, for example. But so even-tempered; she'd just go with the flow. When bad things happen, she just says, "Okay, let's see what this experience is like." Being a natural born writer, she'd make a lot of notes and write up a little story. I wish I had paid more attention to her stories. Maybe I could have seen what was happening.

As for me, I'd always been pretty emotional, but not pathologically so, like my other sister, Jules, who'd go off the deep end over anything and everything back then. Always angry and moody when she was young. It seems like she'd been unhappy since the day she was born. In some ways she's always been the most like my mother, I'm sorry to say. And then Joey, the youngest of our clan, was more like Jenny in that she was calm and smooth-tempered, but easily influenced a lot by those around her. If you were laughing, she'd be laughing, but if you were crying, then so was she. Sometimes, it could be a real bother.

Jules and Joey, taken in by my aunt and uncle, were raised in a relatively normal family environment after the "accident," which is what we euphemistically called the day my mother deliberately ran down her husband and the father of her four daughters. From that point on, I felt responsible for my siblings, and when Uncle Joe and Aunt Sally hinted around that they wanted to adopt my two sisters, I breathed a sigh of relief. I was just sixteen then. I could barely care for myself, let alone them. But being that I was the eldest, and that dear mother would be in the slammer for at least a decade, I felt it was up to me to take care of my sisters the best I could. With Jules and Joey in Morgan Hill, I only had to worry about Jen and me after we were carted off to the children's shelter, which to me was akin to being dropped off at the dog pound. I was on the phone immediately, I tried to get someone we knew to come and get us, but the only likely candidate was my mom's best friend from college, Margaret Ann Dorrington.

If ever there was a woman who was the exact opposite of my mother, it was Aunt Mimi. How those two ended up as best friends has always been a mystery. Where my mother was out-going and extroverted, Aunt Mimi was a shy little mouse, afraid of the world and everyone in it. Easily intimidated by the paperboy, she's also the woman who can't say no. A hundred boxes of Girl Scout cookies can't be wrong.

So when I started asking Aunt Mimi to let us come live with her, at first she said maybe, but it could only be one of us since she had such a small apartment. I then launched into a vigorous campaign to make myself the lead candidate for the position. I pointed out that Uncle Joe had hinted that after I got my driver's license, he might give me Daddy's old VW bug. Daddy had kept the car since he was in college. My mother had tried for years to make him get rid of it, but he loved that old car. It would mean a lot to me to have it. And with transportation, I could drive myself to and from school and Aunt Mimi wouldn't have to worry about taking me everywhere.

Finally she consented. I felt enormously guilty about leaving Jenny behind, but I knew she would understand, being the forgiving person that she was. I completely took advantage of her sweet nature.

But, in my immature sixteen-year-old mind, I felt it was okay because I absolutely hated being at the shelter, whereas Jenny didn't seem to mind that much. She and her buddy Maria were constant companions. She started right in at the new school, making friends and getting involved in school activities. She amazed me, actually. So I took the ball and ran with it. Left her all by herself.

If I had been more worried about Jen, maybe I would have ended up at the Wrights', and I'd have slapped that slimy Tony the minute he tried to lay a hand on me. But that's not the way it happened. If I could take it back, I would.

* * *

Dr. Wheeler tried to get me to see how, from an early age, I had taken on the role of being the adult female in the house. I had to, because my mother refused that assignment.

As a little girl, I adored her. She was more fun than anyone. She always liked to play with me and buy me things. I had a huge wardrobe and lots of toys. But as I got older, I was aware of the tension created in my home whenever my mom went on one of her spending jags. I got an inkling that things were off-kilter at my house, when I started having sleepovers with my girlfriends. I noticed their parents were actually friendly toward each other, and you didn't hear constant bickering, like you did at home. When I was younger, that didn't matter to me as much because I enjoyed all the toys I got from Mother and didn't want to give them up. But when I reached the age of eight or nine, I started trying to get her to scale back on her spending, by telling her I didn't need things. I also tried to get my sisters to go along with me, but that was a hopeless cause.

I remember my parents one time having a huge fight over, of all things, S&H Green Stamps, which were tokens that grocery stores and gas stations handed out after a purchase. You'd lick the back and stick them into little booklets and then could redeem them for household products. My mom always threw ours in the trash and that made Daddy really angry.

"Those are worth something," he yelled.

"What do you think, we're trailer trash? We don't need to save *green stamps*, for God's sake!" she yelled back.

"It's like throwing money right down the drain!" he countered.

Mom just laughed and shook her head. "I'm not wasting my time with those stupid stamps. My mother never bothered with them and I won't either!"

After that, Mom turned the stamps over to us kids and let us redeem them for whatever we wanted, but she always thought it was a gigantic waste of time. "The next thing you know, he'll have us collecting welfare," she grumbled.

And it wasn't just about spending money. My mom didn't like to hear the word "no." When she wanted something, she wanted it, and no amount of logic was going to prevent her from having it. Maybe my grandparents spoiled her, I don't know. But those same parents raised Uncle Joe, and he never behaved that way. My mother was like a kid who doesn't care what she does, even if it hurts other people. So from the time I was ten, she and I were constantly at odds, unless I really needed something from her, and then I'd have to kiss up.

I guess the main problem with my mom is that she was completely selfish. Everything was always about her. One year, she completely ruined our trip to Disneyland.

My father was so busy working that he rarely took time off for family vacations. But in 1963, the whole family went to Southern California for ten days where we planned go to Disneyland and San Diego. My sisters and I were ecstatic. Not only were we all going on vacation together, but due to Daddy's schedule, we got to miss a few days of school. As I mentioned, it was 1963, and my parents were avid Democrats. They both campaigned for John Kennedy when he ran for president. So...you guessed it. In the middle of our vacation he was assassinated, and my mother completely fell apart. There went the rest of our trip. We headed home immediately, my mother in tears the whole time.

As an adult, I can, of course, understand why she was so distraught. But it seemed to me there are some things you should put aside for the benefit of your children. We had been so looking forward to this trip, and she ruined it.

My father, however, was the perfect parent, I thought. He always made me feel special. He told me once, "The day you were born was the best day of my life. The first time I held you, all of my other accomplishments paled by comparison. You were my masterpiece." I'll never forget those words.

He was also was a busy man, so we didn't get nearly as much time together as I would have liked, but the time we did have alone was precious to me. He bought me a guitar for my 12th birthday and spent time patiently teaching me chords. He helped me with my homework when I was struggling. Stuff like schoolwork had always been easy for Jenny, and I envied her for being so smart. I had to study harder and longer to get good grades. I grew up being told I was beautiful, but to tell the truth, I'd love to have traded some of my beauty if I could have had more brains. It would have been be a lot less work.

As I got older, my relationship with my father grew even closer, and I think my mother started getting jealous. She and I had lots of fights. I remember one time we were fighting about something and I yelled, "I couldn't care less!" And Mother said, "Well, you better start caring less!" Right about that time, Jenny wandered into the room and said, "I don't get it. You want her to care *less* than she already does? That doesn't make sense..."

Both Mom and I turned to her and, at the same time, said,

"Shut up, Jenny." It was actually kind of funny. But there were times when I really hated her. And then Daddy moved out and things went downhill from there. She was angry all the time, especially after he started dating Leslie. Then she really had someone to focus her anger on. She was unpleasant to be around all the time. But I never, ever guessed she would kill them. Not once in my wildest dreams.

10

THE DAY MY FATHER DIED was by far the worst day of my life. I couldn't believe it happened. I kept thinking I'd just wake up and realize it was a nightmare. Over and over, I said to myself, "My father is dead," and each time, I felt a jolt. And that he died because my mother ran over him was unacceptable. Unbelievable. Unheard of. You don't just run over somebody because he leaves you. At least, normal people don't. It was actually a good thing my mother was locked up, because I can't imagine how I would have reacted to her if she'd been around.

And the thing is, when you lose somebody, you wake up every morning and it's still the same nightmare. It doesn't get any better. I kept thinking, when I went back to school, I'd be *"the girl whose mother murdered her father."* For the rest of my life, I'd be that girl. It would never change. And I would never get my dad back. It was irreversible. Daddy was gone. So long. Bye-bye. That's that.

How would I ever in a million years be able to forgive my mother? There was no way I could even visualize that possibility. I had, in essence, lost both of them.

But, miraculously, you get by, an hour at a time. Life, somehow, just keeps happening. Fortunately, I had my sisters to tend to. They needed me. And frankly, being sad all the time gets tiring after a while. You might still burst into tears ten times a day. Even today, whenever I see a beige, beat-up

VW bug coming down the road, it brings tears to my eyes.

I gradually adjusted to the idea my parents were gone. Jenny and I went to the children's shelter, and I ended up at Aunt Mimi's. It was crowded at first since she was renting just a studio, but she soon found another apartment in the same complex, and this one had a loft, so I moved my things up there.

It was pretty weird at first. I was used to living with my sisters, where it was always noisy and you could hardly get a moment of peace and quiet. In my new home, it was just too quiet. I'd get home from school, and no one was there. Aunt Mimi worked as a legal secretary, and some nights she had to work late. And, until we knew the outcome of my mother's trial, we were all living in limbo. But the good news was that I was back in school with my old friends. I finally got my license and could drive myself to school. Unfortunately, my dad's car turned out to be in pretty bad shape, so when Uncle Joe bought a new van, he gave the old station wagon to me.

But as I look back on those days, I realize now I wasn't coping nearly as well as I led every one to believe. I'd lost interest in school. It felt as though I was going through the motions of being alive, just so that no one would worry about me.

And then I met Doug. I'd seen him around school for a couple of years, but always thought he was a little square. But this semester he was in my English class and sat right behind me. He wasn't handsome like a movie star, but he was really cute, with gorgeous green eyes, and a little cleft in his chin. He was also very shy, and I totally fell for him. He made funny comments under his breath in class, and I'd start to giggle and tell him to shut up. Walking out of class together, one day he said, "So, I don't want to be forward or anything, but like would you be at all interested in, you know...going out for a pizza and then maybe, going out to my car and having sex?"

I started laughing and he said, "What's the matter? You don't like pizza?"

I was totally charmed. I really needed someone to make me laugh. But he was also sweet and tender and a great kisser! Whenever I started to talk about my family, I'd get all choked up and start sobbing, Doug would just hold me. He was truly the perfect guy. He wanted to meet my sisters and my aunt and uncle, and they were pretty impressed. Uncle Joe asked him a lot about his plans for after high school. He told me later that Uncle Joe said to him, "You break her heart, I'll break your thumbs!" I couldn't believe my uncle would say such a thing, but Doug assured me, with a wink, it was true.

One evening he invited me over to his house for dinner. His parents, both intelligent, educated people, kept up a lively conversation. His dad was an architect and his mother had majored in anthropology, but eventually became a nurse. He had a couple of younger brothers. A very normal family.

That night, as we were all sitting around the dinner table, his mother was telling a funny story about Doug, when he was twelve years old. She'd sent him to the doctor for a physical and when he came home, she asked him how the appointment went. He said, "Fine, except the doctor asked me something funny—he asked me if I moved my *balls* every day." So she said to him, "Are you sure he said *ball*s?" And Doug had answered, "Well, I think he said balls. So am I *supposed* to move them every day?"

By the time she was done, everyone around the table was laughing hysterically. I bet she'd told that story a dozen times, and yet they all still thought it was funny. I could see they were a family who liked to laugh and who really *liked* each other. And suddenly, I was overcome with sadness. My family never laughed like that. Of course, my sisters and I would find things to giggle about, but I could never remember a time when we all sat around laughing with our parents. I felt an overwhelming sense of loss for something I'd never had. I left the table, crying.

Doug rushed out behind me, confused. I was afraid I'd embarrassed him in front of his family. As he drove me home, he asked, "Babe, what's wrong? Please tell me!" but I just couldn't explain it.

That night, in bed, I wondered if I should continue seeing him. Everything in my life was overwhelming, and I seemed to be constantly upset about something. I worried that it wasn't fair to him. He deserved to be with a normal girl. But I needed him so badly right now. He was my reason for getting up in the morning. The one thing I had to look forward to every day. I decided to hang in there for the time being. I just couldn't deal with another loss.

I spent the rest of that year involved in school activities, hanging out with my friends, and working after school at the donut shop. Doug and I would catch a few hours together on the weeknights, when he could get away. Aunt Mimi really liked him and she often invited him to stay for dinner. I tried to go down to Morgan Hill on the weekends to visit with Jules and Joey but a lot of times it was difficult, because I had homework.

I constantly worried about Jules. She was always in a cranky mood when I got there. She'd cheer up for a while, and then get crabby again as I prepared to leave. It made my visits there uncomfortable. Sometimes I brought Doug with me, and he seemed to like playing with my sisters and the twins, and that made me happy. But still, I fretted over Jules. She was seeing a counselor, but I never got the impression that it was helping.

Joey was another matter. She seemed to blend right in with her new family, which I knew was healthy for her, although it bothered Jenny a lot. I guess in a small way it upset me, too, but I had to consider what was best for her. She told everyone that Matt and Mikey were her brothers. When she started calling my aunt and uncle Mommy and Daddy, Jenny nearly flipped out. After the trial, when we knew for sure that my mother wouldn't be coming home anytime soon, there was talk for a long time of Uncle Joe and Aunt Sally adopting them. But my mother put her foot down and said "no way in hell" and that was the end of that. Jenny was greatly relieved. I was confused and didn't know whether to feel happy or sad for them.

The only thing that really concerned me about Joey was that she'd always had a tendency to be a little on the pudgy side, and now, she and Aunt Sally spent a lot of time doing things in the kitchen. She and Joey would make cookies together, or fudge. Joey was becoming quite chubby, and I mentioned my concern to Uncle Joe. He assured me she'd grow out of it. But I'd heard Jules call her "fatso" a couple of times and it bothered me a lot. I hoped Uncle Joe was right.

By that time, my mother had gone on trial. She'd pleaded to a lesser charge and was sent to prison. I didn't feel sorry for her one bit. In fact, I tried to avoid thinking of her at all. She'd often creep into my dreams at night, and sometimes I woke up crying and would be depressed all day. Doug was fantastic at cheering me up. He knew what I'd gone through and was very sympathetic.

Finally, I finished my junior year in high school and spent that summer working and with my friends. When I started my senior year in the fall, Jenny was beginning her freshman year at the same school, so we saw a lot more of each other. My friends enjoyed making a fuss over her, and frequently we gave her and her friends a ride home from school or took them to Dairy Queen for hamburgers. She had a lot of friends and seemed to be happy. I honestly didn't have a clue that anything bad was going on.

Then the unthinkable happened. Beth called one night

saying she and Uncle Joe wanted to come over to talk to me. I felt apprehensive right away, but couldn't imagine what it was about. I usually talked to Beth every other week. She'd call just to chat with me and see how things were going. But for her to make a special trip over had to mean something was wrong.

After they arrived, Aunt Mimi, Uncle Joe, Beth and I sat in the living room. I looked at my uncle, and he seemed a lot older to me. And smaller. The last eighteen months were hard on him, too.

"Jacki," Beth began, "we came over here to tell you we had to move Jenny back to the shelter." She paused. "We…there was evidence found that she was involved in some kind of a sexual relationship with Shelly's brother."

"That's ridiculous," I said. "She's only fifteen. She hasn't even been kissed yet." There was silence in the room. Then I asked, "What kind of evidence?"

Beth glanced nervously at Uncle Joe and then said, "Tony apparently took some pictures of her. Nude pictures. Shelly found them in his room."

"That can't be right," I said. "She's just a baby. Tony's, what, in his twenties? She wouldn't be interested in him…" I felt myself getting hot all over and started hyperventilating. I couldn't picture my little sister, naked, with some man. The idea was repulsive. I felt like I was going to throw up.

"What did Jenny say?" I asked.

"She doesn't want to talk about it. She's refusing to press charges. He could be charged with child molestation, child endangerment, and statutory rape, but if she doesn't cooperate, it would be hard to get a conviction."

The word "rape" was too much for me. I imagined my sweet, innocent little sister, still just a child to me, having intercourse with some jerk. I hadn't even had sex yet! I put my face in my hands and wept.

* * *

I stayed in bed, sobbing, for two days. I didn't eat or sleep. I had no interest in talking to anyone. Not Aunt Mimi, Uncle Joe, Beth, Jenny or Doug. No one. My world had completely unraveled. I couldn't bear the thought of facing another day. Daddy was dead. Mom was a murderer. And my little sister had been sexually abused and I didn't even know it. Mimi didn't know what to do with me, so she called Beth, who showed up with Uncle Joe and Aunt Sally. They'd made an appointment for me to see Dr. Wheeler, the psychiatrist I'd seen once after the accident. I said I didn't care, and I meant it. I just wanted to crawl inside a hole and die. I saw Dr. Wheeler that afternoon. After spending an hour and a half with me, I was admitted to Agnews State Mental Hospital.

I don't remember much about that night. I was so exhausted I hardly paid attention to anything. I do recall the floor was covered in pale green linoleum. A nurse in a white uniform took some blood and made me pee in a cup. I was put into a room with an older woman who sang softly to herself all night long. I remember thinking about Daddy as I rocked back and forth, saying, "I'm sorry" over and over again. The lady in the next bed didn't seem to mind.

In the morning, they came to wake me up, but I'd hardly slept. I didn't want any breakfast, and chose to stay in bed with the covers up over my head, still in my clothes. A nurse came around and asked if I wanted to take a shower or if I needed anything, and I shook my head. I just wanted to sleep. And to be left alone. There was nothing I could see that could possibly happen that would make me feel any better.

That afternoon I had another appointment with Dr. Wheeler. A very serious-looking man in his mid-thirties, he sported a dark mustache and a well-trimmed beard. He wore a suit and tie and I remember that his shoes looked recently polished. After a brief physical exam, we sat and talked about my relationship with my parents and my sisters. He asked about my sexual history, which, other than necking with Doug, was non-existent. We talked briefly about the "accident," and what my life had been like since I'd last seen him, almost two years ago.

After a couple of hours, Dr. Wheeler closed his notebook, sat back, removed his glasses and rubbed the bridge of his nose.

"You've been through a lot over the last two years," he said. "More than most people go through in a lifetime. It's no wonder you feel like you're cracking up."

I sat quietly and listened.

"The thing you should know is that you're NOT cracking up, even though it might feel that way. You've been functioning under quite a heavy load for a long time. What you are suffering from is acute situational depression. Do you know what that means?"

I shook my head.

"A lot of patients in this facility are acutely depressed because of a chemical imbalance in their bodies. But that isn't the case with you. What's going on with you is a normal response to the catastrophic events that have happened to you. You WILL get better over time. I promise you. You might not believe it right now, but you need to trust me on this. I don't think we'll try to put you on any medication right now, except for something to help you sleep, if you need it. That isn't to say we don't have some work ahead of us. We'll need to start dealing with some issues to help you get back on the road to recovery. It won't always be easy. And it might be a slow process. But you *will* get there." And that's when he told me about the camel.

His words didn't really mean a lot to me. At that point it didn't seem like it was possible I'd ever feel any better. But

I felt some comfort in the idea that someone out there was rooting for me. And I really did want to trust him.

11

"Hey, Patsy, eat your own damn pieces, will you?" I complained to the woman sitting across from me at the Monopoly board. One hotel, two houses, and now my little iron had disappeared. Patsy was swallowing them.

The latest admission to the psychiatric unit was admitted two days earlier, after a week on the surgical floor. They'd operated on her after a stomach x-ray revealed several items she had swallowed over the years—pens, pencils, tubes of lipstick, mascara, and a locket on a gold chain. Most of the day, she sat with her arms tied to a chair because she swallowed anything she could get her hands on. She even removed the bandages covering her surgical wound and swallowed them. But the nurses knew Patsy was bored, so they removed the ties on her wrists and allowed her to play Monopoly with us. But once she started slipping the game pieces into her mouth, she couldn't play anymore.

Patsy told us her story that afternoon. Her mom died when she was fifteen. She had a dream one night in which her mother came to her and told her she needed to kill herself so they would be together in heaven. Patsy was swallowing things in the hope that she would die. I liked her a lot and felt terrible she had to be tied down. But then there were so many patients in this unit who had sad stories to tell.

So this is what it was like to be a patient on a psychiatric ward: they woke you up at six thirty in the morning to take your temperature, blood pressure and pulse, which was incredibly annoying, especially since they'd given you something the night before to make you sleep. Then you had to get up, get showered and get dressed and go to breakfast. When you are severely depressed, these are monumental tasks. The idea of breakfast, or any other meal, was totally unappealing.

After breakfast, you attended a round of meetings. In Community Meeting, all the patients and a couple of staff members sat in a circle to discuss either personal issues or stuff pertaining to living on the unit. Then you met with your nurse for the day, who asked how you were feeling, what issues you were working on, etc. On some days you'd get a visit with your doctor for an hour or so. After that, still not hungry, a bland lunch was served. An exercise period followed lunch. You were encouraged you to go out on the patio and play volleyball, but most patients were still walking around in their pajamas, all zombied out from their medication and not the slightest bit interested. After the exercise period, an art therapist came in and encouraged you to do some kind of artwork, supposedly to help you exorcise your demons. Family members could visit or you could go for a walk during the long break just before dinner.

After that meal, the new shift came on, so there was another Community Meeting. In the evening, we watched TV or played ping-pong, if anyone had the energy.

Most of the people on my unit were older, and a huge percentage were smokers, so they mainly just sat around the day room, drinking coffee and smoking. Many of them had been there several times, and they knew all the ins and outs. They could tell you who the good doctors were, which nurses were bitches, who was a lousy social worker, and how to "cheek your meds" instead of swallowing them. The TV was usually on twenty-four hours a day, except during meetings. But a lot of patients just sat and stared at the TV screen, even when it was turned off.

Since I was nearly eighteen, I'd been placed on an adult ward, but there weren't many patients who were my age. One other kid, Danny, was nineteen, but he talked all the time and drove everyone crazy, so I tried to stay away from him. Tall and thin, he had long, stringy hair that desperately needed to be washed. He was actually pretty sweet, but his incessant chatter made him hard to be around. When I asked him why he was there, he said sometimes he'd get so depressed he could hardly move. Other times, he had so much energy he couldn't sit still or stop his mind from racing. They gave him medicine for it, but it made him feel very tired and took away the times when he was feeling really good. So he'd stop taking meds and then get depressed again. I felt kind of sorry for him. But there were times when he would walk around the unit, ranting about LBJ, saying there'd been a conspiracy to kill JFK, and that our current president was leading the conspiracy. And he was sure the Beatles' *Sergeant Pepper* album was part of the plot. He could talk about it for hours, rambling on and on and making no sense at all.

In the beginning, I struggled to just get up and get dressed. Nothing interested me, and I had no motivation to do anything. Everything seemed pointless. I did enjoy my sessions with Dr. Wheeler, but if he was gone on the weekend, I didn't really care. The day was just something to get through. So was the night.

One morning, Dr. Wheeler asked how I was feeling and I said, "Not really sad today. Actually, I'm tired of feeling sad all the time. I feel empty. To tell the truth, I don't believe the opposite of happiness is sadness. It's feeling nothing at all."

"Tell me more about that," he prompted.

I took a deep breath. "I don't know if this really explains it. But, you know how, like when you're little, Christmas morning is really exciting. You keep thinking about Christmas for weeks ahead of time, imagining what presents are under the tree. It's so exciting you think you'll burst. And then, as you get older, it gets less exciting because you know pretty much what you're getting: clothes or jewelry or books, or albums. I mean, it's still really nice, you know? But there's no excitement. My life is like knowing what's under the tree. There's nothing there that I can get excited about. Do you know what I mean?"

"I perceive a slightly different analogy. I think you're more like a kid who wakes up with the flu on Christmas morning. You want to be excited, but you're just feeling too lousy. My job now is to help you get over the flu."

"Good luck," I muttered.

"I need to tell you it's going to be difficult for you to get well until you're willing to work through the issues with your mother."

It was a subject I hated to talk about. He continued: "I think you avoid the subject because you both love and hate your mother, and those conflicting emotions are hard to come to terms with."

I said, "Whatever."

Also, he wanted me to focus on the feeling that I was responsible for everything that had happened: my mother's anger, my father's death and my sister's abuse. I listened to what he said, but they were only words to me. They didn't make me feel any better.

At first I didn't want to have any visitors, except for Beth, who was like an older sister to me. I hated for her to see me looking all ratty. I wasn't into brushing my hair or wearing makeup, and a lot of days I didn't even get out of my bathrobe, so I knew I looked like crap, but she didn't care. Beth was always loving and kind. Sometimes we just sat and watched TV together. She told me that she was really in love with Ken, but he was a hippie type and into "free love." I wasn't even sure I knew what that meant. Ken wanted her to go off and join the Peace Corps with him, so they'd been fighting over that. I really liked that Beth would open up to me about herself.

She also said Jenny was doing well and would come see me when Dr. Wheeler approved. Right now I wasn't sure I wanted to see my sister. I frequently tossed and turned at night, thinking about her, feeling sad and ashamed that I'd abandoned her.

After I'd been at Agnews for a couple of weeks, Uncle Joe and Aunt Mimi came to see me. I felt awkward because I didn't know what we should talk about. Aunt Mimi said Doug had been calling her a lot, wanting to write to me or call me on the phone. But I didn't want to talk to him. Later that night, after giving it a lot of consideration, I wrote to Doug and broke up with him. I told him he deserved someone better—someone who wasn't a nut case. I knew Doug wouldn't think of me in those terms, but it was easier to use that as an excuse. I just felt that being in a relationship right then was too much stress for me. I didn't want to have to be concerned with him. I didn't want him hanging around, waiting to hear from me. While the image of my sweet Doug with another girl brought me to tears, it wasn't fair to hang onto him. Who knew when I'd be ready to see him again? When I gave the letter to one of the nurses to mail, I felt sad, but also felt a sense of relief. One less thing to be concerned with.

That night, I stayed up late with Danny, watching TV, and I made the mistake of telling him what I'd done. He was very sympathetic and tried to put his arm around me. I told him to knock it off. In the following days, he seemed obsessed with the idea of having sex with me, that it would be a tremendous help to both of us. He said guys get this thing called "blue balls" from all of the semen backing up and it was very painful. They needed regular release, and he pleaded with me to give him a "hand job."

"Thanks," I said, "but I think I'll pass."

Late one night, Danny came into my room, opened up his robe, and was naked underneath.

"So, what do you think?" he asked, proudly displaying his erection.

"It looks like a penis, but a lot smaller," I said.

He called me a bitch and left my room. He bugged me a lot less after that. I kind of missed the attention, actually.

Over the next few weeks, I slowly began to feel less like being in my room all the time. I still had long bouts of crying and there were many days when I just couldn't see how I would ever begin to function in the world. But those times were becoming less and less frequent. Dr. Wheeler was right. Eventually, I did start to feel better. One time he told me I had a "spine made of steel," a phrase I've never forgotten. It's amazing how a person can say just one simple thing, and it can make such a difference. With a "spine made of steel," I felt I could handle anything life had to offer.

Now that I wasn't so much into all of my own doom and gloom, I could focus more on the other patients around me. Linda, a woman who wouldn't eat anything, was bone-thin. But she kept saying she was fat, and if she could just lose a couple more pounds, she'd be happy. I never heard the word "anorexia," used, but I'm sure that's what Linda had. Married to an attentive, handsome man with beautiful baby girl, I couldn't understand why she'd do this to herself. Her hair was falling out, and her legs were so skinny her knees looked grossly swollen. The staff monitored Linda during every meal, and yet I frequently noticed that she'd take a bite of food, pretend to cough, and then spit the food into her napkin. Or she'd slip food into her napkin and then drop it on the floor. A lot of times, the nursing attendant wasn't paying attention. One time I even saw her slip some food into her sock.

Then there was Lupe, an older lady from Mexico. Very religious. Lupe already had eight children, and the last time she got pregnant, she'd had an abortion, which she believed was a terrible sin. After that, she was convinced every bad thing that happened in the world was because God was punishing her. A couple of years earlier, three astronauts at NASA had died in a terrible fire, and Lupe *knew* it was her fault. She was finally shipped to another unit where, I heard, she underwent ECT (electroshock therapy).

Still in full use in the 1960s, ECT was the one thing that really freaked out patients. They always talked about it in a whisper. I had never heard about it before, but was told that you would be tied down, something was placed between your teeth so you wouldn't bite your tongue, and then they jolted your brain with electricity. I had a hard time imagining it was true. But patients insisted it was.

There was a man on our unit who was very tall and heavy named Paul. He hardly ever talked; he just shuffled around the unit in his bathrobe and slippers. One day, Paul told a group of us, "ECT isn't so bad. They give you something to relax you, and that's the last thing you remember. You wake up and can't remember much about that day, but you're in a better mood." He'd had it several times. It didn't seem to be helping him very much, I thought.

Danny was discharged one evening and I felt a little lonesome when he left. Even though he could be obnoxious, he was the only young guy on the unit. But a couple of days later, he came back in the middle of the night, screaming at the staff.

"You cunt, you whore, you bitch!" he shrieked, over and over, while being restrained by the nurses and orderlies. ("By the way," I asked in the Community Meeting the next day, "what's a cunt?") They finally injected him with a sedative, but he continued to scream until the medication kicked in and he went to sleep. It was a long night for all of us. That was another big problem being on a psychiatric unit; the other patients frequently kept you up half the night, and then the morning shift came on and they'd be sunny and well-rested, wondering why you were all so sluggish and grouchy.

The next day, Danny was barely able to sit up. He just sat there, drooling. I felt so sorry for him. He had bruises all over, a swollen lip and a black eye. He told me later he'd been in a bar fight and some guys beat him up. I asked what he'd said to cause the fight.

"I told them the government was using alcohol to turn men into queers," he answered.

"Yep, that would do it," I answered.

"Well, it's true," he argued.

The one thing about being surrounded by a bunch of loonies is I eventually started to realize that basically, I was much better off than most people. I knew by then I wasn't a nut case. And started to feel like I might want to consider a career in nursing. I talked to Dr. Wheeler about it the next day.

"I've been thinking lately about going to nursing school instead of law school," I told him. "I think I might be better suited for nursing. But I've really wanted to be a lawyer because I think it's a way that I could honor my father."

"Honoring your father is a very noble idea, Jacki," he answered, "But I'd suggest that you follow your heart. What your dad would have wanted was for you to be happy, and if you think you'd be happier as a nurse, then that's what you should do. Both professions serve people."

I stewed over the decision for several days. I didn't want to give up the idea of law school. I felt that if there was a heaven, and Daddy was watching over me, he'd be so proud if I graduated from law school.

My parents didn't teach us anything about religion. They felt it was something we should decide for ourselves. Mom said the concept of the devil and sinning and going to hell was just something that parents used to get kids to behave. She said it was good that most poor people trusted in God, because it gave them a reason to keep going. So, while I didn't really believe in most religious stuff, it did bring me some comfort to think there might be a heaven somewhere, and that someday I might be reunited with my father. I felt it was like hanging onto the idea of Santa Claus, or the Easter Bunny, but it made me feel good. It comforted me to imagine that Dad might be watching over me and made me feel closer to him. I asked Dr. Wheeler if it was a sign I was crazy if I talked to my dad sometimes, and he assured me it was normal and healthy.

But he also said it was time I started communicating with my mother. He said "You might try writing letters to her, and you don't even have to mail them if you don't want to. Just write down your thoughts and feelings. Think of it as an exercise."

"And you promise you won't mail them?" I asked.

"I won't even read them unless you want me to."

I totally hated the idea of having any contact with Mom, and he knew that, but he assured me it wouldn't be disloyal to my father.

"Children have a special and separate relationship with each of their parents," he said. "I am sure your father would want you to continue to have a relationship with your mother, in spite of what she did."

"But how do you know that?" I asked.

"Because I am a father," was his answer.

I was still doubtful, but I agreed to start writing to Mom, even if I chose not to mail the letters.

That night, I communicated with my mother for the first time.

Mom,

My doctor thinks it would be a good idea if I wrote to you. In case you haven't heard, I am now a patient at Agnew State Hospital. I have been here for over a month. Dr. Wheeler thinks I'll be ready to go home in another month or so. I will have a lot of studying to do to catch up with my schoolwork so that I can graduate with my class in June, but I may not be able to.

I don't know if you heard that Jenny was in a foster home and they found out that she had been molested by a twenty-two-year-old guy who was living there. When I heard the news, I was so upset that I couldn't eat or sleep and I couldn't stop crying, so they brought me here.

Right now I feel that this is all your fault. If you hadn't lost your temper, me and Jen and Jules and Joey would all still be living at home, going to school and leading normal lives. What kind of an example do you think you have set for all of us? Were you even thinking of us at all? I know that you don't believe you are at fault, that it was all Daddy's fault, but that isn't true. And, until you admit it, I don't ever want to see you again.

That's all I want to say for now.
Jacqueline

I had to admit, I did feel better after writing it. I decided not to send it yet, because I knew she would write back to me and eventually I'd have to forgive her. I just wasn't ready for that yet.

One night, when I was feeling particularly blue, I asked to be placed in the "Quiet Room," a place that was grossly misnamed. It was a locked, padded room where patients who were totally out of control would be placed, sometimes in restraints, until they calmed down or until their medications kicked in. I sat there quietly for a little while, and then I began sobbing, then wailing. I started screaming "Daddy" over and over again until my throat was hoarse. I yelled and cried until I was exhausted. I fell asleep and eventually someone came to let me out. I went right to bed, and in the morning, I realized that I actually felt better.

Later, Dr. Wheeler told me the entire nursing staff had been in tears that night as they listened to me calling for my father.

12

Dr. Wheeler finally decided it was time I had a visit with Jenny. He asked if I wanted him there for support, but I declined. I wanted to spend some time alone with her. They put us in a private conference room.

When Jenny walked in, she seemed taller and more mature than the last time I'd seen her, which was only a few weeks before. A lot less like a tomboy, and much more like a young woman. She was wearing bell-bottom blue jeans, with a pink and blue tie-dyed T-shirt that said "Flower Power." On her feet were brown suede moccasins.

"Hey, you little hippie," I said, giving her a brief hug. There was something else about her. "Oh my God! You got your ears pierced!"

"Yeah," she said, turning her head so I could see the tiny peace signs dangling from her earlobes. "What do you think?"

"I think Mom's gonna clobber you," I answered. My mother had always said, "Only tramps get their ears pierced." (To which Joey had responded: "Why would a hobo want to wear earrings?")

"Well, Mom's not here to go spazmoidal on me, now is she?" she said, grinning.

"You got a point there. So, how are you, anyway? How do you like living with Beth?"

"I like it a lot. Beth and Ken are really cool. Ken is a Buddhist. He has a juicer and everything! And they're interested in all kinds of political stuff. They took me up to Berkeley one day 'cause there was a peace demonstration against the war. I really want to go there when I graduate. It's a great place. All kinds of hippies and old beatniks around."

I smiled at her enthusiasm. "And what else is going on?"

"You'll never believe this, but guess what? Maria's having a baby!"

"Oh, bummer," I groaned. "She's not old enough for a baby!"

"I know," Jenny said, "but I think she did it on purpose so she could get out of the shelter and get some welfare money. They're living with Eddie's mom till he gets a job. He was working at Jack-in-the-Box but got fired. I told her she's really stupid, but she's sure it'll work out. If the baby's a boy, she's going to name him Donovan. Isn't that cute?"

"No, it isn't cute. It's pathetic. Or pathetical, as you would say. Anyway, have you seen Mom?"

"I saw her a couple of months ago. She's actually losing weight. I couldn't believe it. She doesn't eat meat anymore. Just fish, if they have it. She'll eat eggs and cheese and stuff, but no meat. She looks better. She's taking some law classes."

I rolled my eyes.

"She's also been teaching some of the other inmates to read. So I guess she's keeping busy." Jenny looked around the room curiously.

"I've actually written a couple of letters to Mom," I told her. "My doctor thought it was a good idea. I've been mostly telling her off. But I haven't mailed them yet. I don't know if I'm going to."

"I think you should," she said.

There was a long pause. I couldn't think of anything to say.

"So, what's it like here?" Jenny finally asked.

"Oh, it's not bad. The food's gross. But the nurses are pretty cool and I like my doctor. He says I'll be able to go home in a few weeks."

"So what are the other people in here for?"

I told her a little bit about Danny and Lupe. I didn't want to talk about them a lot, because you weren't supposed to talk about stuff that people shared in group.

"But there're a lot of whackos here. There's this guy, his name is Jim, and all the time he writes letters to Frank Sinatra. And he signs them 'Love, me.' And in parentheses, he puts 'Jim.' Like Frank Sinatra is going to know who Jim is. And he wears his jacket all the time, even over his pajamas. He never takes it off!"

"Wow, no fooling? That's a gas!"

"Well, not really. It's pretty sad, actually. A lot of people here have been sick their whole lives and they're not going to get any better. They just give them major tranquilizers to keep them calmed down. But it makes their brains all fuzzy and they drool a lot, and shake. There's a girl who was admitted last week, she's like nineteen years old. She was a straight A student, going to college, and she started behaving really weird, and they brought her in. She's, you know, like hearing voices all the time. It's called being schizophrenic. And her family had no idea. One day, she's away at college, doing great, and then, bam! The next thing you know, she's a psycho."

"Man, that's really scary," Jenny finally said.

"Anyway, by comparison, I'm doing really good. I just had some issues to work out... you know, about Mom and Dad and stuff."

"So you're not here because of me?" She looked worried.

"Well, I guess you could say that didn't help. So tell me about it, Jen."

She took a moment before she answered. "It's not as bad as everyone thinks. I was *in love* with Tony. I'm still *in love* with him. He made me feel really special. He was good to me."

"But he took advantage of you; he pushed himself on

you!" I argued.

"It wasn't like that," she said, looking away from me. She stood up and walked over to the water cooler and poured some into a Dixie cup. "I really liked him. He said I was beautiful."

"But what does a twenty-two-year-old man want with a fourteen-year-old girl? That's sick! Not to mention illegal. Why doesn't he go out with girls his own age?"

"He *has* a girlfriend his age! They've been going together for a couple of years now. Her name's Lola."

"So he has a girlfriend and he's still messing around with you? Why would you even go for that? I don't understand at all!"

"I guess I don't really get it myself," she answered slowly. "All I know is that I love him and I want to be with him."

There was silence for a few minutes.

"So," I asked tentatively. "What exactly did you guys do? In his bedroom, I mean."

She glanced away from me again. "We just fooled around a little bit."

She wasn't looking at me, so I couldn't really tell if she was lying. Jenny didn't usually lie, but she didn't usually fool around with older guys, either. I knew about the pictures, but I had never seen them, so I didn't feel right about bringing it up now. Maybe she was still a virgin. There was always that hope.

"So, you know what?" she said. "Becky came over to spend the night with me a couple of times and you'll never guess what she said. It really made me mad. She said Tony had been fooling around with her, too. I said baloney! She's only twelve. Tony would never fool around with her. She's just making stuff up!"

"Why would she do that?" I asked her.

"To get attention, I guess. She's just a big fat liar! So I'm not even speaking to her right now."

Just then the door opened and Dr. Wheeler asked how everything was going.

"Great," I said. He asked if we wanted to go for a walk outside and we both said yes. It was almost May, so the weather was on the warm side. It felt great to be walking around, outside in the sunshine.

"So, any cute guys in your class?" I asked.

"Yeah, there's this guy named Peter. He's really sweet. His parents are Italian. From Italy. He's got long brown hair. He plays guitar in a band. And gets to drive his dad's car sometimes. He gets five dollars a week allowance, so he can either buy a new album or take me to the movies each week. So we go out about every two weeks. We saw 'Bonnie and Clyde.' It was great."

"Well, that's far out," I said.

"Yeah, I like him, but I don't love him. Ya know? So what happened with Doug, anyway?"

"I broke up with him," I told her.

"Aunt Mimi told me. I was bummed. I don't get it. Don't you like him anymore? I thought he was a really groovy guy."

"Yeah, I still like him. I don't know. It's complicated. I can't explain it." Suddenly I was feeling tired. "Let's go back inside, okay?"

* * *

After Jenny left, I felt a little down. I had enjoyed the visit, but I was missing a lot of her life. And I was missing too much of Jules and Joey's lives, too. I decided to ask Dr. Wheeler if I could go to Joe and Sally's for a one-day pass. He said it was a good idea, if I thought I could handle it.

When the day came for me to go out on pass for the first time, I'd been in the hospital for several weeks. I felt kind of jumpy, thinking about being around my family again, but once I got there, I was fine. While we were having dinner, Aunt Sal mentioned that Jules and Joey wanted to take band at school. Jules wanted to play the drums, and Joey wanted to take up the flute. When Jules went for try-outs, the band leader told her that he'd give her a pair of drumsticks, but it was too expensive to provide every student with a set of drums, so until she proved that she could stick with it, she'd have to practice on the bottom of a shoe.

A couple of days later, Sally asked Joey if she had tried out for the flute. She said no, she decided not to, because she didn't want to have to practice on the bottom of a shoe! We cracked up. Joey said defensively, "Well, how was I to know?" And we laughed even more.

It felt so good being with my family. Maybe we were more normal than I thought. Later on, I sat Joey on my lap and told her I thought she'd be great on the flute. She asked me when I was going to be getting out of the hospital. I told her, "Real soon."

After dinner, Jenny's new boyfriend Peter was coming over to visit. Jules loved to tell Italian jokes, so Uncle Joe told her not to tell any Italian jokes while Peter was here. When she protested, he said, "Just make them Irish jokes. We're Irish, so it shouldn't offend anybody."

After Peter had been introduced to everyone, we all sat out on the patio, having dessert. So, of course, Jules had to tell one of her jokes. "There's this Irish guy, see? And he's the head of the Mafia, see?" We all groaned and protested and hushed her up. She kept saying "What?" Peter thought it was pretty funny and kept making remarks about the Irish mafia. He seemed like a really nice kid.

I suddenly wished Doug were there. He would've really enjoyed the evening. I wondered if I should call him. But what could I say? Would he even want me back? What if he already had a new girlfriend? I watched Uncle Joe as he wrestled on the lawn with Joey and the twins. Everything seemed so *normal.* It was an odd feeling, knowing that in a couple of hours, I'd be back at the hospital.

Aunt Sally came up and sat next to me. "How are you feeling, sweetie?" she asked.

"Better than I've felt in weeks," I answered honestly. "But I was just thinking about Doug, if I hurt him. If he'd want me back, when I'm ready."

"Well, I always got the impression he was pretty crazy about you. He's probably sitting at home, thinking about you, right now." My Aunt Sally could really say the perfect thing sometimes. Normally she was pretty quiet and would let Uncle Joe do most of the talking, but when she did say something, it was usually right on.

"Honey, I want to ask you something," she said quietly.

"Okay, shoot."

"Well, do you think you'd have all these problems if we hadn't separated you girls? I mean, we really didn't know what else to do, but now I'm wondering if we should have tried harder."

I was quiet for a few seconds. The back of my throat felt constricted and my eyes were teared up. I had to clear my throat.

"Aunt Sal, I think you did the best you could. You and Uncle Joe have done so much for us. My problems aren't because of you. Honest. You know who the troublemaker is." Aunt Sally had never gotten along with my mom. Come to think of it, no one got along with my mom.

She put her arm around me and we sat there quietly for a few minutes, both of us apparently lost in thought. "I guess I'd better get to those dishes," she finally said, and went back into the house.

Jenny wandered over and sat next to me. I had sensed all day something was troubling her. "So what's up, kiddo?"

I asked.

She hesitated. "Well, you know, I really like Peter. I mean, he's really sweet, you know? All the girls at school think he's really cute. But..."

"Go on," I urged.

"It's just that...I really miss Tony. And I guess I was hoping he'd try to get a hold of me. At least call me or something." Her voice had gone all wobbly.

"Jen, don't you think it's for the best that he doesn't have anything to do with you? I mean, he could get into some serious trouble. You know that."

"Yeah, I know. It's just that he loves me. I know he does. You'd think that no matter what, he'd want to see me."

"If the guy has any brains at all, Jenny, he'd be a thousand miles away from you by now. Sometimes, when you get older, you have to think with your head, and not with your heart. He might love you, but he must know he can't be with you right now."

"You know," she continued, as if she hadn't heard a word I'd said, "In some states, you can legally get married at fourteen."

"Is *that* what you're thinking?" I hissed at her. "Are you completely off your rocker?"

"Well, no. Not really. It's just that...well, when everything else was falling apart, being with him was the one thing I had to look forward to. He made me feel so good. I was *happy* when I was with him. Don't you get it?"

I looked at her and smiled. "Yeah, I do get it. Honest, I do. But don't you think that maybe, eventually, you might feel that way about Peter? Or some other boy?"

We both looked across the lawn, where Peter was playing croquet with the kids.

Finally Jenny said, "The boys at my school all seem so young. They throw spit-wads in class. How immature can you be, you know?"

"Well, it takes boys a little while to catch up with girls. But they do, eventually. When they're about thirty-five." We both laughed.

"I can't imagine Daddy ever throwing spit-wads in class," my sister said.

"Yeah, but I bet he did."

We watched the kids playing. It looked like Peter was deliberately letting the younger kids get ahead. I said, "You know, he is awfully cute."

"Yeah, you're right. And he likes *me*, of all people. Who'd have thought?"

I looked at her. "You know, you're looking pretty cute yourself these days. I meant to tell you after you got your braces off, how great your teeth look. And you're finally getting some boobs!"

"But I'll never be like you," she said.

"No, you'll be better. You'll have both brains and beauty."

"Oh, stop it!" she protested. "You ought to be a therapist, did you ever think of that? Forget law school."

"I've been thinking about it."

When we got back to the hospital that night, Uncle Joe walked me to the front entrance and an attendant let me in. It was late. Almost everyone had gone to bed. I wandered out into the day room and sat by myself. It felt kind of spooky, being there alone at night. It was quiet. No one was around. The hall lights had been turned off. The world suddenly seemed very still.

I was happy I'd connected with Jenny, but I also felt lonely. For days, I'd been trying to avoid a thought that had been tumbling around in the back of my brain: that no matter what my doctor said, no matter what good things might happen to me in the future, I was never going to get my dad back. Nothing could ever make things go back to the way they were. No matter how much I wished for it, or dreamed for it, or hoped for it, it wasn't going to happen. My mother and father and sisters and I would never be a family again. I had to accept the unacceptable. Is that what makes people go crazy, I wondered, having to accept the unacceptable?

Would there ever be a time in the future when I wouldn't feel pain? Or feel there was hole in my heart where my father used to be, and it would never heal? It would always be empty. And it would always hurt. Would I ever get through a day without missing him? Without feeling sad that he died, or for the way he died?

The next day I shared my thoughts with Dr. Wheeler and he pointed out something I hadn't thought of before. He said, "You've been through just about the worst experiences any person could have. Most of the bad stuff life has to offer you from now on will pale by comparison. You are much stronger than you realize. You're going to be fine."

Those words meant a lot to me, and once again he'd reinforced the belief that I had a "spine made of steel."

A week later, I was discharged from the hospital.

13

For my first few days at home, poor Aunt Mimi was a nervous wreck. I'm sure she thought any little thing would set me off. I kept reassuring her I was fine.

One day she said, "All this foggy weather is *driving me crazy*!" She stopped short, a look of terror on her face.

"Aunt Meems, really," I said, "you *must* stop worrying. In the first place, I'm not crazy, so the word doesn't offend me. Secondly, I'm really not that fragile. I'm not gonna break in half. I actually feel a lot stronger now than before they carted me off to the loony bin. And, if I ever do go crazy, I promise you'll be the first to know, okay?"

She smiled and patted me on the head, something I hate. I let out a big sigh.

I started back to school the next week and plowed through a mountain of make-up work to do so I could graduate in June. Fortunately, I'd already earned most of the credits I needed.

Aunt Sally dropped Jules and Joey at our place for the weekend, where they slept on the couches in the living room. The girls wanted hot dogs and fried potatoes for dinner on Saturday and we ate banana splits for dessert. On Sunday, I drove them to the roller-skating rink during the day and we scarfed down hamburgers for dinner that night. Later, while playing Monopoly, Jules asked me, "So when are you going to get another boyfriend?"

I hadn't really thought about it much, but that night, I couldn't get Doug off my mind.

A few days later, I worked up the courage to call his parent' house. I knew Doug was probably away at San Diego State, but I was hoping to get his number. His mother answered the phone and although she was pleasant, I found her to be a little on the cool side. But, true to her gracious nature, she gave me the number at his dorm and said she thought he'd be happy to hear from me.

Five days passed before I had the nerve to call him. I was so afraid he'd already found another girlfriend, but even so, I thought maybe we could still talk. I paced around the living room while Aunt Mimi was at work, and picked up the phone several times before actually dialing the number. He was out, so I left a message. I breathed a huge sigh of relief. Now it was up to him. If he didn't call me back, then I'd know how he felt.

When no call came by nine o'clock that night, I decided to take a bath. I was just soaping up when I heard the phone ring. After a pause, Aunt Mimi threw open the bathroom door, and screamed, "He's on the line! Hurry up! Get out!" I think she was more excited than I was.

I quickly dried off, pulled on my robe, and dashed into the living room. Aunt Mimi handed me the phone and I plunked down onto the couch. She didn't move, so I shooed her away and finally said, "Hello?"

"Oh, Jacki, I can't believe you called!" Doug said. "I'm sorry I didn't get the message earlier. I was out. I hope it's not too late to call."

"No, really it's okay. I'm so glad you did."

Aunt Mimi was still hovering over me.

"Excuse me a sec." I held the receiver to my chest and whispered, "Go! Go! Go!"

She scurried into the kitchen.

"Sorry about that. So…how are you?"

"I'm doing great. But I've been missing you—a lot! There's been so much I've wanted to tell you. But the real question is: how are you?"

"I'm tons better. I really am. I'm sorry for ending it like I did. I just…I didn't really know what to do. I had a million things going on…"

"Listen," he said. "It's okay. I just want to know when I can see you again. I probably won't get home until spring break. Damn. That's still weeks away. I need to see you, honey. When can I see you? *Will* you see me?"

He was talking so fast I started laughing, even as tears flowed down my cheeks.

"Yes. Yes. Yes. Yes," I said.

"Okay. I can't stay on the phone. But I'm going to work something out. I'll get up there as soon as I can. Oh, God, this is so good. Don't, like, get married or anything like that before I can get up there, okay?"

"Okay, I promise, I won't," I said, smiling into the phone.

"Oh, God, this is good," he said again. Then he paused. "Jacki, I need to know something…are you really going to be okay?"

I hesitated. "I think so. I mean, I'm pretty sure I'm ready to go back to school and get on with my life. I really do feel a lot better. Is that what you're asking?"

"I'm not sure. It's just that it was so hard, when I got that letter. I…I just don't want to go through that a second time…"

"I understand, Doug. I really do. You want to be able to trust that I'm not going to go off the deep end again?"

"Yes," he admitted. "I guess that's what I'm asking."

"Well, I don't really know if I can give you a guarantee. I mean, I'm functioning really well. My therapist was wonderful. I have a lot more confidence now. I feel stronger. I feel like I just...I just need to be with you."

"Okay, honey, I'll get there as soon as I can." Then he whispered, "I love you so much!"

With the smile still on my face, I put the phone down. Then I laughed. From the kitchen, I heard Aunt Mimi yell, "Yes!" Doug was right. This was good.

We talked a couple of times a week on the phone, but, worried about the cost of long-distance phone calls, we both started writing almost every day. I told him what I'd gone through while I was in the hospital. Everything I was afraid of. All my feelings about my mother. He, in turn, told me about college life, but mainly he focused on his feelings for me.

"I'm desperately, madly, in love with you," he wrote, and I drank in every word. I loved the feeling of being in love. I told him I was on Clouds Nine, Ten and Eleven.

Unfortunately, he wasn't able to make it home as early as we had hoped, due to his midterms. But we looked forward to spring break so much I thought we might burst. He said he wanted to find a place where we could be alone, and I knew what he meant. I'd heard of a clinic where girls could find something for birth control. I made an appointment.

Doug also encouraged me to think about going to San Diego State in the fall. I'd been so overwhelmed lately, I hadn't really thought much about college or how I was going to pay for it.

Quite by coincidence, Uncle Joe called a couple of nights later, and asked if I'd been thinking about putting in my college applications. I told him I was worried about my financial situation and he just laughed.

"Honey, your dad carried a lot of life insurance and he set up trust funds for you girls. Your college is paid for. I'm sorry. I didn't realize you didn't know that."

"No, I didn't. I guess I should have known Daddy would take care of us." Tears sprang to my eyes. "I sure am glad to hear it. I've been thinking about going to San Diego State. I'd like to be near the beach." Actually, I wanted to be near Doug.

Uncle Joe laughed again. "Sounds like a good enough choice. I think it'd be great for you to get away. But you should apply to several places. I'll help you with your applications as soon as you get them, okay?"

"Great, Uncle Joe. Thanks!"

"Okay, kiddo. You have a good night. I love you."

"Good night, Uncle Joe. I love you too."

Wow! What great news! I couldn't wait to tell Doug.

I sat down on the couch and thought about my father. What a kind, loving and generous man he was. Oh, how I missed him.

Several weeks passed before Doug was able to drive up from San Diego. He told me on the phone he had a surprise for me, and to tell Aunt Mimi he and I would be going away for the weekend.

When he walked through the door on Saturday morning, he looked so good it took my breath away. Since he'd started college and was playing more sports, he'd put on a few pounds. Where he had been on the wiry side before, he was now muscular. And his brown hair was longer, and fell in waves almost to his shoulders. Doug didn't look like a teenage boy anymore. He looked like a man. A very, very sexy man.

I flew into his arms and kissed him passionately. We hugged for a long time, before he finally said, "Okay, let's go!" and grabbed my suitcase.

"So where are we going?" I asked, as we walked down the stairs and headed towards the car.

"I'm not telling," he said, as he opened the car door for me. Before I stepped inside, he turned me around to face him. He grabbed the collar of my coat and pulled me close.

"But I will tell you this," he continued. "I plan to make love to you all weekend long. And there's nothing you can do about it!" He leaned forward and kissed me.

"Then hurry up and let's get there," I countered.

Our destination turned out to be Carmel, a cozy resort town on the coast, south of Monterey. Doug rented us a room in a small hotel, not far from the beach. He picked this particular inn because it boasted having a fireplace in every room. As we pulled in front of the office, he shut off the engine.

"Are you going to come in to register with me?" he asked.

"No way!" I said. I felt very shy about this adventure.

"Come on," he teased. "We'll tell them we're on our honeymoon."

"No, you go!"

Doug sighed and shook his head. "Why do men always have to do the work?" he complained with a grin. He hopped out of the car and went into the office.

I watched him through my window. God, he was handsome! I took in a deep breath, in an attempt to calm my nerves. Doug and I had been together for a couple of years, and all we'd ever done was a lot of making out and some heavy petting. We had never been naked together. We had never made love. I'd been too afraid of getting pregnant. Afraid Aunt Mimi might walk in. Afraid of getting found out. But that was going to change. Tonight.

Doug walked back to the car. "We can't check in until three. We have dinner reservations at five. Let's go for a walk on the beach until then, okay?"

Which was what we did. We didn't actually check into the room until after seven. I'd been so nervous during dinner, I hardly ate a thing. Doug didn't either. We were tempted to leave right in the middle of the main course, but decided it would be rude. As we walked out of the restaurant, Doug said, "That was thirty-seven bucks down the drain," and I punched him on the arm. Light rain began to fall as we strolled from the restaurant to our room. In addition to the fireplace, oil lamps sat on the bedside tables, a soft down comforter on a brass bed, and a fresh bouquet of red roses on the dresser giving the room a quaint, old-fashioned ambiance. I loved it. I took a shower and towel-dried my hair in the bathroom while Doug lit the fire.

"Would you like some wine?" he asked as I came out of the bathroom. "I brought a bottle of the very best stuff that four dollars can buy."

I thought for a moment, and shook my head. "No," I said, looking at him. "I want to be very sober tonight."

Doug looked up from where he was crouched in front of the fireplace.

"Will you do me a favor?" he whispered.

"Anything," I answered.

"Take off your clothes."

I hesitated. "I thought you'd want to do that for me," I said.

"No, I'd like you to do it."

I walked over in front of him and sat on the bed. Watching his face, I slowly unbuttoned my blouse. I was feeling more embarrassed than I thought I would as I slipped it off. Then I reached down, pulled off my boots and socks, as slowly as I could. Doug was sitting on the floor, leaning against the wall. The soft glow of the fire reflected in his eyes as he watched me. I stood up, unzipped my jeans, slid them down, and kicked them away. Then I sat down again, feeling very self-conscious.

"Are you sure you don't want to handle the rest?" I asked softly.

He shook his head, smiling.

I reached behind me, unclasped my bra and slid it off my shoulders. Then tossed it aside. Doug stared at me, drinking me in with his eyes.

I smiled at him. "I know you're thinking of something."

With a husky voice, he said, "There's a line in a poem. By Pablo Neruda. It goes like this: "I want to do to you what springtime does to the cherry trees...""

I sat, smiling at him for a few moments, and then stood up, slid off my panties and sat down as quickly as I could.

"No," he whispered. "Stand up."

I became aware that my whole body was trembling. I stood up but, not knowing what to do with my hands, I crossed my arms to cover my breasts.

"Just let your arms hang naturally. I want to look at you." Doug moved slowly, up onto his knees. "You are even more gorgeous than I ever imagined," he said. "Now turn around."

"No."

"Please?"

I slowly turned around, feeling awkward and silly. Standing there, not knowing what to do, I asked, "What are you doing?"

"Memorizing you." I heard him move behind me, and then he was standing very close. He reached around me with his hands on my hips, and his fingers slowly trailed up, across my belly, up to my ribs, and then he touched my nipples. I let out a gasp. With one hand, he moved the hair off my shoulder and gently kissed my neck. Again, I moaned with pleasure.

Then he turned me around and kissed me. I put my arms around him and began to pull his shirt up. But he gave me a gentle push and we both fell back onto the bed. He kissed my cheek, my neck, my shoulder, and gradually made his way down to my breasts. My heart was thudding in my chest. "Oh, babe," I said, as he took my nipple in his mouth. "Oh, God, this is so great!"

After several minutes, Doug lifted his head and said, "So, you like that?"

"I love it," I said.

"I'm glad. I like it, too. You are so beautiful. I can't even believe I'm with you."

Then he lowered his head again and began to move farther down, kissing my tummy. I held my breath. I loved what he was doing, but felt anxious about him going any further.

"Babe," he said, "spread your knees apart for me."

"No," I whispered. "I'm embarrassed."

"Don't be," he said. "You have such a beautiful body. I want to look at it. All of it."

I did what he asked. He put his finger into his mouth to moisten it, then reached down and touched me gently. Again I gasped. I felt his fingers spreading, probing, examining me. I couldn't help but moan. It felt so fantastic. He slowly rotated his finger in small circles, and I thought I'd lose my mind. "Oh, Doug!" I had never dreamed it would be this good. I felt his weight shift on the bed and then his mouth was where his fingers had been. I continued to moan as his tongue brought me to a place where I thought I might explode.

"Do you want me to stop?" I heard him say.

"No, no...Please...don't stop...oh yeah, that's perfect, just keep doing that!"

And he did, until it felt like my stomach was going to shoot right out between my legs. I arched my back. My whole body shuddered. And then I let out a loud yell. I couldn't help myself. The sensation that washed over me was something I had never felt before. I wanted to laugh and cry, but all I could do was gasp for air.

"Oh, babe! Oh, babe! Oh, babe!" I said, over and over.

Doug got off the bed. He stood, looking down at me for several moments. Then he quickly stripped off his clothes and climbed back onto the bed. He positioned his body over mine, and gingerly guided himself into me. He smiled. I reached up and caressed his face. "I want to remember this always," I whispered.

"I love you," he said. He rocked back and forth, his eyes locked with mine.

"Ohhh, I *like* that!" I exclaimed. "That feels great!" "I'm glad you like it," he said, "I'm *really* glad you like it!" And then he too shuddered and cried out. He collapsed on top of me and stayed quiet for a long time. I thought he'd fallen asleep. Then he lifted his head and kissed me.

"So, how was it?" I asked.

"Not bad," he answered, and we started giggling.

"No, really," he said. "It's the best I've had all day. Honest!"

I tried to push him off the bed, but only managed to roll over on top of him. I sat straddling his stomach, and looked down at him.

"Did anyone ever tell you that you have the most beautiful breasts in the world?" he asked.

"Not until now, but I was hoping you'd be impressed. I've been saving them just for you."

"And I'm so glad you did," he whispered, taking them in his hands. "I will treasure them always."

Doug was right. He made love to me all weekend long. And it was spectacular!

* * *

That summer, I worked part-time as a lifeguard at the local country club, hung out with my friends, and made love to Doug as much as I could when he wasn't at his part-time job. I also made a point of spending time with my sisters.

Jenny took a while to get settled into her new home. She'd gotten used to having no rules or regulations, and was pretty lazy when it came to doing homework or housework. But Beth and Ken were extremely patient with her. They encouraged her academically as well as spiritually. As much as she pretended to be resentful of their supervision, I could tell she respected and looked up to them. I was happy she had them as role models. I knew she occasionally visited Mom in prison, but I rarely asked her about those visits.

Jenny constantly amazed me with her intelligence and

wit. Even after I graduated, she continued to be popular in school and had joined the chess club. She was also on the girls' basketball team. She did, however, jump from one boyfriend to the next, which bothered me. I asked her about it after one break-up and she answered, "He wasn't Tony."

"Thank God," I muttered, under my breath. I never grasped her deep attachment to that guy, so I didn't press her to talk about him. I kept hoping she'd fall madly in love with someone else. But other than that, I was impressed with how well she was coping.

Joey was also blending in nicely with my uncle's family. She was the daughter they'd never had. I worried that, being the youngest, the other kids might pick on her, but it didn't happen. She rarely talked about Daddy, and was always happy to go see Mom, but she was growing much more attached to her new family. That really bugged Jenny, so she frequently took photograph albums when she went to visit. She sat for hours with Joey, telling her the history behind each photograph. Poor Joey must have heard: "Remember, we're the Amazing Graces" a hundred times. One afternoon, she finally said, "This is boring. Wanna see my new Thumbelina doll?" and Jenny got the message.

It was Jules I worried about the most. She never seemed to adjust to being there. She was always unhappy and always in trouble. I talked about her to Dr. Wheeler during my weekly visits.

"Julie will have to find her own path," he told me. "You can be there to love her and offer her support, but you can't solve her issues for her. She will do that in her own way."

I knew what he meant, but I still fretted about it a lot. I loved her and missed her, but when I went for a visit, after ten minutes she was annoying the hell out of me. I could see how she was driving everyone crazy.

The idea of moving down to San Diego, living in a dorm

and starting my college classes excited me, but I felt guilty about leaving my sisters. I could never think about them without feeling some angst. Of course I talked to Dr. Wheeler about it. He tried to help me understand that they weren't my responsibility, they were in good hands with my aunt and uncle, and the best thing I could do for them was to live up to my potential. After my weekly visits with him, I usually felt better for a while, but the feelings would gradually creep back in. Dr. Wheeler arranged for me to see a therapist in San Diego. But I told him I thought I could probably handle things on my own.

He answered, "Making major changes in your lifestyle can be extremely stressful, and while you might not feel like you really need therapy anymore, it won't hurt to have someone to talk to." I reluctantly agreed.

The one thing I'd been feeling particularly anxious about recently was Doug's parents. Since we had started dating again, Doug avoided talking about them, or bringing me to his house for dinner. Before my "breakdown," they often invited me on family outings, but that stopped. They shared a family tradition of going out to a special restaurant for birthday celebrations, but when Doug's birthday rolled around, he simply said he would see me later in the evening. That really hurt.

When he finally showed up later that evening, as nervous as I was, I said, "Doug, we need to talk about this. I get the feeling your family doesn't like me any more. What's going on?"

He took a deep breath and looked away from me. "I'm sorry, babe, it's not that they don't like you. I guess they're just sort of nervous. About...you. About your... mental health. He paused. "I keep telling them you're fine."

I cleared my throat. "You mean, they're afraid I'll have another nervous breakdown? That maybe I'll end up going crazy, like my mom?"

He walked over and put his arms around me. "They just need some time to trust you. That's all. You don't need to worry about it. We'll be fine. They'll be fine. Please promise me you won't worry about it, okay?"

Of course, I made the promise, but, still, I fretted about it. The idea of people worrying about my mental stability really stung. Especially Doug's family. It never occurred to me before that they wouldn't understand what I'd been through. Or think I might follow in my mother's footsteps. I was glad Dr. Wheeler had suggested I continue with therapy. He was right, as usual.

I started my freshman year in September of 1967 and the next two years were probably the best in my life. I loved being at school, making new friends, going to "be-ins," protest marches and concerts with Doug. Life was exciting. I didn't fare that well academically, but did engage in more than my fair share of drinking cheap wine and smoking pot. I traveled the whole summer of 1968 on the road with a group of long-haired friends. The most fun trips were to Yosemite, Santa Cruz, and Haight-Ashbury. We were stoned for most of that time. With my ever-present guitar, we sang peace songs, protest songs and love songs. My friends took to calling me "Jacki Baez."

One night, we were sitting with a group of kids when Doug's friend Peter mentioned the rumor going around that middle-aged people were having "key parties."

"What the hell is that?" Doug asked.

"It's where everyone puts their car keys into a bowl, and then you draw out a key and go to bed with that person!"

"Far out!" my friend Shannon said. "We should do it!"

Everyone was excited about the idea. I quickly excused myself and went to the bathroom. When I came out, Doug was waiting for me. He took my hand and said, "Let's take a walk."

We strolled out into the warm summer night. "So...what do you think of this idea...the key party?" he asked. "Do you want to do it?"

Neither Doug nor I had ever been with anyone else so it would be a huge step for us. I was actually somewhat attracted to Peter but I couldn't help feeling that being with him could radically change things between Doug and me. "Um, I'm not sure. What do you think?"

He took a deep breath and then said, "Well, I want to be totally honest with you."

My heart was racing...

"There's a poem by Richard Brautigan," he began. Richard Brautigan was Doug's favorite contemporary poet. "It goes something like this: 'Everybody wants to go to bed with everybody else. They're lined up for blocks. So I'll go to bed with you. They won't miss us.'"

I said nothing so he continued. "Of course, you know, it would be cool to...experiment with other people, I guess. I won't deny that. But the truth is," at this point we stopped and he turned to face me, "The truth is, I really just want to be with you. You're the one I love and the one I want to—" I jumped into his arms and kissed him for a long time.

"I am so happy to hear you say that! I love you so much!" And that was that.

Of course, over the months we quarreled on occasion, like any other couple, but we never even remotely considered breaking up. It just felt like we belonged together.

Some depressing times still crept up on me. Like every Father's Day. Most people don't realize how painful Father's Day can be for those of us who have lost our dads. So Doug made a point of planning something special for that day, as well as January fourth, Daddy's birthday. And October 1, the day of his death: always the darkest day of the year.

One of the things I most loved about Doug was his ability

to make me laugh like no one else. One time, he had a scratch on his face and Peter asked him about it. He answered, "Jacki and I were having sex and she accidentally kicked me in the face. Again." He had everybody roaring with laughter. He liked to say that sex with me was so good, even the neighbors had a cigarette afterwards.

When summer was over, I headed back to school to start my sophomore year. Majoring in pre-law and not doing very well, I still enjoyed college. The school year passed quickly and the next summer found me back in San Jose. I felt eager for school to start in the fall so I could get my junior year over with. I wanted school to be over with I could go on to the next adventure. After graduation, Doug and I planned to spend the summer in Europe. But that was not to be.

In the middle of the first semester of my junior year, right before Christmas, I left school and moved back in with Aunt Mimi. My sister Jules had run away from home. I needed to go back. I needed to find her.

14

Julie

When I was ten years old, my mom was sent to prison, and I went to live with my aunt and uncle. Two years later, I ran away for the first time, but since I had nowhere to go and no one to go with, I came back home and not a single person even knew I'd left. That's how much they paid attention to me.

I ran away a few more times over the next couple of years, and I always came back. But when I was fifteen, I planned my escape more carefully, saved up some money, and stole away one evening with my best friend, Tiffany.

Looking back on it now, I realize didn't go because Uncle Joe and Aunt Sal were particularly mean to me. They really weren't. To be fair, they probably did the best they could, considering the circumstances. I know I wasn't the easiest kid to get along with. Unlike my baby sister, I just never fit in there.

Joey was only seven when my family was split up. Daddy had died, Mommy went to jail, Jacki went to stay with Aunt Mimi and Jenny went to live with strangers in a foster home. My aunt and uncle took Joey and me in and tried to make us all one, big, happy family, but it didn't work out. At least, not for me. My cousin Kevin got a lot of attention because he was the oldest. Joey got a lot of attention, because she was the baby, and the twins had each other. I had no one. I often felt like I could completely disappear and no one would have noticed.

But Joey was a different story. I think she could have settled in with any family. She was that kind of kid. Or maybe it was because she was so young. She liked having my cousins to play with. In the beginning, she asked about Mom and Dad a lot. Of course we both missed them terribly. But after a while, she seemed happy to crawl into Uncle Joe's lap and snuggle with him, or to go to Aunt Sally if she was upset about something. Aunt Sal would put her arms around her and play with her hair, talking softly to her, and Joey'd just bounce back and be her old self again. I guess she was always a pretty happy person. I wish I could've been more like her. Back then I never really liked being touched. All that huggy stuff made me squirm.

I'd always been sort of restless. Daddy said I had "ants in my pants." It seems like I was born with a lot of nervous energy. I could start on a project or open a book, and ten minutes later, I'd want to go ride my bike. School was always tough for me, having to sit in one spot for hours on end. I liked to get up and move around. See what was happening and try new things. I guess I got bored easily.

Mommy said I never slept as a baby. And from the time I could crawl, I was constantly getting into my sisters' things. I followed them around and pestered them incessantly. They tried to get away from me as much as possible, which I didn't understand. I just wanted them to play with me, but they always said I was too little. I hated that. I couldn't wait to be older and get to play with the big kids. But it seemed like no matter how big I got, they were always one step ahead of me. Maybe I was needier than most kids; I don't know.

I don't recall all the bad stuff about Mom like my older sisters do. I do remember she was fun, always putting on parties and doing things with us kids. She took me and Jen horseback riding several times. We drove to Disneyland once, though we had to come home early for some reason. Christmas at our house was amazing. We each had dozens of presents under the tree. Birthdays were great, too. You could ask for just about anything and count on getting it. But when Jen and I wanted horses, that never happened. And one time I asked for a rifle for Christmas and didn't get it, but I didn't really expect to.

I don't remember my parents fighting a lot. Maybe they did and I just tuned it out. Mommy had a temper, for sure, but as long as it was directed at someone else, I didn't care. She was good to me, bought me things, and played with me when she had the time. What could be better?

And Daddy was really great. He wasn't around that much, but when he was, he'd try to spend some time alone with each of us. I was the only one of his girls he ever took golfing. I loved those mornings. He'd wake me up early, throw his bag of golf clubs into the trunk of his old VW bug, and take me to the country club where he was a member. I followed him and his buddies around the course, bugging them with endless questions, and afterward I'd get to join them for breakfast. Sometimes, just he and I would go to the golf range, and we'd hit a bucket of balls. I was never very good, but he was always patient with me and said he thought I'd make a fine golfer one day.

Daddy also said I was special because I was a rebel and no one was ever going to tell me how to live. One day he said, "You will be a leader," and I never forgot that. I didn't really know why he said it, but it sounded cool. He also said that growing up was going to be rough for me, but once I got there, it would be smooth sailing. I often thought about that.

So I guess I must have been oblivious to all the stuff that was happening between my parents until Daddy moved out and, later on, started seeing Leslie. I remember we liked her and Ben a lot. He was a cute little boy, with brown, curly hair, just like his mom. When we were all together, people would think he was my little brother and I liked that. I called him Benjy when no one else did, and he called me "Dooley." I really loved that kid. And after Mom hit Daddy and Les and they both died, it was Ben I worried about. I wanted to see him, but it never happened. I guess he went to live with his father somewhere in Northern California.

For years, Jenny had me convinced that Mom had accidentally killed Dad and Leslie. She said Mom's foot must have slipped off the brake and hit the accelerator. I told my friends at school she was in jail and it wasn't fair because she was innocent. No way could she have deliberately killed anyone. Moms just don't do that. I knew it was all a big mistake, and once they realize it, my mom would come home to take care of us.

One day a kid at school made some stupid remark like, "Don't make Julie mad or she'll kill you!" and I walked over to him and smacked him as hard as I could on the nose. I'll never forget how the expression on his face changed, from laughter to shock and then tears. I thought for sure I'd be in big trouble over that one, but nothing ever came of it.

I guess you can imagine how tough it was for us after Daddy died. Everything in our lives changed. Our house was sold, we had to move down to Morgan Hill, and my older sisters were gone. I was used to having a big bedroom to myself, and suddenly I had to share a tiny room with Joey. I don't think I would have minded having a room with Jacki, or even Jen, but Joey could be a brat sometimes. Always getting into my stuff and annoying me in general. As long as I can remember, I've been a real fuss-budget about my things. I like everything to be neat and organized. At night, everyone in the family kicked off their shoes in the family room while we watched

TV, and I'd line the shoes up neatly in front of the fireplace. The running joke in our house was "If something's missing, ask Ju; she probably put it away." And Joey would also pester me with questions at night like, "If God is everywhere, can he see me when I'm on the potty?" She always had a lot of questions about God, which was weird since we weren't religious.

For a little while after the accident, she even went through a spell when she started wetting her bed at night. The problem was that many times she'd wake up during the night and crawl into bed with me. Then she'd fall asleep, wet the bed, and later on get back into her nice, dry bed, leaving me soaked. Boy, did that make me mad! Aunt Sally said we had to be patient with Joey, and she gently reminded me that I had also wet the bed until I was six, but Aunt Sally wasn't the one waking up in pee every morning. The boys thought it was really funny and called me "stinky," which made me even madder.

I never really minded the twins too much. Joey fought with them a lot more than I did. One time she came into the house, complaining, "Mikey started a fight with me. He hit back!" But my cousin Kevin was always a jerk and I hated living with him. He was the kind of kid who always used brute force to get his way. And he loved to pick on me. Whenever I complained to my aunt and uncle about it, they'd just say, "Now, you kids need to try to get along." So I stayed out of his way as much as possible. He was thirteen when we moved in, and still involved with Boy Scouts, so he was away on camping trips on many weekends. It was always a relief to have him gone.

As I grew older and started developing, Kevin became even weirder. When we played basketball in the driveway, he'd deliberately throw the ball and hit me in the chest. And he got into this habit of barging into the bathroom whenever I was on the toilet or in the bathtub. Uncle Joe had removed the lock off the bathroom door after Matt got trapped in there when he was little. I swear Kevin would wait until I had pulled my jeans down and then he'd walk through the door without knocking and I'd scream at him. After I complained about it loud enough, Uncle Joe finally put the lock back on.

But Kevin continued to harass me. He was always talking to the twins about my boobs and, even though the twins really weren't particularly interested in female anatomy at that time, they sometimes joined in the fun until I'd grab a wrist and give one of them an Indian burn. Then they'd leave me alone.

I complained to my older sisters a lot. Jacki listened and was sympathetic but said there was nowhere else for me to go. I was just going to have to try to get along with Kevin the best I could. She said I should just avoid him and eventually he'd give up teasing me. Easy for her to say. Then she'd change the subject and try to get me to talk about school.

I didn't understand why I couldn't live with her at Aunt Mimi's, but that was never an option anyone would consider. Jacki did come visit us as much as possible, especially for the first couple of years, before she went away to college. But she had a nervous breakdown and spent a few weeks in the nut house, so I didn't want to bug her too much after that. Aunt Sally said Jacki went to the hospital because she was really sad about Mom and Daddy, but people don't go to the hospital just because they're sad. Even I knew that.

I talked to Jen a few times about how unhappy I was, but she wasn't nearly as sweet as Jacki. Jenny and I never got along that well. She'd tell me to stop whining, that I should be happy because I was living with family and if I wanted Kevin to stop bugging me, I should just hit him between the legs with a frying pan or something. So she wasn't that helpful.

It isn't as if my sisters weren't there for me at all. They came to see Jo and me when they could. Jacki took us to stay at Aunt Mimi's on the weekends sometimes. We were always together on birthdays and holidays. Jen talked about Daddy a lot and reminded us we were still the Amazing Graces. But it just didn't feel that way anymore.

* * *

The one thing I always looked forward to was going to see Mom, which didn't happen very often. It was a lot of trouble for Uncle Joe to drive us all the way down there. The visits were pretty emotional. Mommy would be happy to see us, of course, but she cried a lot. Jacki refused to go, so just Jenny, Joey and I went. Kevin was jealous that we got to see the inside of a prison, and he was mad that he wasn't included. As we got older, Jenny seemed to have a lot of excuses for not going.

"Mom's constantly complaining about stuff. I get tired of her whining," she said once. After a visit with Mom, Jen would bite her nails right down to the quick.

"Yeah, but you'd whine too, if you were in jail all the time," I argued.

"Well, maybe she should stop running over people," she said.

"But I know she's sorry. They should just let her out. She'll come home and show them she can be good." Made sense to me.

"It doesn't work that way. You're so stupid. Besides, she never says she's sorry for killing Daddy. She says he drove her to do it. Like it's not her fault at all."

None of that made any difference to me. I just wanted her to come home. I was hoping we could get our old house back.

"Jenny, do you think little Ben will remember us when he grows up?" I asked.

She thought for a moment before she answered. "Gee, I don't know. He was awfully little. But maybe."

"I was hoping I could write him a letter. I know he can't read, but still."

I asked Aunt Sally at dinner one night if I could write a letter to Ben. At first she said she didn't think so, but I saw Uncle Joe give her a look, and then she said to go ahead and write it, and they'd try to get his address. I don't remember if the letter ever got mailed, but I do recall that whenever I talked about Benjy, they always changed the subject.

I also tried to talk to Mom about what was going on with Kevin, and how unhappy I was, but we had such a limited amount of time together, I hated to bother her. I wanted to cheer her up. It was so hard, seeing her sad all the time. She said she missed us very much, and she hoped that after she got out, we'd all live together again.

Mom wanted to move to Hawaii. She and Daddy had been there on their honeymoon and she fell in love with it. She said we'd get a little house near the beach. Joey and I couldn't wait. Mom said she wanted to get back into teaching. When I mentioned this to Aunt Sally, she snorted and said, "Fat chance. They aren't going to let a woman with two felony convictions go anywhere near a classroom with a bunch of kids. Your mother's going to have to find another line of work."

Still, it was fun to think about a new life in Hawaii. Joey and I laid in our beds at night and talked about living on the beach. I decided I wanted to be a lifeguard when I grew up, and hang out on the beach all day long. You could get a nice suntan and get famous for saving lives. I was surprised that more people didn't want to be lifeguards.

One night Joey announced, "I want to be a garbage man."

I was horrified. "What? Why a garbage man?"

"Because they only work on Thursdays," she answered.

"They do not. They just come to our house on Thursdays. You're such a dope," I said, giggling.

"Same to you, but more of it."

"Shut up!"

"I don't shut up, I grow up and when I look at you I throw up."

I let out a heavy sigh.

After awhile, I thought she had fallen asleep. Then I heard her say, "In that case, I want to be an actress. Like Hayley Mills. Or Perry Como."

"Go to sleep, Bozo," I said.

"Can I sleep with you?" she asked.

"No, you'll just pee all over me."

"No, I won't, I promise. I just went. Please?" she begged.

"Well, okay. But you better not wet the bed this time. I swear, Joey."

"I won't. Cross my heart and hope to die," she said as she crawled into bed with me.

When I woke up in the morning, Joey was back in her own bed. And I was soaked.

15

One reason I liked going to see Mom in prison was that Joey and I got to spend time alone with Uncle Joe. In fact, it was our only chance to be alone with him. My uncle was a great guy and I guess he figured we'd been through a lot, because he was very sweet to us.

The long drive down to the prison in Corona, California, meant we had to leave early in the morning. We'd arrive around noon and visit with Mom for a couple of hours. Then Uncle Joe would treat us to lunch. He always let us choose the restaurant and we could order anything on the menu. Our favorite place was The Burger Pit. Every single time I ordered a bacon cheeseburger, onion rings and a chocolate milkshake. Joey usually got a toasted cheese sandwich (which I thought was dumb because she could always get one of those at home) and a root beer. That Joey really loved her root beer.

After lunch, we still faced five hours on the road to get home. Joey'd fall asleep in the back seat, so I got to ride up front with Uncle Joe. And he did the same thing every time: he'd clear his throat and then start talking about Mom. He'd tell me what she was like when she was young, how all the boys were crazy about her, how she had so many friends. One time he said, "She was so popular in high school, everybody hated her!" And that made me giggle. It was our little joke. By the way he talked, I knew my uncle had been proud of her at one time. But then he'd get real serious and talk about how people change.

"Sometimes they can't help it," he said. "Your mom had so many kids to take care of. It was hard on her, what with your dad working long hours and all. There's no good excuse for what she did, but sometimes people just go over the edge."

I knew he was making excuses for her, but that was okay. It made me feel good, hearing him talk like that. I needed to believe she didn't mean to do it.

And then he would say, "So, how're you? How's school going?"

I think he was trying to find out why I was fighting with the other kids so much, and why I was in trouble at school all the time. I didn't know how to answer him. I honestly didn't *like* being in trouble, but sometimes got so mad I did things without thinking.

"I hate being teased, and when your mom's in jail, guess what? You get teased a lot," I told him.

"Do you ever tell your teacher when the other kids are picking on you?" he asked.

"Yeah, but it doesn't help." Actually, I'd never told my teachers.

"You know, you can always come to me or Sal, if you need to talk," he'd say.

"Yeah, I know." But talking about things wasn't going to bring my mom home from jail any sooner. Or get my dad back. So what was the point? After each one of my talks with Uncle Joe, I vowed I would try harder because I really did want to do better and not be causing trouble all the time. But it never worked out that way. I found myself either mad or sad about something most of the time. And often I'd say mean things to Joey or the boys just because it felt good.

One time I was watching TV and Aunt Sally told me to go to bed. I didn't want to. It was a Friday night and I wanted to stay up later. I was almost thirteen. It was stupid for me to have a bedtime. But she shut off the TV and told me to go to bed right now.

"I hate you. You're that word that rhymes with witch!" I yelled, and she burst into tears. In the morning, she pretended nothing had happened. I knew I should have apologized, but I never did.

I started junior high that year, and things were going downhill for me. I hated all the rules. Aunt Sally constantly wanted our bedroom picked up. And it seemed stupid to me. I mean, what difference did it make if my jeans were lying in the middle of the floor, or folded up in the drawer? In the long run, who cared? Over the summer, Uncle Joe built a shed in the backyard to store the things that were normally kept in the garage, and he turned the garage into two good-sized bedrooms, one for Kevin and the other for the twins. Then I moved into Kevin's old room. He also built a small room off the patio, where he could get away from the noise in the household. It felt good to have my own room again, but Aunt Sally was always bugging me to clean it up. That *really* got on my nerves.

The best thing about junior high was that I met Tiffany Smith, who became my very first best friend. Short, petite, with beautiful red hair, she always wore pretty clothes to school. She lived in what she called a "townhouse," which just seemed like an apartment to me, but it had an upstairs and it was real big and fancy. We weren't even supposed to use the living room. That was for company only. Her parents were divorced and her mother drove a fancy T-Bird. And they had a cute little poodle.

"Her name's 'Coquette, Mon Apricot Cheri,'" Tiff told me the first time I went over to her house to spend the night. "That means, 'Coquette, my Apricot Love' in French. She's registered and everything." Tiffy's brother Andy was three years younger than us. Her mom, a secretary, always dressed up nice to go to work, and wore real pearls and eyeliner, even on weekdays.

From the moment we met, Tiffany and I were inseparable. Our lockers were right next to each other and we were in most classes together. She told me she'd already had eleven boyfriends. I was impressed. I hadn't even had one boyfriend so far. We tried to talk on the phone almost every night and spent our time in class writing notes to each other.

At first, I was afraid to tell her that my mom was in jail because I thought she wouldn't like me, but when I finally did spill the beans, she thought it was cool. "You're lucky," she said. "You have such an exotic past." She said we better not tell her mother, however. She didn't tell me why and I didn't ask. After her mom got to know me, she told me she was happy Tiff had such a good friend. When Mrs. Smith finally found out about my mom, she just looked at me and said, "Oh, you poor thing," and that was that. Mrs. Smith went out most nights with her boyfriend, an older man who wore suits when he came to pick her up and always brought Tiff and Andy a box of chocolate candy. Sometimes that same box of candy would be in the refrigerator for weeks, which amazed me. At my house, a box of candy wouldn't last a day.

When I first met Tiffy, she seemed really classy to me. She always wore expensive clothes, never hand-me-downs. Still a tomboy, I didn't care that much about clothes, but Tiff loved to talk about fashion and how much money her mom spent buying her dresses and shoes. Mrs. Smith had a mink coat, which we tried on one evening after she'd left on a date. Andy was spending the night at a friend's house, so we had the place to ourselves. Aunt Sally would have had a fit if she'd known we were alone, but I never told her Mrs. Smith went out on weeknights.

That evening, Tiffy opened up the sliding glass door to

the little balcony that overlooked the courtyard and pool. It was a real pretty view, but it was kind of chilly so I didn't know why she left the door open. Then she went into the kitchen and came back with a pack of her mother's Marlboro cigarettes. I watched in amazement as she expertly put a cigarette to her lips and lit it.

"You want one?" she asked.

"I didn't know you smoked," I said.

"Oh, sure," she said casually, as she blew a smoke ring. "Everyone smokes. Here; take a puff."

I took the cigarette, put it to my lips and drew a small amount of smoke into my mouth. "It tastes nasty," I said, handing it back to her.

"It always does at first. But you'll get used to it. It's a good thing you didn't inhale, which can really hurt your lungs. I don't particularly like Marlboros, they're not my brand, but that's what my mother smokes."

"Doesn't she smell it on your breath?" I asked.

"No, smokers can't smell anything, but I always gargle before she gets home, anyway. I just have to hide it from Andy, otherwise, he'd snitch on me, the little bastard."

Wow! Tiffy smoked and swore! She wasn't as prissy as I thought. I actually learned she could be real sneaky. Not allowed to wear nylons to school because her mom said she was too young, Tiff would buy a pair at the drug store and hide them in her purse until she got to school and then put them on before first period. She did the same thing with mascara—she'd swipe a tube from her mother's bathroom, put it on in the girls' bathroom at school, and then wash it off before her mother came home from work that evening. Even though I wasn't interested in wearing either nylons or makeup, I thought she was pretty clever.

The first time I brought Tiff over to my house for a sleepover, I was embarrassed that our place wasn't nearly as nice as hers, but she said I was lucky to have both my aunt and uncle living at home, and to have sisters. She really envied me having sisters. She thought the twins were cute, and she fussed over Joey a lot. She even said she thought Kevin was kind of cute! I was in shock!

"He's gross! He's a pig!" I said, horrified. "How could you even begin to think he's cute?"

"Lookit, if he let his hair grow out and wore jeans instead of those stupid cords, he'd look a little cooler. But his face is kinda sweet. I like his dimples. You just need to help him with his wardrobe."

I was shaking my head. "I am going to *throw up*. I swear."

Sixteen by now, Kevin had an interest in girls, but was still so immature, didn't have a clue how to talk to one. I actually saw him walk up to a girl once and say, "I want to lick you all over." Then I watched in amusement as the girl's face reacted in horror. If he had been nicer to me, I might have been willing to coach him a little, but he was still an obnoxious jerk. Besides, he was three years older than me. Let him figure it out.

As soon as I started developing and had to wear a bra, Kevin started calling me "Headlights." I didn't even realize what he was talking about at first. Then he encouraged the twins to call me that, and the first time Matthew tried it, I smacked him right in the face. Of course I got grounded for that, but what else was new?

My grades were so lousy, I probably would have flunked seventh grade if it hadn't been for Tiff. But she didn't want to go on to eighth grade without me, so we spent a lot of time doing homework together, and I just barely managed to squeak by with a D average. Uncle Joe had fits about my grades, especially since he was a schoolteacher. I promised him I would do better next year.

That summer, I spent most of my time at Tiffany's, and I

guess it was probably a relief for my family to have me out of the house. Tiff lived close to downtown, so it was easy for us to walk there, go shopping, and hang out at the local Dairy Queen, where all the kids from school would gather. Except for me, she wasn't supposed to have kids over to her place when her mom wasn't home, but of course she did anyway. As long as we didn't get into too much trouble, her mother didn't pay much attention to us. We frequently had to bribe Andy with money or candy to keep him quiet, but that was easy. Tiff was supposed to be keeping an eye on him, but she let him take off during the day, as long as he was back before their mother got home from work.

Tiffy started dating for real that summer. Dan was a nice kid with long hair. He wore bell-bottom blue jeans and a leather fringe jacket wherever he went. His best friend Gary was kind of cute but a couple of inches shorter than me, so I didn't like him that much. They'd come over and Dan and Tiff would head off to her bedroom.

That left me alone with Gary. We'd usually sit and talk for a while and then go out onto the balcony and smoke. He liked music a lot and sometimes brought his guitar. Other times, he'd bring his newest album and we'd listen to it together.

One afternoon, when Dan and Tiff had slipped off to the bedroom, Gary asked me if I'd had many boyfriends.

"A few," I said.

"So, do you like to make out?" he asked.

"It's okay, I guess." I'd never even been kissed.

"Well, do you think we could make out a little?" He was tapping his fingers on his lap and looking away. I realized he was nervous.

I can't say I was attracted to him in that way, but we had nothing better to do. He scooted over on the couch and put his arm around me. Then he moved his head close to mine, closed his eyes and put his lips on mine. And just stayed there. He didn't move or anything. So I didn't either. *So this is what kissing is all about? It doesn't feel like anything.*

He pulled away and looked at me. "You wanna do it some more?"

"Not really," I answered. "You want some ice cream?"

He followed me into the kitchen. As I was reaching into the freezer, he snuck his arm around me and put his hand on my breast.

"What the heck are you doing?" I said, pushing him away.

"I thought girls liked that."

"Well, I don't, so knock it off!"

"You don't need to freak out," he said. "Dan says Tiffy really likes it."

I thought for a minute while I got the bowls down. "Well, you know, I guess she really likes Dan a lot. Maybe that makes a difference."

"Maybe you're just really weird," he responded.

Later, after they'd left, I tried to get Tiff to tell me what she and Dan were actually doing back in her bedroom.

"Having fun!" she said. I knew she meant making out, but I really wanted to know how far they were going. She wouldn't tell me.

"So Gary kissed me," I finally told her.

Her face lit up. "Far out! How was it?"

"It was okay. Nothing special. I'm not sure he even knows how to kiss."

"Did you French?"

"No, he just sorta put his mouth on mine. It was kinda boring, actually."

"Well, that's too bad," she said. "Maybe after you do it for a while, you'll like it better."

Maybe.

After we went back to school to begin eighth grade, I began seeing less of Tiff. We didn't have any classes together that year, and she was always off with some boy, behind the bleachers or anywhere they could find to be alone. Annoyed with her, I wanted just the two of us to hang out together on weekends, but she always wanted to go look for boys. And then she started getting grounded a lot.

One day, her mom came to school to pick her up for a dentist appointment. Tiff had forgotten all about it and had rolled her skirt up real short. She was wearing makeup, nylons and one-inch heels her mom didn't even know she had. Boy, did Mrs. Smith hit the roof! Tiffy was grounded for a month, which was too bad, because Jenny's sixteenth birthday was coming up. Beth was planning a surprise party for her and was going to bring us over to her house for the weekend. Now Tiff was grounded and couldn't go.

Actually, I was kind of glad she had to stay home. I hadn't spent that much time with my sisters lately. Jacki came home from college for the weekend, so she picked up me and Joey, and the four of us spent all day Saturday together at Beth and Ken's house. Jacki bleached Jenny's hair, and it came out real pretty. Then we pulled out the ironing board, and Jacki tried to iron the curls out of my hair, but it didn't work too well. She put some makeup on me and Jenny let me wear her pretty paisley vest that matched perfectly with my purple bell-bottoms.

Beth told Jenny we were going to have pizza for dinner with cake and ice cream and we'd stay home and have a 'family night.' But around seven p.m., all of Jenny's friends started showing up. I don't know if she was surprised or not, but she acted like it. Her friend Maria showed up, carrying her son around on her hip. Pregnant again, still unmarried, she and Eddy were living with his aunt and uncle. Having Maria there made me feel a little weird because Jenny was only 16, yet she had a friend who already had a baby. It made me feel like we were growing up really fast.

I was kinda surprised that Jenny and Maria were still friends. My sister was so involved in school and interested to going to college, when all Maria ever talked about were her problems with Eddie. We all took turns playing with little Donovan. He was an adorable baby.

Becky, another old friend of Jenny's from her foster home, also showed up. They hadn't seen a lot of each other over the last two years, but kept in touch by phone. I'd never spent much time around Becky. When I did, she always seemed angry. A couple of times she had referred to me and Joey as "brats," so I didn't care for her much. But she was in a good mood that night so she was more fun to be around.

Some kids from Jenny's school were there as well as several people in their twenties, friends of Beth and Ken who Jenny liked to hang out with. The people in the older group were all campaigning for Bobby Kennedy, who was running for president. They even had election signs planted on the front lawn. There was a lot of political talk, which was boring, but Jenny was right in the middle of it. She seemed to know what they were talking about. I was amazed.

I'd never met Jenny's new boyfriend, Craig, before, but he seemed like a cool guy. And he was really cute, like he could be Dr. Kildare's younger brother. He sat listening while everyone talked about the campaign. After a while, he came over and sat with me and Maria.

Reaching for a handful of M&Ms, he said, "These are so good. I could eat them like candy!"

I smiled at his lame joke.

"Kinda dull, huh?" he said to me.

"I hate politics," I said.

"Me, too," he replied. "I'd much rather talk about sports. How about those Giants?"

Maria and I both made gagging noises, and he got up and

went into the kitchen.

Several days after the party, Jenny broke up with him. She was always doing that. She sure went through a lot of guys.

16

When Tiffy and I began our freshman year of high school, we started getting into serious trouble. She was swiping shots of alcohol from her mother's liquor cabinet and replacing it with water. I didn't like the taste at all. Both wine and beer made me gag, and the harder stuff was even worse. I couldn't understand how people could drink it.

One Friday night, Tiff got a boyfriend to get us a quart of Bacardi rum, which we mixed with Coke, and between us we drank the whole bottle. I spent the rest of the night throwing up in her toilet. It was one of the worst experiences of my life. I felt terrible for the whole weekend and vowed I'd never do *that* again.

Another time, I was at Tiffy's house and we wanted to go to a Who concert in San Jose that day. We didn't have any way to get there, so she told her Mom we were taking the bus. She even called the bus station to get the schedule and her mom gave us money for the fare.

But when we got to the bus stop, Tiffy stuck out her thumb.

"What are you doing?" I shrieked.

"We're not wasting money on bus fare," she said.

I stood there with my mouth hanging open, but in no time at all, a van picked us up. Two grungy-looking guys gave us a ride all the way to the concert. When we got out, Tiff gave the driver her phone number.

"You didn't give him your real number, did you?" I asked her.

"No, of course not," she said, "I gave him yours! What do you think—I'm an idiot?" I knew she was being sarcastic, but I was still stunned that I'd done such a dangerous and stupid thing. I'd never even thought about hitchhiking before, but we quickly found it to be an easy way to get around. We were bored with hanging out in Morgan Hill. The action was in San Jose, and even farther away, in the beach town of Santa Cruz.

Waiting in line at the concert, we met up with a couple of girlfriends from school. They suggested we take a walk, and we went around the corner of the building. Sandy pulled a joint out of her pocket and lit up. I'd never smoked pot before, so she had to show me how to do it. At first I didn't feel anything, but a little while later, we smoked some more, right there in the audience, and I started to feel a little light-headed and giggly. I thought maybe I was just imagining it, but as I looked around, I noticed all of my friends were smiling and happy. I had a fantastic time!

After that, Tiff and I tried to get our hands on pot whenever we could. She had a lot more access to money than I did. Tiffy's dad owned a used car dealership in San Jose, and she had a regular allowance. She frequently told him she needed extra money for new gym clothes or school supplies or field trips, and he didn't mind slipping her an extra twenty. As long as she stayed out of her parents' hair and kept out of trouble, they were happy. They never had any interest in what she was doing.

Tiffy and I started getting stoned on a regular basis. In fact, I was only happy when I was stoned. The rest of the time I was depressed because I couldn't find a boyfriend. There were a couple of cute guys at school I kinda had crushes on, but they were dating cheerleaders and weren't interested in me. There were also two or three who said they liked me, but I wasn't attracted to any of them. Tiff changed boyfriends just about once a week. She never had trouble finding guys to go out with. She kept telling me that I was too picky. One time she even started dating this junior just because he had a car. That weekend, he drove us over to Santa Cruz, and after we got there, she broke up with him. I couldn't believe it!

"How are we going to get home now?" I demanded.

"Just relax, mellow out, Ju. Somebody'll give us a ride."

And sure enough, we met some guys who had a car, and they gave us a ride back to Tiff's that night. I did a lot of things with Tiffy that I would've never done on my own, but I didn't want to look like a square.

One time we were at a concert and some kid gave Tiff a couple of pills. She popped them right down. We didn't even know what they were. She lay on the floor all during the concert, just staring up at the ceiling, not responding to anything. I was worried we might have to call an ambulance, but the guys with us said she'd be fine. Later, the boy who gave her the pills said he meant for her to give one pill to me; she shouldn't have taken both of them.

That summer, Tiff and I hitched a ride over to Santa Cruz and we got picked up by a group of older guys wearing motorcycle jackets. They called themselves the "Hellriders," and said their club was "cousins" to the Hell's Angels. These guys took us on all the rides on the boardwalk and bought us lunch. I was starting to get nervous, afraid we might not be able to get away from them. I was riding the roller coaster with Frank, who had started putting his arm around me, and I casually mentioned to him that I had epilepsy, and that if I got scared, I'd have a seizure. I thought it might prevent him from trying anything, and it seemed to work.

Toward the end of the day, we were sitting in the sand, smoking a joint, when Tiff and the guy she was with took off and went under the boardwalk. That left me sitting alone with five rough-looking bikers. Now I was really nervous.

"This has been so much fun," I said. "I don't usually get out much."

"Why is that, honey?" Frank asked.

"Well, my dad's a judge. He's pretty strict."

All the guys started laughing and swearing. One of the guys said to Frank, "You really know how to pick 'em!" I acted all innocent, like I didn't know why that would alarm them. But the story kept me safe, at least that day.

Tiffy wasn't so lucky. When she emerged from underneath the boardwalk, she had a huge hickey on her neck. That was really bad news. Her mother would've killed her if she saw it. Tiff seriously considered burning the spot with a cigarette and telling her mom it happened with a hot curler. Luckily, her mother never saw it because Tiff wore a turtleneck sweater for the next few days. In August.

But her luck couldn't hold out forever. Eventually, her mom found some drugs in her bedroom and she was grounded for the rest of the summer. After that, Mrs. Smith was a lot less trusting and even I was banned from going over to her house for a while. It was during that time that Tiffy started talking about running away and going up to Haight-Ashbury. We both hated school and thought it was totally pointless. We wanted to be out in the world, free to do our own thing. The idea of sitting in class learning about coal production in England seemed totally absurd.

When school began again in September, Mrs. Smith and my aunt and uncle were much more cautious about what we were allowed to do. Tiff could come over to my house if we wanted to spend the night together, but that was boring. We'd tasted freedom and we loved it. We couldn't go backwards now.

Then Tiff had another bit of bad luck. A kid at school

gave her a ride home on his motorcycle and hit a patch of gravel in the road. They spun out of control and Tiffy flew off the back. She broke a couple of ribs and had scratches and bruises all over her body, but it was a miracle she wasn't killed. Her parents were totally shocked that she'd even been on a motorcycle! After all the dangerous stuff we'd done over the last two years, it was funny they were so concerned over a silly motorcycle ride.

Tiff's parents were determined to do something to keep her out of trouble. Mr. Smith lived with his girlfriend who didn't work and was home during the day, so they talked of Tiffy going to live with them for a while. But she didn't want to change schools and be separated from me, so she had a huge temper tantrum and they dropped that idea. Eventually the commotion died down after Tiff promised to bring up her grades. However, now they were keeping closer tabs on us, which was really a drag. Tiffy talked constantly about running away.

There was one thing I was holding out for. Jenny and Kevin would be graduating in June and there would be a big party for them. All of my sisters would be there and I was looking forward to it. But, still, the more I thought about running away, the more it appealed to me.

I didn't want to hurt my aunt and uncle, but I hated living there. I didn't fit in and never would. They weren't my real family. Kevin hadn't let up harassing me. Many times he'd walk by me, reach his hand up under the back of my shirt and snap my bra. Or, if we were fighting, he'd tell the twins that I was "on the rag." Uncle Joe constantly hassled me about my grades. Aunt Sally kept bugging me to clean my room or help with chores, or to watch the other kids when she had to go out. Depressed a lot of the time, I just wanted to be left alone.

I often wondered what my life would have been like if Daddy were still alive. Or if Mom had been acquitted. I'd been to see her a few times, and she always gave me a lecture about behaving myself, doing better in school, and getting along with the other kids. Like she was one to talk! Eventually I stopped going. If Jacki didn't have to see Mom, why should I?

Tiff and I had a vague plan that we would take off sometime in June, although she wanted to leave a lot earlier. Then she met a guy who worked at a gas station. Jim was nineteen and very handsome, with long, flowing hair. He looked like the pictures you'd see of Jesus, except that his hair was the same color as Tiff's--dark red. He was crazy about Tiff and she claimed to be madly in love with him. And when Mrs. Smith found out how old Jim was, she said she'd call the police if Tiff kept seeing him. Of course she kept seeing him.

Then, on the first day of Christmas break, she called me.

"Listen, Jim and I have a plan. There's a place he knows about in the city where runaways can go. He's going to take us up there. I have a hundred dollars saved. How much do you have?"

"About fifty, I think."

"Shit, that's not much. But anyway, come over to my place on Friday night, we'll head over to DQ, and he'll pick us up, okay?"

"Yeah, okay, great," I said, though my heart was thudding in my chest.

"You don't sound too excited," she complained.

"It's just I know my aunt and uncle are going to freak out," I said.

"Look, you keep whining about how they never listen to you. They're hassling you all the time. And your sisters have never been there for you. Fuck 'em! You wanna go back to school on Monday morning, fine. You wanna sit in a boring classroom all day long, fine. You wanna stay in this stupid hick town, fine. But I'm not going to be there. I'm going to start living!" There was a brief pause. "So are you going with me?"

I hesitated. I didn't feel quite ready to take this drastic step just yet, but felt rushed to make a decision. Did I want to get up and go to school on Monday, or be out on the road with my best friend?

Finally, I said, "Yeah. Of course."

"Far out! We're going to have so fun much, Jules. Trust me!"

I worried that I'd start acting weird and give my secret away before Friday. It turned out I was concerned for nothing. My aunt and uncle were fighting with Kevin, for a change. He had just told them that as soon as he turned eighteen, four months before graduation, he was planning to join the Army. He actually had enough credits to graduate early, and was anxious to sign up.

My aunt and uncle were understandably upset. During a time when most young guys were dodging the draft or running off to Canada to avoid going to Vietnam, my retard of a cousin was actually signing up for combat. He was looking forward to it! I listened with a smile on my face as my aunt and uncle argued with him. I was more than happy that the attention was on him right now.

On Friday afternoon, I wrote a quick note to my aunt and uncle and left it on top of my dresser. It said:

Dear Uncle Joe and Aunt Sally,

Tiffy and I are taking off. Please don't worry about us. We just want to be on our own. We have some money saved up and a place to stay. I promise I'll be in touch.

Love, Jules

I wished I could have spent more time writing the note, but I knew Tiff was in a hurry. It was December, so I wore a T-shirt, a sweater and a jacket over that, plus my jeans. I packed a small bag with extra underwear and socks, makeup and toothbrush. It didn't seem like much.

Kevin had recently gotten his driver's license, so I talked him into giving me a ride over to Tiff's. From there, we walked to the DQ. Jim was waiting for us in the parking lot. It was so easy.

17

JIM STARTED THE CAR and we pulled onto Highway 101, heading north toward San Francisco. He and Tiffy were so excited! She put an Iron Butterfly tape into the 8-track player and cranked it up real loud.

"This is *far out*!" Tiff said. "Now we can do whatever the hell we want! No one to answer to!"

Jim took a joint out of ashtray and handed it to Tiff to light. She took a hit, then passed it to me. I had a toke and, after a few minutes, started feeling all floaty and warm. By now, it was dark and cold outside. We turned the heater on and the three of us rode up in the front seat. The back seat of the car was filled with sleeping bags, pillows and our meager belongings. We were on our way, and we didn't even have to hitchhike.

I tried not to think about what it would be like at home after they got my note. Or the Christmas presents that were waiting for me under the tree. Tiff might have been thinking the same thing.

"My old lady's going to croak when she finds out I'm gone. Serves her right, the bitch." She took another hit, held it in for a long time, and then slowly exhaled. The car started filling up with smoke. "So where exactly are we going, Jimmy?" she asked.

Jim cranked down the window to let in a little air. "There's a guy I know, works some light shows around the city. He knows of a place we can crash for now. But the thing is, you girls, if anyone asks, you gotta tell them you're seventeen, dig it?"

"Sure, but why?" Tiff asked, lighting a cigarette.

"'Cause if you're close to turning eighteen, the pigs aren't going to be too concerned. But at fifteen, you're trouble. Probably no one will even ask, but just in case...you're seventeen, okay?"

"Got it," we both said.

It took a couple of hours to get into San Francisco and find the Haight-Ashbury district. We parked and walked up the street. An old yellow school bus sitting on the corner had been turned into a fish and chip shop. We bought a couple of orders, and sat on the curb, eating our hot, greasy dinner.

"Far out," I heard Tiff say again. She said that a lot.

After we finished, they smoked a cigarette while Jim looked at an old map. "It's only a couple of blocks from here," he said, and led us up the street and into a building where the front door windows were covered with newspapers. A guy at the door was taking money. Jim whispered in his ear, and the man let us in without paying. We went down the hallway, through another door into a room that was totally dark. Most of the walls were painted black and covered with black-light posters. On the far wall, however, colorful images danced around in tune to the sounds of Jimi Hendrix. I had never seen a "light show" before and was impressed. I could just make out the images of people lying around on pillows watching the show. The smell of incense and marijuana filled the room. We settled down to watch and I promptly fell asleep. When I woke up, I didn't see Jim and Tiff anywhere. I fell right back to sleep, but was awakened later when Jim shook me.

"Come on, they're closing, we gotta split," he said quietly. We walked back into the cold. The street was deserted.

"Where we going now?" I asked, dazed and sleepy.

"Jim can't find his friend," Tiff said with a touch of annoyance. "We're going to have to sleep in the car until tomorrow."

"Oh, crap," I said.

Jim moved some stuff into the trunk and I crawled into the back seat with a sleeping bag over me. Jim and Tiff spent a while trying to get comfortable in the front seat. I don't know how they did it.

As I was dozing off, I heard Tiff whining to Jim. His voice was low and muffled, but I heard him whisper, "Don't worry about it, babe. We'll find something in the morning."

When we awakened, the sun was just coming up and we were stiff, tired, cold, grimy and hungry. We found an open coffee shop and ordered breakfast. Tiffy and I went into the bathroom to try to wash up. I wished I'd brought a washcloth and towel. We did the best we could with paper towels.

When we came out, Jim was sitting in a booth, smoking a cigarette. "Well, you two look ravishing this morning!"

Tiff stuck her tongue out at him. She was always kind of cranky in the morning, and sleeping in a car all night didn't help.

The waiter, a young guy with long, greasy hair and a tie-dyed T-shirt, brought some menus over.

"Hey, you wouldn't happen to know a cat by the name of Carl?" Jim asked. "Carl Murphy, I think."

"Oh, you mean Crazy Carl? Sure, I know the guy."

"You know where I can find him?"

"Oh, I think he mighta got busted. Haven't seen him around for a while."

"Shit," Jim muttered. "Well, you know a place where we can crash for a while?"

"Hold on," the guy said and disappeared. He came back with a piece of paper. "Here, look for this address. Chick by the name of Lucy owns a place where kids can stay. Kind of a dump, but at least you're out of the cold."

"Great! Thanks, man!" Jim said.

After breakfast, we drove around until we found the address, not far from Haight Street. It looked like an old warehouse with green and yellow peace signs painted all over it, and sayings like, "There's love in Haight."

Once inside, we found lots of kids hanging around, sitting on the floor or in beanbag chairs. They welcomed us and directed us upstairs to the kitchen. That's where we found Lucy, a very fat middle-aged lady with long brown braids and a headband. She stood kneading a loaf of bread, and was covered with flour.

We introduced ourselves and Jim told her we were looking for a place to stay. The first thing she asked was, "How old are you two?" and we both said seventeen. "Sure you are," she said. "Well, I don't want no troublemakers around here. But you kids look okay. I think there's some space on the second floor. Just watch your stuff. I can't be looking after it. And clean up after yourself. I'm not running a motel here, ya know what I mean?"

We found a couple of empty mattresses and arranged our sleeping bags there. Jim and Tiff wanted to spend some time alone, so I wandered down to the main floor. Five or six people sat around the living room, listening to The Doors on the stereo. They looked pretty spaced out. Someone passed me a joint and I took a hit. I introduced myself, and everyone was pretty friendly. Marcia was a small, black-haired girl who I thought was younger than me, but turned out to be almost nineteen. Todd, a tall, skinny guy wearing just a pair of bell-bottomed blue jeans, said, "Hey, beautiful lady." One woman called herself "Butterfly." She was always stoned. Then there was Maggie, an older woman who was very talkative and always complaining about the "war machine." People would come in and out, smoke something, take a nap or bring in a bag of potato chips to pass around. I really liked the vibes there.

That evening, Lucy put out the fresh-baked bread she had made and served it with a big pot of beef stew. She said, "Some of the kids who come in here don't like to eat meat, but I just say fuck 'em! I cook what I like, and if you don't want to eat it, you don't have to! No skin off my nose!"

I found out later that Lucy had been married for a long time to a guy with a lot of money and she won a big settlement when they divorced. She'd moved to San Francisco, bought this warehouse and turned it into a place where people could just hang out. She liked to talk tough, but she was actually very sweet and loved having young people around.

Jim and Tiff came downstairs, looking rested, and joined us in the living area, sitting with big bowls of stew in their laps. We hadn't eaten since breakfast and were starving. Maggie was asking us about our background, when Tiffy just suddenly burst out: "Julie's mom killed her dad. On purpose. Her mom's in jail now. Her dad was this big hotshot attorney, but he was having an affair." There were murmurs of sympathy from everyone in the room. Todd crawled over and gave me a big hug. I was a little embarrassed.

"You're welcome to stay here as long as you want," he said, which I thought was funny, since it wasn't even his place. Later that night, when we were settled into our sleeping bags, I turned to Tiff and said, "You didn't have to tell everyone about my parents!"

"Why not?" she asked. "It's interesting. It's not your fault; why should you hide it?"

"I'm not trying to hide it, but I don't want to advertise it, either!"

"Well, I don't know why you're getting all bitchy about it. You need to relax, go with the flow."

"I just don't like standing out like some kind of weirdo!" I had never realized until that moment that I really *did* feel like a weirdo where my family was concerned. "And I sure the hell don't need anyone telling me to go with the flow!"

Jim, snuggled up next to Tiff, lifted his head and said, "Actually, Jules is right. You two should try to keep a low profile. They might've sent the cops looking for you."

I hadn't even thought about that. I buried down into my sleeping bag, still annoyed. Tiff could really get on my nerves sometimes!

The next day, I met Denny. We were all sitting in the living room again smoking a joint, when a tall, slender handsome boy walked through the door and I fell flat on my face in love! He took one look at me and said, "I must be dreaming."

He sat down and introduced himself. He was seventeen, and had been living at Lucy's since he ran away from home in New Jersey six months ago. He worked part-time in a restaurant, and said he thought he could get us some work "under the table," as he called it. We chatted for a while and then it started to rain. More and more kids were coming in off the street, and the living room was really crowded. With the music blaring, it was hard to talk. Denny asked if I wanted to take a walk and I grabbed my jacket. We wandered out into the cold.

I'd never really spent much time in San Francisco, but at Christmas, it was truly beautiful. The storefronts, decorated with Santa Clauses, reindeer and lights, beckoned shoppers inside. An older guy, wearing a Santa's hat, sat in front of a stove on the sidewalk roasting chestnuts and gave me a free sample. Everywhere we went, young people greeted us by saying, "Peace, brother!" or "All you need is love!" The air was thick with the rich scent of incense, patchouli oil and marijuana. The energy here made me feel so good.

Denny had a lot of friends and introduced me to dozens of kids. He knew of a place where we could get a bowl of soup for a quarter and where we could get used clothes for really cheap. He pointed out the free clinic where you could go if you got sick. As we were walking, I had my hands in the pocket of my coat to keep them warm, and Denny reached inside my right coat pocket and took my hand in his, intertwining our fingers. My heart almost jumped out of my chest.

"You have the most incredible hair," he whispered in my ear. "Every other girl I know has long, straight hair. I love your curls. Promise me you'll never cut them?"

I looked up into his face and smiled. He leaned down and kissed me. It was magical!

We stood on the corner, kissing, for a long time. I remember feeling happy for the first time in ages. It was the perfect place for me to be right then and I was so glad I'd come. Arm-in-arm, we walked back to the house.

I found Tiffy upstairs, fresh out of the shower.

"I hate this place," she said, combing her hair in the mirror. "There's not enough hot water, and I had to dry myself off with a dirty towel. And I hate sleeping on the floor. I don't know if I can live like this. Jim needs to get a job so he can get us out of here."

"You should stop acting like a spoiled brat," I said.

She turned to me, surprised.

"I like it here," I said, as I sat on the edge of the bathtub, watching her.

"Why?"

"Because Denny is here. He kissed me. A lot!" I was beaming now.

Tiffy was so happy she threw her arms around me. "That is so cool. He is so cute! But don't call me a brat just because I don't want to share a towel with a dozen other people, okay?"

I went downstairs and was floored when I saw Denny sitting with his arm around Marcia. I didn't know what to think. He saw me and waved me over. "Hey, Julie, you've met

Marcia, right? She's been my buddy ever since I got here." I breathed a sigh of relief. "So we're all gonna drop some acid tonight. You want some?"

I hesitated. "I've never done acid. I don't know..."

"Oh, it's great. It'll blow your mind. I'll stay right beside you so you'll be safe. Okay?" I nodded.

That night, I took LSD for the first time. There were six of us altogether, lying around the living room. I didn't notice anything at first, but then I started feeling light, tingly and a little jumpy, like my stomach was in knots. After a while, I noticed if I gazed at a poster on the wall, all kinds of images jumped out, like a little mouse, or a flower. I looked at the rug and watched as it moved in waves across the floor. If I closed my eyes, I saw lots of beautiful colors, purples and greens, spinning around. But if I sat up and looked directly at something, the images went away. I felt safe and warm, like I was in a cocoon. People were talking and laughing around me, and the sounds seemed to come from far away. I noticed Denny was looking at me with a smile on his face.

"What?"

"Nothing. You just look like an angel. Floating on a raft of baloney." Everyone started laughing.

"Julie," I heard someone say, "you're the Baloney Angel."

I liked the feeling, and seeing the colors, but after a couple of hours, I kind of wanted to come down. My stomach was still jumpy and I had started feeling a little restless. I didn't want to be high anymore. Denny suggested we go upstairs.

The second floor was empty, which was pretty unusual, and we settled down on my mattress. Denny started kissing me, but I didn't feel like making out. Every now and then, an ugly image would pop into my head and it scared me. Then I thought about my dad, about him lying in the road, dead, and I started crying.

"What, the matter, baby?" he whispered.

I started telling him about my parents, but he kept saying, "Don't focus on that right now. Think about something else. Don't let your mind go there."

I couldn't stop crying.

"Here," he said. "Let me make me you feel better," and he started to push up my T-shirt.

"No, what are you doing?" I pushed him away.

"What's the matter? Why not?"

"I just don't want to! You're scaring me. Stop it!"

"Jules, you are really bumming me out. Do you want me to leave?"

"No, don't go. I'm just scared. Hold me!"

He put his arms around me, which felt good, but then he put his head against my chest and his hand on my breast.

"Denny, you know, I'm only fifteen," I finally said.

"You're what? Shit!" he sat up. "You're fifteen? Oh, Christ, Jules. You're still a teenybopper!"

He rummaged around his pants pocket and pulled out his cigarettes and a lighter. He lit one for each of us. I wasn't into smoking yet, but I took it anyway, and started making circles with it, watching the smoke curling up into question marks.

Finally he said, "I really wish you would've told me."

"Jim said we should lie about our ages. Besides, what difference does it make? You're only two years older than me."

"Actually I'll be eighteen next week. But that's not the point. I wanted to make love to you. Real bad. But I'm not going to push myself on you. You'll just have to let me know when you're ready, okay?"

And that was how we left it.

When I woke up the next morning he was gone, and I didn't see him for a few days. It was Christmas Eve and we spent most on the day on the street, hanging out with our new friends, who were begging shoppers for money. I was surprised at the generosity of people. Tiff and I still had some money left, so we didn't have to do any begging, but since Lucy cooked only one meal a day, we knew we'd need some money soon. Jim worked occasionally doing light shows, but spent most of his money on grass, beer and gas for the car.

That night, I thought a lot about my family, knowing they'd be worried about me. I told Tiff I wanted to call home and she freaked out, saying they'd be able to trace the call, but I said, "Bullshit!"

She stormed off down the street while I found a phone booth. I really wanted to talk to Jacki, but Joey answered the phone.

"Hey, kiddo," I said.

"Hey, back. Merry Christmas. Who is this?"

"It's Jules, you dope. Don't say anything. I don't want—"

"Aunt Sally! Julie's on the phone," I heard her shriek.

"Godammit!" I yelled and hung up. *Oh, well, at least they'll know I'm alive.*

* * *

What I learned about running away from home was that you just trade one set of problems for a whole new set. I'd imagined it would feel like being free, but every day you have to think about food, and doing your laundry, and needing money to buy some more pot. A lot of older guys hanging around the Haight were happy to share their drugs with you in exchange for sex. I always avoided those guys, but Tiff did go off with a guy once and came back with a little baggie of pot. I didn't even want to ask what she'd done to earn it.

I also realized we were stupid for leaving home in the middle of winter. It rained a lot, so we tried to stay inside as much as possible, which was really boring. The best times were when we could hang out on the street, talking with our friends, laughing, singing, being silly, getting stoned, and always watching out for "the man."

Tiff discovered she really loved dropping acid and would do it whenever she could get some, but I preferred to stick to pot, although it made me incredibly hungry at a time when I didn't have that much access to food. We started buying large bags of rice and beans, something I had never eaten before, just so we'd have food in our stomachs. Occasionally, Lucy would take off for a few days at a time, so we'd be on our own when it came to food. I noticed my jeans were getting a little loose around the waist. I was too embarrassed to beg for money. I'd rather just go hungry.

After a couple of weeks, Denny showed up again. I was so happy to see him. I threw my arms around him and we kissed for a long time. I'd really missed him.

"Wow, you've gotten skinny. Have you been eating?" he asked.

"Not too much. Got to keep my girlish figure, you know!"

"Well, let's go get a hamburger, okay?"

We walked over to a nearby Doggie Diner. It was the first meat I'd had in a while. Hot dogs never tasted so good.

"So where've you been, anyway?" I asked, sipping on my milkshake.

"At my uncle's in Montana. He's got a small ranch. I did some work for him. He's a cool dude. I love it up there, man. It's like the old west. Ranches and horses and cows."

"It sounds great," I said.

"But it's so damn cold. You wouldn't believe it. The wind blows right through you. But I want to go live there. I want to be there in summer."

"So why'd you come back?"

"I was kinda hoping I could talk you into moving to Montana with me."

"Me? Really? Wow!" I was so surprised I didn't know what to say. "When?"

"Should I take that as a yes?"

"How soon do we leave?"

"I need to find some work around here and save up enough bread to get a car."

"That's okay, because I don't feel like I'm really ready to leave here right now, anyway."

"Cool," he said, leaning over to give me a kiss.

That night, someone passed around a large jug of red wine that was spiked with downers. And later, Denny and I made love for the first time. But I was so high, I don't remember it at all.

18

While Jim and Denny were out hustling for work during the day, Tiff and I were on our own. We usually slept in late, then got up and looked for leftovers from the night before. Afterward, we'd head out onto the street to see what was happening. We hooked up with our friends and exchanged gossip, sharing cigarettes and pot, if we had any. When Jim was around, and it wasn't raining, we'd drive over to the beach and hang out there. After we ran out of money, Tiffy started shoplifting.

To tell the truth, Tiff had always done a little stealing. A tube of lipstick, a candy bar, a pack of cigarettes. I never did, because I was too afraid of getting caught, but Tiff thought it was fun. We had a couple of fights about it because she thought I should be contributing something, but I didn't want to end up in jail. She accused me of being paranoid. I just shrugged.

I did swipe a candy bar every now and then, when I got really hungry, but never anything more than that. Tiff actually stole a bottle of vodka from a liquor store once. I was astounded at the stuff she got away with. It was a constant hassle, trying to get money for food. When you're young and still at home, you never think about food. It's always there. But living on the streets, suddenly it became a huge issue.

And, I have to admit, after a couple of months, I started to get a little bored with just hanging out all the time. We really had nothing to do. Occasionally someone would get excited about a protest march happening over in Berkeley and we'd try to get a ride across the bay, or to a concert in Santa Cruz, and sometimes we had a blast. But often it turned into one big headache. We might be left to get a ride back on our own, and I really hated hitchhiking, out in the cold and the rain. Many times, Tiff and I would look at each other and say, "It still beats going to school," but I often wondered. Frequently, I'd see a car go by with little kids inside, and I was envious that they had a place to go home to, a warm bed and food. The part of living on the streets I loved was being on my own, and being with my friends. Sometimes it felt like one big party. But, more often than I cared to admit, I was miserable.

One night, Tiff and I were crashed on someone's living room floor in Oakland, when I was awakened by a man climbing on top of me. He started tugging at my jeans and I let out a shriek, waking up everyone in the house. There was a lot of yelling and confusion, and the guy keep saying "Sorry, I didn't know, man," whatever that meant. They finally threw him out, but I hardly slept for the rest of the night. After that, I tried to stick closer to Lucy's.

Then I started feeling a little homesick. I wished I could get hold of Jacki, but she was in San Diego at school and I didn't know how to reach her. And Jenny was living with Beth and Ken. I didn't want to call home because I was afraid Uncle Joe or Aunt Sally would answer and I didn't want to deal with them. I thought about sending a letter, but then they'd know I was in San Francisco.

Just when I was feeling really down, Denny started hassling me. He said I only wanted to have sex when I was stoned, which I denied at first. But eventually, I realized it was true. We were high so much of the time, I hadn't even noticed. But the truth was, smoking pot made me feel relaxed and sexy. It put me in the mood. When I wasn't high, I wasn't that interested. I knew it was odd, but didn't know what to make of it. He asked what I thought about us being with other people. I surprised myself by telling him it was okay with me.

"You are so groovy, Jules," he said. "I can't believe it. This is just perfect. I'm so lucky to have you!"

I really liked Denny a lot, but I had slowly come to realize that I wasn't in love with him. I wanted to be around him all the time and didn't want to break up, but if he wanted to sleep with someone else, that was fine with me.

One day in April, I started vomiting. I thought I had the flu. Jim asked me if I could be pregnant. I said no, because Tiff and I had gone down to the free clinic and gotten birth control pills. But I knew I hadn't been taking them consistently. When your life is chaotic, you just forget sometimes. I was throwing up all the time, not just in the morning, so I was sure I wasn't pregnant. Then my breasts started getting sore, and Tiff insisted I go down to the clinic to get tested. I was in total shock when the test came back positive. So was Denny.

"So what do you want to do?" he asked.

"Well, I don't know what I *can* do," I answered. "I'm too young to have a baby. You're too young to be a father. You don't have a job, we don't have any money..."

"Would you consider having that procedure...you know? To make you not pregnant anymore?"

I had never thought about the subject of abortion before, but now it seemed like the only thing to do.

"I guess so," I answered slowly.

He visibly relaxed. He put his arms around me and kissed me.

The next day I called the clinic and was told the only way to have the procedure was if the doctor said it was medically necessary. We spent a couple of days freaking out, and then Lucy gave us the number of a doctor she had been to once. I called and made an appointment. They said we'd need three hundred dollars. I started crying again, but Denny told me not to worry. He'd get the money somehow. I wanted to get it over with as soon as possible, but they couldn't get me in until the following Wednesday.

After I made the appointment, there was nothing else I could think about except for this baby I was carrying. It was amazing—I had someone inside me! I looked down at my flat stomach, and wondered how it would feel to watch it grow big. A little person was actually growing in my belly. Someone who would look like me, and Denny. I wondered if it was a boy or a girl. I thought about names. If it was a boy, of course I would name it after my dad. Jeff. Little Jeffrey. For a girl, I wasn't sure. Maybe Molly.

I was so restless, I couldn't sleep. I kept tossing and turning. Finally, Denny woke up.

"What's the matter, honey?"

"I can't sleep. I keep thinking about the baby."

He rolled over and sat up. "It really isn't even a kid right now. It's just a little blob of nothing," he whispered.

When I didn't say anything, he said, "Are you thinking about keeping it?"

"You know I can't. We don't have any money," I started sobbing. "I can't even take care of myself right now!"

He snuggled close to me and stoked my hair. "Shhh, it's okay. You'll have plenty of time to have another baby."

"I know, but this one is here right now. And it's yours. It's ours. That means something to me."

He held me as I cried myself to sleep.

I spent the next five days thinking a lot about my situation, wishing something would happen that would change things, but I knew it was hopeless. There was no way I could have this baby. Denny borrowed money from everyone we knew and even donated blood until we had the three hundred dollars.

When Wednesday finally rolled around, Tiff and Denny went with me to the clinic. The waiting room was filled with women, young and middle-aged, and a few couples. We were all there for the same reason. I couldn't make eye contact with anyone.

The nurse called my name, and when I got up to the counter, she gave me a little pill to help me relax.

"I was kinda hoping you were going to put me out for this," I whispered.

"General anesthesia would cost you a lot more money, sweetie," the nurse answered. "But it's a very short procedure. You'll do fine."

I went back to the waiting room and sat, not speaking. Eventually I was called again and the nurse led me to a room where she told me to take off everything below the waist and get up on the table. She covered me with a warm blanket. Then she put my feet in stirrups. I had never been in this embarrassing position before.

A few minutes later, the doctor walked in. While putting gloves on, he asked how I was feeling.

"Okay," I said. But, truthfully, I was scared to death and afraid that any minute I was going to burst into tears. He went to the end of the table and said he needed to give me an exam. I was so nervous, I was trembling. No one had ever seen me down there except for Denny, and even then, it was usually in the dark.

He told me to relax and then began the exam. "I need you to spread your knees for me," he said. He asked the nurse for some instruments and she brought them over on a tray. I felt cold metal sliding into me and nearly jumped off the table.

"Now, Julie, try to relax," he said again. "Take some deep breaths and let your legs go slack." As he began working, the doctor said I needed to think seriously about using contraception. He said, "Abortion is the very worst form of birth control." He also asked if I was using anything to prevent venereal disease. When I said no, he told the nurse to be sure to give me some printed materials before I left.

I felt a sharp pull, and then the worst cramp I had ever felt. I gasped and stared up at the ceiling as warm tears trickled down the sides of my face and into my ears. When I couldn't stand the pain any longer, I cried out, and the doctor said, "We're almost done. You're doing great." It didn't feel like a short procedure at all.

When it was over, the nurse gave me a pill for pain and told me to go home and rest. She said I'd have some bleeding and cramping. And she gave me a date for my follow-up appointment.

So that was that. I was in and out in less than two hours. No more baby. Feeling groggy and tired, I wanted to go home to a nice warm bed, not a dirty mattress on the floor. We trudged back to Lucy's. I lay with the sleeping bag over my head, wishing my mom was there with me. If I couldn't have her, then I wanted to be left alone.

For the next few days, I was grouchy and irritable. I tried not to think about the baby. The nurse had said I needed to avoid sexual contact for six weeks and that was okay with me. I just wanted to sleep, anyway. Tiff did her best to cheer me up. But Denny kept telling me I needed to snap out of it. I told him to go to hell.

I was just starting to feel a little better when Lucy called me to the phone one evening. It was Jim.

"You're never going to believe this," he said. "Tiffy got busted for shoplifting! I'm at the jail right now but they won't let me see her!"

"Oh, my God!" I yelled. "What happened?"

"She put a ham under her jacket and tried to walk out with it! Can you believe that? A ham, for Christ's sake!"

"So what's going to happen now?" I asked.

"I'm not sure. But I think they're trying to contact her parents. I can't believe she was so stupid!"

A couple of days later, Jim found out that Tiff's dad had driven up and taken her home with him. She hadn't been allowed to contact us. She was gone!

So now I was really bummed! What was I going to do without my best friend? She and I had been through so much together. I hoped she'd at least think to call my family and tell them I was okay. It occurred to me she might just run away as soon as she could and head back here. I was in such a funk that Denny finally said, "Hey, babe, let's give some thought to heading to Montana, okay?" The idea cheered me up enormously.

We took off on the first of May. I had some misgivings about leaving my new friends behind, but was looking forward to doing something new. It was springtime, and a lot warmer. I was starting to feel better.

Denny finally managed to save enough money to buy an old red Ford Fairlane. It was pretty beat up but had a good engine, he said. All I cared about was the heater and radio, both of which worked great.

Being out on the road was a blast. We bought a used tent from the army surplus store, and some camping supplies. We had enough money so we could take our time. This was the first time Denny and I had spent time alone —we'd always been surrounded by other people. I loved it!

We drove north, through the upper part of California, into Oregon, and then through Idaho. I loved seeing parts of the country I'd never seen before. We picked up hitchhikers and shared our food and pot with them, when we had it. The people we picked up were always a trip. A couple of college girls we gave a ride to one morning ended up paying for a whole tank of gas, as well as buying us a new tire to replace one that was completely bald.

A couple of days later, we picked up a middle-aged man by the name of Hank, who offered to take us to breakfast. We were sitting in Sambos, enjoying our pancakes, when Hank suggested we check into a nearby motel room and take a shower together—the three of us! Denny just said, "No, I don't think so, man!"

Hank then said that he'd be happy to just watch Denny and me "get it on." I thought Denny was going to choke on his coffee. Hank went on to say he was a famous photographer and had studios in Paris, New York and L.A. And that he was just hitchhiking for the fun of it, that he actually owned several cars. As soon as he got up to go to the men's room, Denny and I made our escape and drove off without him.

"I sure hope he has the money to pay for our breakfast," I giggled as we sped off.

The next day, we picked up a boy who introduced himself as "Stoney." He was really a sweet kid, but so nervous and hyper; he talked continuously. I mean he *never* shut up! We dropped him off near Boise, and a couple of hours down the road, I realized he'd left a baggie of Quaaludes in the back seat. I felt bad for him and wanted to go back to try to return it, but Denny thought we'd never be able to find him. "It must be divine intervention," he argued. "Those 'ludes are meant for us!"

As much as I loved the adventure I was having out on the road with Denny, I was still feeling weird when it came to sex. I just wasn't interested. I tried to fake it, but Denny was worried. He hoped this trip would help change things.

We pulled into Helena five days later. Denny's uncle owned a couple hundred acres of ranchland about an hour outside of town. Whenever he'd talked about his uncle, I'd imagined an older man, but "Uncle" Steve turned out to be in his early twenties. He was the tallest person I'd ever met, nearly six foot five. Almost entirely bald, he had a little fringe of light brown hair that he combed regularly with a small, black comb he kept in his front shirt pocket.

Steve had a crude but funny sense of humor. He liked to make jokes about being bald. On the back of his truck was a bumper sticker that said, "The more hair I lose, the more head I get."

Steve's wife, Kelly, was tiny, barely over five feet tall. They were an odd-looking couple, with such a large difference in their heights. I commented about it, and he chuckled. "It makes for interesting sex," he said. "I have no trouble getting on, but once I do, I got no one to talk to!" Steve said such hilarious things he constantly kept me in stitches. They had a little boy, Dylan, who was a year old.

I really liked these people a lot. They seemed genuine and down to earth. They had a huge garden, several chickens and a small herd of cattle. Kelly spent her time working in the garden, milking cows, baking and sewing. I had never met anyone like her. She said her parents were from Sweden, which explained her platinum blonde hair and blue eyes. Their house was old, but comfortable. Out back was a small cottage, connected to the garage. That was our place.

It was a small apartment, with a tiny bedroom and bathroom, and an average-sized living area and kitchen. After having lived at Lucy's, it seemed like heaven to me. Our very own bed! And our own bathtub! Privacy! It was perfect. It even came with dishes, pots and pans and some bath towels. Anything else we needed would have to wait for Denny's first paycheck.

I was hoping he wouldn't have to work right away so we'd have a few days to get settled in, but Steve had projects for Denny to start on the very next day.

About a week later, they invited us over for dinner. Kelly made a big pot of chili and hot corn bread. Steve lit some logs in the fireplace. It was so warm and cozy. What a change from being on the streets! After dinner, they pulled out an old jar filled with pennies and suggested a game of poker. I'd never played before, but I picked it up pretty quick. Kelly'd been playing with her brothers for years and that was how she met Steve, at a poker party.

Steve explained, "My buddy invited me over. I walked in expecting to find a bunch of old farts, and here was this beautiful blonde sitting there. I was so surprised I almost dropped my dick in the dirt!"

I laughed so hard I nearly choked.

Kelly asked what I planned to do the next day and I told her I needed to go grocery shopping. She suggested I take Denny's car, but I didn't have a driver's license. I was sixteen now, the legal age to drive in Montana, so she said, "Let's go practice tomorrow!"

I'd never driven before and was pretty nervous, but fortunately the car was an automatic, and maneuvering on country roads was easy. Kelly sat next to me with little Dylan on her lap, which wasn't exactly safe, but she wasn't worried. The next day we went into town, where I got a copy of the driving rules and regulations, and after a few more days of practice, I got my license. Denny was worried about it, wondering if my family would be able to track me down now, but we were so far away I didn't let that bother me.

Living on the ranch was pretty cool in the beginning. It was such a different environment than I was used to. I missed my friends, and I constantly worried about Tiff, but enjoyed helping Kelly with her chores around the house and babysitting Dylan. Eventually I asked Steve if I could start doing some work on the ranch, and he taught me how to milk a cow. At the end of the day, Denny and I were tired, dirty, and happy. Our first paycheck, which wasn't much, was spent on new clothes. We both needed jeans and shirts and good boots and gloves.

One day I asked Kelly if I could use the phone and I called Tiff's number, but the phone just rang and rang. I knew her mom worked during the day but I wondered where Tiffy was, if she was in school or if she had run off again. Finally, feeling bored and lonely, I called home. I was shocked when Jacki answered.

"Hey, it's me," I said.

There was quiet on the other end of the line. Finally: "Jules, is that you?"

"Yes, it's me. How're you doing?"

"Oh, my God, where are you? We've been looking all over for you! Where have you been? Are you okay?"

"Yes, I'm okay! I'm fine! I'm doing really good, in fact!"

"God, Jules." My sister was sobbing now. "We've been so worried about you. How could you just leave like that? How come you didn't call? Didn't you know we'd be freaking out?"

"I'm sorry, but I did call, you know. On Christmas."

"But you didn't talk to anyone. Anyway, where are you?"

"I'm in Utah," I lied. "I'm living with a very nice family. I really like it here."

"Utah? How did you get there? Did you join the Mormons?"

"No, no. I just came here with some friends. Anyway, why are you at home? Why aren't you at school?"

"I dropped out of school. I came back when you ran away. I went to look for you."

"Oh, no! Why did you do that?" I moaned.

"Because I needed to find you. Obviously, I never did. We spent time over in Santa Cruz looking. Doug and I even went up to the city several times. I put posters out."

"What made you think I was in the city?" I asked.

"I didn't know for sure, I just guessed. Then, when Tiff came back, I called her."

"How is she, do you know?"

"Her mom's got her in some kind of residential treatment facility. I only got to talk to her once."

"So how is everybody else?"

"On pins and needles. Always worried about you. Jenny graduated early so she's at San Jose State now. Joey's doing good. She misses you. When are you coming home?"

"Oh, I don't know. Listen, I've got to go. I can't be running up the phone bill. But I promise I'll call you again."

"No, Jules, wait—"

But I hung up.

It felt great to talk to Jacki, but it was a bummer she'd dropped out of school. I hadn't even asked what she was doing now. I wished I hadn't hung up so quickly.

I continued to feel sad and homesick for my sisters over the next few weeks. There wasn't a lot for me to do during the day, so I hung out with Kelly as much as I could, which was fun. We laughed a lot. We baked cookies together and she showed me how to run her sewing machine so I could make curtains for our little apartment. At night, Denny was pretty tired from working all day, but I was bored and wanted to go out and do something. Unfortunately, it was a long drive into town, and I was afraid to drive in the dark. So I just sat and watched TV, although way out there in the boonies, we only got a couple of stations. Denny encouraged me to go into town with Kelly, which I sometimes did. We'd go shopping or to the movies, if we could afford it. Since I was underage, I couldn't get into any bars or clubs, so she'd take off with her girlfriends every now and then, for a night of drinking and dancing. I was envious.

One evening, out of the blue, Denny asked me if I knew what it meant to be bisexual.

"No, what?" I asked.

"It's when you like both sexes. I mean, when you want to have sex with both guys and chicks."

"You're making that up," I said.

"No, it's true. There are people like that. In fact, Steve says that Kelly is a bisexual. Before they got married, she had a couple of girlfriends."

"You lie!"

"As God is my witness!"

"I'm going to ask her about it," I threatened.

"Go ahead. Supposedly, she's not ashamed of it. And to tell you truth, I think it's kind of sexy."

"Well, I think it's weird," I said.

The next day, as I was helping Kelly hang clothes on the line, I wanted to ask her about it, but I was kind of nervous. So I just blurted out, "Denny says you're a bicycle!"

"A what?" Kelly stopped hanging clothes and looked at me. "He said what?"

"I don't mean a bicycle. He said you're a ..."

"A bisexual? Is that what he said?"

For a minute I thought she was going to be mad.

"Yeah, it's true. I enjoy both men and women. They both turn me on. Of course, it's not something I advertise, especially in this neck of the woods. There's a shitload of rednecks around here. But you know what, Jules? I am what I am. Can't help it. Don't want to help it."

I thought about it for a moment. "Then why are you married to Steve?"

"I love him. He loves me. He's a fantastic guy—a good husband, a good father, great in the sack. *And* sometimes I like to be with women, too. It's the best of both worlds."

I just shook my head. But that night, I couldn't stop thinking about it. It both intrigued and repelled me.

A few nights later, after dinner, Kelly put Dylan to bed and invited us to come over to the house for a drink. The guys had beer, which I never liked, so Kelly made a pitcher of Harvey Wallbangers, something I'd never tasted before. They were great! After two rounds of drinks, I was feeling pretty good. Better than I'd felt in weeks.

"So, Jules," Steve said. "What did you think about Kelly's little secret?"

"I don't know," I said, putting down my drink and snuggling up to Denny. He put his arm around me and caressed my hair. We hadn't made love in a long time, and I honestly didn't miss it, but alcohol always made me horny.

"There she goes," Denny laughed. "You get a few drinks in this girl and it goes right to her crotch!"

"Well, then, tonight might be your lucky night," Steve said with a grin.

Everyone laughed. Kelly looked at me and said, "I wish it was my lucky night!"

I didn't exactly know what she meant, but I felt flushed all over. The room got quiet for a minute, and Denny said, "Kelly, why don't you come over here?" As she moved toward us, Denny reached around the front of me and started undoing the snaps on my shirt. I watched Kelly's face as she kneeled in front of me. She was smiling. She reached up to help Denny undo my top.

"Is this okay?" she asked. I nodded, feeling nervous, and a little embarrassed, but also very excited. When my blouse was open, Denny unhooked my bra and lifted it slightly. Kelly reached over and gently touched my nipples. I gasped. It was the most wonderful thing I'd ever felt! She leaned over and took me into her mouth and sucked. It felt like sparks were going to shoot out of my body. The only sounds in the room were my loud moans. I opened my eyes and looked over Kelly's head at Steve, who was watching us intently. I smiled.

Then the baby started wailing from his bedroom.

"Fuckin' A!" Kelly muttered as she got up. "What timing!" She went into the back room and I nestled even closer to Denny. "Let's go home," I whispered to him. I was so aroused

I could barely contain myself. A few minutes later, back in our own bed, making love, I thought about Kelly. And climaxed. For the very first time.

The next morning, I felt like shit. I had the worst headache. I was embarrassed about what had happened the night before, but Denny just said, "So I guess you had a good time last night?"

I'd promised Kelly I'd come over in the morning to watch Dylan while she ran into town, and I was nervous about seeing her. As soon as I walked through the door, she came over and gave me a kiss on the cheek and a big hug.

"Are you okay?" she asked.

I nodded.

"Are you sure? I was afraid maybe I scared you off last night."

"No, I liked it," I said, looking away from her.

"It's okay, Jules. You don't need to be shy about it. It just *is.* Love is beautiful, no matter which way it comes. It's always good."

Out of the blue, I burst into tears. She led me into her bedroom and we lay down on the bed. She held me while I cried, stroking my cheek. It was so sweet and tender, I couldn't stop sobbing. Then she asked if she could undress me, and I nodded. She stood up, slipped off her robe, and then slowly removed my clothing. We kissed and caressed each other, and stayed cuddled together for a long time. It felt so perfect being there. And so *normal.* We fell asleep like that.

A little while later, we got up and had breakfast together. I felt so incredibly happy and also extremely confused. We drove into town, with her behind the wheel and little Dylan on my lap. I wanted to be with her as much as I could.

When we got into town, I felt a sudden urge to call home again. I wanted desperately to talk to Jacki. I was actually surprised when she picked up the phone.

"Jules! Thank God! You have to come home. Right away!"

"Why, what is it?" I immediately knew something was wrong, and thought of Uncle Joe. *Please don't let it be Uncle Joe.*

"It's Kevin. He was killed, in Vietnam. Can you come back? Please?"

I was on the next plane home.

19

Johanna

When my cousin Kevin died in Vietnam in 1971, I was thirteen years old and had been living with him and his family for over five years. Kevin and the twins were like brothers to me. So when we got the news that we'd lost him, it was more devastating to me than losing my father when I was just seven. It was hard for my older sisters to understand that.

It had already been an eventful year, even before we got the news about Kevin. My oldest sister, Jacki, was in San Diego, finishing up her junior year of college. My sister Jenny had graduated from high school a semester early and had moved to San Jose, where she was going to San Jose State. My next oldest sister, Jules, always the troublemaker, had run away right before Christmas, and we didn't have a clue where to find her. Then Kev enlisted in the Army and was sent to Vietnam. My aunt and uncle were ready to flip out.

The strangest thing was that Jacki, when she heard the news that Jules was gone, just dropped out of school and came home to look for her. Uncle Joe and Aunt Sally tried to talk her out of it. They said there was nothing she could do, and it would be better to stay in school and graduate.

But she moved back to San Jose and in with Aunt Mimi,

saying she was tired of college and wanted to get a job. She planned to spend her days off looking for Jules. Sometimes, she even took me with her. We'd drive over to the beach in Santa Cruz or up to San Francisco, hang up flyers and talk to kids on the street. It was always a treat for me, just to be able to hang out all day with Jacki. But we never found any sign of Jules.

Jacki had always been pretty emotional. She had this mini-breakdown right after Daddy died, and went away for a couple of weeks. Then, a year or so later, she had another nervous breakdown and was sent to the nuthouse again, for a few months this time. I guess she always took things pretty seriously.

To tell the truth, after Jules ran off, it was actually a lot quieter around the house. Of course, Uncle Joe and Aunt Sal were upset about it, but I didn't mind that much. Having Jules in the house was like living with a time bomb. You never knew when she was going to go off. And, after Kevin joined the Army, it was just the twins and me at home, which was even better. I was pretty content.

I guess I was a pretty happy kid. Daddy used to call me his Sunshine Girl. He said I was special because I was the youngest of the family, and I would always be his baby.

What I remember about my father most was that if he wasn't working late, he would come in and sit on my bed and read to me until I fell asleep. Even if I picked the same story over and over. After he died, I missed that a lot. Another memory was when I was real little, I fell off my trike and lay in the dirt, crying. Daddy came, scooped me up and carried me into the house. I felt so safe in his arms.

I don't remember being nearly as upset when he died as my sisters were, but they were a lot older than me. I do remember being sad. I couldn't understand why Daddy wasn't coming home, or why Mommy had to stay in jail. But I had my aunt and uncle, my sisters and my cousins, so it wasn't too bad.

With Jules and Kevin out of the house, Aunt Sally and I got a lot closer. She had gone back to work, teaching part-time, but she frequently picked me up after school and took me shopping, or roller-skating. One time Aunt Sal looked at me and said, "You're the little girl I always wanted." I loved that. And Uncle Joe used to say I was the only one of the girls who never gave him any trouble. I was the good one.

When I was little I played with my cousins, Mike and Matt a lot, but as we got older they started excluding me. They built a treehouse in the backyard and put a sign on it saying, "No girls allowed." It bothered me at first when they kept ditching me to run off and play with their friends, but there were other girls in the neighborhood for me to play with. Sometimes I played with Jules, but we fought a lot. One time she got a set of Lennon Sisters paper dolls for her birthday and she wouldn't let me play with them, so I bit their heads off. She holds that against me to this day.

Kevin was already a teenager by the time Jules and I moved in. He wasn't around much and when he was, he'd be busy with his own things, or bugging Jules. He got to be more fun after he got his driver's license and could take us places, like to drive-in movies when his parents were busy or too tired.

Uncle Joe continued to drive me down to see Mom every few weeks. Jacki wouldn't go. Jen was away at school and only came home occasionally, and Jules had run away. So Uncle Joe started including Kevin and the twins every now and then on our trips, but I liked it better when it was just me. Then Mom and I could talk and I had all her attention.

We often talked about what we would do after she got released. She was hoping she'd be out by the time I graduated from high school.

"I think we should move to Hawaii," she said one day. "You can go to college there. What do you think?"

"Yeah, that'd be cool," I said. "But it would be a long way from home."

"Well, we would just have a new home," she said.

I wasn't sure I liked the idea of moving way across the ocean. But I decided not to worry about it just then. There was plenty of time before that day came.

Mom always asked a lot of questions about how we were all doing, and she sent home letters for everyone. One time she told me she was writing to a man who wanted to marry her when she got out. He was the brother of a woman Mom knew in prison. When I told Aunt Sally about Mom's boyfriend, she said, "That figures. Janet never did have a lick of sense."

The thing that bugged me about seeing Mom was that she was always trying to tell me what to do. That I needed to behave. That I needed to work hard in school. Silly stuff like that. I was already doing well in school and I didn't need her to tell me how to behave. When I complained to Uncle Joe about it, he said, "Your mom just needs to feel like she's still your mother. That she has some control over how you're growing up."

"Well, I don't need another mother. I already have Aunt Sally," I remember saying.

* * *

The day that Kevin was killed, we were all in school and Aunt Sally was home alone when she got the news. I guess some army people came out to the house to tell her. I'd stayed late after school, working on a project, and by the time I got home, some friends of the family and teachers that Joe and Sally worked with were already there. Aunt Mimi met me at the door and gave me the news. I looked through the living room and saw Uncle Joe on the couch, holding Matt in his arms. Matt's head was buried in Uncle Joe's chest and I could hear muffled sobs. Uncle Joe was crying, too. Whenever I hear of someone dying in Vietnam, that's the image I always think of, my cousin and uncle, holding each other, weeping. Right then I had a bizarre thought: first Daddy, then Kevin; who would be next?

That evening, Jacki came over after work. Jenny had a final exam the next day, but said she'd be down as soon as she could. The phone was ringing constantly, and one time, by sheer coincidence, it happened to be Jules. Jacki talked to her for a while and then Uncle Joe got on the phone and made arrangements to wire money for her to get home. She'd be coming in the next day. Jules had rarely called home after she ran off, and she said later that she'd had an odd feeling that day that made her pick up the phone.

It's funny how different people react to bad news. Aunt Sally looked stunned, but kept busy in the kitchen, making snacks for everyone, and making sure we all had something to drink. Every time I walked by her, she would grab me, give me a big hug and say, "I've got to get busy." Uncle Joe's face was red and swollen, and for days it was constantly wet with tears. Matthew and Michael were scheduled to go on a camping trip with the Boy Scouts that weekend. Matthew decided he wouldn't go, but Mike definitely wanted to, which Aunt Sally was against at first. She thought we should all be together. But Uncle Joe convinced her it was a good idea. At the last minute, Matt changed his mind and went with him.

That whole weekend, I was constantly thinking about Kevin. Did he die instantly, or did he lie there, knowing he was going to die? Did he think about us? Was he proud to give his life for his country? Or at the last minute, did he think, "Boy, joining the Army was a stupid idea?" If he had it to do all over again, would he do the same things? It wasn't the idea that my cousin was gone that upset me all that much. After all, he was dead, so he didn't know what was going on. But everyone around him was left feeling so incredibly sad. Every time I saw Uncle Joe in tears, I had to duck into the bathroom and cry for a little while.

The next day, Uncle Joe and Aunt Sally drove to the San Francisco airport to pick up Jules. Jacki and I both wanted to go, but they said no. Jacki got really pissed off about it but she didn't want to give them a hard time, so she stayed home with me. I was worried that she might have another melt-down, but she was actually pretty calm.

"As horrible as this is," she said, "at least it's bringing Julie home."

I actually had mixed feelings about having Jules back. I was glad to hear she wasn't dead or anything, and I wanted to know what she'd been doing all these months. But I worried over how she would fit in here now. I wondered if my aunt and uncle would start yelling at her as soon as she got off the plane, or if she would take off again as soon as she could.

That afternoon, before they all got back from the airport, Jenny showed up with her friend Maria, who had her two kids with her and was obviously expecting a third.

"Wow," I said, giving her a hug, "you just keep popping them out!"

"Yeah, it's the one thing I'm good at! So how ya doin', squirt?" she asked.

"Well, it's been pretty sad around here, I guess you could say."

"I'll bet. Always something going on with you guys. But I'm so sorry to hear about Kev."

I looked at Maria closely. She was real skinny and had dark circles under her eyes. She smoked constantly and I knew, from talking to Jenny, that she also did her share of drinking. She wasn't with Eddie anymore. He never did marry her. Now she was pregnant by another guy, Ralph, who was already married to another woman. Maria didn't have much luck with guys.

Jenny came through the door, carrying a big basket of dirty laundry. Even though it was obvious she'd been crying, she looked great. She'd grown taller than the rest of us, and she was very slender and shapely. Her hair was long, almost to her waist, with blond streaks, thanks to Lady Clairol. It looked great. Besides coloring her hair, she'd also traded in her glasses for contact lenses when she started college. She was wearing a peasant blouse and a long, flowing skirt. With her large, dangly earrings, Jenny looked like a model right out of a fashion magazine. She came over and gave me a long hug. I started crying and then she did too. It felt good to be hugging her.

"So when is Jules getting here?" she asked, after we finally broke apart.

"Uncle Joe thought they'd be back around five or so," I said, taking Maria's baby out of her arms and sitting at the kitchen table with her.

Jacki came through the door then and gave both Jenny and Maria a hug.

"I swear, your baby girl looks just like you," she said to Maria. Jacki started pulling items out of the cupboard to make lunch while Jenny went to put her clothes in the washing machine. "You guys want a tuna sandwich?"

"No, I'm okay," Maria said. "But if you've got a Coke, I'll have that."

"It's going to be really weird, having Jules back," I said to Jacki.

"Yeah, this place has gone to Helena Handbasket," she teased me.

Jenny came back into the kitchen and got out some potato chips. "So, Jacki, what are you going to do now that Jules is back?"

Jacki sat at the table and began assembling the sandwiches. "You know, I've been seriously thinking for a long time about going to nursing school. I realized I never really wanted to be a lawyer. Honestly? That's the main reason I dropped out of school. I was just totally not interested, ya know?"

"So why were you planning to be a lawyer, then?" asked Maria.

"Because my dad was a lawyer. Because I thought it would please him. I talked to my therapist about it years ago. He said I should follow my heart and do what was best for me. Even back then I had an inkling I wouldn't enjoy being a lawyer. But I just couldn't let go of the idea that I would somehow be honoring Daddy if I followed in his footsteps."

Jenny and I were listening attentively. We had never heard Jacki talk about this before.

She continued, "Dr. Wheeler even said nursing was a noble profession. That Daddy would be very proud of me. But it's taken me all this time to realize he was right. And now, for the first time, I'm excited about something! I really do want to be a nurse. In fact, I'm going back to school in September. To San Jose State. With the credits I already have, I'll be finished in a couple of years."

"That is so cool!" We all chimed in.

"Good for you!" Jenny said. She was wiping her eyes.

"And what about Doug?" Jenny asked.

"Well, he has a couple more years of grad school. We should both be finishing up about the same time. And then, I'm guessing we'll probably get married!"

"Wow, that's bitchin'!" Maria said.

We sat in silence for a few minutes, as if we were all trying to think of something else to talk about so we didn't have to focus on Kevin. This concept, that he had actually been killed, was so new, so raw, it didn't even seem real.

Finally, Maria said, "Man, this war. It's totally fucked, isn't it?"

Jenny answered, "That's for sure. Jane Fonda's right. Those people don't want us over there, and we shouldn't *be* over there."

"I'm so glad girls don't have to worry about getting drafted," I said.

"Well, don't talk about Vietnam in front of Joe and Sally, okay?" Jacki took the baby out of my arms and walked across the kitchen floor, jiggling her up and down. "They aren't in favor of the war, but I'm sure they don't want to think Kevin might have died in vain."

"Which is true," Jennifer said softly.

We sat around the kitchen, talking, for the rest of the afternoon, until we heard the car pull into the driveway.

Jules walked through the front door, her face red, eyes bloodshot. I was surprised she'd been crying. She never got along with Kevin all that much.

She dropped her suitcase on the floor and everyone squealed and got in line to give her a hug. She was followed by Uncle Joe and Aunt Sally, who gave hugs to everyone. There was a lot of commotion. The baby started crying and Maria took her into the other room to feed her. Jenny went with her. Aunt Sally told Jules to put her bags in her old bedroom. Jacki and I followed her. She took off her jacket, and stretched. She looking taller and thinner since the last time I'd seen her. Her hair was all wild and curly, but even with no makeup on, she still looked gorgeous.

"Oh, man," she said. "It's good to be home. I didn't think it would be, but it is!"

"So, where were you?" I asked.

"Oh, all over! But as of yesterday, I was in Montana."

"Montana!" I said, looking at Jacki. "We sure never

thought to look there!"

"Well, why would we, dopey?" she answered.

"I heard you guys were looking for me. I'm sorry about that," Jules said softly.

"I actually had fun," I told her. "Jacki and I went all over the place. It was pretty groovy. So what were you doing all that time?" I asked.

"Oh, a lot of stuff. Mainly hanging out with other kids up in the city. I got a boyfriend. His name's Denny. We went to Montana to work on a ranch."

"So are you going back? I mean, after the funeral and everything?"

She shook her head. "No, I don't think so. I was getting ready to break up with him anyway and head back to the Haight." She looked tired. "I'm kinda wasted. I think I'll just hit the sack."

Jacki and I got up to go. "Okay, goodnight, then. We're glad you're back!" I said and awkwardly gave her a hug.

"Okay, thanks. I'm glad to be back. I love you guys!" she said as she closed the door.

Wow, that was a first!

20

Although we didn't know exactly when Kevin's body would be shipped back to the States, Uncle Joe and Aunt Sally decided to have a memorial service for him the following Friday afternoon. I guess maybe they figured it would be better to get it over with. Or maybe they simply didn't know what else to do at all.

The twins came back from the camping trip on Monday. They were both pretty upset after they got home. I think, being gone, they were able to put off thinking about Kevin, but once they walked through the door, there was no way to avoid it.

I'd always had a special relationship with the twins. For one reason, I was the only one in my family who could tell them apart, even when I was little. Don't ask me how. It's like I just grew up knowing who was who. And for another reason, the twins were pretty protective of me, especially after Jenny was moved into the foster home. They never let anyone pick on me. Kevin had always picked on Jules, teasing her or calling her names, but he never did that with me. The twins wouldn't have tolerated it. Go figure.

Of the two of them, I was always closer to Matt. He didn't seem to mind playing with me if the other boys weren't around. Mike was a little closer to Kevin, especially when it came to manly things, like playing army or detectives. But we always teased Mike because he was head over heels in love with Jacki. She doted on him constantly, and he ate it up.

"Mikey and Jacki sitting, in a tree," we'd sing. "K-I-S-S-I-N-G. First comes love, then comes marriage, then comes Jacki with a baby carriage!"

"So what," he'd say. "I *am* going to marry her."

* * *

On Saturday morning, I wandered by Kevin's room, and Matt was in there by himself, sitting on Kevin's bed. I didn't know if he wanted to be alone or what, so I went in and sat on the opposite twin bed. He was just sitting there, tossing one of Kevin's baseballs into the air and catching it.

"It sure is strange," I finally said, "to think he isn't coming back."

"I wonder where he is," Matt said.

"What do you mean?" I asked.

"I mean, I know he's dead and all, but, if there is a spirit or something, you know, like his soul, hanging around? It has to go somewhere, right?"

"You mean, like a ghost?"

He thought for a moment. "No, there's no such thing as ghosts." He paused. "I guess, I mean, like is he still around, watching over us?"

"Well, Jacki says that sometimes she feels like Daddy is looking out for us. Like a guardian angel. Like she feels that he really didn't leave, just his body left. I know she talks to him sometimes. She says it makes her feel better."

Matt was still for a moment. "I wonder if he's with Uncle Jeff," he said quietly. Mike walked by the doorway right then and I thought he would just pass on by, but he stopped and slowly entered the room. He walked over to the dresser and picked up Kevin's baseball mitt. Then he sat on the bed with me. He and Matt began to toss the ball back and forth.

"What you guys talking about?" he asked.

"Kevin," I said.

"I hate those gooks who killed him. I want to go over there and stab every one of 'em. Over and over. I would if I could!"

I knew how he felt. I think we were all feeling the same way. There was someone on this planet who had fired the gun that killed our brother. Some nameless man, with dark hair and eyes. I pictured him with a real mean look on his face.

"I bet he never, ever thought this was going to happen," Matt said.

We were still sitting there when Aunt Sally wandered by and joined us, sitting on the bed with Matt, putting her arms around him.

"I like to come in here, too," she whispered. "I feel closer to him in here."

"Maybe we should keep his room just like this. Never, ever change it!" Mike said.

Aunt Sally gave a sad smile. "Well, we'll see about that. As hard as it is to believe, life does go on. We know that all too well, don't we?"

At that moment I felt closer to them than I ever had.

Later that afternoon, Uncle Joe once again asked us girls if we would sing at the funeral. Of course, we said yes. We decided on "Amazing Grace." Jacki brought over her guitar, and we practiced in front of the mirror, which we hadn't done since before Daddy died. I have to admit, we actually sounded pretty good.

The morning of the service was sunny and warm. I was surprised at the number of people there. Kevin wasn't very popular in high school, but an awful lot of kids from his school showed up. So did a bunch of Vietnam vets, and people from the community. Uncle Joe and Aunt Sally were pleased, I think.

We sang beautifully, if I had to say so myself. I was afraid we might start crying and ruin it, but we were all too nervous to feel sad just then. Afterward, back at the house, several people approached me to say how sweet it was that we had sung for Kevin. I was really happy we did it.

Only a small number of people came to the house. A man I didn't recognize came up to me and said he was Norman Green, Daddy's old law partner. He and his wife kept commenting on how much we'd all grown. Doug, Jacki's boyfriend was there. He'd been around a lot all week, helping Uncle Joe with anything that needed to be done. I'd always liked Doug. I thought he had to put up with a lot, being with my crazy sister and all.

Jenny's friend Maria was there, too. Then I saw a real tall black girl come in. I didn't recognize her at first. It was Becky. I hadn't seen her in years. She was slender and pretty, wearing her hair in an Afro. She had large, gold hoop earrings and looked very chic, I thought. I knew Jenny had kept in touch with her, though I didn't understand why.

"Well, if it isn't Angela Davis!" Jules said when she saw her. Becky spotted us from across the room and came over to say hi. She gave us both a hug, which surprised me.

"I'm glad to hear you're back, Julie," she said. "You gave your sisters quite a scare."

"Yeah, well, you know how that goes," Jules said, which was the dumbest thing I ever heard her say.

"Do you know if we can smoke in the house?" Becky asked.

"Out back," I told her. I followed Becky and Jules out to the patio. Maria was already there, having a cigarette. Jules and Becky both lit up. I was surprised Uncle Joe had allowed Jules to continue smoking since she got home, but he only said she couldn't smoke in the house. It looked so cool, the three of them sitting there, smoking. Like they were all grown-ups.

"It's a hell of a thing, isn't it?" Becky said, blowing smoke out of her nose. "Kevin getting killed, I mean. We need to get the hell out of there!"

"We were just talking about that the other day," Maria said. "I never could see why he went and enlisted. Makes no sense. I guess we'll never understand that."

"So, what've you been up to, Becky?" Jules asked.

"I'm going to Berkeley in the fall," she answered casually. "Majoring in Poli Sci."

"Well, good for you!" Jules said.

"What do you mean, good for me? You think black girls can't get into Berkeley?"

"No," Jules said very slowly. "I meant that a lot of kids who've been in foster homes don't end up going to a good school, that's all."

"Well, you're right. Most of them don't. Especially black foster kids. I'm going on scholarship."

"Well, that's what I said. Good for you!" Jules clearly sounded irritated. She mashed out her cigarette and went back into the house.

"So how're the twins doing?" Becky asked Maria. I was sitting right there and she didn't bother to ask me.

"They're doing okay, I guess. What would you say, squirt?" Maria said to me. "How do you think the twins are doing?"

I just shrugged.

Back in the house, I found Jules sitting on the stairs by herself. She'd been very quiet since she got back.

"That Becky!" she complained. "She's always bugged the shit out of me."

"Yeah. She always annoyed Jenny, too. I don't get why she still hangs around her. It's a mystery to me." I sat down next to her.

"Me too," she said.

"Hey, what happened to Tiffy? Have you talked to her since you got back?"

"No, but I did talk to Andy for just a minute. I guess she

was locked up somewhere for a while and now she's in a group home. Her mom doesn't want to her to have any contact with me. The bitch. Like she ever cared about Tiff at all."

"What's a group home, anyway?" I asked.

"I'm not sure. But I think it's a place where you go to live and they keep an eye on you twenty-four hours a day. Like, if you do okay there, then you can go home."

"I bet you miss her," I said.

"Yeah, I guess so."

"What about Denny? Do you miss him a lot, too?"

Jules thought for a moment before she answered. "I really liked Denny. I guess I loved him. But I didn't *love* love him, you know? I mean, he was cute and everything. It was kinda scary, being out on the street. And he was there for me. He kind of rescued me, I guess. But it was time for me to go, you know what I mean?"

I really didn't, but I pressed on. "So, what did you do when you were up there? Did you have a job, or what?"

"No, we just hung out on the streets. Got high a lot. On pot. Dropped acid a few times. Don't tell anyone, okay? Sometimes it was a lot of fun. Like you could just do whatever you wanted to do. But sometimes it was a drag. Nothing to eat. Nothing to do. No money to do anything. You had to watch out for people on the street who'd try to hustle you."

"So you aren't planning to go back then?" I asked.

"I'm not sure what I'm going to do yet. I know I'm not going back to regular school. I told Uncle Joe I just couldn't handle it. I might get a job and go to night school to get my high school diploma."

"What did he say about that idea?" Uncle Joe was really focused on getting a good education. I'd have been surprised if he agreed to that plan.

"You know, Uncle Joe is really a square sometimes. But other times, he can be pretty hip. He wants me to talk to a guidance counselor, and a shrink. And that's cool."

"Are you sure you're okay? You still seem kinda weird to me. And I don't think it's about Kevin."

"Yeah, I'm okay. Or at least I think I will be. I just have some stuff to work out, you know?"

I bit my bottom lip. I didn't really know what she was talking about. I wondered if she'd ever tell me.

After everyone finally left that evening, all of us kids hung out in the living room. I got the feeling that Uncle Joe and Aunt Sally didn't know what to do next. Aunt Sally worked in the kitchen, and we helped Uncle Joe straighten up the rest of the house. I got the feeling they must be thinking, "Okay, we had a son, he died, we had a service for him. Now what do we do?"

Jacki picked up her guitar and started playing. We sang, "Michael Row the Boat Ashore," "Lemon Tree" and "Puff, the Magic Dragon." Then my aunt and uncle came in and joined us. We sang every old folk song we could think of. Even the twins joined in, which was unusual. It was almost like we didn't know what to say to each other, so it was easier to sing. It was very sweet. Jacki's eyes were bright with tears.

Then the phone rang, and Uncle Joe went to answer it. I could tell it was Mom. I hadn't talked to her since we got the news about Kevin, but I'd heard she was real upset. She hoped she'd get permission to be released for a day to come to the service, but it was denied and she was really angry. To tell the truth, I don't think anyone even wanted Mom to be there. Then the focus would be on her, as it always was. But she was crying and carrying on and wanted to speak to each of us.

I talked to her first, just briefly. I told her who had been at the service. She kept sobbing and saying that she wished she could have been there for us. I didn't want to hurt her feelings, but honestly, no one needed her to be there. As quickly as I could, I passed the phone off to Jules, who kept shaking her head "no" before she finally took the receiver. I think she was afraid Mom would start yelling at her or something, but it sounded like they had a quiet conversation. Then Jenny talked to her for a long time. When that conversation started to wind down, Jacki made a beeline for the bathroom, where I heard her running water in the tub. There was no way she was going to talk to Mom.

Three weeks after Kevin's memorial service, Uncle Joe and Aunt Sally flew to Washington, where Kevin was buried at Arlington National Cemetery. They brought home the flag that had covered his casket, all folded up in a neat little triangle. Uncle Joe had it framed and hung it in the living room over the fireplace.

* * *

On Monday morning, Jacki headed back to Aunt Mimi's and to her new job as a nurse's aide at a small hospital in San Jose. She planned to work there over the summer, until she went back to college in the fall. She'd been accepted into the nursing program, and thought it would be a good idea to get some experience taking care of patients before she actually started school.

Jenny left on Sunday afternoon, returning to her dorm to get some studying done before classes started up on Monday. I cried when she and Jacki left. It had been a long time since the four of us spent time together, and even though it had been a very tearful week, it still felt good having them around.

A quietness settled over the house in the days after everyone left. The twins and I started back to school. Uncle Joe and Aunt Sally returned to work, but when they were home, were pretty much in a fog. Especially Aunt Sally. One evening she made a meatloaf for dinner, but instead of putting it in the oven, she put it into the pantry. Another day I went grocery shopping with her, and after the cart was filled with food, she headed out the door without paying. I had to grab her arm and guide her back to the checkout counter. But the strangest thing of all was when I mentioned to her how nice it was that so many kids had shown up at Kevin's service. She looked surprised and said, "Oh, really. I didn't know any kids came." When I mentioned this to Uncle Joe, he just made a joke: "I don't think either of us is functioning at full capacity right now!"

Jules got a job at a local record store and jumped right in to taking classes at night school for her high school diploma. She kept to herself a lot. Occasionally, she's suggest that we clean up the house or do laundry for Aunt Sally, which I'm sure was appreciated, even though my aunt didn't seem to mind housework. She said it helped to keep her mind off things.

The twins kept busy with baseball and other sports. Uncle Joe mounted a basketball hoop over the garage and soon a gang of kids showed up to play on the weekends. My girlfriends and I sat on the curb, watching the boys play, cheering them on. The twins also found an old go-cart and asked Uncle Joe to help them fix it up. The three of them spent hours in the garage together working on it. I think it helped Uncle Joe to have something different to focus on.

Jules really liked her job in the record store, and also started waitressing part-time at a 24-hour diner, saving up all of her money so she could buy a car. She came and went at odd hours and sometimes I thought I could smell alcohol on her breath. It was pretty calm around the house since she wasn't being a pain in the butt like before. As long as she stayed focused on getting her high school diploma, Uncle Joe didn't seem too concerned about her. I guess he had other things to worry about.

A couple of months after Kevin's funeral, school let out

for the summer. I didn't have much to do besides hang around with the twins or my best friends, Megan and Martha. We'd walk into town and meander through the shops, stopping for a burrito or some French fries at Dairy Queen. I asked Aunt Sally if we could plan a family vacation, maybe to Disneyland or the Grand Canyon, and she said it was a good idea. But nothing ever came of it. Whenever Jacki or Jenny had a couple of days off from work and school, they'd come down and take us over to the beach.

In August, Aunt Sally took us up to San Jose to shop for school clothes. I'd gained some weight over the summer and didn't fit into any of my old clothes. I suggested to Aunt Sally that we start on a diet and she agreed.

I was excited about starting high school, and even if the twins didn't come right out and admit it, I think they were, too. Always a little on the short, puny side, over the last year they'd gotten taller and now girls were starting to show an interest in them. Megan and Martha were madly love with the twins, couldn't tell them apart, so the twins liked to play tricks on them. Martha and Meg went around writing "M&M" on everything and started collecting M&M candy wrappers, which they Scotch-taped to their lockers. After a while, it got pretty obnoxious. The twins had a friend, Brad, who I had a crush on. But he already had a girlfriend who went to another school. Still, the six of us hung out together as much as we could, goofing around and being silly.

21

After Kevin died, Mom started calling the house a lot. Maybe she was scared she could lose one of *her* kids, too. She kept pressuring us to come see her. In fact, she wanted us to visit every two weeks, but it was a long way down there, and even once a month was sometimes too much for Uncle Joe. She suggested we take the bus down, but we had no way of getting from the bus station to the prison.

One weekend, Jenny borrowed her boyfriend's car and we drove there together, just the two of us. We had so much fun! On the way down, we played our favorite 8-track tapes of Bob Dylan and The Byrds. We drove by a couple of young guys who were hitchhiking.

"Maybe we should give them a ride," I suggested.

"Picking up hitchhikers is *not* a safe thing to do!" Jenny protested.

I thought about it for a while and then said, "We're driving down to see our mom who is in prison for murder. Don't you think maybe *they* might be afraid of *us?*"

Jenny laughed. "I guess you do have a point there!"

It felt good to be able to laugh about the situation sometimes.

We stopped at a McDonalds for lunch. Jen was almost twenty now, but she still liked to be silly and goof around. She dressed like a stylish hippie, with long skirts and pretty blouses. During the summer, she always wore sandals, and her legs were long and tanned. I asked her about her latest boyfriend, Phil.

"Have you ever heard of the expression 'built like a brick shithouse'?" she asked.

"I thought only girls were brick shithouses," I argued.

She sighed. "In the official rulebook, either gender can be described as a brick shithouse, okay? Anyway, that's Phil. Plus he's got beautiful dimples and a great butt! He's a psychology major. And he likes to play volleyball on the beach. Any more questions?"

"Yeah, just one. How come you always break up with guys and then find someone else? I mean, it's like you're never with a guy for more than a month or two."

"I don't know. Well, yes, I guess I do know. The truth is, there was this guy a long time ago. You never met him. His name was Tony. He was like my first real crush, you know? I mean, I was madly in love with that guy. And no one else has ever measured up to him. And this is gonna sound a little weird, to tell you the truth..." She paused. "But some of the boys I've been with were actually better than Tony, you know? I mean, like smarter, or treated me nicer, or had more money. Whatever. And yet, I haven't fallen in love with anyone since Tony."

"So, whatever happened to him?" I pressed on. "Why did you two break up?"

"It was complicated. He was a lot older than me. Actually, Uncle Joe made me break up with him."

"No kidding? Wow! That must have been something. Were you really mad?"

She paused, looking in the rearview mirror before making a lane change. "I guess I was at first. But eventually, I accepted that Uncle Joe was right. It hasn't been easy for them. Dealing with Mom. Dealing with Jules. How is it with Jules these days, anyway?"

Now it was my turn to take a minute. "I think she's kind of depressed. She hangs out with those weird kids from the record shop. She's not home that much, but sometimes I hear her crying. And, can you keep a secret?"

"Of course."

"Sometimes I smell smoke coming from her room. I think she's smoking pot in there."

"Dammit!" Jenny said. "Uncle Joe and Aunt Sally don't need any more grief right now. I wish she'd just cool it."

"Well, I know she's going to therapy. Once a week, I think. But I can't tell if it's doing any good."

"I don't know what it is with Jules," Jenny murmured, shaking her head. "Sometimes I think she was just born unhappy."

* * *

It was different visiting Mom this time, because Uncle Joe wasn't around. She was very happy to see us. She'd lost weight since she'd been in prison, but now she looked pale and dried up. As usual, she complained that Jacki wasn't there. She wanted us to pressure Jacki into coming down, something neither Jen nor I were willing to do. Then she asked about Jules.

"She wanted to come today, Mom," I told her, "but she had to work."

"It seems like they would let her off work if it meant coming to visit her mother," she grumbled. Like Jules would have told anyone at work where her mother was.

"So, how're you doing, Mom?" Jen asked.

"I guess I can't complain," she answered. "Same old thing every day. The boredom is the worst. Occasionally we get a new inmate, and it's always interesting to hear her story."

"Why are most people in here, anyway? I mean, what is the most common crime?" Jenny asked.

"Actually, most women are here for non-violent crimes: fraud, forgery, selling drugs. Of course there are the ones who've abused their children, or killed someone." She looked down at her fingernails before she continued. "But most of their crimes are almost always connected to a man. Wouldn't you know? My current cell mate was coerced by her boyfriend into robbing a bank!"

"That's so sad," I said.

"Mom!" Jenny broke in. "You should write a book! All the stories the women in here have to tell! It would be a bitchin' book to read!"

"Well, I don't know, Jennifer," Mom answered. "I'm not really a writer."

"That's the cool thing about it!" Jen argued. "You wouldn't have to do that much writing. Just have them dictate their stories to you. It'd give you something to do. I bet a lot of the women would really like to tell their stories."

"Well, it's a thought," Mom said.

I could tell Jen was disappointed by Mom's lack of interest.

"Maybe I should just write about myself. Everything I've been through," Mom finally said.

Jenny and I exchanged glances. At some point during every visit, my mother would manage to turn the conversation to herself, and how hard things had been for her. It always made Jenny mad because Mom never talked about how hard it had been on us. Then Jenny said, "Well, maybe you could start off the first chapter about yourself, and then move on to the others. A variety of stories would be more interesting to the reader."

"Perhaps," Mom responded.

On the way home, Jenny was really aggravated. "Our mother is the most self-absorbed person I've ever met!" she fumed. "I swear to God, every time I visit her, I come away thinking, why do I even bother? Did she ask you anything about school? Your friends? Your life?"

"Well, it must be hard, you know, living in a room the size of a broom closet. Having to pee in front of everyone. Maybe it makes you become selfish," I reasoned.

"No, she was that way long before she went to jail. You just don't remember."

"I think Mom is a good person, really," I argued. "She was just, I guess, kind of out of her mind that day. I don't think she did it on purpose. She wouldn't deliberately hurt anyone."

Jenny didn't say anything.

"I remember she was always fun," I said.

"She's always fun as long as she gets her own way and is the center of attention," Jen responded. "I'm glad none of us turned out like that."

"Except for Jules," I said.

That made her giggle. "Yeah, but even Jules isn't that bad. Thank God! But still, sometimes she can be a real pisser."

I burst out laughing and almost choked on my gum. "A pisser? That's a funny word. Like, isn't everyone a pisser?"

Jenny snickered. "No some people are pissers and some are a-holes."

"Don't forget nimrods," I said.

"And douche bags," she countered.

"Ewwww…that's gross!"

A mile or so down the road, Jenny had to slam on the brakes. "Dammit!" she said. "The traffic's all backed up!"

"Yeah," I said, giggling. "What a pisser!"

* * *

After I got home that day, I went into my room to write in my diary. Jenny had turned me on to keeping a diary when I was little. She called it a "journal." After visiting with Mom, as usual, I felt a little sad. I knew she wasn't perfect, but it always bothered me when my sisters talked bad about her, like she was just a big pain in the neck. Like they didn't love her anymore.

I heard Aunt Sally's car pull into the garage, and a few minutes later, she knocked softly on my door. Aunt Sally was always really sweet to me after I had been on a visit to see Mom.

She came into my room and sat on the bed with me.

"How'd it go today, honey?" she asked.

"Going down with Jenny was really fun. I'd like to do that again. But visiting with Mom was just okay. Nothing special."

"So you had a good day?" she continued.

"Aunt Sally, can I ask you something?"

"Sure, sweetie, what is it?"

"When Mom gets out of jail, do you think she could come live here? With us?"

She looked shocked. "Why? Is that what she suggested?"

"No, not at all," I answered. "It's just that she's mentioned a few times that she wants to move to Hawaii when she gets out. And she wants me to come live with her. And...I'm not sure. I mean, living in Hawaii would be fun and all, but I don't think I want to leave *here*."

Aunt Sally shook her head. "In the first place, your mom *can't* move to Hawaii for a long time, because you *can't* leave the state when you're on parole. In the second place, by the time Janet gets released, you'll be heading off to college, living in a dorm a thousand miles from here!"

"But what if I don't want to move away? What if I just went to the junior college down in Gilroy? Couldn't I stay here and live with you?"

"Joey, you're only thirteen now, so the idea of moving away from home is probably pretty scary. But five years from now, you'll be chomping at the bit to get away from us. Trust me. And even if you aren't, you'll be welcome to stay with us as long as you want." My aunt put her arm around my shoulders and gave me a gentle squeeze.

"But what about Mom?" I asked.

"We'll just have to see what happens. It's a long way off. You really don't need to worry about it right now, okay?" She leaned over and kissed me on the cheek. "It will all work out okay. I promise."

She always knew what to say to make me feel better. That night I wrote in my diary, "I really love Aunt Sally."

22

Jennifer

After I dropped Joey off in Morgan Hill and got back on Highway 101, heading for home, I started feeling blue. Leaving my sisters behind always made me sad. It just never felt right.

But this time, I was more down than usual, after Joey brought up the topic of my love life. I'd known for a long time that something was wrong with me, but tried not to think about it. I thought I'd managed to fool everyone, but now even my baby sister had picked up on it.

As I looked back on my high school years, I realized I was exceptionally lucky to have been taken in by Beth and Ken. They not only provided me a safe and healthy environment, but they'd encouraged me scholastically and socially. With lots of liberal, freethinking people around the house, my friends were always welcome to come over and join in the conversations and debates. They were both interested in what I had to say. And while they didn't exactly allow me to run wild, they did teach me the value of integrity, discretion and a good education. I respected them enormously.

After I moved in, Beth tried to get me to open up about my relationship with Tony, but I was never comfortable talking about him. Maybe because my feelings for him were so complex I didn't understand them myself. As I grew older, I was able to see that he'd definitely taken advantage of me, and yet I still loved him. I dated lots of boys in high school, but found them to be too young and immature for me, especially when it came to sex. Most of them were fumbling, insecure, and nervous. I wanted a strong partner, who took the lead and wasn't afraid of passion. I wanted Tony.

It was amazing to me that, at a time when most boys were focused on sex twenty-four hours a day, in reality many of them were cautious and tentative. A couple of times I'd be making out with a guy I was really attracted to, and he'd start pawing at my shirt, and when I didn't try to stop him, he'd panic and make some excuse to stop. There were even a few that I went all the way with, but I was always disappointed by their inexperience. Many times after my date dropped me off, I'd go to bed and dream about Tony's muscular, tanned arms around me. The way he would slowly undress me. The way he touched me, kissed me, licked me, teased me and savored me. That's what I wanted. That's what I needed. And teenaged boys just didn't cut it.

So I spent most of my free time hanging out with girlfriends, and focusing on my grades so I could get into Berkeley. I was fairly happy, although there were many nights after my father died when I cried myself to sleep, thinking how unlucky I was with my mother in jail for killing my father. No one else in school was in my shoes; I stood out in the worst possible way.

My friends all knew not to bitch at me about their folks, because I'd tell them they were lucky to have a normal family. I'd have given *anything* to be normal. Beth and Ken were great substitutes, and I truly appreciated them, but no one can ever take the place of your real parents.

The one person I did confide in about my relationship with Tony: my roommate at college. Kate Delacroix was a tall, big-boned blonde from Texas. She talked loud and laughed a lot and in the beginning I thought we'd never get along—that she was way too extroverted for my taste. But within a matter of days I'd grown extremely fond of her and we became best friends. Kate was friendly and compassionate with everyone, and people gravitated toward her. She could be completely non-judgmental, while on the other hand, she also said exactly what was on her mind.

A few weeks after school started, Kate met Tom, a big, burly sophomore from Ireland and they fell in love. With Tom's thick Irish brogue and her southern drawl they were quite a pair.

Kate, a psychology major, planned to go on to get her Master's degree and become a therapist. When I told her about my background, she was thrilled. I was perfect material for her to practice on.

We spent long hours discussing my past when we should have been studying. She pestered me to talk about what it was like when I found out my father died, how I felt when Mom went to jail, and how I dealt with being separated from my sisters. When I told her about Tony, she wasn't surprised.

"So there you were," she said. "You'd lost your dad. The one man who was the most important to you. The one male figure who'd given you attention. And then Tony comes along. No wonder you fell for him; a strong, handsome older guy, who's giving you attention."

"Now don't turn this into some kind of weird Freudian thing. Tony wasn't a father figure to me," I argued.

"I wouldn't be so sure about that," she countered. "Of course you didn't *think* of him as a father figure. But I'll bet he was. And then things got sexual way before you were ready. So now you've got this pseudo-father-figure who you've been pressured into having sex with. Woo-wee, girl, it's no wonder you're totally fucked up when it comes to men!"

I laughed. "I really don't think it's quite that simple, thank you very much. Why don't you wait till after you graduate before you try to therapize me? You're just a beginner, remember?"

"Some lucky doctor's going to be rolling in dough after you walk through the door!" she answered.

"I think I've actually coped quite well, don't you? All things considered, I could have turned out a lot worse. Look at my sisters. Jacki's been in the nuthouse and Jules is a mess. I think I'm doing really well!"

Kate thought for a moment before she spoke. "Did you ever hear that joke about a guy who's driving along when he suddenly gets a flat tire? He gets out of his car and just happens to be in front of a mental institution. He sees a patient behind the fence and he calls the guy over. He tells him he has a flat tire and asks for the nearest telephone. They start chatting and the patient seems normal to him. So the driver says, 'Hey, when are you getting out of here?' and the patient tells him, 'Next Tuesday.' So then driver says, 'I'll tell you what. You seems pretty okay to me. I can give you some work, if you want.' He gives the guy his card and says, 'When you get out of here, give me a call and I'll get you a job.'

"As the driver starts to walk away, the mental patient picks up a huge rock and throws it at him. It beans him right on the head. The guy turns around in shock, and the mental patient says, 'See you Tuesday!' That's what you remind me of. One day you're going to bean me right on the head with a big ol' rock!"

After I stopped laughing, I said, "Yeah, because you totally deserve it!"

It was Kate's boyfriend Tom who introduced me to Ian, who was from Scotland. He and Tom met on the plane back to America the summer before our junior year. They became instant friends, in spite of their constant rivalry. They bantered about sports, politics, music, you name it. Sometimes their accents were so thick, Katie and I would look at each other and say, "Did you understand *any* of that?"

Ian was short and stocky, with thick, curly brown hair that was never combed. He was cute, funny and very sweet. Tom first introduced us at a night football game. We were standing in a circle of several friends when Ian walked up, took one look at me, and said to Tom, "Who is this fucking gorgeous bird?" We'd been together ever since.

It was Ian who had lent me his car so that I could drive down to see Mom. I liked him a lot, but I wasn't quite in love with him. So what else was new?

I was attracted to Ian in part because being a foreigner, he wasn't caught up in all the political commotion that was common in Berkeley in the early '70s. Having lived with Beth and Ken for so long, I'd had my share of political rallies and protest marches in high school and my first two years of college. In 1972, the year I met Ian, Nixon was still president and we were still in Vietnam, but I was burned out on politics, and didn't even realize it. Not until I started dating Ian, and he wanted to spend his time hiking.

Ian loved the outdoors, and couldn't get enough of exploring California. He was shocked that I'd never been hiking at Muir Woods or Mount Tam or driven up the coast. We enjoyed a trip to Yosemite early in our relationship, and a few months later, spent four days in the Southern California desert. Ian loved anything physical: skiing, horseback riding, scuba diving, you name it. Enthusiastic about everything new and adventurous, it was easy to get caught up in his excitement. Ian loved to eat, drink, and get stoned, and he loved making love to me. I have to admit, I let him distract me from my studies on more than one occasion.

Ian was the first guy I was nervous about introducing to my family and friends. Beth and Ken took to him instantly.

Ken later said that Ian was very "grounded" and an "old soul." I took him home over Thanksgiving that year, and my sisters thought he was adorable. He, Uncle Joe and Doug played darts with the twins and wouldn't let the girls join in. Uncle Joe pulled me aside later and quipped, "I think you've got yourself a lovely chap there, old girl," in an exaggerated English accent. Of course, being that we were staying at Uncle Joe's house, Jacki and I had to sleep in Joey's room, while Doug and Ian slept in with the boys, a situation neither of them was very pleased with.

"This is just bloody awful," Ian complained as I kissed him goodnight. "The next time we come here on holiday, we better be married. I don't particularly fancy sleeping with Douglas."

The only person who had any trouble with Ian was Becky. She'd started her freshman year at Berkeley when I was a junior, but I only saw her occasionally. She hung out with other students in the Black Student Union, a place I never felt very comfortable.

Becky was now a very attractive young woman. She was also smart, and excelled in her classes. I'd encouraged her to apply at Berkeley, since she was living with her brother in nearby Albany. Her first couple of weeks there, she wanted to hang out with me a lot, but as she started meeting other students, she came around less and less, which was okay by me. She was still a pain in the ass.

The nicest thing Becky would say about Ian was that he was "okay, for a white guy." Even though he did his best to win her over on the few occasions we were together, she continued to be snotty toward him.

"What is your problem?" I asked her on the phone one day.

"What makes you think I got a problem?"

"Because you're always such a little bitch. To me. To Ian.

To every white person you meet. You've been that way since the day I met you. It's really tiring, if you want to know the truth."

"Well, why wouldn't I be?" she answered.

"I don't know what you mean."

"Jenny, did you ever stop to think what it was like for me, to be taken out of my home by white people, put in a damn foster home with a bunch of white people, put in a school where I was the only black person? Can you even begin to imagine what that was like?"

"No, I guess I can't really," I answered. "I never even thought about it before. You never talked about it."

"Well, let me tell you, it was fucking awful, okay?"

"I see that now. But I was just a kid back then. There wasn't anything I could do about it."

"I didn't say you were supposed to *do* anything. Just maybe try to understand where I was coming from." Becky's voice was cracking.

"Look, I'm sorry," I said. "I truly am. I wished we'd talked about this stuff a long time ago."

"Yeah, me too," she said softly.

"You know, I've never really understood why you've kept this relationship going. Why didn't you just end our friendship a long time ago?"

Becky paused before she spoke. "I guess I don't think of you as a friend," she finally said. "I really think of you as a sister."

"Oh, Becky," I said.

"You know, I grew up in a family of flakes. For the most part, all of my brothers and sisters were pretty fucked up. Pregnant at fifteen. On drugs. In jail. You know the story." She stopped for a moment and I heard her take a drag from her cigarette. "You were the first person close to me that had her shit together. I saw it right from the beginning. So I respected you. I know you don't buy that. But I really did. You came from a fucked-up family too, but you were still above it all, you know?"

"Well, I don't know if I was above it all—"

"You know what I mean. You weren't going to let yourself get dragged down by it."

"I was pretty lucky," I said. "I've had some good role models. Uncle Joe. Aunt Sally. Beth. Ken."

"Yeah, some of it might have been luck," she countered. "But I think a lot of it was just you."

"I can't believe you're telling me this, Beck. I always thought you just tolerated me, at best."

She chuckled. "Well, you can be an uppity little bitch sometimes, too!"

We both laughed. "I think I learned that from you!"

"I'm glad I could be a good influence on you!" she retorted.

That evening, I was talking to Kate about my conversation with Becky, and she asked if I'd ever talked to Becky about Tony.

"No," I said. "Why would I?"

"I thought you mentioned to me one time that Becky had been molested by Tony," she answered.

"No, what I said was I was pissed at her for a long time because she copied me and *said* that Tony molested her. She just wanted the attention."

"But, honey, how do you know she wasn't telling the truth?" Kate persisted.

I found myself getting hot. "Because she was a little liar, that's why. And because Tony wouldn't have done that. I know it's hard for you imagine, Kate, that this older guy was in love with me. But he was. We were in love. Sure, in some ways I guess he was a jerk. He was immature. He'd come from a broken home, too. His dad was abusive. But he wasn't a child molester, okay?"

"Okay," she answered. "But from the emotion in your voice, my guess is that deep down inside, you've worried about it."

I shook my head. "Not in a million fucking years."

"I know you won't mind if I change the subject," she continued. "But Tom has been talking about us going to spend the summer in Ireland with his folks. We thought maybe you and Ian could come too. Maybe not for the whole summer, but for a few weeks. Have y'all made any plans?"

"Actually, we haven't talked about this summer yet, but he did suggest that I move in with him next semester!"

Ian came from a fairly wealthy family and didn't have to live in the dorm. He was renting a one-bedroom bungalow near campus. I'd been reluctant to bring up the subject with Kate, because it felt like I'd be abandoning her. We'd really enjoyed being roommates for almost three years now.

"Oh, my stars!" she exclaimed. "That's wonderful! Oh, you definitely should! That'd be so great, living off campus. Think of the parties we'd have!"

"You wouldn't mind if I left you?" I asked.

"Well, of course, it wouldn't be the same as being together every night...but I'd get used to it somehow! Tell me you're going to say yes!"

"I'm going to have to think about it. Let's get through the summer first. You know my history with guys. This may not even *last* until summer!"

"I think Ian is just the sweetest guy. He's perfect for you. He's handsome and sexy as all get-out. And he adores the livin' shit out of you. Y'all would be crazy to break up."

"Yeah, I know," I said quietly.

* * *

Over Christmas break that year, I decided to have a little party back home to celebrate my twentieth birthday on

December 30. Kate, Tom and Becky drove down to Morgan Hill together. Maria and her three kids were there, plus Ian and my whole family. Kate kept everyone laughing with her stories of growing up on a big ranch in Texas. The twins always enjoyed having the older guys around. I think they really missed Kevin, and having them there helped with that. The small house was packed with people. Most of us were enjoying the holiday spirit. Jules was subdued, as usual. She'd become somewhat reclusive when it came to family functions. I was worried about her, but since she wasn't causing a lot of commotion, I'd decided to leave well enough alone. She had her friends at the record store who she hung out with; she was taking night classes and saving up for a car. I knew she occasionally talked to Jacki on the phone, so I wasn't that concerned about her.

Jacki and I were making a salad in the kitchen. Becky was buttering some garlic bread, and Maria was sitting at the table, nursing her new baby, Carly. As always, the conversation turned to sex. Maria was complaining that her new boyfriend, Pete, Carly's father, was always asking her about her previous boyfriends, and she was too embarrassed to tell him.

"So you're saying you have babies by two different men and he's nervous about the fact that you've had sex with other guys?" Jacki asked.

"Nervous ain't the word for it," Maria said. "That man is so uptight he could open a Coke bottle with his butt!" Everyone burst out laughing.

"He wants to hear all the details, like the very first time I did it, but when I tell him, he gets pissed off. It's so weird," she continued.

Then Becky joined in. "When I tell my friends my first time was with a white guy, and I was only twelve years old, they really freak."

I stopped slicing carrots and stared at Becky. Jacki and

Maria both stopped what they were doing and looked at her as well. She continued, oblivious. "But you know, that Tony, he actually made me feel good about myself. One time, he had me stand naked in front of a mirror and look at myself. He made me see how beautiful I was. I never forgot that!"

I felt like I'd been punched in the stomach. I was aware that I was staring at her with my mouth hanging open. Becky stopped talking when she noticed everyone looking at her.

"What?" she said. Then she looked at me. "I can't believe after all this time you still don't accept the idea that Tony wanted me, too! But, trust me, he did!"

Everyone turned to look at me. I felt my face get really hot. I thought I was going to throw up. My knees gave way and I sank to the floor.

23

Later that night, I sat in the living room with Jacki, Kate, and Aunt Sally. Jules had gone to work and Joey was spending the night with a friend. Ian was shocked that I'd sent him home on the night of my birthday. The term he used was "totally gobsmacked." I didn't even try to explain. It was hard enough hanging around, trying to pretend I was enjoying my birthday party, when I felt like I was crumbling inside. I was so relieved when the party broke up and people started leaving.

I sat on the couch sobbing, and rocked back and forth.

"I just can't believe I was so stupid," I said. "How could I not have known?"

"You were in love with him, honey," Aunt Sally said.

"I should've had the bastard arrested. I should've thrown his ass in jail!" I wiped my eyes. "I probably still would, if I could find him."

"Did you ever try to contact him after you went to Beth's?" Jacki asked.

"I thought for sure he would try to get a hold of me, you know?" I answered. "After a few weeks, I called Shelly, but the number had been changed. A couple of years later, after I got my driver's license, I drove by the old house and I saw a Mexican couple come out, with some kids. So I knew they'd moved. I looked up the name Robert Wright in the phone book, and there were, like, five or six of them, and I called them all. But none of them were Bob and Shelly." I reached for more Kleenex. Then I said to Kate, "How did you know?"

She looked at me sympathetically. "Girls don't usually lie about being molested. I mean, they do on occasion, but it's rare. And I figure Becky didn't really have any motivation for sticking to her story if it wasn't true. And if he molested you, then what was to stop him from molesting her?"

"But she was only twelve!" I wailed. "There's a big difference between being twelve and being fourteen!"

"Not to him, there wasn't," Jacki said. She came over to the couch, sat down and put her arm around me.

"For five years I've been thinking about him. Missing him. Wanting him. Hoping that somehow, he was going to show up. Now I find out, on my birthday, that he was actually a sick son of a bitch. I feel like such a dope!"

Kate came over and sat on the other side of me.

"Jenny, darlin', please don't be so hard on yourself. You were just a kid. And extremely vulnerable then. He was a handsome young guy who took advantage of that. There isn't anything you can do to take it back. It happened. And it's going to be painful to think about for a while. But I really think you'll be able to move on now."

"You know, I feel really bad about Becky. For not believing her." I blew my nose. "I thought there was no way he'd have anything to do with her. She was twelve. And she was black. That's a shitty way to think, isn't it?"

"Jenny," Aunt Sally said, "no one could have guessed what was going on. You and Becky were both young and innocent. You need to forgive yourself."

"Oh, God, I'm tired of talking about this," I finally said. "Let's go clean up the kitchen."

"No, you girls stay here," Aunt Sally said. "I'll do the dishes."

"No, I really need something to do," I protested. "You go

to bed. Jacki and Kate will help me clean up."

"Well, if you're sure." She hesitated.

"I'm sure. Honest. I'll be fine."

Aunt Sally went to bed while the rest of us headed into the kitchen. I sat down on one of the chairs and stared at the floor.

"I still can't believe it," I said. "That piece of shit! You know, I've never told Ian about him. Or any other guy I've ever been with. It blows my mind that for so long, I haven't wanted other boys because they weren't Tony. Tony was a 'real' man, I thought. Jesus Christ!"

Around midnight, Jacki drove home and Kate and I went to sleep in Joey's room. But I was feeling restless, so I got up and went back into the living room. I kept the overhead lights off but plugged in the Christmas tree. For a long time, I sat in the dark, just looking at the twinkling lights. Over the years, I'd learned some meditation techniques from Ken, so I did my best to try to quiet my mind, and focus on something pleasant, but it wasn't easy. I couldn't stop thinking about Tony, and I'd feel the tension creep back into my body. I'd take a deep breath and start all over.

I heard someone drive up and stop out front. A car door opened and I heard young girls, probably drunk, laughing and talking. The car door slammed and footsteps headed towards the house. Jules opened the front door and stomped into the living room. She stopped when she saw me sitting in front of the tree.

"What are you doing?" she asked. "Where is everybody?"

"Shhhhh," I whispered. "Everyone's gone home. Everybody else is asleep."

"Jeez, early night. Why aren't you with Ian?" She came in, took off her coat and sat next to me.

"It was a bad night for me," I whispered.

"What do you mean, 'bad night'? I didn't think you ever

had any 'bad nights.' What, turning twenty has been hard for you?"

I ignored her at first. Jules and Joey had never been told about what happened to me when I was in the foster home, so I very briefly explained the situation to her.

"So all this was going on and no one even bothered to tell me?" she hissed.

"This isn't about you, for God's sake!" I answered.

"So let me get this straight," she said. "You were boinking this guy when you were, what? Fifteen?"

"Actually, it was right after I turned fourteen."

"Oh, my God!" she exclaimed. "And here I thought you were the perfect one all this time! What a hoot!"

"You can really be a bitch sometimes, Jules, you know that?" I asked.

"Yeah, well, I guess it goes with the territory," she said.

"What's *that* supposed to mean?"

"Never mind. It doesn't matter." She got up. "Is there any birthday cake left? I'm starving."

"You know, I can't believe you're such a jerk. I just shared something really painful with you, and you're acting like it's no big deal."

Jules sat back down on the couch. "Look, you were playing around with this older guy. It turns out he was also playing around with someone else. My guess is he must have been doing a lot of girls. Like most men, he was a big jerk. So what else is new? But that was a long time ago. You've got a great guy now. You've got friends. It seems like you're pretty happy. What are you whining about?"

I couldn't believe she was being so callous. Typical Jules.

"I'm going to bed," I said. "Good night, *Bane.* And thanks for listening!"

"No problem. Sure you don't want some cake?"

* * *

The next day was rainy and windy, and my aunt and uncle tried to convince Kate and I to stay over another day. But it was New Year's Eve and we wanted to get back to the guys. As it turned out, we decided to take the twins and Joey to an early movie, and didn't get on the road until almost four.

I was quiet on the drive back to Berkeley. The conversation I'd had with Jules was still bothering me. But in a way, she was right. I did have a great guy, and a relatively good life. Lots of friends. Family I loved. Why dwell on something that happened such a long time ago?

We checked into the dorm around eight. After dropping our bags in the room, Kate went in to get cleaned up before meeting up with Tom. I planned to head over to Ian's. It was still raining, and very windy, but I decided to walk. The wet and cold felt good. It somehow matched my mood.

It was raining harder than I thought, and by the time I had walked the several blocks to Ian's, I was drenched. I hadn't taken time to call him, so I worried he might not be home.

I saw a dim light through the window as I knocked on the door of his cottage. After a few minutes, he opened it. By the bewildered look on his face, it was obvious he'd been sound asleep.

"Did I wake you?" I asked.

"No, no," he said. "I was just studying. But bloody hell, what happened to you? You look like something the cat threw up."

I entered and shrugged off my coat. "We just got back. I decided to walk over."

Ian closed the front door. "Yeah, nice night for a walk." He gave me a kiss. "You must be freezing."

"Yeah, can I take a shower?"

"Lovely idea," he said. "I think I'll join you."

I went into the bathroom and turned on the water. Ian took a couple of towels from the hall closet and put them in the dryer. We got undressed and stepped into the shower. The hot water felt wonderful. Ian took a washcloth, soaped it up, and began rubbing my back.

"Oh, my God, that feels great," I said, closing my eyes. He did a thorough job of washing me all over, and then I took the cloth from him. "Now it's my turn," I said.

"Okay, but this is my first time. Be gentle," he quipped.

I scrubbed his back and legs, and then had him turn around so that I could work on his hairy chest and arms. By the time I was done, he had an enormous erection.

"Perfect!" I said. "I needed a convenient place to hang the washcloth." I draped it over his penis.

"You're not going to let this go to waste, are you?" he asked. "That's the saddest thing I've ever heard!"

I reached for the shampoo and he said, "Oh, let me."

He dumped some shampoo on my head and began to lather it up. It felt so soothing, having him tend to me.

We stepped out of the shower. Ian retrieved the towels from the dryer and began drying me off. It was such a nice touch, those warm towels.

"You are so good to me," I said to him

"Bloody fucking right I'm good to you. And you'll be expected to put out later on, I hope you realize that."

I smiled at him and gave him a kiss. "Why else would I be here?" I teased.

I picked up a comb and tried to run it through my tangles.

"Oh, bollocks, just sit down," Ian said. "Must I do everything for you?"

I sat on the toilet and he reached into the medicine cabinet. He pulled out a large, purple comb.

"This is my very special Charles Antel Curl-Relaxing Comb. I brought it all the way from London." He began to comb through my hair, starting at the very ends.

"You are full of surprises," I said. "I had no idea you ever actually combed your hair!"

He reached down and gave my nipple a playful squeeze.

"You'll pay for that later, you cheeky bitch!" he whispered in my ear. "So are you going to tell me what was going on last night?"

I took a deep breath. I had never told Ian about Tony because he wasn't the kind of guy who liked to get into deep, personal stuff. It made him uncomfortable. So I told them the story as briefly as I could. He continued to comb out my hair and listened quietly.

When I was done, he said, "That bloody fucking wanker. If I ever run into him, I'll knock him on his arse." He paused. "He isn't real big, is he?"

I smiled and took the comb from him. "You are really adorable, you know that?" I said.

"How adorable?" he asked.

"Bloody fucking adorable," I said, kissing his chest.

"Well, I don't really want to be adorable. Could I trade that in for being, say, handsome? Or manly? I prefer manly."

"Yes. You got it. You are the manliest man I know, okay? Now do you have *anything* in this place to drink besides beer? Like maybe a shot of Amaretto?"

"Yes, right. Of course. I'll get that straight up. Actually, you put on my robe and go make us a drink, and I'll get a fire going."

Later, as we were snuggled up on the couch, Ian asked if I wanted to go out to a party to celebrate New Year's Eve.

"No, I want to stay right here," I said.

"What time do you have to get back to the dorm?" he asked.

"Midnight. But I have a feeling I won't make it back there at all tonight." I took a sip of my drink.

"So then," he said, "you'll get kicked out, and I suppose I'll just have to take you in."

"I suppose you will," I whispered.

He set his drink down and put his arms around me. "Banner idea. So you can just stay here and relax."

"Are you kidding me?" I asked. "If I were any more relaxed, I'd have to wear a diaper!"

"You're a very funny girl, anyone ever tell you that? You ought to think about being a writer."

"The idea has come up," I bantered.

"Speaking of things coming up? Your washcloth holder is starting to need some attention," he murmured.

"That's the most erotical thing you've said all night," I teased.

"Well, I'm a very erotical kind of bloke," he said, kissing me.

The next day, Ian moved me out of the dorm and into his place. I was worried about bailing out on Kate, but since I'd paid in advance with the money my father had left me, that meant she got to have the room to herself for the rest of the term. She was delighted.

I now had a longer walk to class, so I decided to buy a bicycle and Ian helped me find one. On weekends, we rode up to Tilden Park in the Berkeley hills, overlooking all of San Francisco Bay.

Moving in with Ian was a great distraction from my thoughts about Tony, but I still obsessed about him sometimes. I felt so used, so hurt and betrayed. Kate seemed to know instinctively when I was thinking about him, and she'd approach the subject gently and let me vent. As the weeks went by, I grew weary of thinking and talking about Tony. Eventually, I stopped thinking about him at all.

As summer approached, Ian and I made plans to go to Scotland to visit his family, who lived right outside of Edinburgh. We'd be there for a month, and then fly to Ireland and visit with Tom and Kate for two weeks. Then the four of us planned to spend another two weeks in Greece. Ian had been there before, and was looking forward to "turning me on to the islands." This would be my first trip to Europe, and I was so excited, I could hardly stand it.

A week before the term was over, I got a call from Jacki. She'd been on the phone with Aunt Sally and was upset. Aunt Sally said she'd found a bag of pot in Jule's room, along with some pills. She and Uncle Joe confronted her, and they had a big fight. Jules packed up her belongings and took off in the old Corvair she'd purchased recently.

A week later, Jules called Jacki from San Francisco. She was back living near the Haight-Ashbury area, working in a free clinic and renting a room from a friend. She said she was happy, and wasn't planning to come back. Jacki thought she sounded good. We all breathed a sigh of relief. I really hoped she was happy.

24

Julie

It wasn't exactly an accident that Aunt Sally found my stash of drugs. I wasn't being all that careful. Maybe I wanted to get caught. I don't know why I didn't just pack up and leave rather than let myself get booted out. But then I wasn't thinking very clearly. I'd been either stoned or drunk or a little bit of both almost every day since I got back from Montana, eighteen months earlier. If my aunt and uncle hadn't been so overwhelmed by their grief for Kevin, they might have caught on. But as long as I was being "good" and not getting into trouble, they pretty much left me alone. Which was exactly how I wanted it.

Things had been so screwed up when I returned home. I was barely able to make it through the day. Denny had called several times, and I told him that I didn't want to be with him anymore. I said I was sorry over and over again, but he wanted a better explanation. During our last conversation, he asked if I still loved him, and I told him no. He never called after that.

The thing with Kevin was really a trip. Everyone was crying and talking about him all the time. It was "Kevin this" and "Kevin that" and I thought I would lose my mind. I tried to spend as much time alone as I could, and everyone thought it was because I was in mourning as well, when the truth was, I hated my cousin and thought he was an idiot for joining the army. Of course, I couldn't tell anyone that.

I tried several times to contact Tiffy, because I knew I'd be able to talk to her, but her mother's phone had been disconnected. I called a couple of my old girlfriends from school, but none of them had heard from her. I'd lost her.

Finally, Jacki came over one day and insisted I tell her what was going on with me. We went for a drive up to Uvas Meadows, a park near our house in Morgan Hill. We sat in the car beside a grove of eucalyptus trees. I rolled down my window and inhaled the pungent scent. It was so hard. I didn't know where to begin.

"Look," I said, "everyone is real upset over Kevin. I get that. But it's weird because he was so mean to me the whole time I lived here. He constantly tormented me. And now I'm supposed to be sorry that he went off and got himself killed?"

"I know you guys didn't get along," Jacki responded, "but that's normal with siblings."

"No, it was worse than that. He was really a jerk."

"But he was your cousin. He was family," she argued. "And, yes, it was pretty dumb that he volunteered to go to Vietnam. But he believed it was for the right reason."

"Well, I just can't pretend to be as upset as everyone else," I said. "You never liked him. Neither did Jenny. You guys thought he was a square. You laughed at him all the time. And now everyone's acting like he was a big hero or something."

Jacki was quiet for a while. "Kevin *was* a square. Sometimes it seems to me he was just a big, dumb kid. Even when he was little, he liked playing Army. I think he glorified it in his head. I don't honestly believe he had a clue what he was getting into. And I bet if he could do it all over again, he'd think twice."

"Maybe," I agreed. "But it still doesn't make me miss him much. He was horrible to me and whenever I tried to tell you and Jen about it, you just ignored me. I wanted to get away from him so bad, I used to wish I'd be put into a foster home. And you guys just didn't care!" I burst into tears.

"Jules, I'm so sorry. It was a hard time for all of us. I know I should have paid more attention to you. But we were all coping the best we could. Which, for me, wasn't very well. You remember that I had to be admitted for a while? *To the nut house,* as you used to call it. I just couldn't handle anything else. All I can say is I'm sorry."

I sat, wiping my tears.

She continued. "And I don't expect you to grieve for Kevin. But it's not good to keep stuff bottled up, either. You can talk to me. You really can. And I wish you would. You know my psychiatrist, Dr. Wheeler? He said that emotions are real. They aren't good or bad. They just are. The way you feel about Kevin is the way anyone would feel if they had grown up with someone who abused them all the time."

"Do you really mean that?" I asked.

"Yes. But I don't think now would be a good time to bring all that up with Uncle Joe or Aunt Sally. I mean, they're in a lot of pain, you know? They can't take back what happened, either. They were doing the best they could."

We were both quiet for a while. Finally, she asked, "Is there anything else bothering you?"

I shook my head. I did feel better, after talking to her about Kevin, but there were other things too awful to speak of out loud.

* * *

For the next few months, I tried to stay away from the house as much as possible. Uncle Joe and Aunt Sally were pretty cool about letting me get a job in town, as long as I was taking classes toward getting my high school diploma. Since Kevin died, they'd really made an effort to take lot of family outings with the twins and Joey, and they always invited me along, but I usually told them I had to work. I didn't want to hurt their feelings, but there was no way I wanted to go camping for a whole weekend when I wouldn't be able to have a drink or get high. That was much more important to me.

For several months, I really loved my job at the Calliope Record Shop. There were a lot of other freaks like me working there: people who had dropped out and spent their free time getting stoned. In fact, the owner of the shop, an older guy by the name of Pete, was our main supplier of pot, but he didn't like people smoking while we were at work, which we did anyway when he wasn't around. It wasn't a hard job. During the week, it was pretty quiet and we had a lot of time to goof off. On the weekends it was busier, since the local kids had nowhere else to go.

A lot of my old friends from high school would come by the shop just to visit and let me know where the next party was and I'd pass the information along to other kids as they came in. After the shop closed, we'd hop into someone's car and head off to a party in town, or up to San Jose. The few times that Uncle Joe caught me coming in late, I'd tell him we had to stay over to do inventory, or some kind of bullshit like that, and he just let it go. I don't think he really wanted to know what I was up to, as long as I wasn't getting into trouble.

A couple of boys who worked at the shop flirted with me a lot, and guys who came in off the street would ask if I had a boyfriend, but I told everyone I had a guy back in Montana. The truth was, I wasn't interested in anyone. When I was stoned or drunk, sometimes I'd make out with one of them. Sometimes I'd let it go even farther than that, I'm not proud to say. The truth was, when I was high, and feeling good, and a guy was groping me, I liked to imagine it was Kelly.

It was Kelly who haunted me. It was Kelly I thought about when I was horny. And, late at night, in the dark, parked in a car with some guy I didn't care about, I closed my eyes and pretended it was Kelly who was touching me.

During the day, of course, when I was sober, I didn't allow myself to think about her. The idea was repugnant. I had known a couple of girls in my class who were rumored to be lesbians and we'd always made fun of them. Or, if I or one of my girlfriends liked a certain guy who didn't like us back, we'd say, "He must be a queer!" Queers were rejects, losers, and oddballs.

There was a kid who worked part-time in the record shop, Billy, who was flamboyantly gay. He was also very funny and a real party person. Everyone liked Billy. He was never shy about who he was. It couldn't have been easy, living in a small town, to be the first to "come out." I admired him for that. We became friends, and whenever I overheard someone refer to him as a homo or a fag, I got pissed.

In spite of my respect for Billy, there was no way I was going to talk about, or even allow myself to think about my own sexuality. I decided it was simply a result of the antagonistic relationship I'd had with Kevin, who'd teased me incessantly when I'd started developing. I figured when the right guy came along, I'd fall in love and have a normal relationship. That's what I wanted to believe. Anything else was unacceptable.

Eventually, I got fired from Calliope. I'd been high so much that I missed a lot of work, or came in late too many times. I worked for a while at a women's clothing store and then lost that job, too. I realized then I really needed to keep a job because I desperately wanted a car so I could get out of town more often. I got hired as a waitress at a little diner in town, the only place that was open twenty-four hours a day, and was amazed at what I could make in tips on the weekends. I tried to curtail my drinking and smoking to my days off, but it wasn't easy. The only time I was happy was when I was high.

* * *

Four months before my eighteenth birthday, Aunt Sally found the baggie in my bedside table and threw me out. In all fairness, what she said was I needed to stop using drugs and stop drinking or I'd have to leave. The choice was obvious—I'd have to leave. Only this time it would be easier, because I finally had a car, a little Corvair I'd bought for eight hundred dollars. Uncle Joe and the twins had tuned it up for me and it ran great. I loved that little car. I named it Günter.

That night, I packed all my stuff into the trunk and back seat. This time, I was careful to pack some warm winter clothes. Of course I was a little wasted at the time, so I decided to spend the night at a girlfriend's house. In the morning, I took off for San Francisco once again.

I was a little nervous when I got on the freeway. I'd never driven around San Francisco by myself and it had been a couple of years since I'd been there, but I was also excited about going back. This time I was prepared. I had a couple of hundred dollars, a car and a lot more clothes with me. Plus, I was sure I'd find a job pretty quickly. I decided to head to Lucy's, hoping she'd still be there and could put me up for a couple of days.

I arrived in the city around noon, and pulled over to grab something to eat. Afterwards, I drove around for at least an hour, looking for Lucy's place. When I finally stumbled across it, I was stunned. The house had been completely renovated, and was now an office building! I stood in front of it with my mouth hanging open. *Dammit!*

I decided to drive a couple of blocks over to the Haight and walk around. I hoped I'd run into some familiar faces. Again, I was in for a shock. The neighborhood was packed with tourists and I had a hell of time trying to find a parking place. I had to leave my car several blocks away. But it was an unusually warm day in May, and I didn't mind the walk. In spite of all the changes, it felt good to be back. There were still lots of hippies and other young people hanging around on the streets. There was also something I had never seen before: same-sex couples walking arm in arm together, mostly men. You'd never see that in Morgan Hill! For some reason, it made me smile. I was kind of hoping that Tiff had managed to get away and that I'd run into her on the street one day. Although I was much better prepared this time around, the one thing I didn't have was Tiffy.

I decided the best thing to do was to start looking for a job right away, so I walked up and down the streets, looking for help-wanted posters. There was a little Italian bakery that was looking for help. I went in and grabbed a job application, and continued walking. The only other sign I saw was for a bartender, but I knew I had to be eighteen to work there. Then, on a side street, I saw a small sign in the window of a Planned Parenthood clinic, advertising for a part-time receptionist. I went in and asked the girl behind the front desk for an application. She was a tall, pretty woman; about twenty, I guessed, with short, reddish hair. Her nametag read "Kim."

"Do you have any experience with typing, answering the phone, filing?" she asked.

"Well, I just came from a home where there were four teenagers...so, yeah, I have experience answering the phone!" I said.

She laughed. "Okay. Fill out this application and my boss will call you for an interview."

I took the form, but hesitated. "Well, actually," I said, "I just came into town. I don't have a place to stay yet, so I don't have a phone number to give you. But I have lots of job experience already. I've worked in a record store, a clothing store and a restaurant. I'm real good with customers. Do you think I could get an interview today?"

She looked me over carefully, and said, "Okay, hold on, let me go ask my boss. I really think she's looking for someone a little older...but I'll put in a good word for you. Go ahead and have a seat."

I sat in a green vinyl chair next to a plastic fern. The vestibule was small, but as she walked out the door, into the next room, I caught a glimpse of several young women sitting in chairs, all staring straight ahead. No one was talking. It brought back unpleasant memories. This wasn't the type of environment I was used to working in, but I hoped the hourly wage would be better. And, working part-time would give me the opportunity to look for something more interesting.

When Kim returned, she said, "Can you be here tomorrow at three p.m.?"

"Sure!"

"Okay, make sure you have the application filled out. And, if I were you, I'd go out and get a nice pair of slacks, maybe in black? And a pretty blouse. You need to look a little more professional to work here, okay?"

That surprised me because, while she was wearing a white lab coat, it was unbuttoned, and underneath she wore faded blue jeans and an Iron Butterfly tee shirt.

"Oh, okay," I said.

"There's a used clothing store around the corner. You might be able to find something there," she suggested.

"Great, thank you. Um, one other thing. I'm looking for a place to stay. Do you know where I could rent a room?"

She thought for a moment. "About half a block down, across the street, on the right, there's a coffee shop. They have a bulletin board that sometimes has ads for roommates. I'd try there."

"Cool. And thanks. See you tomorrow."

"Be sure not to be late, okay?" she called out as I opened the door.

"I won't," I answered.

I walked down to the coffee shop. It was a business that obviously catered to the younger crowd. I heard Carole King singing, "It's Too Late" on the radio in the background, and the walls were plastered with posters of Janis Joplin and Jim Morrison. I found the bulletin board and saw some places listed, but I didn't recognize any of the addresses, nor did I have a map. I ordered a cup of coffee and loaded it with cream and sugar, then dug a pen out of my purse and started filling out the two applications.

I sat there for along time, trying to figure out what to do next. I could always drive around and look for a cheap motel, but that idea unnerved me. I was afraid of getting lost. Plus, I didn't want to waste my money on a motel if I could avoid it. Maybe I'd have to sleep in my car. That would be a drag.

As I sat there, pondering my situation, a news bulletin came over the radio. George Wallace had just been shot. The longhaired guy behind the counter turned up the volume and people crowded around to listen.

"Finally, they got a bad guy," someone said. I looked out the window. It was starting to get dark. At home, Aunt Sally would be fixing supper. I'm sure they'd have the TV on, watching the news. It seemed a long way away. Was it really only this morning I had left? The image of Aunt Sally, standing in the hallway, crying as I packed my clothes, haunted me. I'd need to call her soon to let her know I was okay.

The door opened and closed. More people came and went. I bent over the applications, trying to decide what I should put down for the address and phone number. Just leave it blank?

I heard a soft voice. "Hey."

I looked up. It was Kim.

"I was wondering if you'd still be here. Did you find a place to stay yet?" she asked.

"Actually, no," I said. "I mean, I saw some ads, but I don't know how to get there...Do you want to sit down?"

She took off her lab coat and draped it over the back of the chair. "I'm going to get some tea. Do you want something?"

I shook my head. When she returned to the table, she said, "You know, I think I forgot to ask your name."

"I'm Julie. My friends called me Jules."

"I think Julie's a beautiful name. I had a doll named Julie when I was little. Actually, it was a 'Poor Pitiful Pearl' doll. Did you ever have one of those? Her name was Pearl, but I called her Julie. Isn't that silly?" she laughed and blushed.

"I didn't really play with dolls that much," I said. "Me and my sister Jenny really liked horses. Playing cowboys and Indians. Climbing trees. Tomboy stuff."

There was an awkward pause. Then Kim set her mug down and said, "I thought about you all afternoon."

My heart start to flutter. Now it was my turn to blush.

She continued, "I thought, if you hadn't found a place yet, you might want to come hang out at my pad. It's small, but I have a couch you could sleep on. Until you find a place of your own."

"Man, that would be great," I said. "I was thinking about sleeping in my car tonight."

"Okay, cool. So, you wanna go?"

May 15, 1972. The day George Wallace was shot. The day Kim came into my life. It was a Monday.

We went back to her place. I never did sleep on the couch.

25

That first night, Kim and I stayed up till dawn, just talking. She kept yawning and saying she needed to go to bed. But then we'd chat some more. She told me her mom was dead and her dad lived back east. He retired from the Army as a Lieutenant Colonel. Her older brother, Don, still lived near their dad. She moved to California right after high school, and was going to school part-time at San Francisco State. She planned to go to medical school.

Kim was totally open and free in talking about herself. She didn't hold back anything. She said she knew from an early age that she was somehow different from other girls.

"All my girlfriends would look at the boys in teen magazines, but I was more interested in the girls. I never had a crush on a boy, like they did. They'd talk about how cute some guy's butt was, but I just couldn't see it. I never talked to anyone about it. But I knew I was different. That's why I wanted to come to San Francisco. It's just more acceptable out here."

"Does your family know?" I asked.

"I think my dad figured it out before I did, and he didn't freak out or anything. Which is pretty surprising, considering how straight he is. But he's old, you know. Almost seventy. My parents got married late. So nothing much bothers him any more. Except Nixon. He hates Richard Nixon. That's a surprise, too.

"And my brother. He's almost six years older than me and

he's never paid much attention to what was going on with me. He's married now and having a baby. I guess he thinks this is just a rebellious thing I'm going through."

Kim told me she'd never been with a man, but had been involved in a couple of relationships with girls before she moved to San Francisco. Since she'd been so busy with school and work, she hadn't made time to meet anyone lately.

Then she asked about me. I said I'd had trouble finding a boyfriend in high school, and always felt alone. Then I told her about running away and meeting Denny and having an abortion. She was very sympathetic. She asked if I'd ever been with a girl, and I explained what had happened in Montana. It was the first time I had ever told anyone about Kelly.

"Have you talked to your family about being a lesbian?" she asked.

"No," I said, "because I'm not sure I am. I mean, I don't know what I am. I haven't wanted to even think about it. You know, that one night when I was with Kelly, I was drunk. I don't think I'v ever been with anyone when I wasn't drunk or stoned."

"So, you get high a lot?" she asked cautiously.

I was afraid to tell her the truth. "No, just when I'm partying with friends. You know, socially."

"You know a lot of girls come into the clinic who are pregnant or have a venereal disease because of stupid things they've done when they were stoned. Or drunk. It really puts a crimp in your decision-making process. So, anyway, I'm not trying to pass judgment or anything, but I try to stay away from stuff like that. It just ends up fucking you over in the long run."

I was disappointed. I'd been hoping she'd have a joint we could fire up. But I was attracted to Kim in a big way. It felt so good, sitting in her little apartment, sipping tea. I looked around and noticed she had a lot of tapestries on the walls.

There were macramé hangers holding ceramic pots of plants dangling from the ceiling. A wooden loom stood in the corner. Her bedspread and curtains were especially colorful.

"I batiked them myself," she explained.

" How do you do that?" I asked.

"With hot wax, dye and lots of rubber bands," she answered. "I'll show you sometime." I smiled at that.

I also noticed several cookbooks on the counter in the tiny kitchen.

"My mom really liked to cook," I said quietly.

"She did? Is she no longer around?" she asked.

I took a big breath. "My mom is in prison. She killed my dad when I was ten years old."

"Oh, my God! Julie! I'm so sorry!" Kim put down her cup and moved closer to me on the couch. She put her arm around me. "Is this okay?" she asked.

I nodded. "She's been in jail for almost eight years now. She might get paroled in a couple of years. It'll be so weird to have her out."

"So where did you live after she went to jail?" she asked.

I told her the whole story. About my sisters, my aunt and uncle, Kevin, the twins, living in Morgan Hill, running away. Everything. By the time I was done, it was almost four o'clock in the morning. We were both falling asleep.

"Come on," she said, helping me up off the couch. "Let's go to bed."

She pulled back the covers. I slid my jeans off, and climbed under the blankets, wearing my T-shirt, underwear and socks. She turned out the light and joined me. I was lying on my right side, and she snuggled up close behind me, with her arm across my waist.

"I'm so glad you're here, Julie," she whispered.

"Me, too," I said.

She kissed the back of my head.

The next morning, Kim overslept, so she was rushing around, trying to get ready for class. She encouraged me to sleep in and help myself to anything in the fridge. She said she'd see me at the clinic when I came in for my interview.

"Do I really need new clothes?" I asked.

"I told you that because my boss, Mrs. Butler, will probably be hesitant to offer you a job since you're so young. She doesn't like to hire kids who come in off the street, because they don't usually stick around very long. But if she thinks you're serious about working, you'll have a better chance."

"Gotcha."

She kissed me briefly on the lips and said, "I wish I didn't have to run off. I'd love to just stay here and hang out with you all day. I'm sorry."

"That's okay. I'll see you this afternoon."

After Kim left, I hung around the apartment, looking at her stuff. It felt so fantastic being there. I just couldn't believe my good luck.

That afternoon, I showed up for my interview looking as straight as possible. I had found a pretty white blouse, and a pair of black polyester pants. I'd never worn polyester in my life. Luckily, I had a pair of black boots in the trunk of my car and I found a purse for two dollars at a consignment shop. I tied my hair back and put on a little lipstick. Looking in the mirror, I thought I looked older and more sophisticated.

I needn't have worried. Mrs. Butler looked at my application but barely even glanced at me. She hired me on the spot at four-fifty an hour. It was more money than I had ever made on an hourly basis. She put Kim in charge of training me. We were both thrilled. I'd only be working twenty-four hours a week to start, but I'd be able to pick up more hours in a couple of months when one of the other girls was on maternity leave. I could start on Wednesday. As I left, I said to Kim, "Maybe we could celebrate tonight?"

"I'd love to, but I'm afraid I have to study. You could go out and get to know the neighborhood, if you want."

I liked that she was so thoughtful. I didn't really want to go out without her, and since I wasn't eighteen, I couldn't get into any bars or clubs anyway. But I did have a pot of spaghetti waiting for her when she got home that night, and she had a big grin on her face when she walked through the door. It wasn't until a few days later that she admitted to me that she didn't eat meat. She was too much!

I adored Kim right from the start. She was kind and sweet and so patient with me. She was someone who knew exactly what she wanted and where she was headed. Exercising was a big deal for her, so we hiked a lot through Golden Gate Park, and walked along the beach on the weekends when she wasn't studying. She had a lot of friends who were both young and older women, most of them lesbians, and they dropped by frequently. I loved hanging out with them. I felt so comfortable, so safe.

And being with her in bed was great. At first I was really shy and embarrassed. I felt clumsy. But we took it slow and I got over feeling awkward. And I didn't have to be high on something to enjoy it. For the first time ever, being with her felt right—like this was how it was supposed to be. Like how it had been with Kelly.

The morning after we first made love, I got up to go to the bathroom and then crawled back into bed with her and said, "Wow. My mama never told me it could be this good!"

"You're lucky," she said quietly. "You had a mama to talk to about sex."

"Oh, are you kidding? My mom never talked to us about sex. One time I was reading one of Jacki's romance magazines—I was about nine, I guess. And I came across the word 'orgasm.' But I didn't know how to pronounce it. So I went to my mom and said, 'What's an or-jasm?' And you know what she said? She said, 'When you learn how to pronounce it, then come ask me.'"

"Oh, man," Kim sympathized. "That's mean! If I had a daughter, I'd tell her about sex if she asked. So how did you learn?"

"I guess Jacki told me. I think we each passed it down to the next one. Except for Joey. When she was about, I don't know, maybe nine or ten, she started asking questions, and Aunt Sally wasn't comfortable talking to her about the birds and the bees, ya know? So Jenny goes and gets this book from the library. It's called 'Molly Grows Up,' or something like that. And she's going through this book with Joey, telling her all about the sperm and the egg and the nest inside the mother's womb, all that shit, and my baby sister, all blonde and cute, looking like a little princess, looks at her and says, "Is this anything like fucking?'"

Kim burst out laughing.

I continued, "Jenny just about blew a head gasket. She couldn't believe those words were coming out of little Joey's mouth!"

We stopped talking and snuggled up together.

"So, in the mood for another or-jasm?" she whispered in my ear.

I was.

* * *

I ended up really liking my job at Planned Parenthood. Many of the girls coming in wanted advice on birth control, but a large part were there to have an abortion. I knew the pain they were going through. Kim had an old typewriter that I practiced on because the job required a fair amount of typing. It was fun answering the phone and filing—that was the easy part. She and I frequently worked opposite hours and when she needed time off for studying, I was able to pick up extra shifts. When I called home the first time, I talked to Aunt Sally, who tried to get me to come back, but I told her I had a job and a place to stay with friends and was really happy. She didn't exactly sound convinced, but she didn't try to bully me.

There were two problems that came up after the first couple of weeks. One was that the apartment was so tiny it distracted Kim if I was hanging around all the time when she needed to study. I tried to stay away when I wasn't working so I wouldn't bother her, but I really had nowhere to go. I wandered around the neighborhood and went into record stores where teenagers could hang out. A couple of times I got together with friends of Kim's and went out for coffee with them. I wanted to be with her a lot more, but she was usually at school, at work or studying.

One day I ran into my old housemate Marcia. I was really happy to see her. But then she told me that Lucy had died of breast cancer. I was shocked. I had been gone for only two years, and yet so much had changed. We traded phone numbers and I promised to keep in touch.

The second problem was I really missed drinking and getting high. A few of Kim's girlfriends smoked pot, so I'd drop in on them if they were home, but I was afraid I'd make a pest of myself. I bought a lid from a guy on the street one day, but Kim didn't want anyone smoking in the apartment because she had asthma, so that was a pain in the ass. Sometimes I had to go sit in my car to toke up, which was a hassle because I frequently had to park several blocks away. Kim had encouraged me to sell Gunter since we didn't really need it, but I was reluctant to do that. It was my very first car, it was paid for, and besides needing a quart of oil a week, it ran great. But she hated it whenever I went out to smoke out on the street since I could get busted, and, if I did, I'd probably end up in Juvenile Hall. She tried as much as she could to be a good influence on me, but I'm afraid I was incorrigible.

Four months later, things came to a head on the morning after my eighteenth birthday. I'd got real drunk the night before and acted like a jerk in front of Kim's friends. The next morning, she was in a foul mood and barely speaking to me. Finally she said, "Look this isn't working out for me."

"Ok, I'm sorry," I said. "I got a little carried away last night. I don't usually drink that much..."

"No, it's more serious than that. You and I are just at different places in our lives right now. I need to work and study. You want to party all the time. It's not a good mix."

I started getting pissed. "Look, I said I was sorry! I didn't mean to embarrass you. Maybe you need to lighten up a little bit!"

Now she was pissed. "No, I do *not* need to lighten up! I need to study. I need to work. This is a really intense time in my life right now. What I need is a partner who respects that!"

"I do respect that," I argued. "I try to give you space. But there's no reason why we can't have fun too!"

"Getting drunk or stoned all the time is not my idea of fun...maybe if I was 15 or 16 I'd think that falling down in the street and making an ass of myself was a great way to spend the evening, but frankly, it bores me!"

"So I bore you?" I yelled. "Is that what you're saying? How ironic, that I bore you!!! You're the one with the stick up your ass. Sitting around with your dyke friends drinking tea! Now's that's the way to have a good time!"

"I think you need to get the hell out," she yelled back. "I don't need this shit right now."

"Fine! I'm out of here today. Maybe I'll find someone who understands me better. Someone who gets why I need to get high all the time."

"Ok," she said, "but I'd suggest you stop using what happened with your parents as an excuse. It's not an excuse! We all have shit to deal with. Get over it!"

"And I'd suggest you go fuck yourself!" I screamed.

She grabbed her purse and stormed out of the apartment. I burst into tears. I couldn't believe she could be so mean. She'd been so sweet and so understanding before. What made her completely turn on me?

That afternoon I moved in with Hazel, a gay friend of ours who had two little boys. I rented a small room at the back of her large Victorian house. She was very clear that I couldn't smoke pot or drink in the house, but I could sit on the porch in back to smoke cigarettes.

At first, I kind of liked having my own little space. I could come and go as I pleased and I didn't have to explain myself to anyone. But I desperately missed Kim. I still saw her at work occasionally, but we worked different shifts and I heard she was taking extra time off to study for her exams. I cried myself to sleep a lot.

One Saturday night, about 3 o'clock in the morning, I got high with some friends and was missing her so much, I called her from a pay phone. When she picked up, I could tell she'd been sleeping and was clearly annoyed. I hung up without saying anything.

About eight weeks later, she called me on a Sunday afternoon. "I just wanted to see how you're doing," she said softly.

"I'm okay," I said. "I miss you a lot."

"I'm really sorry about everything," she said. "I guess I didn't handle things well. I should have tried to be more understanding."

"No, it's not your fault," I said, sobbing. "I'm just so fucked up. I don't blame you for not loving me anymore."

I heard her start to cry. "It isn't that I don't love you. I do love you. It just feels like we came together at the wrong time in our lives. You need someone to play with. I need someone to be strong for me."

"I *can* be strong for you! I know I can. I know now that I really fucked up. Please, Kim, let me come back!"

I listened as she cried for a few minutes. I could tell she was wavering. "Jules, if you come back, there's one condition."

I held my breath. If she said what I feared most, that I'd have to give up getting high, I didn't think I could do it. In the beginning, maybe for a little while, I could. But not for long.

"You have to agree to get into therapy. I know you don't have any insurance, but somehow, we'll find a way. You *have* to see someone!"

"Yes! Yes!" I agreed. I packed my meager belongings and was on her doorstep in two hours. It was the happiest day of my life.

That evening, as we lay in bed together, she told me how much she'd missed me.

"You know, I have felt like a freak my whole life," she said. "I didn't think I'd ever find anyone who'd love me. When I was growing up, and in high school, I didn't know anyone who was like me. I felt so completely alone."

I snuggled up closer to her as she continued. "Did you ever see that movie *Splendor in The Grass*? With Natalie Wood and Warren Beatty?"

I nodded.

She said, "I so much wanted to be loved the way that Bud loved Deanie. They yearned for each other so much it was tearing them up. I was desperate for that. But I just knew it was never going to happen for me. That it only really happens in the movies. Or to normal girls. And then I met you. You were so beautiful and funny and smart. And for the first time, someone I really wanted, wanted me back! Bud and Deanie found each other!"

I held on to her as my tears flowed across her shoulder.

"We will get through this, babe," she said. "I'll help you.

Whatever it takes."

We held each other for a long time. Then I said, "I'm confused. Am I Bud or am I Deanie?"

"You're a pain in the ass, that's what you are."

I was home at last!

* * *

The next week I made an appointment with a therapist Kim knew of, who also happened to be a lesbian. Kim was getting a monthly check from her dad as long as she was in school, and she wanted to use some of that money to pay for my treatment. She also started applying for student loans. We argued a lot about it, but finally, I relented.

Dr. Kendra was a tall, older woman who dressed in East Indian-style clothing and wore her gray hair pulled back in a single braid. She was a very calm, quiet person who would sit and nod a lot. I had been to a lot of therapists as I was growing up, and was tired of hearing the words "And how did that make you feel?" Sometimes, she'd just ask me what was going on and I'd burst into tears.

"I know Kim loves me a lot, but I think it's really unfair of her to ask me to give up drugs," I whined. "It's the only thing that makes me feel good, outside of sex."

"Maybe we should start thinking of other ways that might make you feel good," she offered. But, of course, I ignored that suggestion. Over the next few weeks, I screamed, I cried, I yelled, I swore, I pounded my fists on a pillow, and was generally as obnoxious as possible. But still, she encouraged me to come back.

"You just want my money!" I accused her. "You make your living off of sick people! You ought to be ashamed of yourself!" I was cruel, relentless and vicious at times. I don't know how she stood it.

One day, I asked her if she had to take a Valium before one of our sessions. She smiled.

"Your anger is not unfounded," she said. "You have a lot to be angry about."

"So I guess you're going to tell me my anger is really about my mother. I'm directing it at you, but it's really about Mommy, right?" I said it with as much sarcasm as I could. We had already talked about my parents many, many times.

"I think you are a very wise girl," she answered.

"What else do you think?"

She hesitated before she spoke. "I think you are very afraid of your anger. Afraid of what you might be capable of."

I was quiet for a while, looking at my fingernails.

Then she asked me, "Which one of you sisters takes after your mother the most?"

"Physically, Jacki does. But I have her personality."

"So if you take after your mother, and your mother is a murderer, what does that say about you?" she asked.

I started weeping.

"Tell me what's going on?" she prompted.

It took a while for me to calm down. Then I whispered, "I had an abortion. I killed my baby."

She handed me a box of tissues. "So you equate abortion with murder?" she asked.

I blew my nose before answering. "You know I work with a lot girls who are coming in for abortions. Some of them are in really bad shape. They can't afford another baby. They're addicted to drugs. They're too young to be mothers. They have boyfriends who are assholes. And for them, I think abortion is the right answer."

"But for you, Julie, abortion wasn't the right answer? For you, it was murder?"

I nodded. "I know it doesn't make sense."

Dr. Kendra smiled again. "A lot of times, emotions don't

seem to make sense. But underneath it all, there's a good reason why you feel the way you do."

I thought about what she said, and then continued, "I really felt at that time it was the right decision. But sometimes I wish I could take it back. Because it was *my* baby. It was something I did to *my* baby. Do you understand?"

"Yes. Abortion is a very painful decision. It can come back to haunt you. But it doesn't mean you made the wrong decision. In your case, it was more significant than most."

"Why?"

"Because the children of criminals often fear they will follow in their parents' footsteps. And I think you've carried that fear with you for a long time, even if you didn't realize it. In your young mind, having had the abortion is proof to you that you are like your mother. Which isn't true, but it feels that way to you now."

"So you don't think I'm a murderer?"

"Julie, I'm not going to tell you if abortion is right or wrong. It's something that every woman must deal with on her own terms. I think you did what was best for you at the time. Do I think it's likely that you're going to go out and run your partner over with a car? No, I don't. I think you are a very special person. I see you as being very strong. A leader. With a lot of potential to do good things in your life."

"That's what my dad said," I told her. "He said I would be a leader."

Dr. Kendra smiled. Her eyes sparkled. "I'm sure you must have inherited your wisdom from him."

Our time was up. It had been a good session.

I won't lie and say that from that day on, I was "cured." But I continued to work with Dr. Kendra and slowly began to experience a shift in my mood. I found I needed to get high less often. I met with her for over a year. Sometimes I talked about Kevin. Sometimes I talked about being gay, and what it would be like to come out to my family. A few sessions I talked about little Ben, Leslie's son, and how guilty I felt whenever I thought about him.

One day she asked if I'd ever talked to my mother about the day of the accident. I told her no.

"Why not?" she asked. "It seems like a good idea for you and your sisters to know what was going on in her mind that day."

"You don't know my mother. She gets hysterical in an instant. She starts talking about what a jerk my dad was, and how he abandoned us, and how it was all his fault. She doesn't take responsibility for what happened at all. She believes if Daddy hadn't had a mistress, we'd all be fine. We'd still be a family."

"What do your sisters think?"

"Jacki thinks Mom did it on purpose. That she planned it. But that couldn't be true, because when she drove over to my dad's office that day, she wouldn't have known they'd be walking across the street at that exact moment. Jo, on the other hand, is positive it was an *accident.* That mom was upset and *accidentally* ran over them. Jenny doesn't like to think about it at all. With her, it's more like okay, it happened, let's get on with our lives."

"And what do you think?"

I took a moment to collect my thoughts. "I like to think it was an accident. That my mother would be incapable of just putting her foot down on the accelerator and running over two people, no matter how upset she was. You know, I've been pissed off all my life. But I've never been so pissed off that I could ever kill someone. When I'm really drunk, or high, sometimes I get sad and weepy, but I never think about going out and hurting anyone. When I'm sad, it's about me, not about other people."

She nodded but didn't say anything. I thought about it

some more.

"To be honest," I finally said. "I think I don't want to know the truth. I'd rather just believe it was an accident. Anything else is just…unbearable."

We sat in silence for a few moments. I listened to the sound of the clock ticking on the wall.

"What are you feeling right now?" she asked.

"I'm not sure. But I feel like there's this little shift going on in my brain. I don't know how to describe it. But it's like I realize now that I've made this decision: I don't want to know the truth. And somehow it makes me feel a little bit lighter, you know?"

Again, she nodded. Then she said, "You've taken control of how you are going to deal with this pain. That must feel very empowering."

"I guess that's what it is," I said.

She paused. "Julie, you mentioned you've been angry all of your life. So what are you angry about today?

I thought for a few minutes, staring at the floor. And then I looked at her and smiled. "I'm not angry today. I can't believe I'm saying that. I am not angry today. Wow!"

Dr. Kendra nodded. "I think we're making some progress here."

"No shit!" I exclaimed.

26

I continued to see Dr. Kendra for another few months before I finally told her I thought I was done. She agreed, but said I could come back if I needed to. In the meantime, Kim and I had moved into a bigger place, a two-bedroom apartment. She used the second bedroom as an office so she'd have a place to study. I'd been calling home once a week and when I finally told Uncle Joe I'd been in therapy for over a year, and that Kim had been paying for it, he said there was money from my dad's insurance policy to cover it. He promptly sent Kim a check for five thousand dollars. The day it came in the mail, we jumped up and down. The money would come in really handy if Kim got accepted to med school.

I'd also been thinking seriously about becoming a social worker. I loved my job at Planned Parenthood. By then I was teaching classes in birth control to groups of young men and women, and I got a tremendous sense of satisfaction from counseling them. I applied to and was accepted at San Francisco State and would start school in September of 1974.

That July Fourth weekend, I took Kim down to meet my family. I'd never actually come out and said "I'm a lesbian," but I'd told them, in the beginning, that I had a "good friend." Then she became my "special friend." That Christmas I signed my cards: "With love from Julie and Kim." I guess Jacki and Jen eventually figured it out. One day, all three of my sisters came up to visit, and I showed them around the apartment.

Joey looked into the bedroom and said, "You both sleep in the same bed?" And I said, "Well, of course!" She looked dumbfounded for a moment and then shrugged her shoulders.

The day I took Kim down to Morgan Hill to spend the weekend with my family, I had something to propose. When I got time alone with my sisters, I said I wanted us all to go on a little vacation, maybe take a week together and go somewhere. And there was something else, I added.

"I know this might sound a little weird, but it's been on my mind a lot lately," I began. "I really want to try to track down Benjy. Leslie's son. I want to find out what happened to him. If he's okay."

"Yeah," Jacki said. "I've thought about him over the years, but I don't know if we could find him. He must be living with his dad somewhere."

Then Jenny added, "You know, I've mentioned him to Uncle Joe and Aunt Sally, and it's really odd, because they're always so negative when Ben's name comes up. It's like they just want us to forget about him, like he never existed."

"Well," I said, "I looked up Norman Green in the San Jose phone book this morning."

"Who's Norman Green?" Jo asked.

"Daddy's old law partner," I explained. "He might be able to steer us in the right direction."

"All right, let's give him a call!" Jacki said.

"We'll have to wait till Monday," I answered. "I'm sure they're closed on the weekend."

"So how old would Ben be, anyway?" Joey asked.

I thought. "Let's see, in 1965, he was three. So I guess he'd be about eleven now."

"He's not going to remember us at all, you know," Jacki said. "And what do you plan to say to him? 'Hi! Our mother killed your mother. So how are you, anyway?'"

"I don't exactly know," I answered. "Maybe he won't even

want to see us. But I guess I just want him to know that we think about him and that we care about him..."

"We're going to have to do this pretty soon," Jenny said. "I'm leaving at the end of August." Jenny had graduated from college in June and was going into the Peace Corps. For the next two years, she'd be living in a remote village in Guatemala.

"And I'll be starting my job in September," Jacki added. She'd just finished up the nursing program and had been hired to work as a pediatric nurse at San Jose Hospital. But she'd delayed her starting date for a few weeks so she could take some time off and do some traveling.

"Doug and I were planning to go camping that week," she continued. "But he wants to take a bike trip through the Sierras with one of his college buddies, and I definitely don't want to do that. So I'm sure he won't mind if I take off with you guys."

"Oh, man, this is so cool!" Joey said. "I can't wait! We're going to have a blast!"

On Monday morning, I called Norman Green's office. He was away on vacation, but I talked to the receptionist.

"I was a friend of Leslie Tilson," I explained. "She used to work there. I'm looking for an address or phone number for her ex-husband. I want to send a birthday card to her son..." I hoped I sounded believable.

"Oh yes, " the woman on the other end of line responded. "I started working here right after she...passed away. What a shame! I heard she was a lovely person."

When I didn't say anything she continued. "Well, let me go through my files and see if I can find an address for you. What did you say your name was again?"

I gave her just my first name and my phone number. A couple of days later, she called back. She said she couldn't find any paperwork that mentioned Leslie's ex-husband, but she did have a number for her parents. It was a Santa Cruz area code.

I paced nervously around the room for a couple of hours before I had the nerve to pick up the phone.

When I dialed the number, an older man answered.

"Hello, I'm looking for someone by the name of Ben Tilson?"

There was a pause. "Well, we have a Ben here, but his name isn't Tilson."

"His mother's name was Leslie Tilson," I said.

"Yes, Leslie was our daughter. She's no longer around, I'm sorry to tell ya." There was another pause. "Well, Ben's not here right now. He's in school. What ya want with him, anyway?"

Fuck-a-rooney. What do I say now?

"Ah, I went to grade school with Ben. I wanted to get in touch with him." *Oh, yeah, like that's believable. I sound like an idiot.*

"Well, call back after three," he said. Then he hung up.

I put the phone down and pondered what to do next. Santa Cruz would be a fun place to spend a week with my sisters. We could hang out on the beach and boardwalk during the day. Go to restaurants and bookstores in the evening. Do some shopping. Jacki and Jen were old enough to go dancing in clubs, but Joey and I were underage, so we'd have to find other things to do. And we could try to see Ben. After talking to my sisters about it, we decided to wait until we got there before we contacted him again.

The day I met up with them in Morgan Hill was a beautiful Saturday morning. We decided to take Jacki's van, since we all had suitcases. We were excited and happy. Uncle Joe and Aunt Sally were pleased that the four of us were taking a trip together. And the twins were out of town that week as well, so they'd have the house to themselves for the first time in years.

We hopped into the van and got on the road as quickly as possible. Joey had nicknamed our trip "The Amazing Graces on Tour." I watched my sisters as we drove down the highway. Jacki's hair was down past her shoulders, blonde, thick and wavy. Jenny's was also long with light brown with streaks of gold. Joey's honey-blonde hair was tied back in a ponytail, and I was the one with curls. I wondered what we'd look like when we were in our seventies. It was hard to imagine us ever having short, white hair. Jenny put an 8-track tape in the player and we rocked out to Rod Stewart as we cruised down Highway 17.

It took us a couple of hours to get from Morgan Hill over to Santa Cruz, where we checked into the Dream Inn, a large hotel overlooking the water. We were anxious to get to the beach and start "working" on our tans. After a late lunch on the boardwalk, we rode the roller coaster, screaming our heads off the whole time. Jacki, Jenny and I pigged out on cotton candy and candied apples. Joey was doing really good at sticking to her diet. She had already lost quite a bit of weight.

That night over dinner, we were talking about Daddy when Jenny said, "I used to imagine that Daddy was actually alive. That for some reason, they wanted us to *think* he was dead!"

I was flabbergasted. "I know exactly what you mean! I used to pretend he was like an FBI agent or something and he had to go into hiding. And that one day he'd just walk through the front door, smiling at us."

"I bet a lot of kids think that way," Jacki said. "Especially when your parent just goes away and you don't get to say goodbye. It's like he just disappeared. I know they didn't want us to see Daddy in the casket, but, in a way, I bet it would've made it more real for us."

"I'm glad we didn't see him dead," Joey added. "I wouldn't have wanted to remember him that way."

"Yeah, that's a good point," Jenny said. "I was thinking something weird the other day. I was thinking about Kevin." She hesitated, looking at Joey.

"What?" I prodded her.

"Well, this is going to sound creepy, maybe, but I was wondering if Kevin ever got to...you know...be with a girl before he died."

We were all speechless, considering the thought.

"I really hope so," Jacki finally said.

"I don't really care," I said at the same time.

Jacki continued, "I know he was little doofus, but I hope for his sake he got to experience some fun before he died."

"He had fun driving his car really fast," Joey added, sipping on her root beer.

"That's not the kind of fun we're talking about." I grinned.

"I know what you're talking about, I'm not a baby, you know!" She stuck her tongue out at me.

"You'll always be a baby to us!" I leaned over and hugged her.

"Stop it!" she complained. "You're grossing me out!"

The next two days were a repeat of the first. We were, in fact, amazed that we hardly fought at all, except for whose turn it was to use the bathroom, and who left wet towels on the floor. We also carefully avoided talking about Mom , Dad or Kevin or anything else that could bring us down.

On the second evening, I called Kim from a phone booth to see how she was doing.

She said, "I just had the funniest call from my dad. You know how he's always thinking there might be something that 'helps' gay people to not be gay anymore?"

"Yeah," I said.

"Well, he just said there's a new type of doctor he wants me to see—a *homopath*!"

Kim and I laughed hysterically. When I got back to the

room and told my sisters, they also thought it was hilarious.

The next day was Monday, and Jacki called Doug a few hours before he was leaving on his bike trip. The rest of us were lying on the beach, slathering each other in baby oil, when she returned with some interesting news.

"You're not going to believe this," she said, "but apparently, the receptionist in Norman Green's office told her boss that someone named Jules had called, so he called Uncle Joe. Uncle Joe called Doug. Uncle Joe wants us to call him. Doug got the impression that he does *not* want us to go see Ben!"

"Wow," Jenny said. "That is really freaky. I mean, what's the big deal?"

"Maybe we *should* call Uncle Joe first," Joey offered.

"Look," I answered. "I know Uncle Joe means well, but really, is it any of his business what we do? In the first place, he never spent time with Ben like we did."

"Yeah," Jenny agreed. "Well, maybe he just doesn't want to be digging up stuff from the past. Maybe he thinks we should just, you know, get on with our lives. Or he thinks we'll be traumatizing Ben if we go see him."

"I don't want to call Uncle Joe," Jackie said. "This is about us. And Ben. Not about him!" She had finalized the decision for us.

"Let's make the call this afternoon," I said, "before Ben gets home from school, okay? I'd like to get it out of the way so we can enjoy the rest of our week."

After lunch, we headed back to our room to make the call. For some reason, they all decided that I should be the one to talk.

"Chicken shits," I called them.

But they all crowded around to listen in. The phone rang, and a woman answered.

"Hello. Um, I'm sorry for bothering you," I said, "but my name is Julie Grace. I'm trying to reach Ben."

Silence. Then the woman said softly, "Oh, my." She sounded elderly.

"I know this is really weird. But my sisters and I are here, in Santa Cruz, for the week, and we wanted to come by and say hello. I don't think he'll remember us, but...we'd like to see him."

Again, there was silence. And again she said, "Oh, my."

Then she said, "Hold on a minute, would you?" And I heard her say to someone, "It's the girls. They want to come see Ben."

The television was on in the background and I heard a man answer her, but I couldn't hear what he said.

Then she came back to the phone. "Were you planning to come today, honey?"

"Um, yeah, I guess so. Would that be okay?"

"Well, alrighty then," she said. "Could you get here before he gets home from school? Like around two?"

"Okay. Sure," I said.

She gave me an address, and I scribbled it down on the hotel stationary. My hands were shaking.

"Boy, is *this* a trip," I said, hanging up. "But she sounded really sweet. She called me honey."

We still had an hour to kill before we were due at the house, so we got into the van and drove around. We were all fairly quiet, lost in thought.

"You know another thing that's weird?" I said. "When I called the other day, the man said that Ben's last name wasn't Tilson. Why would Ben have a different last name than his mother?"

Jacki answered, "Maybe she decided to take back her maiden name. A lot of women are keeping their maiden names these days."

" Yeah, I guess that makes sense," I said.

An hour later, we parked in front of a faded green house.

The neighborhood was run down, but the yard was neatly landscaped. There was a basketball hoop over the garage.

"This is, by far, the strangest thing I have ever done," I said, looking at the house.

"Come on, you guys!" Joey slid open the van door. "Stop freaking out. Let's just go in!"

We piled out of the car and walked up to the front porch. Jacki knocked softly on the door.

A woman who looked to be about sixty-five opened it. She was wearing a housecoat, and had her hair piled up in a bun.

"Come on in, girls!" she said. "My, you've all gotten so big!"

We entered the living room and a man walked in from the kitchen.

"Hi, I'm Frank. This is Edith. Come on in and have a seat. We was wondering if you was ever gonna come around."

Jacki and I sat down on the living room couch, and Jenny chose the love seat. Joey remained standing. The house was small, but neatly furnished. There was a shelf next to the TV stand that held what looked like baseball trophies. So Ben was a Little Leaguer. None of us knew what to say.

Jacki finally broke the ice. "Well, you're probably wondering why we're here. I guess you know who we are. Who our mother is, I mean. It must seem strange, us coming out of the blue like this. But, you know, we've thought about Ben over the years. I guess we just wanted to see how he's doing."

"Does Ben even remember us?" Jenny asked.

"Well, not really," Frank answered. "He's seen the photos, and all. He's knows about you, but he doesn't remember that much."

"What photos?" Joey asked.

Edith walked down the hallway and took a picture off the wall. She handed it to Joey, saying, "Well, here's one of them." Joey knelt down next to me and we looked at it together. It was a shot of the four of us standing around Dad and Leslie, who were sitting on chairs in the center of the picture. Ben was on Leslie's lap. I had forgotten all about that picture. It brought tears to my eyes.

"I don't remember this," Joey said and then passed it to Jenny and Jacki.

"I do," Jacki said. "I remember exactly when it was taken. It was Leslie's birthday. We had cake. Joey stuck her fingers in the frosting and then said Ben did it."

"Did not," Joey argued.

She handed it back to Edith, who looked at it for a few moments before putting it down on the coffee table.

"So, do you think it will upset Ben?" Jenny was asking. "Seeing us now? I mean, all things considered?"

"No, I don't think so," Frank answered. "All we told Ben was that your mother was real upset one day and caused an accident. He let it go at that. But he's asked about you girls a few times over the years."

"Hey, what's this?" Joey broke in. She was holding one of the trophies in her hand, looking at the inscription. "It says 'Benjamin Grace!' Why does he have our last name?"

There was dead silence in the room.

Frank looked at Edith, and then at Joey.

"Well, of course he has your last name. He's your half-brother. What name would he have?"

Someone gasped. I'm not sure who. We were all staring at Frank.

"Ben is my brother?" Joey said. "How cool! I didn't know we had a brother!"

"Oh, my," Edith said. "We thought you girls knew! We thought that's why you came! To see your brother!"

I looked at Jacki. Her face had gone completely white. Jenny stood up, took the trophy from Joey and looked at the name, as if for verification. She sat down on the couch with it still in her hand.

"No," she said slowly. "We thought Ben was Leslie's son, from her first marriage."

"Oh, no," Edith said. "Tom, that's Leslie's husband, he was sterile! Had the mumps as a boy. Leslie married him right out of high school. We tried to tell her, didn't we, Frank? But she wouldn't listen to us. He had such a drinking problem, that boy. They weren't getting along at all. So when Leslie went to work for your dad, well, I guess she fell for him. When she found out she was expecting, she left Tom. She and Jeff were going to get married. You kids knew that, right?"

"Except he already had a wife," Jacki said coldly.

"Look," Frank said. "I feel real bad you girls didn't know. I guess maybe they was gonna wait 'til after they was married before they told you. It must be kind of a shock."

"Kind of?" Jacki said.

At that moment, the screen door opened and Ben walked in. He stopped when he saw us sitting there.

"What's up?" he asked. He looked strangely familiar, and then I realized I was looking at a male version of Jenny when she was about eleven years old. He was tall and slender. His brown hair, which had been curly when he was little, now hung long and straight. He had Dad's green eyes. But his face was Jenny all over again.

"Hi, I'm your sister, Joey. Actually it's Johanna, but everyone calls me Joey. We didn't know until a few minutes ago that you're our brother. I think everyone's sorta freaked out, except for me. I think it's wild."

Ben stood in the middle of the room, staring at us.

Joey continued, "We've always wanted a little brother. I don't understand why Daddy didn't tell us. Can I give you a hug?"

Before he could answer, Joey had thrown her arms around Ben and was giving him a big embrace.

"Joey, knock it off," Jacki said. "Maybe he doesn't want a hug."

"It's okay," Ben said shyly. "Which one are you?" he asked Jacki.

"That's Jacqueline, she goes by Jacki," Joey answered. "And that's Julie and that's Jenny. Jacki's the oldest and I'm the youngest. There's nine years between us!"

"That's a lot of Js," he said.

"You used to call me Dooley, remember?" I asked.

He shook his head, and pushed the hair out of his eyes. God! I'd seen Jenny do that a hundred times.

"Would you girls like something to drink? A soda, maybe?" Edith asked.

Joey and I said yes. Jen and Jacki both declined.

Edith went into the kitchen.

"You knew about us, Ben?" Jenny asked. "That we're your half-sisters?"

He nodded.

"Where did you think we were all this time?" I asked him.

"Grandpa said you lived out of state. I was thinking I'd go look for you when I got bigger. But I guess I'm pretty happy you came to find me. I never had brothers or sisters to play with. But I always told my buddies I had a bunch of sisters. I have baseball practice in an hour, so I have to go pretty soon. Can you come back on the weekend, maybe?"

"We won't be here on the weekend," Joey said. "We have to head back on Friday. But maybe we could come see you again tomorrow, after school?"

"Yes, why don't you girls come for dinner tomorrow?" Edith said, as she handed the drinks to Joey and me.

"Well, we'll see," Jacki said, I didn't know why she was being so cold.

We stayed there for another half an hour. Joey asked Ben more questions about his life. I found it hard to talk to someone I didn't know anything about. It was so weird to think of him as our brother. He was just this kid, someone I would pass on the street without really noticing. And, after answering Joey's questions, Ben seemed to lose interest. He was anxious to get to his ball game.

As we left, we all gave him a stiff hug and promised to call the next day.

Back at the van, Jacki told Jenny to drive.

27

Jacqueline

When we got back to the van, I was so agitated I felt like throwing up. It had taken all my willpower to remain calm when we were in the house. Now I leaned over in the back seat and put my face in my hands.

Joey, in front with Jenny, was oblivious.

"Wow, this is so bitchin'," she said. "I just can't believe it! We have a brother!"

I collected myself and sat up.

"You just don't get it, do you?" I said to her. "Our father was not only having *an affair* on the side, he had *a child* on the side! He had a whole other family besides us! Doesn't that *bother* you? Just a little bit?"

Joey was quiet.

Then Jenny said, "Sure explains why Mom was pissed."

And my world came to a standstill.

"Oh, my God!" I said. "You think she knew?"

"I'd bet anything she did," Jenny answered. "Don't you see? That's probably why Uncle Joe didn't want us to find Ben. He must have known, too!"

"Pull over!" I yelled to Jenny. "Find a phone booth! I'm calling him right now!"

"I am *not* pulling over and looking for a phone booth. You

can call from the hotel room," Jenny said firmly. I decided not to argue.

When we got to our room, I dialed the phone as fast as I could. Aunt Sally answered.

"Aunt Sal," I said. "It's me. Jacki. Did you know? Did you know Ben was our brother?"

"Honey, we didn't want you to find out this way...Wait, Joe, get on the line."

I heard my uncle pick up the extension.

"Hi, sweetheart," he said. "Look, I tried to get a hold of you—"

"So you knew!" I broke in. "You knew and you didn't tell us! How could you keep something like this from us? Didn't you think we had a right to know?" By then I was yelling.

"Jacki, calm down," he said. "Sal and I thought you girls should be told the truth. Right from the beginning. But your mom didn't want you to know."

"But it wasn't her choice," I argued. "He's *our* half-brother. He's our father's son. We had a right to know. This isn't about her!"

"Honey, this is something you're going to have to clear up with your mom. It was important to her that you girls not find out the truth. She didn't want you to hate your father. You girls loved your father. She didn't want to take that away from you."

Oh, Mom.

"Uncle Joe?" I asked. "When did Mom find out? That Ben was Daddy's."

He was quiet for a minute. Then he said, "That morning. October 1."

Oh, Mom. Mommy. I put my face in my hands and wept.

* * *

My sisters gathered around me. I'm sure they were worried they'd have to cart me off to the loony bin again.

"What'd he say?" Jenny asked, handing me a box of tissues.

I wiped my eyes. "He knew. He wanted to tell us, but Mom said no. She didn't want us being angry with Daddy."

"How could *she* be so mad at him, but not want *us* to be?" Joey wondered.

"I don't know," I said, "but I am furious. I can't believe he did that! He betrayed Mom! He betrayed us! He lied. By not telling us the truth, he was actually lying to us. That *asshole!*"

"I don't think Daddy was an asshole," Joey said.

"Really?" I said, sarcastically. "What do you think?"

"That he loved us. All of us. I know he did. And I guess he loved Leslie, too. And they had a baby. Maybe they didn't plan it, but it happened. Maybe Daddy was afraid we'd stop loving him, I don't know. But I can't be mad at him. 'Cause I just don't know. And besides, I don't *want* to be mad at him. He loved us. I know he did. That's all that matters. To me, anyways."

"Well, I wish I felt like you, Jo. I really do." I got up and looked out the window at the ocean. "But I am so pissed! What about you two?" I asked Jules and Jen.

"It's amazing," Jenny said. "I hear both of you. I agree with both of you. But I'm not sure if I'm angry. I feel really sad that Daddy felt he couldn't tell us. I guess he must have had his reasons. Maybe he was afraid of how Mom would react. He had every right to be. I just can't sort it out right now. What about you, Jules?"

Jules looked at Jacki. "What I'm thinking about is how Mom must have felt. She was probably a lot angrier than you are right now. She must have felt sad. And betrayed. I'm sure she would have been overwhelmed."

I went into the bathroom and grabbed a washcloth. After

soaking it in cold water, I put it on my forehead. My temples were throbbing.

"Hey, are we going to get something to eat?" Joey asked. "I'm starved."

Walking back into the room, I said, "No, I'm not hungry. You guys go ahead without me."

" We're not leaving you," Jenny said.

"Look, I'm okay. I'm not going to do anything. You guys can trust me, you know. I'm not gonna go wacko."

"We're not gonna leave you alone," Jules argued. "We came on this trip to be together, and we're gonna be together. Maybe we could just have a pizza delivered. Why don't one of you call? I'll get some Cokes from the machine."

"See if they have diet root beer," Joey said.

"No kidding. Like I would get you anything besides root beer."

* * *

We sat on the two beds, wolfing down a large pepperoni pizza, as we watched a baseball game on TV. None of us were even remotely interested in watching sports on TV, but it was the only channel that came in clearly. I said, "You know what's really funny? For a couple of years now, Doug has wanted to get married. And I keep putting it off. You want to know why?"

"Yeah, why?" Joey asked.

"It's not that I don't want to marry Doug. I do. I'm twenty-six. We've been together forever. And I really love him. He's the guy I want to be with for the rest of my life. But the thing is, whenever I think about getting married, I remember that I always imagined Daddy walking me down the aisle. And I've been afraid that, on my wedding day, I would just be feeling sad he wasn't there. I don't want to feel that way on my wedding day."

"So it isn't marriage you're afraid of," Jenny said. "It's just the wedding?"

"Well, maybe," I answered, "although I never realized it before."

"So why don't you get married on the beach and not have anyone walk you down the aisle?" Joey asked.

"I hadn't thought of that before," I mused, "but what a great idea!" I looked at my youngest sister who was staring at the TV. I leaned over and kissed her on the cheek. "You can be so brilliant, sometimes, you know that?"

"Yeah, I know," she grinned. "That's what I keep telling everyone!"

"So," Jenny said. "Are you gonna go see Mom?"

All three of them turned to look at me. "Yeah, I guess so," I said.

"For real?" Jules asked.

I nodded. Then I remembered something. "You know, I talked to Daddy once about getting married. He said, 'Just don't marry the first boy you fall in love with. Because that's lust, not love.' He said, 'Lust can *feel* a lot like love in the beginning. But you need to wait until you know for sure that he's someone you truly want to be with for the rest of your life.'"

There was silence in the room. The air suddenly felt very heavy.

When Jenny finally spoke, her voice was tiny. "So. Another mystery solved."

We all stared at the TV screen.

* * *

The next morning, every time I thought about my dad, I felt restless and angry. But I didn't want to spoil the week. The last vacation we'd all been on was the year we went to Disneyland, and it had been a fiasco. I wasn't going to let that happen again.

We did go back to see Ben, and stayed for dinner, and everyone seemed to have a good time. He was a sweet kid but, at eleven, didn't have a whole lot to talk about. He was interested in sports, mainly. We didn't talk about Daddy or Leslie. Joey brought up the fact that Mom might be getting out of prison in a couple of years and I thought Ben might get upset about that, but he barely reacted.

I mentioned it to Edith when we were alone in the kitchen, doing dishes.

"Ben doesn't remember his mother at all," she said. "He knows *of* her, and sometimes he's curious about her, but he grew up with Frank and me as his parents. He's not concerned about the past right now. He might have had stronger feeling towards your mother if he remembered Leslie. But she's just someone he's heard about over the years. I guess, in the long run, it's better that way, don't you think?"

"I'm really happy you let us see him," I told her. "I know it probably wasn't easy."

"Well, you're his family. And Frank and I won't be around forever. It's a good thing he knows you now. I hope you won't be strangers to him."

"We won't. I promise."

When we left that evening, we exchanged phone numbers. It was pretty sweet, actually. We'd come to check up on a little boy we used to know, and we came away with a brother.

When I told Doug all about it on the phone that night, he said, "You girls are really something. You're like no other family I've ever known."

"Yep, that's us," I said. "We're the 'Amazing Graces.'"

"Someday there'll be a soap opera about you. Bet you anything," he said.

* * *

We spent the rest of our trip hanging out on the beach. My sisters had a good time. They laughed a lot. Julie was lighter and funnier than she'd ever been. We had never seen her so *happy* before. I kept expecting her to lapse into one of her foul moods, but she never did. She talked about Kim a lot, and even though it had been hard to accept in the beginning, I guess we all eventually realized on our own terms that this was who Jules was. Our sister was a lesbian. After everything else this family had been through, it seemed a minor oddity.

Right before we left to head home, Jen and Joey were downstairs loading up the van with our suitcases so Jules and I were alone for the first time. I asked her, "So, what was it like for you? To be with a woman the first time?"

She stopped packing her bag, looked at me and smiled. "Like being turned inside out," she answered. "Better than I ever imagined it could be. Was it like that with Doug?"

"Absolutely!" I laughed. "I am so happy for you, I really am!"

On the drive home, I sat in the backseat with Joey. Jen put the Creedance Clearwater tape, "Bad Moon Rising" in the player. She turned the volume way up and the three of them sang, "There's the bathroom on the right!"

When the song was over, I shook my head. "You guys are a bunch of retards," I said.

They all cracked up.

Driving back to Morgan Hill that afternoon, I decided I'd drop them off and head down to L.A. to see Mom. The idea made me nervous and edgy. I wasn't sure I could entirely forgive her for what she had done, but at least now, I understood her rage a little better.

I planned to tell her why I'd been so angry with her for all of these years. That she'd never taken responsibility for what she'd done. That she never apologized. That she always blamed Daddy.

But the minute my mother walked into the room, I was a sobbing wreck. She looked so much older now, small and fragile. Her hair was starting to gray. She held me tight and we both cried. "There, there," she repeated, smoothing my hair. I felt like a little girl. Like I was five years old.

"Mom, why didn't you tell us about Ben?" I asked, when I could finally compose myself.

"Oh, honey. You girls really looked up to your dad. You admired him. Everyone should have at least one parent they can respect. I had taken everything else from you. I had to leave you with something. I'm not a complete monster, you know."

"Ben is really a sweet kid, Mom. He looks a lot like Daddy. And Jennifer. And Joey is thrilled to have a brother."

Mom smiled, but it was a sad smile. "Well, I'm pleased for her," she said. "But he must wish I'd gone to the gas chamber."

"No, Mom, he really doesn't. His grandparents said he doesn't talk about you at all, actually. He's kind of like Joey that way. Very forgiving. Life just goes on, you know?"

"Well, I'm happy about that. This has been such a gift, having you here. You'll never know how much I've thought about you. Now I want to hear all about you. Tell me about Doug. Did you bring any pictures?"

I spent the rest of my visit talking about him. She asked a lot of questions about his family and his interests. I told her I thought we'd be getting married one day. She said it would be great if I could wait until she got released. I said, with a smile, that I'd think about it.

Of course, I cried all the way home. For five hours. Thinking about everything Mom had missed. Thinking of the nine years she had spent behind bars while we were growing up. I thought of Ben, who would live his entire life never knowing either of his parents. I thought of Daddy, and how sad it was that he'd missed knowing his children as adults. I wondered about the likelihood of there actually being a heaven, and if we would all be together again.

Crying can be a good thing. It helps to wash away the grief. After a while, I started thinking about all the stuff I had to look forward to: a life with Doug, starting my career as a nurse, Mom getting out of jail, watching my sisters as they matured, having a brother in my life.

Dr. Wheeler said once, "There are three things that make you happy: having people that you love, having work that is meaningful, and having something to look forward to." And I had all three.

28

Johanna

The year after our trip to Santa Cruz, my mom finally came home, although Morgan Hill wasn't exactly "home" to her. I'd been nervous about her return because, as it got closer and closer to her release date, she started getting more insistent that I should go live with her. My aunt and uncle said it was normal, that my mother had been without her kids for so long, and this was really important to her.

But there was no way I was going to leave Morgan Hill. In my senior year of high school now, I was very involved with cheerleading, the Pep Club and choir. The twins were really popular, so we had kids over to the house all the time. Uncle Joe finally relented and got a second phone line installed. He said he hadn't been able to make a phone call for three years because one of us was always on it. Unfortunately, with all my socializing, I wasn't spending that much time studying and my grades reflected it. I decided I wanted to go to Gavilan Junior College a few miles away in Gilroy, and live at home for my first two years of school. Unlike my sisters, I had no desire to move out and live in a dorm. Besides my college plans, I had a boyfriend, Greg, who I spent most of my free time with. There wasn't going to be a whole lot of room in my life for my mother. I didn't even have much time to spend with Aunt Sally, but we did go shopping together occasionally. I was always worried about spending money, but Aunt Sally said to me one day, "Don't worry, honey. It comes out of your trust fund."

We were having lunch at the mall that day. I took a sip of my diet root beer and said, "I thought that money was just for college."

"Well, that's not exactly true," she answered. "Your father had an extremely good life insurance policy that included a double indemnity clause."

"What's that mean?" I asked.

"It means that it paid double for accidental death. And Joe was appointed executor of the will to decide how it should be used."

I felt shy about asking but finally worked up the courage. "So how much was it anyway?"

She hesitated before she answered and then said, "A couple of million dollars."

"Holy-moley!" I exclaimed. "I had no idea!"

I thought about it as we continued to eat. "Aunt Sally, I don't get it. Since we had all that money, why didn't we just move into a bigger house so we could all live together?"

She look on her face was one I'd never seen before. She seemed totally *stricken.* I didn't know what was going on. Finally she said, "Now isn't the time to talk about it." And I let it go.

I probably would have forgotten all about it except for the fact that over the next several days, I noticed Aunt Sally seemed troubled. She wasn't her usual perky self.

Then, one afternoon as I sat on my bed doing math homework, she came into my room and asked if we could talk.

"Sure," I said, laying down my pencil.

She sat on my bed and stared at the Led Zeppelin poster on the wall. "I don't really know where to begin," she said. I couldn't imagine what was coming.

She continued. "I don't know if I ever told you that both my parents were full professors. And when I was growing up, I wanted to be just like them. I dreamed of working at a big university like Vassar, or Yale. I imagined I'd be married to another professor and we'd have a little house on campus. We'd have students over for intellectual or political talks. We'd spend time writing papers and getting published."

This was all news to me. I guess I had never thought much about Aunt Sally's life.

She went on. "I never really cared too much about having kids. I guess if I did at all, I thought about having maybe one child, a girl. But I was much more drawn to having an academic life, than being a wife and mother.

But then I met Joe in college, and we were in love. We got married after graduation. I was still planning to go on and get my Master's degree...but then I got pregnant with Kevin. I wasn't exactly thrilled, but Joe was so excited about being a father! Your sister Jacki was two already and he just adored her. And your mom was expecting Jenny. So *everyone* was enthusiastic about my pregnancy. I guess after awhile I got used to the idea as well. And, of course, after he was born, I was so happy. Kevin was such a beautiful little baby. We were completely smitten with him. I still thought we'd somehow manage to get our graduate degrees, but by then, of course, we needed money. And then the twins came along... and the course of our lives just changed. It happens that way, I guess."

She stood up and began rearranging the items on my dresser. She was quiet for a few minutes, but then continued. "So we had our little family and our little house. It was nice, I guess. But it wasn't what I had planned, you know? I had to stay home and take care of the kids...Joe worked two jobs for a while just to make ends meet. I guess I was pretty lonely sometimes. I'd be folding diapers and sterilizing baby bottles and think about what I was missing. But I really loved my sons and I guess I gradually began to accept the situation. I still thought that once the kids were grown, maybe I'd go back to school…Anyway, it was okay. I really didn't dwell on it that much. Who had the time? I was exhausted from running after three little boys all day long. I guess a lot of mothers are. It's just the way it is when your kids are little."

I still didn't know where this was heading, so I said nothing. She opened up the top drawer of my dresser and began organizing my socks, with her back to me.

"And then," she finally said, "came the day of the accident. We were, of course, all in shock. We knew Janet was a little *off*-- sorry about that, honey. But we never dreamed she'd do something like that! And then, we had these four little girls to deal with. Don't get me wrong—we loved each and every one of you! But when Joe said we'd have to take you all in…well, it was too much for me. I was already feeling overwhelmed by the kids I had. I just couldn't see how we could take in four more. It was… well, I just couldn't do it! Joe and I fought about it a lot."

She sat down on the bed, wiping tears with the back of her hand. "I'm not proud of what I did. I wish I would have handled it differently. We really did love you girls so much. But I finally threatened to leave Joe!"

"Oh, my God, Aunt Sally," I said, putting my hands to my face, "I had no idea!"

"So we fought about it some more, but then we finally reached an agreement," she continued. "We would take you and Jules. It was the most I felt we could manage. It was a very painful decision for both of us—but especially for poor Joe. He never wanted to separate you girls. But he didn't want our family to fall apart, either. I'm afraid I put him in a position no one should ever have to be in. But that's what happened. I don't think we'll ever stop feeling guilty about it. I just hope you girls can forgive me one day."

"Oh, please don't feel bad," I told her, putting my arms around her. "I think you had to do what was best. It wasn't your fault we got dumped in your lap. And it all turned out okay, didn't it?"

"Well," she smiled. "Maybe. It's hard to tell. But it looks like you girls will be okay. You especially. You've always been so precious; you are the silver lining in my life."

We hugged for along time. When we finally pulled apart, I said, "Aunt Sally, I really think you should consider going back to school after we all graduate. You could still be a professor one day!"

"Okay, I'll think about it," she promised.

* * *

The day Mom was released, I was in school. Uncle Joe picked her up and brought her home. When I walked in the door, she was sitting there on the couch, and I ran over and hugged her. She was crying and smiling all at once. She looked so small and uncertain. Like she didn't know what to do. I kept offering her things, to get her something to eat or drink, but she just sat there. Finally she said, "Is it all right if I go for a walk?" and that blew my mind. That she would even ask!

Uncle Joe planned a little family party for that weekend. Jacki had to work during the day, so she would drive down afterwards.. Jules was in school but had the weekend free, so she arrived on Friday night. Jenny was, of course, away in Central America, but would call if she could get to a phone. Uncle Joe and Aunt Sally were there, along with the twins, Aunt Mimi and me. I wanted to invite Greg, Martha and Meg, but Mom said she thought it would be too much. She wanted it to be just family. I was disappointed because I wanted my friends to finally meet her. But I think Mom was overwhelmed with everyone there and went to bed early. The next morning she was happy and cheerful and said it was the best party ever.

I think my friends got tired of listening to me talk about my mother over the next two weeks. But it felt so good to be able to say something simple, like, "My mom and I went shopping," rather than, "My mother is in prison."

Mom kept trying to corner me to talk about "our" plans and I kept trying to avoid the subject. Aunt Sally told me I was going to have to be honest with her.

During the time Mom was away, both of her parents died. It didn't mean a whole lot to us kids, because they were already quite old when we were born. By the time I got to know them, they were pretty frail, and my grandmother was senile. When she died, Uncle Joe took us to her funeral, but when my grandfather passed away a few months later, there was no service for him. The "good" news was that they had a left a small amount of money, which went to Mom and Uncle Joe, so Mom had some cash to get by on until she could get a job. Of course, she wasn't going to be able to move to Hawaii like she wanted. Her next plan was to rent a house in San Jose, and have me come live with her. We would be close to Jacki, and not too far from Jules.

I came home from school one day and she was real excited. She'd found a place for us.

"Mom," I said quietly. "I don't want to move to San Jose. I'm in the middle of my senior year. I'm just not going to change schools."

"Honey, this would be so perfect," she argued. "It's a darling little house, not far from Jacqueline's and close to your Aunt Mimi. And they've just built a beautiful new high school. I'm sure you'll love it!"

"Mom, you don't get it! I am *not* changing schools! I have my *friends* here, I have *Greg,* and my *life* is here. I'm going to *stay* here and go to Gavilan next year. That's my plan!"

"Don't be ridiculous," she said. "You're too smart to waste your time going to a junior college. You should be applying to universities."

"My grades aren't good enough. Besides, that's where Greg and Martha are going. I want to be with my friends! I want to go to Gavilan."

"Johanna," my mother said patiently, "you don't pick the college you are going to based on what your friends are doing!"

"Mom, this is my choice and this is what I'm doing!"

"Well, you are still a minor and I am still your mother, and if I say we are going to move to San Jose, then that is what we're doing!"

"You haven't been my mother in over ten years!" I yelled at her. "You can't just come back and throw your weight around! You lost that privilege a long time ago!"

I was shocked at the words coming out of my mouth. I had never, ever stood up to an adult before. Much less my mother.

She seemed to wilt right before my eyes. She went into the living room and sat down. I followed and sat next to her.

"Look," I said gently. "I do think it would be good for you to take the place in San Jose. For you to be close to Aunt Mimi. And Jacki. And I'll come up and visit you on the weekends. Jules can come down to see you, too. But my life is here, Mom, in this house. This is where I want to be."

She sat quietly, staring out the living room window, before she spoke. "But you're my daughter. You should be living with *me*."

"I'm sorry, Mom. I know this is hard. I hate to disappoint you..."

She looked at me for a long time. "So, you'd really come visit me?" she asked.

"Yes, of course," I assured her.

"You'd think, after spending all this time living with other women, I'd want to live alone right now. But I don't," she said. "I was really hoping we'd live together."

I leaned over and kissed her forehead. "Guilt isn't going to work either. But nice try."

"You've developed quite the attitude, I must say, Johanna," she remarked.

"Yeah, I wonder where I got it from," I answered, smiling. "Now I've got to study."

That weekend, we got Mom's stuff out of storage and moved her into her new place. For all those years, I'd never realized that our belongings from the big house in Almaden had been stored away. I assumed everything had been sold a long time ago. Jacki, Jules and Kim were there, helping. They'd open a box and then squeal with delight, finding bits and pieces they'd forgotten about over the years. I'm afraid we let Uncle Joe and the twins do most of the work, while Mom, my sisters and I pored over scrapbooks and picture albums. Going through all of our old stuff was sweet, but also very sad. Looking at a picture of my mother taken a couple of years before Daddy moved out, I realized with a shock that she had aged considerably. Her once lustrous blonde hair was now thin and dull. She had deep lines in her face and her skin was a sickly shade of gray. I quickly shoved the picture back into the box.

That evening, Doug came over with a bucket of fried chicken. He knew we'd be too exhausted and dirty from moving all day to do anything about dinner. As we sat around the tiny living room, Jacki and Doug kept exchanging glances.

"So what's up with you two?" I asked, munching on a chicken leg.

"We have an announcement," Doug smiled.

"Finally!" Jules exclaimed and everyone laughed.

No one was surprised when Jacki said, "Doug and I are

planning to get married this summer!"

"About damn time!" Matt said.

"The only thing is, we don't know if Jenny'll be able to get away. She's committed to spending two years down there, and I don't know if they'll let her take a break."

"Well, we'll just have to pull some strings to get her home for a little while, I guess," Uncle Joe said.

As it turned out, Ian called a few nights later with some disturbing news. Jenny had contracted hepatitis and was in the hospital. The good news was that she was expected to make a full recovery and would be flying home when she was well enough to travel. When Jenny did return, she was even thinner than usual, and quite weak, but in good spirits. She'd decided she wanted to go back to school to get her teaching credential, and then teach English as a second language. She was proud of all the Spanish she'd picked up during the year she was in Guatemala.

More than anything, I think she had missed Ian the most while she was away. He was going to law school at Santa Clara University and had two more years before graduation. She decided to move in with Mom until she was well enough to start school, so of course, Mom was delighted.

After Jenny recovered, Mom made another decision. Since none of her daughters would be living with her, she decided she still wanted to live near the beach, and found a bungalow in Capitola, a little town south of Santa Cruz. She'd be moving in on June first.

She also got a job as a receptionist in a law office, and wanted to become a paralegal! After moving to the coast, Mom met a guy she was interested in. I guess I expected him to be a lot like Daddy, but Milt was a small, shy man, retired from the post office. He also had a quiet sense of humor. When Mom told him she was an ex-con, he'd just looked at her and said, "I stole a watch from K-Mart once."

With Mom living in Capitola, Jacki naturally planned to have her wedding there. On September first, she and Doug were married on the beach at two o'clock in the afternoon. No one walked her down the aisle. Instead, we all stood in a circle around them. Counting all of Doug's family, plus our family and friends, there were about forty people in all.

Jacki was breathtaking in her beautiful, white, off-the-shoulder dress. Everyone kept saying they had never seen a prettier bride. And Doug looked so handsome in his rented white tuxedo with its green and purple paisley cummerbund. Jenny, Jules and I wore violet granny dresses and flowers in our hair. We each carried a bouquet of lavender roses and baby's breath ferns.

The minister started out the service by giving a short prayer for Kevin. As soon as he was finished, a pigeon flew over and dropped a load on Milt's shoulder. "Story of my life," he said, pulling a handkerchief from his pocket and wiping it off with as much dignity as he could. Everyone was giggling and we heard Aunt Sally snorting. Then we laughed some more. The ceremony was short and sweet. Doug surprised us all when he made a little speech before they exchanged rings.

"As most of you may already know," he began, "I am the one guy on the planet who actually *likes* poetry, corny or not. So, for this special occasion, I wrote something for Jacki that I want to read today. It's called: 'My Amazing Grace.'"

I've always known I'd find you
I could feel you everywhere.
The gentle rain of autumn
Left your perfume in the air.

Sometimes I'd catch your spirit
In the golden morning sky.

At night the silver moon would wrap
Around you with a sigh.

So here you are, my sweetest prayer
The proof that dreams come true.
For in your eyes I find my worth
When looking back at you."

By the time he was done reading, everyone was smiling and wiping their eyes.

* * *

Afterward the wedding we had a reception at the Crow's Nest Restaurant on the water. I sat with Becky and Maria on the outside deck while Maria smoked.

"Man, I never thought this day would come," Maria said. "Jacki, in the same room with her mother! Everybody getting along. Hell must have frozen over!"

"It's amazing you've stayed friends with Jenny for so long," I remarked. "How many kids do you have now, Maria? Five? Six?"

"You little brat!" she said. "I just have the three. And I ain't having any more, I can tell you that! I got my tubes tied. But I'm still waitin' for Mr. Right to come along."

"So why *have* you two stayed friends for so long?" I asked.

"I don't know," she answered. "I guess we got together during a really tough stage in our lives, and that experience kept us friends. We never really talked about it back then, but it was a scary time. I've always admired Jenny. She has a lot of spunk. And she can always make me laugh, even when I'm really down."

"I'll bet she'll be the next one to get married," Becky said.

"Yeah, I can't believe she finally settled down with one

guy. That's one girl who really knows her way around a mattress!"

"Becky, that's a terrible thing to say!" I protested, but we all laughed. Just then, the photographer motioned for me to come over to have pictures taken with my sisters.

Jacki sat on a chair in the center, while Jenny, Jules and I stood around her.

"Hey, Jacki, are you Mrs. Palmer now?" Aunt Mimi asked.

"No way!" Jacki exclaimed. "I'm keeping my last name. There's no way I'd break up the Amazing Graces!"

"Girls, look this way," the photographer said.

We all turned to the camera and grinned. It was a great picture. For the first time in years, we were all smiling at the same time.

Epilogue

Janet

I'd like to be able to say that after Jacqueline got married, we all lived happily ever after. But real life just doesn't work that way.

Of course, having my freedom, being with my four beautiful daughters on that glorious day with a very sweet man by my side, was more than I'd ever imagined possible during the previous ten years. That Jacqueline would ever speak to me again, much less invite me to her wedding was a dream come true. Don't think for a minute I didn't consider it an unexpected gift. In fact, I couldn't stop smiling. But beneath the surface lurked an overwhelming sense of melancholy.

I watched each of my girls as they talked, laughed and joked around while brushing each other's hair, sharing make-up tips and trying on each other's shoes. I was so proud of them. All my daughters had grown into gorgeous, outgoing, graceful young women. But they had turned into these incredible creatures without me. Or perhaps, in spite of me. I wanted to be able to take credit for them. To somehow feel that it was because of their mother that they'd turned out so well. But it simply wasn't so.

I'd always imagined that on the day of Jacqueline's wedding, I would be standing in the front row as my handsome husband walked her down the aisle. I knew it must have been on her mind as well. The morning Jacki was born, I would never have guessed in a million years that things would have ended this way. But life rarely turns out the way you expect it to, and sometimes, exactly the opposite.

* * *

When I was a little girl, I always dreamed of having a large family: two boys, then two girls, and then a boy. I spent hours picking out their names. I would stay home and take care of them, and be there when they came home from school. I knew beyond all doubt I would be a good mom. I envisioned a family much different from the one I'd come from.

My parents were in their early thirties when they got married, and I was born when my mother was almost thirty-eight. My brother, Joe, came along two years later. Back in those days, it was almost unheard of for a woman to have children so late in life. But my parents were determined to make a lot of money before they started a family and by the time I was born, they owned a very successful business, selling commercial real estate. My mother didn't let having two kids slow her down. Father used to call her the "brains" of the outfit. She was smart, educated, and a shrewd businesswoman.

I have no doubt my parents loved Joe and me, but quite frankly, they were lousy at raising kids, so that responsibility was handed over to our nanny. We wanted for nothing, except attention from our parents. They traveled a lot, and even took us with them on occasion, but we'd often be left alone in the hotel room while they dressed up and went out in the evenings.

In prison, I learned early on not to dwell on my childhood. At least not out loud. The other women would call me "poor little rich girl" and had no sympathy or compassion for me whatsoever. And I know that my parents probably did the best they could. So I'm not blaming them. I just grew up knowing that I wanted something entirely different for my family.

* * *

When I started college in 1944, I had almost no interest in academia. I wanted to go to parties, meet boys and have fun. I only majored in education because my best friend Mimi said she thought it would be easy. I probably put, at most, a grand total of fifteen minutes into thinking about my career choice. All I really wanted to do was to settle down and start raising a family.

My parents were appalled that I, and then later, Joe, would go into teaching. I guess it's normal that most children tend to follow in their parents' footsteps when it comes to career choices, but neither Joe nor I had an interest in business.

I met Jeff at a party during my junior year at San Jose State. I remember the evening so well. I was standing in a circle, talking with my girlfriends, telling some wildly funny story, and I looked over and noticed this tall, handsome boy beaming at me. That's the only way to describe it. Beaming. We kept making eye contact over the next hour, and finally he approached me and said hello. He told me later he was so nervous his knees were shaking. That he'd never been so smitten with a girl before.

Jeff and I started dating, and he seemed like the perfect guy for me, except for being a little on the introverted side. I liked going to parties and skiing with my friends. Having fun was my top priority. Jeff was very serious about school and spent a lot more time studying than I did. We dated off and on over the next two years, occasionally breaking up when one of us decided it was time to start dating other people. But we always got back together. The bottom line was that we were crazy about each other. I overheard him talking to his brother on the phone one night.

"She's beautiful, smart and funny," he said. Then he laughed. "I guess you're right. Opposites do attract. I can't wait till you meet her!"

After graduation, I got a job teaching at a private girl's academy while Jeff went to law school. For the next three years, he was busy with classes, studying and working part-time. We tried to see each other as much as possible, but it was frustrating for me, because I wanted us to travel and enjoy life while we were young. I had a temper tantrum over it and we broke up for several months. But during his last year of school, we got back together and he gave me an engagement ring with a tiny diamond chip in it. It wasn't the engagement ring I'd always dreamed of, but I was thrilled he'd asked me to marry him. My parents and Joe loved Jeff. My dad told him, "You're just the type of man to rein her in."

After Jeff graduated from law school, he went to work for a law firm in San Jose. A year later, we were married. Jeff thought we should hold off starting a family so we could save up money to buy a house and, initially, I agreed. But three months after we were married, we came home from a party one night and we were both a little tipsy. We made love without using protection. It wasn't exactly an "accident" on my part. Nine months later, Jacqueline was born.

When we found out I was pregnant, Jeff was upset at first. He was the type of person who liked to make a plan and stick with it. His dream was that we'd be living in our own well-furnished house before we brought our first baby home. So he was a little moody for a couple of months, but I was so excited about my pregnancy, eventually he got caught up in the excitement, too. And from the moment we brought our little girl home, Jeff was crazy about her.

There were two things that I'd looked for in picking a mate. I wanted a man who would support me, and I wanted a man who would be a great father. With Jeff, I got both. I was the luckiest girl on the planet.

Of course, I had to quit my job when my daughter was born, but that didn't bother me at all. We were living in a tiny one-bedroom apartment that quickly became too crowded, so we moved into a two-bedroom place near downtown. Jeff could walk to work. Money was tight, since we were still saving for a down payment on a house. I wasn't used to living on a limited income, and we frequently squabbled over our financial situation. Other than that, we were happy. Jeff loved coming home at night to be with me and our beautiful baby. We met other couples in the neighborhood who had children. Occasionally, we'd all go out dancing on Saturday nights.

When Jacqueline was two years old, I discovered I was pregnant again, and again, Jeff got upset. He felt we were just spinning our wheels financially, but all that changed when my parents gave us an unexpected gift—the down payment on a house. Jeff didn't want to accept it at first because he felt it was his responsibility to come up with the money. But he finally broke down and reluctantly, but graciously, accepted the offer.

We found a cute, three-bedroom home in the suburbs of Willow Glen, and I immediately began to decorate. A month after Jacqueline's third birthday, our second daughter, Jennifer, was born. Even though we'd both been hoping for a boy, we were delighted with this new baby. Jeff thought two kids made a perfect family. I was content at first, but envied my girlfriends who had sons.

Three years later, Julie was born. We couldn't believe our luck. Three perfect little girls. I no longer cared that I didn't have a son. Everywhere we went, people complimented our daughters. Each one was so different and so very special.

Unfortunately, Jeff and were squabbling a lot. He obsessed over our finances, which irritated me, because he was making a pretty good income by then, and my parents were always willing to help out if we needed it. He didn't like taking money from them, which I thought was stupid, because they were loaded. I didn't think his pride should stand in the way of our having nice things. I've always believed that life should be enjoyed. I'd suffered because my parents were always so focused on making money and it would be different for my kids. I loved to spoil them, to dress them up and buy them toys. Sometimes my mother would slip me some money, which I never told Jeff about. It would've just made him crankier.

The other area I was more concerned about was our sex life. All through college and the early years of our marriage, Jeff and I had made passionate love as often as possible. Once, twice or three times a day sometimes. In every room of the house. On the beach. He had the strongest libido of any guy I ever dated. But after our third daughter was born, his interest dropped off drastically. He was working long hours, and when he came home at night, he spent time with the girls, if they were still up, and then fell into bed exhausted. I'd gained weight with my pregnancies, but I still dressed nicely, did up my hair and put on makeup. It bothered me that he wasn't after me all the time, but then I was tired as well. I talked to my girlfriends about it, and they admitted that they rarely had time for sex.

In spite of the trouble we were having in our marriage, Jeff and I adored our daughters. He frequently complimented me on my mothering skills, although he did feel that I was spoiling them too much. I loved to play dolls with them, and I taught them board games. They had swimming lessons and riding lessons, as well as tap and ballet. He read to them every night and tried to foster an interest in playing chess.

Jacqueline and Jennifer were both well-behaved little girls. Jules, however, was fussier, even as a baby, and I wondered if she was picking up on the tension between her dad and me. She was more difficult to potty train than her sisters, and had frequent accidents. She also sucked her thumb until she was almost six, a habit we desperately tried to break.

Jeff was adamant after Julie was born that he didn't want any more children. He was happy with the three we had, but I often wondered if he was disappointed in me because we hadn't produced a son. He denied it, of course. I didn't have the guts to tell him, but in all honesty, I wanted another child, a boy. We weren't having sex very often, and when we did, Jeff was adamant about using a condom. But one night, on our anniversary, when I knew I was ovulating, we went out to dinner and drank several glasses of wine. That night, I seduced him and he was too drunk to think of using a condom. Three months later, I announced I was pregnant again. He was furious!

"You did that on purpose!" he yelled. "This was no accident!" I'd never seen him so angry. And while I did feel a little guilty that I had tricked him, I felt justified. I wanted another child. What right did he have to deny me that? I had always wanted five children, but I would settle for four. I prayed this one would be a boy.

Things between us were tense for several months. He continued to work long hours, sometimes on the weekends, and occasionally had to go out of town. I hated it when he traveled. With the girls in school, I couldn't go with him. This pregnancy was different from the first three. Jeff wasn't around to support me, and with the other girls to care for, I was exhausted and crabby all the time. I wanted to hire a nanny to help, but Jeff flatly refused. My mother frequently sent her housekeeper over to clean when he was out of town, and when Jeff found out about it, we had another huge fight.

Then Julie started wetting the bed again and her doctor couldn't find a medical reason for it. He asked if I thought she might be picking up on any stress in the household. When I told Jeff about it, he immediately apologized. "The last thing in the world I want to do is hurt our kids," he said. After that, he made an attempt to be around more. I was beginning to realize that getting pregnant this time might have been a mistake.

When I was six months along, my blood pressure shot up and my ankles were so swollen I could barely walk. My doctor put me on a low-salt diet and insisted I stay in bed. My mother immediately hired a woman to help with the housework and cooking, and we found a girl in the neighborhood to come watch the kids when they got home from school. It was the longest three months of my life. But as soon as Johanna was born, I knew it had all been worthwhile. She was a beautiful, sweet baby, and Jeff totally fell in love with her. I'd expected that we'd both be disappointed if I had another girl, but, honestly, I was so proud of all of my daughters, it didn't bother me at all. My doctor warned me that if I got pregnant again, I would be putting my health at serious risk and might miscarry. I knew Johanna would be my last baby.

Jacqueline was now nine, and Jennifer was six. They were both very helpful with the new baby, especially Jen, who tried to take over her care. Julie resented her new sister and acted out more, wanting attention. Jeff reluctantly agreed to keep Mrs. Grant, our housekeeper, on a part-time basis. Our house was now too small for a family of six, so I found us a beautiful five-bedroom home out in the country, in an area known as New Almaden. It was on half an acre and had a large patio and built-in pool, with room for a vegetable garden and fruit trees. I fell in love with the house as soon as I saw it. Jeff was worried about the mortgage payments, as usual, but he, too, loved the house. He now had a much longer drive to work, which meant less time with us, but felt it was a sacrifice he'd have to make. We had to give up Mrs. Grant, but found another woman who lived closer. She came in three days a week to clean and do laundry.

The first year in our new house was probably the last time that Jeff and I were happy as a couple. We increasingly fought over money. He even suggested I go back to work, which made me hysterical.

"I have four daughters to take care of!" I screamed.

"Jacki and Jen are in school during the day, and the other two can stay with a baby-sitter," he argued.

"I did not have children so that I could turn them over to someone else to raise!" I shrieked. "What the hell could you be thinking?"

Eventually Jeff apologized, and admitted I was right. He wanted me to be home, taking care of our girls. And the money I would make teaching would barely cover the expense of a baby-sitter and gas. His constant harping about money was really getting on my nerves.

More and more I realized there was no passion in our marriage. He'd barely touched me since Johanna was born but, even worse, we never had fun together. He no longer wanted to go dancing. He worked twelve-hour days sometimes, spent his weekends doing things with our girls, and had recently taken up golf, which I resented. I wanted some time alone with him. After a while, I started feeling as if I were living with an older brother who picked on me all the time. If that wasn't bad enough, I was heartbroken that his disdain for me was showing up in our eldest daughter. Jacqueline was becoming surly and argumentative with me.

I had spent the last nine years being the best mother I could be to my daughters. I drove them to and from school every day. I gave them lavish birthday parties and took them on vacation. I played with them, I bought them toys. They had become my best friends. But instead of being appreciative, Jacqueline now favored her father and treated me with scorn. It infuriated me and I didn't know what to do.

The only thing in life I'd ever wanted was a happy family.

To have a loving, lifetime partner and some healthy, happy kids. Now I had a husband who rarely spoke to me, and a daughter who was following in his footsteps. Julie was wetting the bed again, which frustrated me to no end. I talked frequently on the phone to Mimi, who assured me that all couples went through difficult times, and there was no such thing as a perfect family. I didn't want to hurt her feelings by asking her what the hell she knew about having a family, since she was single and didn't even have a boyfriend, but I did want to take some solace in her words. They were all I had. I suggested to Jeff that we try marriage counseling, but he just looked at me like I was a crazy person and shook his head.

* * *

Things continued to deteriorate between Jeff and me over the next few years. No matter what I did, he wasn't happy. I tried to diet and exercise, but it was a constant struggle. I focused my energy on the girls, frequently taking them on trips by myself. I kept the house clean, and prided myself on being an excellent cook. But we fought a lot, and between fights were long periods of silence.

Jacqueline entered puberty, and continued to be rebellious towards me. She was a lot like her father—quiet, serious and sullen. She was so pretty; looking at her, you would have thought she was a beauty queen, although she never seemed to notice. She always went to her father when she had something to talk about. She never shared anything with me. And now Jennifer was starting to get bitchy on occasion, which floored me, since she'd always been such an easygoing kid. I had done nothing but pamper and adore my girls, and couldn't understand why they were turning on me.

And then Julia, with all of her little quirks and tics; my heart went out to her. Not only had she experienced problems with thumb sucking and bed-wetting, but in second grade she started tugging on her eyebrows, and after several months had managed to pull them all out! Her pediatrician said it was something that kids went through, that Julie was just more high-strung than the other girls, and she would grow out of it. In the early 1960s, no one had heard of Attention Deficit Disorder, but I believe now that Julie had ADD. She was fidgety all the time, and wouldn't listen to her teachers.

Johanna, however, was the total opposite of Julia. She was a sweet, outgoing, friendly little girl who rarely got upset over anything. I never for a moment regretted my decision to have her.

But after she started kindergarten in 1963, Jeff began spending more and more time at the office. His job also required him to do a lot more traveling. This was infuriating to me. I hadn't married Jeff and had children with him so I could raise them on my own. When I complained about it, he just said he needed to take on additional clients in order to pay for our lavish lifestyle. That made me even angrier. He was making an excellent income now. I knew it wasn't about money.

One morning, when Johanna was in first grade, I walked around the house in tears. The bottom line was my husband didn't love me anymore. That was the awful truth. He simply didn't love me. Yet I was the same person I had always been. I hadn't changed that much. We'd been together for over twenty years and married for the last sixteen, but now it was evident that somewhere along the line, for some reason I couldn't fathom, it was over. I stayed in bed for two days, thinking, "He doesn't love me anymore." I don't know why it had taken me so long to see it. It left me reeling with grief. That was why he refused to go to marriage counseling, even though I'd suggested it repeatedly. Why try to save your marriage if you don't love the person you're married to? Then my sadness turned to anger. I felt cheated. I wanted to have a wonderful, loving family and a husband who adored me. I didn't want my children to grow up with parents who fought all the time. I desperately needed to do something to save my marriage.

When Jeff got home that night, I told him we needed some time alone so we could talk. He avoided looking at me, but agreed. On Saturday morning, he drove the girls down to Morgan Hill to spend the weekend with their cousins.

When he walked through the front door, from the look on his face, I knew our marriage was over. We sat down in the living room and, without any prompting, he started to talk.

"We can't go on like this anymore," he said quietly. "We need to be apart for now. I've been thinking about renting a small place near my office."

When I didn't say anything, he continued, "This has been going on for a long time. It just isn't working out."

My throat closed off, but I managed to squeak, "Why haven't you been willing to see somebody with me? You don't want to save our marriage?"

He refused to look at me. When he didn't answer, I got angry. "I just don't understand. You need to *make me* understand. You just need some time apart? Or you want a divorce, what?"

He still didn't say anything. Then I yelled, "Do you want a divorce but are too much of a coward to say anything? Is that it? You're just a big chicken shit?"

"Let's not do this," he said. "I don't want to fight anymore. But, yes, I want out. I haven't been happy for a long time. You haven't been happy. I didn't want to admit it. God, I never wanted to do this to our kids." He put his head in his hands and wept.

I went over and sat next to him, putting my arm around him.

"Jeff, it doesn't have to be this way. There are things we can do. I know we can work it out. I don't know why you're so unhappy, but we need to try to figure this out. For me, for you, for the girls. We're a family. You can't just bail out on us."

He sat there quietly for a long time. Then he sat up and looked at me.

"I'm sorry," he said. "But I've already taken an apartment. I've had it for a while. I'm going to stay there during the week. I'll come home on the weekends to see the girls. It's the best I can do for now."

Then he went upstairs and started packing. I sat there, stunned. I didn't even know what to think. He'd gotten an apartment and didn't even tell me? What else did I not know? I was so bewildered I couldn't think straight. It was obvious he had no desire whatsoever to work things out.

After he left, I called Mimi. I was so devastated that she came over to the house to spend the rest of the weekend with me. I alternated between incredible sadness and outrage.

* * *

So my husband moved out of the house and left me with four kids to raise. In the beginning, he came home on Friday nights, but slept on the couch. Then he started picking the girls up on Saturday mornings and taking them back to his place for the weekends. That was even worse—being totally alone for the first time in my life. I absolutely didn't know what to do with myself. I walked around the house, crying. I sat in front of the TV, eating bowls of ice cream.

Six months later, I got papers in the mail saying Jeff had applied for a legal separation. I called him at the office, crying. We were already separated, I told him. Why did he need to file papers? "To make it legal," was his response.

I knew I was being hysterical, but every move he made hurt me even more. Mimi kept trying to get me to accept that my marriage was over, that I needed to move on, find a job, and get a new lover. But all I could think about was Jeff. I couldn't understand it. How can someone love you, marry you, have children with you, and then one day just wake up and decide that it's over? How is it possible for that to happen? I had always been there for him. Always been faithful to him. I had ruined my figure by giving him four beautiful daughters he adored. What had I done to cause this? I couldn't get the idea out of my head that I didn't deserve it. Jeff had torn our family apart and didn't seem to bother him!

One morning, he came to the house to pick up the girls. They were going on a four-day skiing trip. In the middle of winter, Jeff looked lean, tan and healthy. And happy! He looked happy! He obviously wasn't grieving at all. We got into a huge screaming match. Right then, as much as I loved him was how much I hated him.

A couple of weeks later at breakfast, Johanna mentioned that Daddy had a "new friend." The other girls looked stricken that she had let the secret out. The "new friend" turned out to be Leslie, a young woman I had met at a few office parties. She was a paralegal who was separated from her husband and had a young son. The fact that Jeff was already seeing someone else infuriated me. We weren't even divorced yet, and he was already moving on.

I have to admit I wasn't the best mother during the next few months. I was depressed and angry. My world had been turned upside down and now I faced an uncertain future. I did the best I could, but my mothering skills failed me. I yelled at the girls a lot. I was impatient and rude to them and their friends. It took all my strength to keep from kicking the cat. I wanted to lash out at anyone, at everyone.

And Jeff wouldn't talk about it. He would only mumble, "Things are different now." He never accused me of anything, at least not in the beginning, but would only say that *he* had changed, that he had different needs now. That was unacceptable to me.

Six months later, on a crisp, fall morning, I was going

through the mail when I stumbled across a medical bill that was addressed to Jeff. When I opened it, it was from a pediatrician's office, a doctor I didn't recognize. It was for services rendered to "Benjamin Grace." I called the number.

"Oh, yes, Mrs. Grace," the receptionist answered. "That bill was from when you brought Ben in for his ear infection. I know we usually just send the bill to your husband's office, but we have a new girl working in billing and she must have sent it to your home instead. I apologize. How is little Ben doing, anyway?"

I hung up the phone. The only Ben I knew was Leslie's son. I kept staring at the bill. Benjamin Grace. Suddenly, it all made sense. Jeff had not only left me for Leslie, but already had a child with her! I gasped for air, feeling as if all the wind had been knocked out of me.

I don't know how long I sat there, holding the bill, my eyes blurred with tears. He had a new family. A new woman, a young son. How old was Ben, anyway? He must be three by now. My husband has a three-year-old son? This has been going on for over three years? All this time, he's been lying to me? To the girls? Surely they didn't know Ben was their brother? I knew that was impossible. They were crazy about Ben and could *never* have kept that a secret. I shook my head. That bastard!

I dressed slowly. Methodically, I gathered up my purse, jacket and car keys. I don't know what I was thinking as I got into my car and headed in the direction of Jeff's office. I didn't have a plan. Maybe I just wanted to talk to him. To both of them. To tell them how betrayed I felt. I had to keep wiping the tears from my eyes with the sleeve of my sweater. I could hardly see. In all honesty, that's all I remember about that drive, until I turned the corner onto the street where Jeff's office was. I spotted him walking across the intersection with his arm around Leslie. She was wearing a lovely pale blue suit.

Her long, brown hair was blowing in the wind. They looked like the perfect, happy couple.

I remember feeling a rush of heat surge through me. But I don't recall what I was thinking. As my car made the turn, I stepped on the accelerator. There were no thoughts in my head that I was going to hurt them, that I was going to kill them, that my life would forever be ruined, that my daughters' lives would be ruined. There was only rage. Pure, unadulterated, blinding rage. As my car hit them, I watched in amazement. Jeff glanced in my direction with a look of bewilderment before he disappeared under my car. Leslie sailed clumsily through the air and landed in an awkward heap on the sidewalk. It all took just a few seconds.

I sat there in shock. How had that happened? Someone was yelling at me. I heard voices and saw people gathering. I was confused. I thought my car had somehow malfunctioned and lurched forward all on its own. It seemed unreal that my foot had actually been stepping on the gas pedal.

I heard a man yell, "She deliberately ran over them! I saw it with my own eyes! She turned the corner and just sped up!" He kept shouting and I wished he'd shut up. No one deliberately runs over people. Surely he had to know it was an accident?

In the distance I heard the wail of an ambulance. I wondered where it was going. The next thing I remember is sitting in the back of a police car with my arms handcuffed behind me. As we drove away from the scene, I leaned forward to tell the police officer, "I have to be home by three to pick my daughters up from school."

* * *

My memories of the days following the accident are just a blur to me now. I couldn't believe what I had done, or that I was in jail. That I faced going to prison. How could I ever explain to a jury what had happened when I didn't understand it myself? The enormity of the situation was so overwhelming I simply couldn't deal with it rationally.

In the beginning, all I could focus on was getting out of jail and returning home. Of course, that never happened. Instead, I spent the next ten years in prison.

Every single morning when you wake up in a cell, it's a nightmare. It's like something that might happen to someone else, but not to you. Unless you experience it yourself, you can't imagine how horrible it is.

When I was a little girl, I used to have dreams at night in which something scary was happening, and I'd opened my mouth to scream, but nothing would come out. That was what those years in prison were like for me. I wanted to scream, to tell the world it was an accident, it was all just a huge mistake, that I wasn't a monster, that I wouldn't deliberately kill the father of my children, that I wouldn't have killed Leslie, no matter how much I hated her. I wasn't a bad person! I loved my husband, and it was because of my intense feelings for him that I'd reacted the way I did. Some days I felt like all I wanted to do was scream and scream and scream. But I couldn't get out a sound.

I knew my daughters would have liked to hear me say I was sorry, but in all honesty, I couldn't apologize. Because I felt I had no control over the situation and therefore *couldn't* have done anything differently.

What weighs on my mind the most these days is that I missed so many of my daughters' crucial years. That I wasn't there for them when they needed me. They had to find their way in the world without me. I am more than proud that they have each developed into their own person, and each one has her own distinctive charm. But, of course, I continue to worry about them.

Johanna is a sophomore in college now down in Gilroy,

majoring in pre-law, and appears to be the most well adjusted of all my girls. She shares a closeness with Sally that I envy. Sometimes I feel she thinks of me more as a sweet aunt who pops by every now and then to check up on her. But slowly we are growing closer as she becomes less resistant to my attempts to mother her.

We did have one huge argument after the wedding, when she told me, "You screwed up your life so bad! What makes you think you have the right to tell me how to live mine?" I guess she had a good point. But she later apologized and I have learned to back off.

Jennifer is now teaching English as a second language and continues to write. She's had a few articles published in women's magazines. I am so proud of her. She is strong, independent and very funny. She is still trying to get me to write a book about my experiences. Maybe one day I will. She's been with Ian for a long time now and I am guessing she'll be the next one to get married.

And Julie. I think I will always worry about my third daughter, although she is much happier as an adult than she was as a child. She and Kim are still together and she's working on her Master's degree in social work.

It breaks my heart that she prefers to be with women. While I was in prison, I saw a lot of women turn to each other for comfort. But prison life is different from the outside world. It will be hard for her. I would love to see Jules settle down with some nice man and have babies, but that isn't my choice. She does go to AA meetings, although she has slipped up occasionally. She calls me regularly to ask for advice, even if she doesn't take it. I think she just tries to humor me, and I appreciate that.

Jacqueline seems to be happily married, and Douglas is the son-in-law every mother dreams of. She loves working as a pediatric nurse. She still seems fragile to me at times and has lashed out at me in anger on more than one occasion. But I think we have made a truce.

She came over to Santa Cruz to visit me recently. We walked across the road and sat on a log, watching the ocean. Once again, she talked about her father.

"The thing that's so hard for me to accept," she said, "is that, in so many ways, he was such a good dad. I mean, all of us loved him and respected him and admired him. He really was a good person. Except for totally betraying us, I mean. How can someone so perfect turn around and do something so awful?"

I smiled at her. "You could probably ask the same question of your mother."

"Yeah, I guess you're right. So what's the answer?"

"I'm not sure, sweetie. I just don't have all the answers. I guess Milt has the right idea. Whenever it comes up that I've been in prison for killing my husband he says, 'Well, no one's perfect!'"

Then she smiled. "I sure can't believe that's the answer I'm looking for—that *'no one's perfect'!"*

I stood up and stretched. "Well, if it was, would it be too hard to accept?"

We watched the waves as they crashed against the shore.

"I guess I won't ever really understand what happened," she whispered.

"Me neither," I answered. I put my arm around her and we headed back toward the house.

The End.

About the Author

Darlene Shorey-Ensor is a writer and playwright who lives in Jacksonville, Oregon with her husband and Golden Retriever Jessie. She did grow up with her sisters in an old rambling house in New Almaden, but the similarity ends there. *The Amazing Graces* is her first novel.

Made in the USA
Charleston, SC
05 June 2013